The Guardians
of
Warad
The Lost Tribes

Idius Kane

PublishAmerica
Baltimore

ISBN: 1-60474-429-4
PUBLISHED BY PUBLISHAMERICA, LLLP
www.publishamerica.com
Baltimore

Printed in the United States of America

Chapter 1

A small village rested peacefully inside the territory of Cavell. Cavell was a land known for its farming and high population of humans. The large land consisted mostly of dense forests and large mountains that took travelers many weeks to cross. In these parts only deer and sometimes bear were seen roaming the forests. Most of the human hunters as well as the other races hunted these two species to feed their families and sell to the others that lived in their village. Most of the Westside of Cavell was farms and villages just like this small one not far from the ocean. The human empires were many weeks and months further east. These villagers had no money to be able to live among the city folk far away. They lived by themselves relying on their neighbors and other races that lived among them for comfort.

Hundreds of villagers surrounded the many huts and taverns located inside this village. Chimneys exhaled smoke from the fires blazing inside the huts to keep the homes warm. The winter years were coming and the farming would be stopped for some time. In this small village, races of many kinds lived. Halflings, who were small humans, humans themselves, and elves. Most elves were part of the ever increasing empire across the great land of Tullian, but the elves here believed in the old ways. They didn't want a king to rule them, and knew an empire of elves would be surrounded by politics.

The farmers were returning from the great fields getting many crops and wheat to be sold to the others. Hundreds of men, woman and children surrounded fires outside their huts and talked with the other people of the village. Hunting was just about down for the day as several men could be seen returning to their homes. The animals though were declining in these regions for some time and all that could be spared was the ever decreasing crops. The villagers knew they would need to move out to other areas of the world to fend for food and better shelter with the winter coming.

An elf hunter with three of his sons was returning from the forest with a wooden cart carrying many deer. His eldest son was about twenty in human years but it was known that elves aged far slower than humans. He was a few hundred by his race, and rather handsome.

The two younger sons were on the wooden carriage their older brother pushed as many farmers and hunters around them returned to the village with the sun setting not to far away. Darkness in these parts was frightening to the villagers and many evils dwelled once the sun set.

The farmer was an old looking elf. His face decreasing of age and was getting wrinkles. Many scars were all along his face but his tan skin made many look as if they weren't there. He wore light armor on his chest to protect him from an attack from any type of wild animal or possible another being. His blonde hair hung freely as he walked with his sword in hand fresh with blood. He had used it to begin skinning a deer he had killed earlier in the day. He wore ragged cloths around his body just under his armor along with his three children. The wooden cart was carried by his eldest son and he seemed to be straining from the process. The two younger children were on top of it staring down at him as he tried to push it.

"Come on Cloron," The youngest teased, "You can do better than that."

"It's hard enough to push this thing with four deer on it but with you two it's near impossible," Cloron replied.

"Hecorus, Halouse," The old elf called.

The two younger boys looked at their father as he spoke with a purpose.

"Get off there at once and stop teasing your brother," Their father commanded.

Hecorus and Halouse jumped off at once as they heard their fathers command.

"Calbrawn," A fellow hunter called to the old elf.

The elf looked over at a human farmer who didn't have a catch for the day.

"How many?" The human farmer asked.

"Four," Calbrawn told as he looked over.

"How did you manage that?" The human farmer asked, "There are so few even in these parts."

"I had to travel far," Calbrawn told, "Even ran into some hunters from other villages."

The old elf talked with many of the villagers as he returned and was well known among them. The humans and others knew the sword he carried could be used for other purposes.

The youngest brother, Halouse looked over at another farmer family as they reached the many huts. There was an elf family much like his with many children. One of them, a girl, about his age looked at him as he walked past. She was dressed in a white dress and her blonde hair was tied back. Her blue eyes seemed to captivate him as they glanced at one another for many moments. He knew nothing of beauty and love, but this young girl seemed to make him know what it was instantly.

Hecorus saw this as he hit the shoulder of his younger brother playfully. Halouse turned as the sharp pain took over his shoulder and hit back. Hecorus looked as if he was about to retaliate but was grabbed by the back of his shirt by his father and pulled away. Calbrawn placed them side by side with him to make sure they didn't fool around.

"You two start that up again and I'll whip you," Calbrawn warned.

"We were only playing father," Hecorus assured.

"Playing or not you will not act that way in public," Calbrawn told.

Halouse turned to see the little girl still looking over at him as he turned back and continued to walk toward his home. They all stopped at a small hut in the center of the village. Standing there awaiting them was an elf warrior.

He was dressed head to toe in armor. A sword to his waist and a cape draping behind him. He wore a horned war helm that he surly used to protect himself in battle. A blue dragon was crested on the center of his clean armor and the remaining parts of his clothing were clean as well. He looked very presentable even for a warrior and had many necklaces around him. He was alone and seemed to be waiting for quite sometime.

The boys looked at him in fear as he looked to Calbrawn with a small smile. Calbrawn didn't seem too happy to see him as Cloron rested the wooden carriage near the house. Still looking at the warrior, Calbrawn commanded his eldest son.

"Take three of the deer to the center of the village and give it to the others," Calbrawn commanded, "The first one we will keep for ourselves."

"But father we caught them all," Cloron reminded.

Calbrawn's head shot over to his son and replied, "Do as I say boy. There are some here not as privileged as we are."

Cloron looked down ashamed at his father's tone toward him. He just nodded as he took the first deer and tossed it on a table outside the small hut. He began to push the cart away as the two youngest stayed where they were.

"You two inside," Calbrawn commanded.

The two youngest children went in quickly but soon went to a window to hear what his father was going to talk about.

Calbrawn looked the warrior over and replied, "I see you wear the mark of Tamian."

"Royal Elves," The warrior informed.

Calbrawn looked at him queerly at the statement.

"Tamian is calling his followers Royal Elves," The warrior told.

"Interesting name," Calbrawn told as he placed his sword down and leaned it against the hut.

"I see you still haven't spoken to the other clans," The warrior replied.

"No," Calbrawn said as he faced the deer and took out a small dagger, "I haven't spoken to the others since they decided to join Tamian."

"A warrior like you will be considered a noble," The warrior informed.

"Is that so Dalian?" Calbrawn asked.

The warrior looked at Calbrawn as the old elf began to skin the deer.

"And who is it that says who is of noble blood and common?" Calbrawn asked, "The same man who will call himself king once his great city is built?"

"It is being built," Dalian informed, "There are millions in his empire and more to come. A warrior like you is a noble because of your legend and skills in the battlefield."

"I only fight to protect my family," Calbrawn assured, "As well as the less fortunate. Who will protect the humans and Halflings in these parts? This village is my home now and the home to my children."

Dalian looked at the old elf and said, "I know you've been at odds with the tribes since she died."

"Do not bring that up." Calbrawn warned as he looked over at the warrior, "It is because of this false dream that she died. She thought we could be protected."

Dalian saw the look in his eyes and knew he crossed a line.

"You should take your children and come with me," Dalian told, "You will be a great voice in the empire."

Calbrawn looked at him as if ready to answer but felt a cold chill in the air. It was something odd to him as he turned slightly toward the forest just off in the distance.

"Calbrawn?" Dalian asked, "What is it?"

Calbrawn didn't say a word as he dropped his dagger and got his sword. Dalian pulled his blade as well as he knew the old elf had felt something.

Calbrawn looked to the huts beside his and yelled, "Get the children away from here."

The villagers looked at him as if he were mad not understanding the sudden yelling.

"Get the children out of here," Calbrawn yelled to the villagers, "Warn the others at once."

The villagers began to scatter around his hut as the men went inside their small homes and brought out swords.

"Something wrong Calbrawn?" A human asked as he walked up.

The fields ahead had eyes to them as Calbrawn looked at them.

"Hecorus and Halouse," Calbrawn called.

The two young boys came outside quickly to their fathers call.

"Go to the center of the village and find your brother," Calbrawn commanded, "Go to the mountains and wait for me there."

They didn't question his command as they quickly went.

Calbrawn began to walk toward them as word began to go all around the village. With Dalian beside him Calbrawn walked with many men in the village toward the feeling he got. Humans and elf hunters who had never fought in a battle walked with the experienced Calbrawn and Dalian. Behind them the villagers went inside their huts for safety not knowing what the old elf was warning them about. With about forty men with him Calbrawn stood with his sword in hand and looked to the forest.

"I feel it too," Dalian told.

"Feel what?" A human asked beside them.

The sound of a loud war horn was heard echoing from the forest. The ground rumbled and the earth seemed to shake. Small balls of light soon came to the eyes of the farmers that stood watch. It seemed an evil was coming toward them that they weren't prepared for. The eerie air chilled their very soul as the sound of the horn continued.

The villagers all screamed in fear as dark figures emerged from the forest in an overwhelming number. The balls of light were arrows that had the tips of them on fire. They were quickly shot into the air by the mysterious creatures as they landed on the many huts inside the village. The huts quickly caught fire and the village was filled with anarchy.

With only a force of forty farmers, Calbrawn knew they didn't stand a chance. He had to stay and fight anyway as he had to protect all those in the village. The dark figures came toward them and yelled an unnatural scream as they held weapons in their hands. One of these beings came toward Calbrawn with an ax in one hand and a small sword in the other. Calbrawn blocked the attack and quickly countered slicing the unarmored being in the chest.

"Goblins," A human yelled as he fought them off as well.

The small beings just a foot smaller then they were began to come in at alarming numbers. They were reckless fighters and without a doubt stupid. They were green and ugly in their faces. No sign of hair on their heads and filled with earrings on their faces. Most of their face looked dirty and scratched up from some other encounter. They all had long noses and razor sharp teeth as they yelled when they attacked.

The warriors of the village put up a great fight though, slaying anyone of the goblins that came near them. Only a few got past and began to cause carnage in the village. A few of the human men who didn't join Calbrawn quickly killed them with no casualties coming to the village so far.

Calbrawn went through each goblin quickly as the bodies of the ugly beings began to pile up around him and the others. Blood flew through the air and began to fill his clothing and body armor. No goblin stood a chance against the skilled elf as he and Dalian showed the human warriors around them what skills they possessed.

"Kind of like them old days huh Calbrawn?" Dalian asked with a smile as he killed another goblin.

The hunters manage to keep up with their elf friends killing as many as they could recklessly. Dalian and Calbrawn seemed to be the only two that had enough experience in these types of fights, and their blades showed. Each swipe was accurate and hit their target. They blocked quickly and effectively assuring a quick counter to take their foe out.

Soon though the goblin force stopped coming in such large numbers. A few of the hunters had died defending their village but the task was done. Calbrawn stood side by side with the others with his face covered in the blood of those he killed.

A loud crack was heard from the forest as Calbrawn's eyes got wide. Larger beast that towered over even them emerged slowly carrying axes and swords as large as a man. They were massive in muscle and girth and their faces just as ugly and hideous as the goblins before them. They were bald too, and had pointed ears. Their skin was dark green and able to blend in with the night skies that were soon coming over head. They didn't wear armor, but by the looks of them didn't need to. They could withstand the force of a powerful swipe and still stand to fight. They used this when fighting humans, but the elf that stared at them now knew what strikes to use to put them down quickly.

They slowly walked toward the hunters that had gathered to protect the village in massive numbers. Each towering beast seemed larger then the other as the hunters were filled with intimidation.

"Orcs," A human said softly.

The orc in front of them all was the only one wearing a helm. Around his chest was a sash filled with the heads of elves and other beings it had killed. Most of the orcs gathered the heads of the many people they murdered just to intimidate the next race they encountered. This technique was working as the hunters began to scatter beside Calbrawn.

The humans wanted to make sure their families got a good running start as they left the old elf alone with only a few humans and Dalian. Calbrawn just looked at the first orc coming his way with rage in his eyes as it stared at him.

"I think we should run," Dalian whispered.

Calbrawn kept his eyes fixed on the massive orc as he seemed to ignore Dalian.

"Calbrawn," Dalian yelled, "There are too many of them."

"Is that what you will say to your king?" Calbrawn asked.

Dalian stayed his ground as the first orc swung hard toward Calbrawn's head. The impact of the swipe shifted the wind as the old elf ducked quickly. With no fear Calbrawn swung and sliced the orc in the chest as the orc backed off and yelled in pain. Calbrawn just came in again and swiped as the orc blocked. Calbrawn then countered and sliced the orc again in the chest, stepped to the side and removed its head. The fearless elf wasn't going to let its large body and ugly face stop him from defending the village he called home. He had encountered many of these beasts and knew that their skills didn't match their hideousness. They were just as stupid as the goblins they traveled with and only relied on their power. The skilled elf began to go through them like they were nothing with Dalian at his side.

The humans and elves that stayed and fought with them were overcome with fear. They put up a valiant effort but were no match for the powerful orcs. With one swipe the orcs cut them in half and knew their size and looks made the humans fear their very presence. A few human warriors tried to crawl away, missing an arm or a leg. Goblins ran in back of the orcs and finished the job as the two elves couldn't help the fallen farmers.

Standing back to back Dalian and Calbrawn made sure they couldn't get killed with an attack to their blindside. They were surrounded by dozens of orcs and the others ran into the village and caused havoc among the once peaceful village.

In the center of the village women and children began to scatter away trying to run further east away from the assault. Hecorus and Halouse ran as they final saw their brother trying to run back to where the village was being attacked.

"Where's father?" Cloron yelled in the carnage.

"He said to head for the mountains," Hecorus replied.

Villagers scattered all around them as they heard a sound of screaming. From the sides of the village in every direction goblins and orcs began to ride in. They swung down on innocent villagers with no care or compassion. Human men and women were slaughtered by their swords and axes. Halouse just watched in a state of shock as an orc swiped at a human man cutting him in half. The blood flew through the air and landed on the ground as the young elf was in a state of shock. A human warrior had a sword and managed to kill a few goblins. Once a large orc came at him though, he was sliced in the throat as he dropped to his knees. Two goblins came in and stabbed him in the chest over and over until he no longer moved.

Halouse watched as a small girl grabbed her dead mother's hand and cried as the village began to get filled with the evil beasts. Goblins jumped on the backs of fleeing women as they took their weapons and stabbed the defenseless villagers. Men tried to go to their aid but were quickly slaughtered by the towering orcs that struck fear into their hearts. Each goblin that tackled a victim slammed their swords into them over and over as blood flew from the wounds. Every chop had a sickening sound as the bones crushed and the flesh ripped. Halouse shook with fear at the sight of all the death around him.

Cloron pulled his sword and looked to his two younger brothers.

"Go now," Cloron screamed.

Halouse and Hecorus ran quickly as their brother sliced a goblin in the chest and then stabbed it in the back as it bent over from the first wound. He fought furiously as he tried to save as many people as he could.

The two elf children ran past many goblins and orcs as they continued their slaughter on the villagers. Their speed was helping them along with many other villagers that ran away. A goblin jumped in front of the children as they stopped quickly and saw the drooling beast smile at them. He raised his sword to swipe at them but another blade exploded out of his chest. The blood flew forward and landed on the faces of Hecorus and Halouse. When the goblin fell a human warrior looked to them.

"Run," He yelled.

Hecorus and Halouse did as they were told once again as the intense heat from the burning huts began to take over the village. Some engulfed their vision as they tried to see the direction they were going in. Halouse stopped in his tracks and watched the human that saved him and his brother get swarmed and killed by many orcs.

"Come on Halouse," Hecorus yelled.

Halouse saw the young girl who had captivated him before. She was by her fallen father as she tried to revive him. Blood covered the ground he laid in and the young elf knew he was dead. The young girl cried as she begged for her father to get up. Halouse stood in shock not knowing what to do as his brother called to him a few feet ahead.

Halouse then saw many goblins begin to make their way toward her. He ran toward the little girl as his brother yelled for him to run. Halouse went to a dead human and picked up his sword. He had to hold it with both hands as it dragged behind him. He tried to reach her just as the goblin grabbed her by the back of her hair. She screamed loudly as Halouse was now only a few feet away. Raising the sword with all his might the goblin turned just as he swung. The blade smacked into the side of the goblins face and killed it instantly as it fell to the ground. The little girl's hair was let go off the goblins grasp as Halouse stood in front of her. They exchanged glances like they did before as she sat silently by her dead father.

Hecorus ducked under a swipe from a goblin as he tried to make his way to his brother. He ran quickly as the goblin followed holding his sword high and ready to strike.

"Halouse," The frightened boy yelled.

Halouse turned as the goblin charged at him. Halouse panicked and didn't know what to do. The goblin got closer and closer as Hecorus helped his brother raise the sword. The goblin ran right into the blade as the two held it out. They saw the life escape the goblins eyes and still had a face of absolute fear as it died in front of them.

Halouse saw a dead human on the ground with a bow and several arrows.

"Hecorus," He said to his brother as he pointed.

Hecorus saw it as he ran to the bow and arrows quickly. He ducked under another blade from a goblin that passed. He slid to the bow and arrows and grabbed them. He ran back and landed in front of his brother as Halouse just stayed his ground with the little girl in back of them. She cried out loud almost asking for the goblins to find them.

The sights around them were more hideous as they could barely watch the other villagers get killed so viciously. Halouse just watched as the blood flew through the air from the swing of the swords by the goblin and orc beasts. He cradled the little girl in his arms as she buried her head in his chest.

A goblin saw them as he began to walk toward them slowly.

"Hecorus," Halouse yelled.

The young elf took an arrow and began to place it on the bow string. The goblin picked up his pace as he raised his sword. Hecorus pulled back the string and fired. As the goblin was struck in the face he fell to his knees and dropped in front of them. Hecorus quickly loaded another arrow still shaking in fear as he pulled back and fired again. He looked all around him and tried to help those who were in need of help. Each shot hit its mark as the young elf had experience in firing an arrow. Every goblin that came anywhere near them was met by an accurate arrow hitting them in the head or chest. Hecorus reached his last arrow and aimed. A goblin tackled a woman a few feet away from them and raised its ax. Hecorus fired hitting it perfectly in the chest. The goblin fell back as the woman ran from the body but was quickly killed by another not far away. Hecorus began to cry in fear as he looked at the empty sack.

More goblins began to swarm them as Hecorus went to his brother while he held the young elf girl. The goblins seemed to laugh at Halouse holding the sword as they knew he couldn't hold it upright with all his strength. Many of them surrounded Halouse, Hecorus and the young girl as the two young elves looked on in terror. The young girl wanted to look but Halouse shifted his body away so she couldn't see the faces of the horrible beings that stalked over them. They waited to strike knowing that the young elves were defenseless.

"Feisty one," The goblin hissed as his unnatural voice made the three shake in fear.

"Give me the blade boy and I'll kill you quickly," Another said as he went toward them.

Halouse picked up the sword and swung wildly. The goblin jumped back out of the way of the sluggish attack as he laughed.

Two orcs walked up and began to throw the goblins out of their way. They towered over the young elves as their shadow covered all three of them with room to spare. They grunted at the sight of them and stared curiously.

"Leave them to us," a goblin said to the orc.

The orc threw out his elbow hitting the goblin in the face as he fell back. The orc then picked up his ax as the three all prepared for the worst. Hecorus grabbed his brother as Halouse grabbed the little girl and covered her.

Just as the strike was about to come a large spear landed in the center of the massive orc's chest. It grunted in confusion as it looked at the large spear. The orc looked forward as a sword was coming right for it. The warrior wielding it cut off the orcs head and began to engage with the other.

Hundreds of elfish warriors came from the east end of the city and began to fight off the orc and goblin forces. Hecorus and Halouse had never seen these warriors before and knew that they just arrived. Dressed in armor and holding shields they were definitely skilled. Warriors stood in front of the children as they protected them from the orcs and goblins.

Two of the warriors looked down as the three frightened children looked up. The two warriors were elves by their long blonde hair and pointed ears. One the chest plate of one warrior was four red slash marks going from right to left. The other warrior had a dark red crescent moon on the center of his. The one with the slash marks held out his hand to the children.

"It's alright," He replied, "We are here to help."

Hecorus, Halouse and the young girl all rose as the girl looked down at her father in tears.

"Papa," The young girl said.

The other warrior dropped to his knees in front of her and said, "Your papa is gone."

The little girl looked at him as her eyes pored with tears. The warrior wiped them away for her as he pulled the young girl in and picked her up. With the village now filled with hundreds of these strange warriors, the orcs and goblins were quickly getting killed.

"Come with us boys," The elf with the slash marks replied.

On the other side of the village Calbrawn and Dalian had dozens of bodies surrounding them as they were filled with blood. None of it their own as their swords were ready to strike again at the orcs that surrounded them. Arrows flew in from every direction as the orcs began to fall to their death. Calbrawn and Dalian rested as they saw hundreds of elf warriors emerge from in back of them and attack.

Calbrawn looked on in disbelief as these warriors seemed to come to their aid. Calbrawn and Dalian killed several other orcs before finding that they were surrounded by elves now and not the beasts that attacked their village.

Cloron found his brothers in the company of the two elves as he reached them.

"You're alright," Cloron said in relief.

"Sure they are," The elf with the crescent moon told as he held the little girl.

"Who are you?" Cloron asked.

The two elves looked at one another as the one with the slash marks asked, "Where is Calbrawn."

The village was put out of all its fires. The orc and goblin army that attacked was no more. They had ran off and been pushed out by the elves that showed up and helped the remaining villagers. Hundreds of bodies laid all over the village grounds as Calbrawn walked through it with Dalian beside him. Calbrawn reached down to a woman who was face up and her eyes still open. Covered in her own blood she had been killed with no means of defending herself. Calbrawn closed her eyes as he stood up and examined the others around him.

"This never would have happened if you were with us," Dalian told.

Calbrawn grabbed Dalian by his shirt and began to shake him violently.

"Did you bring them here," Calbrawn yelled, "Did you know they were coming."

"No," Dalian assured as he pushed Calbrawn away, "I came here for you. I have no ranks with me it is only me."

Calbrawn was enraged as he looked at Dalian and fought back his anger.

"Tamian asked you to find me?" Calbrawn asked.

Dalian nodded and replied, "Zesordan is speaking with him soon as well for his tribe to join the empire."

"Zesordan will say no," Calbrawn knew, "Just like I am saying no."

"And you will let this happen again?" Dalian asked, "Not in this village my friend but another. We need an empire."

"For what?" Calbrawn yelled, "We will be great the first few years until the politics take over. Every elf I have ever encountered except a slim few have become engulfed with their power. Tamian is just like his father."

Dalian just looked at him and knew he couldn't convince the old elf.

"I have to find my children Dalian," Calbrawn told.

"Father," A voice called.

Calbrawn watched as Cloron ran to him past many of the elf warriors. Calbrawn was relieved once he saw two elves walking with Hecorus and Halouse.

"Thank Warad," Calbrawn replied hugging his eldest son.

Calbrawn then looked to the one warrior with the slash marks on his chest who walked with Hecorus and Halouse.

"Hadenmere," Calbrawn called.

"Calbrawn," The warrior replied.

Calbrawn reached in and hugged him as well.

As they broke Hadenmere asked, "How have you been?"

Calbrawn looked around and said, "Not so good."

"Sorry," Hadenmere replied, "We knew they were coming and had been tracking them for days."

"You couldn't send word?" Calbrawn asked.

"We didn't know how," The warrior with the crescent moon said.

Calbrawn looked at him and saw the young girl in his grasp.

"Bramodor," Calbrawn said.

"Calbrawn," Bramodor greeted with a nod of his head, "We need to talk."

The living villagers were all being attended to by the elf warriors with both the marks of their chest. They were a tribe like most elves that had joined together over the struggles that had happened over the years. Maybe once they were bitter rivals, but new times called for new actions.

Dalian and Calbrawn were in a tent with many other elf hunters that survived the attack. They seemed to be the voices of the remaining villagers. The two leaders who had seen them earlier were commanding their forces outside and making sure no other attack would come. There were hundreds of these elf warriors now and the number seemed to be getting greater by the moment.

"Who are those two you spoke with before?" Dalian asked Calbrawn as he ripped a piece of bread and ate it.

"The one with the slash marks is Hadenmere," Calbrawn told, "He is the leader of the Lycans. The other is Bramodor; he is the leader of the Murkildens. The slash mark is known as the mark of the Lycan, and the crescent moon is the mark of the Murkilden. They are tribes of elves that Tamian hasn't gotten to yet."

"He will soon," Dalian assured, "He wants to unite all of them."

"The Lycans and Murkildens believe in the old ways," Calbrawn informed, "They won't go for it."

"How do you know?" Dalian asked.

"I used to lead the Lycans," Calbrawn reminded, "They were my clan remember."

Just then Hadenmere and Bramodor entered the tent and looked at the others inside. Hadenmere had a basket filled with bread as he tossed it toward some of the other elves.

"We brought this with us," Hadenmere informed, "We figured you'd be hungry."

Calbrawn took a loaf and just placed it on his legs as he sat. He looked up at the two warriors that came to his aid and knew they were there for other reasons.

Hadenmere and Bramodor sat across from him as some of the others ate the bread they were given.

"What is it?" Hadenmere asked seeing Calbrawn's glance.

"What news?" Calbrawn asked.

Bramodor and Hadenmere looked at each other for a few moments then back at Calbrawn.

"Most of the clans have joined with Tamian," Hadenmere told, "The Crasions were the newest to go. They joined him in his attempt to build the elf empire."

"The Overlanders?" Calbrawn asked.

"They and the Underlanders are now one as well," Bramodor told, "They are lead by an elf named Rakar. He plans on moving to Cagore to get away from these parts."

"And you two?" Calbrawn asked, "Do your clans plan on walking away as well?"

The two leaders looked at one another as Hadenmere said, "You are the true leader of the Lycans."

"I left a long time ago," Calbrawn reminded.

"Since your wife died," Bramodor remembered, "You have to get past that now my friend."

Calbrawn looked at him as the rage filled in his eyes soon went away. He knew he didn't mean to bring her name up out of disrespect.

"Tamian's idea of one empire is good," Dalian jumped in, "We should join him in the upper lands and create this empire. He's building a city as we speak."

"Human's have cities," Hadenmere reminded, "Look at the history of our world and you will see what has happen to them."

"We are elves," Dalian reminded, "We will give the people protection and they will not live in fear of The Dark Lord's forces."

"So you're here for Calbrawn as well," Bramodor knew looking at him, "It seems everyone is looking for you old friend."

Calbrawn looked at the Lycan and Murkilden leaders and thought to himself.

"How many do you have?" Calbrawn asked.

"A few hundred thousand," Hadenmere told, "Some were killed in the resistance."

"What resistance?" Calbrawn asked.

"There are more orcs and goblins all over the Cavell Territory," Bramodor informed, "So many tribes have been wiped from the earth."

"Zesordan and the Lucian tribe?" Calbrawn asked.

"Still around," Hadenmere informed, "Not for long though he says he's leaving Tullian."

"Leaving Tullian?" Calbrawn asked as if the statement was mad, "Where will he go."

Bramodor shrugged and replied, "Who knows."

Calbrawn took a small piece of the bread he had and began to eat it. The two leaders just looked at him as they looked ready to ask him something else.

"What?" Calbrawn asked reading their expression.

"A lot of the Lycans and Murkildens think it is wise to join Tamian," Hadenmere informed, "Being the leader of the Lycans I have agreed."

"So have I," Bramodor told, "The Murkildens want nothing but to survive not get killed."

"What about us?" Another elf asked not far away, "Our tribes have been killed. We can only find refuge with the humans in these villages."

"These villages are easy to attack," Calbrawn told the elf as he looked at Hadenmere and asked, "You think it wise to join Tamian?"

"We came looking for you because some of the men still think you lead them," Hadenmere replied.

"And what do you say?" Calbrawn asked.

Hadenmere shrugged and said, "They are your tribe. I only took over after you left us. They will follow you to the ends of the earth."

Calbrawn looked at them all and simply replied, "Our ways have never been for an empire ruled by a king. We have always lived our lives with no one being of better blood then the next man. Every ones family have shed blood and spilled it in the name of elves. I will not join a power hungry boy."

"You're making a mistake," Dalian assured him.

Calbrawn looked at his converted friend then back at Hadenmere and Bramodor.

"Where will we go?" Bramodor asked.

"I know a place," Calbrawn said, "Hunted across it many times and it is a secret."

"The woman and children are northeast of here," Hadenmere informed.

"We will get them," Calbrawn said, "We leave in the morning."

"What about the rest of us," An elf on the side of them asked.

Calbrawn looked at them and replied, "You can either go with us to where I'm going, or go with Dalian to the empire northeast of here. A man named Tamian promises an empire and if that's what you feel is best for your family then go."

"Will they give us protection?" An elf asked.

"He builds a city with large walls," Dalian informed, "You can find a home inside for a small fee."

"A fee that will get larger with every passing season," Hadenmere replied softly.

"Please," Calbrawn said to him, "Let these families chose their way. I will not force any of them to follow us."

"What will I tell Tamian about you," Dalian told, "He sent me to find the one warrior he heard so many rumors about."

Calbrawn looked at Dalian and said, "Tell him you heard I died."

Calbrawn got up as Hadenmere and Bramodor followed. The two leaders looked at Dalian for several moments before they followed Calbrawn out of the tent.

Halouse, Cloron and Hecorus sat by a carriage as a few Lycan warriors looked after them. The young girl Halouse had saved was still with them as she still had glassy eyes and looked to have been crying the entire time. Calbrawn took the bread in his hands and tossed it to Cloron.

"Split that with your brothers," Calbrawn commanded.

Calbrawn looked down at the young girl who had lost her family. She looked up at the old elf as he saw something in her eyes he had never seen before. He seemed captivated by her as she looked up at him sadly.

"Calbrawn," An elf yelled from in back of him.

Calbrawn turned to see a neighbor of his walking up to him.

"How's it going Famon?" Calbrawn asked.

"Alright," Famon said, "You have my brothers adopted daughter."

"Is that so," Calbrawn replied as he looked down at the young girl, "Are you her only family left?"

"Seems that way," Famon told, "I take my family to the empire being built."

"Is that so," Calbrawn asked as he looked at the little girl and just nodded to her.

She began to walk slowly toward the elf Famon but was grabbed on the arm by Halouse. She looked at him with a shocked look as Halouse stood in front of her and stopped her from going to Famon.

"Seems my boy has quite a liking toward her," Calbrawn replied, "Are you sure you'll be able to look after her?"

"On my brother's honor I will," Famon assured.

Calbrawn kneeled down to his son and made the boy face him.

"Halouse," Calbrawn called, "Let her go my boy. I have a rough time taking care of the three of you."

Halouse just looked at his father then back at the little girl. She just looked at him with her face down. She began to walk toward her uncle as she stopped for a moment. She turned back around and began to take off a necklace she had around her neck. She opened Halouse's hand and placed it in.

"Thank you Halouse," The little girl said.

She turned quickly and went to her uncle as Famon walked her away from the young boy.

Calbrawn saw the sadness in his son's eyes as he made Halouse face him.

"What's wrong?" Calbrawn asked.

"I think I loved her," The young boy replied.

Halouse kind of chuckled and asked, "Truly?"

"Yes father," Halouse said.

Calbrawn just nodded and said, "Then if you truly love her, the gods will make sure you see her again."

"Do you think so?" Halouse asked.

Calbrawn smiled at his son and said, "Yes. For one day you will see your mother again and so will I."

Calbrawn got up and began to walk with Hadenmere and Bramodor. Cloron followed his father as Hecorus stood next to his younger brother.

"You sound so stupid," Hecorus told, "You know nothing of love. We're just kids Halouse."

Halouse looked for her through the darkness but couldn't see her. He was so captivated and intrigued by her and he couldn't explain it.

As the night stars shined above the many elves that remained in the village began to move out with the Lycan and Murkilden warriors that saved them. Dalian had gotten a few of the elves to follow him back to the city that was being built not too far away.

Halouse sat in the back of a carriage and looked out at the village he once called home. Smoke still came in the air from the many fires that burned earlier. With his brothers sitting beside him he wondered if he'd ever see that girl again. Opening his hand he saw a gold necklace with a small star as the charm. He slowly placed the necklace around his neck as he sat forward and looked to the open land the large force was traveling toward.

He knew he'd see her again.

One day.

Chapter 2

In a land that only exists in the imaginations of those who chose to
see it; lives the land of Tullian. In this numinous world of magic
and beasts that haunt the nightmares of every living man, the
races of this land battle the evils to keep peace amongst the world. In
this land though there are races of such beauty and grace long lost in
the minds of everyday men. Brave warriors who are bound by their
word and honor, as well as beautiful women who are as loving and
elegant as their striking presence.

At first the god Warad had only created humans. For thousands of
years their kingdoms fought back and forth one kingdom claiming
rule to the world and then another. The humans soon became greedy
of ruling the world and ultimately destroyed themselves. To protect
them from the other human forces Warad created six creators of a
superior race. They were elves. The six were giving blessing from each
god of the six realms. Each warrior cast out to protect the kingdoms
from the evils of the world and themselves. Protecting the human
forces known as the Falmores was Fayne. He was Warad's warrior of
the six created elves and was to be champion of the six.

Warad realized that the six could not even control all the kingdoms
of Tullian and decided to create more elves to create balance amongst
the world. The six created elves though were the most powerful. The

elves created after them could never stand to put up a fight against them and only the bloodline of the original six could defeat the others. These six chosen elves though soon began to make their own tribes of the elves created by Warad as they too became greedy with power. To prove who was the ultimate champion of all the world, each of the original six cast out to find the others. In the end Fayne was the only one that remained. Taking each blessing by each god from the corpse of the other five. Torn by the war each tribe cast away from him and scattered all over the lands of Tullian. It would be thousands of years before the tribes would reunite once again.

Starting from the beginning the god Warad decided instead of making a world of just humans that he'd create a whole world of many races. Races that would keep the world of Tullian balanced and unable to drop to one kingdom then another. The chosen race of the god Warad was the elves. Elves unlike most creations were a people of their word. They were honorable and respectable to even their most hated enemy.

Being champion of the original six elves Fayne was defender of all the world and would go to great lengths to stop the evils made by Warad's three evil sons.

The three sons The Dark Lord, Greco and Korack were once gods to protect the world of Tullian. Each of his sons were Guardians of this sacred world to protect it from the other gods. There was Korack the Guardian of Fire, Greco the Guardian of Shadows and the eldest The Dark Lord, his original name long lost, the Guardian of Darkness. They were each given kingdoms to rule and people to love them, but each god was not satisfied with all the gifts given to them by their loving peaceful father. After becoming greedy with their life style they struck out against the god and tried to destroy him for full control of Tullian. The three brothers were easily defeated by their father and cursed for the remainder of their days. Banished to The Dark Realm, a world created by The Dark Lord in his own image was a realm plagued with darkness and would never feel the embrace of the sun ever again.

The fourth member of this family, The Guardian of Light, was also cast out into the world so it could not be corrupted by the other three. If the fourth Guardian went against Warad then the mighty god no matter how powerful would be killed. For its own protection The

Guardian of Light was born among the races of Tullian and raised unknowing of its true fate or identity.

Sent to defend the world of Tullian from The Dark Lord, Korack and Greco; Fayne, believed at one time to be the Guardian of Light was the greatest champion the world had ever seen. A dark day soon came to the warrior as The Dark Lord cast a spell on him and forced him to murder his own wife. The Dark Lord getting into the mind of the mortal, easily convincing the feeble minded elf that it was Warad's fault Fayne turned his allegiance over to The Dark Lord. Once again trapped and unable to kill his creation Warad cast Fayne from the world of Tullian forever. In his last words to Fayne he told him he could only return if he killed a king of the elves. At the time there were no kings and it never seemed there would be because of the mass hatred of all the tribes. After his banishment Fayne forced the humans he was protecting; The Falmores to be banished with him. They soon came to the island known as Fadarth and were soon known as a myth among the races in Tullian.

Elves had always believed that a king would make their race corrupt and able to be defeated if an injudicious king took the throne. After thousands of years of fighting in tribes one elf who went buy the name of Elamorn wanted to combine the tribes. He thought it best to make an empire that could defend against the evils of the world. He knew that with all the elves separated into tribes that they were only weaker. After his death, his son Tamian followed in his fathers dream. He combined the tribes to form his own kingdom. With a leadership quality born to him by the gods he reunited every tribe he could to join as one immense force. After ages of building the great city for the army was built and the Royal Elves were born.

Many tribes who disagreed with this concept soon heard the rumors about the great empire being built. Still believing in their old ways and not wanting a king to rule over them, they fled to other parts of the Tullian world. They were soon lost to the minds of all the other elves and never heard of again.

Many years of being king of Royal Elves, Tamian began to make many enemies. They all lived around him, and as the empire expanded into the great force it is today, many of his enemies fled his city and made their homes in other portions of the empire. They plotted to this day, to remove him from the throne and take place as king of the elves themselves.

In the land of Tamian which took up most of the north and center of Tullian was the home of the mighty Royal Elves. Able to live thousands of years with no look of aging coming to their face, they all stood at an average of six foot, had blonde hair and either blue or green eyes. There most distinct quality was of course their pointed ears.

Tamian was the land and also the name of the largest city in the world. Fitting millions of Royal Elves inside its gates, it always protected them from the evils in the outside lands.

Inside the city of Tamian the Royal Elves were going about their lives as if usual. The city was filled with many soldiers to make sure everything in the city was kept in order. Markets and shops were set up all around so many people inside the villages of the city could get the usual things to feed their families.

Tamian had four castles that raised high in the heavens and could be seen many miles away from the Royal Elves capitol. The tallest of them belonged to Tamian and his wife; Queen Drizell. The three other castles were his safe havens where he met with the nobles and other high authority figures among the Royal Elves to discuss any agendas going on around the world.

He stood in his high tower looking out in the courtyards below. Wearing a mighty crown on his forehead he was being dressed by many of his servants. As they surrounded him they were fitting him for that days outfit. Only the most expensive robes would do. They quickly placed on a sheet of light armor and a royal blue cape. He also wore a royal blue sash that had armor around it as well. The servants quickly placed his sword around him as he finally looked at himself in a mirror.

He looked like most Royal Elves. Blue inescapable eyes that caught the attraction of every woman he passed. The top half of his long blonde hair was pulled back but some of it still dropped freely behind him and on the sides. He had several scars on his face from past battles but his name and reputation made him the fiercest and most known man in the entire world. The royal blue dragon crested on his armor was the symbol of his people. Designed by his late father when his people were still tribesmen, this symbol represented all those who had died before him who wanted an empire like the one he was king of. This wasn't just a symbol of his people, it was the lives of many lost before this great empire stood in the world today. It was a reminder to him that he owed his kingship to many before he was even alive.

"What do you think my lord?" One of his servants asked.

"Fine for today," Tamian agreed as he began to tighten the sash around his waist, "Make sure General Lyncade and Nagarth are waiting for me in the throne room."

"Of course my lord," A servant replied.

Tamian looked himself over for several moments before he turned away and began to walk out his chambers. After reaching the hallway dozens of guards surrounded him as they escorted him to the throne room. As he passed other guards in the castle they quickly dropped to their knees. When he was out of his sight they rose again and went on with their daily duty. All the guards in the castle were dressed head to toe in armor. Only their upper arms and thigh were without it. Even those portions of their body had blue robes covering them. The royal blue dragon as well was on their chest and hung all around the halls of the great castle they guarded. Their faces were hidden behind cone shaped helms and their faces covered with the steel of a faceplate. Only the eyes of each warrior were seen as they kept them open to anything unusual in the empire.

As Tamian reached the throne room the doors were opened and even more guards stood inside. They smashed the bottom of their spears in the ground as he entered and all dropped to one knee.

Awaiting him on the throne platform was his wife Drizell. Drizell's beauty and grace was becoming legend as the years of her rule continued. Dressed in an all white robe that glistened with the diamonds around it she sat patiently for him. She wore a small crown on her forehead with her long blonde hair dropped freely in back of her. Her purity and embellishment was seen in just her body language. Her love for her people was almost as strong as her love for the king. Her beauty was envied by women of every race and fantasized about by the men of every race.

The white gown she wore was tight around her body showing off her curvy figure. The bust line of the gown wasn't too low but showed just enough for those to see. She wasn't to show too much, being a woman of royalty but still enjoyed showing herself off to any eye that wanted to look.

Tamian slowly made it to his throne as he turned and looked at the hundreds of guards standing inside the throne room. All at the same time they turned and faced him as they all dropped to their knees in worship. Tamian took the hand of his wife and sat in the large throne next to hers.

"Rise," Tamian softly said.

Each did as two warriors made their way to the king.

They dropped to their knees once again but rose quickly as they looked up at him.

The first was Lyncade, the High General and a High Lord of the Royal Elf Empire. He was looked at and worshipped like Tamian by all those he encountered. For the many years of service to the king he was given lands and servants of his own. Choosing to stay in the city and teach he was given one of the four castles that stood high in the heavens of the great city.

Lyncade was by far the most skilled with a blade and able to take on legions of orcs and goblins by himself. He was also the leader of the Royal Guard. The Royal Guard was Tamian's personal body guards. Each warrior of this regiment wore heavy armor from their neck to their feet. Each of them had hundreds of years of training under their belts and had fought in many battles in the years past.

Lyncade was always dressed ready for a battle like most warriors in the city. Their constant dressing in armor was to let everyone in the city know who they were. Lyncade's face though was no secret to the people, built on the many battles he had won through the years. He wore a long blue cape with the blue dragon on his back outlined in white.

The second general was Nagarth. He led the forces of foot soldiers that walked into battle. These warriors were the frontline of the Royal Elves but with him next to them they always fought nobly. His armor was freer and not as heavy. With just light armor protecting his chest, he also wore shin guards and forearms guards. The rest of his body was free and scars from the past proved he had experience.

Tamian looked around and the many guards in the throne room and said, "Leave us."

After many moments the guards inhabiting the throne room shifted toward the doors and quickly left the king and queen alone with the two generals.

"What news?" Tamian asked.

"An orc and goblin force was spotted hitting the shores of Cavell a few days ago," Lyncade informed, "A small regiment was sent out the moment we heard of it."

"Any news of them?" Tamian asked.

"They were supposed to send word if they engaged," Nagarth told, "So far nothing has come back."

"Was a number counted on how many orc and goblins there were?" Tamian asked.

"No my lord," Nagarth informed.

"What do you suggest?" Tamian asked.

"A large force," Lyncade said quickly, "I will lead them."

"Very brave of you," Tamian replied, "But Nagarth will go. Lyncade you have been away from the city long enough and are due for a rest. I wish for Nagarth to go with his regiments."

"How many my lord?" Nagarth asked.

"Take five hundred," Tamian suggested.

"My lord," Lyncade quickly cut in, "I do not suggest that his regiment is weak but the last force we sent was about three hundred. I think we should make it a force of at least a thousand. We don't know how many forces are coming."

Tamian looked at him for a few moments and replied, "Agreed. Good suggestion. Do you think this is an all out invasion of The Dark Lord?"

"Hard to say my lord," Nagarth told, "The scouts who spotted the orc and goblin force said it was just a small war party. Nothing to be concerned of as an all out invasion."

Tamian thought to himself and just nodded slowly. He seemed to be thinking to himself about the situation.

"Orc and goblin forces haven't had a major army in many years my king," Lyncade reminded, "Last we heard from the city of Arawon, General Xanafear had won many battles against the orc and goblin forces that came to their portion of our lands."

"Arawon," Tamian said with a small laugh, "His armies haven't felt the wrath of an orc and goblin force. He stays high in his city and stays away from conflict when we fight the real armies of The Dark Lord."

"What is his word to us about the amount of forces he is encountering?" Lyncade asked.

Tamian shrugged and replied, "Don't know. Arawon hasn't spoken to me in many years. He seems to think my ways of ruling *my* kingdom are wrong. He has his General Xanafear and he will fight off what ever armies go his way."

"Why hasn't he spoken with you?" Nagarth asked.

Tamian looked at the general for a brief moment and replied, "The hunting grounds in Celladom have become overrun with the other races. The Forest Elves, the humans, and the dwarves. The amount of animals they are killing is becoming too much and we may have to back away for a while. Arawon seems to think that we should be the only race able to hunt in Celladom and that the others should stay away. Matter of fact he's killed many and almost caused a war between me and some of the other races."

"He should be dealt with accordingly," Nagarth suggested.

Tamian shook his head and replied, "Arawon has many allies even in our city. The senate and the nobles even here hold him in high favor. He controls most of the trades in the known world and is a powerful man."

"He is not king," Lyncade reminded, "You are."

Tamian looked at his dedicated general and glanced over at his wife.

"Would you leave us dear," Tamian said softly, "I doubt you want to hear about politics."

"Of course my lord," Drizell said respectfully, "I will be awaiting your call."

The queen reached in and kissed him gently on the lips as when she rose, Lyncade and Nagarth dropped to one knee in respect. It was only when she headed for a side door in the throne room did they rise. Tamian rose as well and stood on the platform in front of his two most trusted generals.

"Her dedication to me is undeniable," Tamian replied, "But now it seems I can't even trust her."

"Things among the nobles that bad?" Nagarth asked.

Tamian looked at them and slowly nodded as he said, "Maxus may be in alliance against me."

"The High Nobleman of Tamian?" Nagarth asked.

Tamian nodded and regretfully said, "Yes."

"For what purpose?" Lyncade asked.

"It seems that many of the nobles and those among the senate think that the lands should be ruled by elves," Tamian said, "In theory they may be right but our ways are to the gods. Not to rule over the races but the live among them as our god intended."

"They sit high in their large homes surrounded by servants," Lyncade reminded, "They eat large amounts of food, stuff themselves with fruits and indulge is escapades with many of their friends wives. A man of power always wants more."

"They are taking too much from the races that live around us," Tamian told, "It's no wonder that they hate our kind."

"The dwarves live too far away to be a problem," Nagarth reminded, "The Forest Elves have their own kingdom and the humans are still without a king. They have nobles running them and couldn't go to war with our kind even if they wanted to."

"My fathers dream was an empire of peace," Tamian reminded, "Those nobles and senators of our empire are causing a lot of trouble. There are so many of them into the idea of ruling the entire world that they may think me being king is in their way."

"We will never let anything happen to you," Nagarth assured, "You have many other generals besides me and Lyncade that will assure that."

"I know," Tamian knew, "But with Maxus here and many others in alliance with Arawon the future of our kingdom could be in danger. If my life is taken and one of them has the throne you may see evil in which not even The Dark Lord can show."

"We have problems with them and they are trying to control the world themselves," Lyncade added, "It's hard to know who is with us and who is against us."

"We will know in time," Tamian assured, "Those trying to take me from my place with show themselves through their actions."

"What does Boleadar say?" Nagarth asked.

"Boleadar's allegiance is with whom ever is strong," Tamian knew, "He will show me allegiance if I win, and the others allegiance if they win."

"Doesn't really show him to be one we can count on," Lyncade stressed.

"Boleadar is just like them but not as corrupt," Tamian informed, "At least he isn't after my throne."

"Have the other races shown any indication of wanting a war with us because of their actions?" Nagarth asked.

"None yet," Tamian replied, "Then again if you were about to attack us, would you inform us?"

The two generals just looked at their king and knew he had a great deal on his mind.

"So this orc and goblin force is really the last thing we need," Tamian replied as he sat sluggishly on his throne and looked down at them.

"Is that why you wanted me to stay?" Lyncade asked.

Tamian nodded and replied, "With you here and knowing of your reputation they will surly know that I am on to what they may or may not be planning."

"Have you assured the other races that you do not condone what Arawon is doing?" Lyncade asked.

"I have sent word," Tamian informed, "But because of the threat of them I had to dispatch a few thousand men all around the kingdom to assure no one tries to attack."

"That's why we haven't seen the other generals," Nagarth realized.

Tamian just exhaled in frustration then looked at Nagarth and replied, "Get your men prepared and go out on your task."

Nagarth and Lyncade nodded their heads, turned and slowly began to walk away.

"Lyncade," Tamian called.

Lyncade looked at Nagarth and nodded as he turned and faced his king.

"Walk with me," Tamian replied as he got up.

The two slowly began to walk out the east exit of the throne room as they left guards in the halls followed their king and Lyncade, but at a distance. Knowing the king wanted a few moments alone with his general they stayed far behind.

"Yes my lord?" Lyncade asked as they walked.

"I didn't mean to offend you in there before about the sending only five hundred men," Tamian assured, "But you have been out of the city for some time."

"I know," Lyncade replied, "The orc and goblin force don't seem so strong right now. I figured if I went my regiments would make it quick."

"Of course they would," Tamian replied, "But I have something else I need to ask."

"Of course," Lyncade said as he stopped and looked at his king.

Tamian looked down for a brief moment and replied, "Drizell wants to have a child."

Lyncade looked shocked a little as he said, "That's great news my king."

"Indeed," Tamian agreed, "But the problem is he is surely to be the one to take the throne when I'm gone."

"Of course," Lyncade said.

"Any thoughts of getting a wife yourself?" Tamian asked.

Lyncade studied his king and asked, "What are you suggesting?"

"Me and Drizell were talking and agreed that among all my nobles and generals that you should get a wife and have a child of your own," Tamian explained.

"Like a daughter," Lyncade said.

"Yes," Tamian replied, "With my blood and your blood together the future of our people would be at its strongest. The son of Tamian and the daughter of the Royal Elves greatest general joined in marriage. With the recent alliance against me with the other nobles and senators, if I am to be slain I want an heir to take my place that believes in the same things I do."

Lyncade just nodded as he said, "You must give me some time my lord."

"How much?" Tamian asked.

"Well I will need to find a wife," Lyncade informed.

"Why not have one of your servants?" Tamian suggested.

"This type of proposal from you my king, I will go about in the purest form," Lyncade told, "I will not mate with just a random servant."

Tamian nodded and replied, "As you wish."

Lyncade watched as Tamian walked away from him slowly. Lyncade quickly began to walk out of the castle.

"Lyncade," a voice called.

Still walking Lyncade looked back to see Nagarth running toward him.

"Don't you have a regiment of goblins and orcs to kill?" Lyncade asked.

"Of course but I have to at least ask where it is you're headed," Nagarth replied.

Lyncade smiled at him as he said, "Home for a few moments."

"Then to the temple?" Nagarth asked in a teasing matter.

"Maybe," Lyncade replied.

"Let me follow?" Nagarth asked.

"You have to leave," Lyncade reminded.

"Not for a few moments," Nagarth said, "Besides some of the men are still getting there things together."

"Come if you wish," Lyncade replied.

"What did you and Tamian discuss?" Nagarth asked.

"That is between me and our king," Lyncade reminded.

"Who will I tell?" Nagarth asked.

Lyncade hesitated for a few moments then began to tell his closest friend, "He wants me to find a wife so when he and the queen have a child they will end up married to one another. He wants both our bloodline to continue and be the future of this empire. I don't know why he didn't ask Boleadar."

"It's because of the fight he and Boleadar got into," Nagarth told.

"Fight?" Lyncade asked, "He didn't say anything about a fight."

"He wouldn't. Tamian wants us to think that the problem among him and the others has nothing to do with him," Nagarth told, "Some of the nobles who live in that city got into a very bad disagreement with him. Some of the evils that plague Porian came onto the lands near Boleadar and killed thousands. Tamian told them that there was no way they could fight the evils in Porian."

"Some say they're ghosts of warriors that have died unnaturally and never accepted their fate," Lyncade said.

"How can you kill a ghost?" Nagarth added.

"When did this disagreement happen?" Lyncade asked.

"When you were away," Nagarth told, "Boleadar himself told Tamian to handle the situation or he wouldn't go to the king's side if ever there was a need."

"That's treason," Lyncade told.

"Not if it's by a High Noble," Nagarth reminded, "Especially if he has a rule of agreement from most of the nobles. As you know to get away from Tamian's rule here most of the nobles go to Boleadar to get away from him."

"And Arawon?" Lyncade asked, "His hatred is just?"

"No," Nagarth said, "Arawon is drunk with power and just wants more. He hates Tamian only because Tamian has the crown. Arawon has everything else except that."

The two generals walked through the crowded streets making their way to a temple located in the center of the city. It was a temple where the god Warad was worshipped daily by the people. With hundreds in the courtyard in worship the two generals quickly walked up the stairs to get inside. Only Royalty and Lords of the Elves were aloud to go inside. Guards in the front of the temple quickly knew the generals and let them pass.

Inside servants were washing the floors on the temple. It was done daily to make sure it was kept clean. Inside were mighty columns, pillars and statues of the god Warad as seen in the minds of artists who imagined what the god looked like. Several fountains were also inside with beautiful gardens surrounded by flowers. All around them priest and priestess walked around keeping watch of the sacred temple.

The two generals stood next to a column as they looked down several hundred feet at a servant girl cleaning the floor.

"Is that her?" Nagarth asked.

"I think so," Lyncade replied softly.

The woman they stared at was facing away from them working like a slave to clean the floor. Her long blonde hair hung in back of her as she was wearing a white robe filled with dirt from her hard days work.

"Can I help you," A priest asked as he walked up to them. As he realized who they were he quickly replied, "General Lyncade, General Nagarth I'm sorry for my rude greeting."

"It's alright," Lyncade asked still looking toward the girl, "Who owns these servants?"

"A Royal Elf names Farian," The priest told, "They come once every other day to wash the floors."

"That will be all," Lyncade said.

The priest bowed his head and quickly walked away from the two men.

"Farian?" Nagarth whispered.

"I've heard of him," Lyncade said, "He's the one who handed Tamian his servants. He's nothing but a shop keeper. Takes the orphaned children of those who died in battle and sells them as slaves. With the fathers of the homes dieing in battle being a servant is all they can afford to do."

"It's a real shame," Nagarth replied, "That one has a face I have never seen before."

The servant girl got up and turned to them slowly. Her face captured them instantly despite the fact that it was filled with dirt. She looked tired and exhausted from her work as she made eye contact with Lyncade. Her face was so pure and her blue eyes seemed to capture him in a way he could never explain. Lyncade had seen beauty before but this girl he looked at now made everything that he once called beautiful seem so ugly.

She was young for an elf, maybe a few hundred years old but a late teenager by their standards. Royal Elf woman reached a peek of their beauty at about one hundred and look that way for most of their remaining days. Only elves who reached into the eighty thousands began to decline in looks.

As the girl looked she quickly looked away and went back to cleaning the floor.

"Good luck," Nagarth replied as he hit Lyncade in the shoulder, "I'm off to battle."

Lyncade just nodded still looking at the back of the girl as Nagarth walked away. Lyncade slowly made his way to the girl and stood a few feet in back of her.

Scrubbing the floor the girl looked in back of her slightly and went back to work. Lyncade just paced looking at her as the girl finally stopped and wiped the sweat from her face.

"Am I in your way my lord?" The girl asked.

Lyncade didn't answer as he kept studying her.

The girl looked at him for a moment than back forward.

"Your name," Lyncade quickly replied.

The girl just faced forward not doing any work as she replied, "Mayreon."

"How long have you been a servant Mayreon?" Lyncade asked.

"All my life my lord," Mayreon replied as she scrubbed once again.

"You can speak freely," Lyncade assured.

"That's alright my lord," Mayreon said, "If my master hears me address a man of your stature in such a way I will be whipped."

"Farian?" Lyncade asked, "I know him."

Mayreon ignored him as she went back to scrubbing.

"You ignore me?" Lyncade asked.

"I mean it as no disrespect my lord," Mayreon assured, "But I have a lot of work to do before I'm aloud to leave."

"Where do you live?" Lyncade asked.

"With all the others," Mayreon told, "In the servant's chambers inside the village by Tamian's castle."

Lyncade just nodded as he watched her work away. Lyncade quickly walked around so he was facing her. She kept cleaning as she quickly noticed him. She tried to look up at him but she shyly looked down.

"It is I that should be shy to you," Lyncade told.

"How?" Mayreon asked.

Lyncade went to his knees and said, "I have never seen a woman as beautiful as you."

Mayreon stopped scrubbing as she looked at him for a moment. Quickly looking away she went back to work.

"Why do you not look at me?" Lyncade asked.

"It is said to be disrespectful to look at High Lord in the face," Mayreon said.

"You can look at me," Lyncade assured.

"My lord please," Mayreon said, "If I'm caught even talking to you I will be dealt with in a way you can't imagine."

"How so?" Lyncade asked, "Looking at you I can tell that you are still pure."

Mayreon looked at him slightly and replied, "You have no idea what they do to us when we are caught misbehaving."

"Talking to me is misbehaving?" Lyncade asked.

"Very much so," Mayreon replied.

Lyncade looked at her hand as a cut of some short was seen on her forearm. Lyncade quickly snatched her hand and lifted it up. The robe covering her hand fell down as Lyncade began to see what she was talking about.

Angered, Lyncade got up quickly.

"My lord I beg you," Mayreon yelled as she jumped up as well.

"Keep scrubbing," Lyncade yelled.

Lyncade quickly walked out of the temple and went to the main square of the city. There he walked passed several small shops and an armory building before walking into a tavern.

The dozens of soldiers in the tavern all stopped as the general walked in. They quickly got silent as Lyncade looked around. Many woman dressed in reveling clothing were surrounding the many soldiers. The tavern was no stranger to the warriors and the owners knew they'd pay good money for the company of woman. A bar was at the far end with many warriors and commoners sitting in front of it drinking wines and ales. Around the rest of the tavern was tables surrounded with more people. The High General was no stranger to those in the tavern and they all knew his reputation. They had all served or been ordered by him at one time or another. They saw the angered expression on his face and knew there was something wrong.

"Who is Farian?" Lyncade asked them all.

All the Royal Elves seemed to look at one another. When the general of the army comes in asking for a name it's not to make small talk. Finally a Royal Elf got to his feet.

"I am," Farian replied arrogantly.

He was wearing nobles clothing. Exotic robes worn by those of title and power among the city. He was surly a senator as well as a slave owner. It was obvious in his tone that he didn't know Lyncade's face but if he heard his name he might have checked his tone. Lyncade slowly walked over to him with his head down as he said, "I was just in the temple not too long ago."

"Yes," Farian replied.

"Took a look at some of your servant girls," Lyncade told.

"And what can I help you with?" Farian asked.

"How much for one of them?" Lyncade asked.

"Depends on who it is," Farian told.

Lyncade thought for a moment and replied, "Mayreon."

"Mayreon?" Farian asked, "She's one of my best."

"Is that so?" Lyncade asked, "If she's one of your best why do you whip her?"

Farian looked at him concerned as he said, "I never..."

Lyncade's back hand came up quickly smacking him across the face. With no attempt to fight back Farian just touched his lip.

"Sometimes I'd..." Farian began.

Lyncade once again threw up the back of his hand smacking him across the face.

"I can do with them what I like," Farian screamed.

The soldiers inside the tavern all turned their heads as he raised his tone to the High General. Lyncade threw up his knee hitting Farian in the stomach. He grabbed him and tossed him over several tables as Farian landed hard on the ground. Lyncade picked up a goblet and began to drink from it. Farian quickly got to his feet and rushed toward Lyncade. Lyncade stopped drinking and threw back his elbow nailing Farian in the face. As Farian fell to the ground Lyncade finished the drink and turned back around.

Lyncade pulled out his sword and pointed it toward Farian as he was on the ground. In a state of fear Farian just looked up at him not knowing what was going to happen.

"How much?" Lyncade asked.

"Five gold," Farian replied scared, "That's nothing for her."

Lyncade took a pouch around his waist and tossed it at Farian, hitting him in the face.

"That's five hundred," Lyncade told, "You couldn't get that from Tamian himself."

Lyncade placed his sword away as everyone in the tavern had their eyes locked on him.

"All the warriors in here who fight under me better enjoy the drinks they are receiving and the pleasures of a woman's company," Lyncade replied, "You deserve it and should be thankful you are alive today. You all know what terrors we've seen in the fields." Lyncade then looked at the commoners, "But for all you slave owners and senators in here. Let me find out that one of you whips them in a matter I don't like or disrespects any woman at anytime. I will be back to deal with you."

Lyncade quickly walked out and as he did the warriors all looked at Farian still on the ground. As if ignoring what just happened they went back to normal as if Lyncade hadn't entered. They knew their general meant what he said and wouldn't speak of what happened to anyone. Lyncade was above the laws of commoners and they just pretend like it didn't happen.

Lyncade began to make his way toward the temple once again. Lyncade went inside and walked back over to Mayreon still scrubbing the floor.

"Get up," Lyncade commanded.

"But I'm not finished," Mayreon told.

"Yes you are," Lyncade told, "That is the last floor you will ever scrub."

"How so?" Mayreon asked.

"You belong to me now," Lyncade replied as he held out his hand.

All the other servants in the temple looked over as Lyncade held out his hand.

"All of them are looking," Mayreon pointed out.

"Let them look," Lyncade replied, "Their looking at a woman of royalty now."

Mayreon held out her hand as Lyncade helped her up. Quickly Lyncade began to walk her out of the temple.

Back in the castle Lyncade walked into his chambers as several of his servants were inside awaiting him.

"Ladies," Lyncade replied, "This is your noblewoman, Mayreon."

"My lady," They all replied with a curtsy.

"Have her cleaned up at once," Lyncade commanded.

Mayreon just stared at him as Lyncade quickly walked out. Lyncade made his way down the hall and walked up to several guards as they stood in front of Tamian's chambers.

"My lord," They replied bowing their heads slightly.

"Is the queen inside?" Lyncade asked.

"She is resting," a guard informed.

"I must see her at once," Lyncade informed.

"Your sword," A guard requested.

Lyncade untied the case around his waist and handed the blade to the guards. As he walked passed them they then again bowed their heads. Lyncade entered as Drizell was on her bed with a maiden braiding a few strains of her hair.

"General," Drizell greeted as she looked to him slightly.

Placed in front of her were a book and a cup of herbal tea. She picked up the cup and sipped from it slightly. Lyncade walked over and kneeled before her.

"Rise," She commanded as she continued to read.

"Can I borrow you for a moment?" Lyncade asked.

"For what purpose?" Drizell asked still reading.

"I need some assistance," Lyncade told.

"For what?" Drizell asked.

Lyncade just looked at her for several moments.

Drizell looked to him and rolled her eyes as she replied, "A few more pages."

"What are you reading?" Lyncade asked.

"The early text of our people," Drizell informed, "Before Tamian's time it speaks of his father and grandfather before the tribes formed the kingdom."

"I'll help you threw," Lyncade replied, "The next few pages talk about Rakar and how he joined together the elf tribes in the south and formed the Forest Elves."

Drizell looked at him kind of angered as she asked, "What is this task you want me to do so bad?"

"Can you just please come with me?" Lyncade asked.

Drizell looked at her maiden braiding her hair as she stopped and picked up her cup of tea. Drizell held out her hand as Lyncade took it and helped her up. Lyncade walked with Drizell out the door as the guards walked beside them down to Lyncade's chambers.

The guards in front of his doors opened the doors quickly as Lyncade walked in with Drizell. Drizell stopped her guards from entering assuring them with her hand that she'd be safe.

They entered a room inside Lyncade's courtiers as Lyncade's maidens were bathing Mayreon in a bubble bath. The young servant girl almost jumped from where she was as they entered. The dirt in her blonde hair still seen as well as many of the dirt spots on her face. Only her shoulder and neck were coming from the bath as the bubbles covered up her naked body.

"What is this?" Drizell asked.

"Mayreon," Lyncade told.

The young servant looked up at the queen shyly as the maidens continued to wash her.

"I wish for you to pick out something for her to wear," Lyncade replied, "A woman as beautiful as you my queen should be able to pick the proper attire."

Drizell studied the young girl as she replied, "I don't think I've ever seen a young woman this beautiful before."

Lyncade looked at Mayreon and replied, "That's your queen who speaks to you."

"Thank you," Mayreon shyly replied.

"It's quite alright," Drizell assured, "Servant girls are never suppose to address the queen," Drizell looked at Lyncade and asked, "What do you intend to do with her?"

"Make her my wife," Lyncade told.

Both Mayreon and Drizell looked at him in shock.

"Are you out of your mind?" Drizell asked as she grabbed Lyncade and pulled him out of the bathing area.

"Why?" Lyncade asked as he looked at her.

"Do you know what the nobles and other generals will say when the main general of the army picks a servant girl to be his wife?" Drizell asked.

"Do you really think I care about the nobles or the other generals?" Lyncade asked, "They are meaningless to me."

"You are a high lord," Drizell reminded, "Many of the nobles have daughters of noble blood that you can breed with."

"I've seen all of them," Lyncade replied, "None of them have captured me the way that girl has."

Drizell looked in toward the room and replied, "I admit that she is quite beautiful."

"And she isn't even dressed up yet," Lyncade reminded, "Imagine what she'll look like when she isn't dirty."

"She's a slave," Drizell reminded.

"Was," Lyncade informed, "I bought her today."

"From who?" Drizell asked.

"Farian," Lyncade informed.

"Farian!" Drizell replied in shock, "He gives Tamian and I our servants and you just go and buy one for a wife? Lyncade your intentions might be pure but I assure that this rash behavior will be looked down upon."

"Like I said before I don't care what the others think," Lyncade assured, "If any word is echoed loudly enough for me to hear I will cut the throat of the man who says it."

"Go around killing the nobles!" Drizell replied.

"My lord," A guard replied as he entered, "Tamian wishes to see you."

Lyncade looked at Drizell and replied, "My queen please. Do me this one favor."

Drizell looked at him and rolled her eyes as she replied, "See what my husband wants and meet me back here in an hour."

"Thank you," Lyncade replied as he kissed her on the cheek and walked out of his chambers.

Lyncade walked into Tamian's other chambers in the high tower of his castle. There several Royal Elf nobles handed him sheets of paper that he signed and handed back.

Lyncade walked in as Tamian looked up at him for a brief moment. He raised his pointer finger and looked at the nobles.

"Maxus thinks we need to speak to the nobles in Boleadar at once," A Nobleman replied, "This distain they have for you for not responding to the evils in Porian is very upsetting. Without their forces any major invasion of The Dark Lord, Korack and Greco will be devastating."

"Is Boleadar angry with me or Arawon?" Tamian asked, "Boleadar might own that city but we all know Arawon is the one that runs it."

"Both," The Nobleman assured.

"The only thing The Dark Lord commands is orcs and goblins," Tamian reminded, "I do not know about you but the last time I was in battle with them they didn't put up much of a fight."

"The nobles are concerned with the evil in Porian," The nobleman said, "What evil commands them? If not The Dark Lord then who? It is now that territory that is the most threatening to our kingdom."

"The Dark Lord would have invaded from that territory if it was in fact him that commanded those evils," Tamian assured, "The evil that is killing the lands of Boleadar and the farmers only happens when the farmers go into Porian. The nobles from Boleadar are trying to tell me that they are being invaded. Why invade Boleadar if it was The Dark Lord. That city has nothing to give The Dark Lord, Korack or Greco. If it was The Dark Lord he would strike out against us."

"Maxus believes it is The Dark Lord," The nobleman told.

"Is Maxus king or am I?" Tamian asked.

"You," The nobleman said.

"Never forget that," Tamian replied, "The nobles in Boleadar, Arawon and Boleadar himself are only making a problem for me because they wish to have more land."

"Are they not worthy of it?" The nobleman asked.

"They are but there comes a point where the more you ask for only makes you greedy and not honorable," Tamian told, "Go to Maxus and tell him yourself that I will make peace with the nobles in Boleadar my way and not giving in to their unreasonable demands."

"Of course my lord," The nobleman replied.

Finally looking at Lyncade again Tamian said to the nobles, "Leave us."

The nobles walked passed Tamian and bowed their heads as he did the same. Tamian adjusted himself in his chair as he looked at Lyncade and smiled a bit.

"What?" Lyncade asked.

"I'll get to that in a moment," Tamian assured, "What do you have to say about the matter I was just discussing."

"You're doing it the way you like," Lyncade replied, "I have nothing to say about it."

"I value your opinion," Tamian told.

"You are doing what you feel best," Lyncade said, "In time I know you will deal with it your way. Now about your smirk?"

Tamian sat back in his chair and placed his hands together.

"I heard a rumor not too long ago when I was signing a bill," Tamian began, "That's all that gets placed in front of me lately. Bills about wages for servants. Now the nobles and traders have agreed that those who have not been born of royal or noble blood shall serve the first five thousand years in service to either the queen, myself, you or any other noble or general.

"Then something funny came to my attention," Tamian replied, "It seems a nobleman told me a story that a certain general went into the public and beat one of the traders. When the man was described to me as looking just like you I choose to believe that it wasn't true."

"It is true," Lyncade informed quickly.

"I didn't expect such a quick answer," Tamian admitted, "May I ask why?"

"I was in the temple and saw a servant who had been whipped," Lyncade informed.

"And the problem with that is what?" Tamian asked.

"She was whipped badly," Lyncade told, "So badly I was surprised that she was cleaning the floor so well."

"Traders are aloud to do what they like with their servants," Tamian told.

"I know that," Lyncade replied, "But this girl deserved a better life than that."

"That is why they serve," Tamian told, "After years of service they are granted freedom from that life and are aloud to do what they like."

"I couldn't wait that long," Lyncade informed.

Tamian took a deep breath and asked, "What should I say about this incident to the noble that brought it up to me?"

"Ignore it," Lyncade told, "Tell him to make sure Farian treats his servants a little better."

Tamian just nodded as Lyncade turned to walk out.

Chapter 3

On the west part of the world was a sinister land called The Dark Realm. The creatures who roamed this world would rip apart the likes of every race that lived in Tullian. Everyday inside this land the clouds above were always pitch black. Under those clouds was the night sky that would forever stay there because of the monsters that lived in this land.

Deep inside the dark continent stood a large black castle. Outside thousands and thousands of orcs and goblins roamed around waiting to go about and cause carnage. They were a civilization like any other race just filled with hatred and rage. It was said that they were once elves and their bodies when killed in battle were resurrected by The Dark Lord to do his bidding. They though had changed through their transformation. Orcs were beasts that were all seven foot and very muscular and wide. They had green skin, bald heads and pointed ears. Their mouths were filled with razor sharp teeth with two long ones sticking out of the bottom of their lips and raising to just below their eyes. Their intimidating stature scared many that came in contact with them. Their strength and scary looks were their only ways of winning battles. They didn't have much skill with the swords and axes they went into battle with. A warrior who lacked fear of them could easily use the skills he learned to defeat them. Their goblin partners were much smaller than they were, but looked similar.

In the highest tower of the black castle stood the lord of the land. Standing out on a large balcony he looked out at the army that he ruled.

His name was Korack, the Cobra King. He had the head of a cobra that was ready to strike. His snake tongue shot from his mouth from time to time. His skin was purple with the scales of a cobra all over it. He had the body of a man with long pointed nails coming from his fingers. He wore black armor with a purple colored cape falling from his back that dragged on the ground as he walked. His powerful magic sword was in its case tied tightly around his waist. He reptile type eyes that gazed upon the army he commanded. The sight of a nose was just two holes where his nose should have been. He was decorated in armor that was blessed by his hand. No mortal sword forged by any of the races could even penetrate it. The sword around his waist could cut through heavy armor as if it wasn't even there and he could match even the most skilled warrior.

He didn't like to fight that way though. He preferred magic, and he was gifted with it. If he had the power he could take on forces with the abilities he had. He like his brothers was in fact a god.

As Korack looked out into the landscape he held out his hand as lightning shot from it. In the empty land ahead the lightning struck the ground as thousands of more orcs and goblins began to emerge from the dirt.

"Your forces grow by the day," A voice replied from in back of him.

Walking out was a large creature that had a black hood over its head. The black robe covered the being entire body. It stood about eight foot and was massive in width. The creatures face was not seen. Only two long black horns coming from its forehead and shooting out of the hood.

"The more the better," Korack replied to the dark figure behind him.

"How many do you have risen?" The figure asked.

"Fifty thousand," Korack told, "After these forces rise from the ashes."

In the distance a few of the orcs and goblins began to fight one another.

"They seem restless," The dark figure told.

"They will see battle soon," Korack assured.

"Any word from our brother?" The dark figure asked.

"Greco hasn't said much to me these past years," Korack told, "His forces are small and it seems he has no drive to want to invade Tullian."

"I will speak to him," The dark figure told.

"The more forces the better," Korack replied, "These orcs and goblins are nothing compared to a large fleet of Royal Elves."

"That's why we will need him to raise more forces and attack beside yours," The dark figure replied.

"What about you?" Korack asked.

"My forces are around," The dark figure replied, "They don't need to be raised."

"Small forces have already been sent to Tullian," Korack informed, "Keep the Royal Elves on their toes."

"You should have them back off," the dark figure informed, "Surprise them."

"I will handle my forces the way I like," Korack replied, "Make them think it is only small forces then when they have small regiments there to attack them the full army will be there to wipe them out."

"Interesting strategy," the dark figure replied, "My army will not be far behind."

The dark figure vanished into a blast mist as Korack looked out into the landscape at the thousands of orcs and goblins that were ready to do his bidding.

Lyncade sat silently on a small chair next to Tamian's throne. Tamian and he seemed to be waiting for something as the king looked off into the distance. Drizell was next to him as the rulers held each others hand. Inside the throne room the hundreds of nobles and general stud as if awaiting something. The whole throne room was in silence as no one dared say a word.

The throne room doors slowly opened as the hundreds in there turned their heads quickly to the entrance. Servant girls began to make their way in as a shadowed figure began to walk slowly toward the throne.

In a white dress with blue strips a gorgeous woman began to make her way in. The dress was so long that two maidens in back of her held it up to help the woman walk. With her hair done up to perfection the woman wore a vale over her head with a white see threw cloth. The dress complimented her bust and was tight enough to show off her body. With glitter all over her sleek elegant body it was hard to keep eye contact.

As the woman walked in gasps were heard from all who laid their eyes on her. In a state of shock the nobles and generals stared at her as if in some trance.

As Tamian laid his eyes on her for the first time Drizell's hand seemed to drop from his grasp. With an enchanted look he gazed at the woman as she made her way closer to them.

A Royal Elf approached the king and kneeled slightly. As he raised himself he replied, "May I present Mayreon of Tamian."

Drizell looked to Tamian as he still looked at her uncontrollable. In a state of anger Drizell rose from the throne and walked toward the east exit. Tamian didn't even notice his wife had left as he continued his unnatural lustful look toward Mayreon.

Mayreon went to one knee as she stood in front of Tamian. Lyncade slowly walked to her as he held out his hand. She took it with hers and stood up straight once again.

Her eyes as well became locked on Tamian. The vale in front of her face was taken away as a blue gemmed circlet was around her forehead. The once dirty look of her face was completely gone as the stunning look of this servant girl captivated the king. Her blue eyes were more intense than any other. She almost demanded a glance as you saw them. Even a man who sculpted the face of a goddess couldn't perfect hers. It was the face of a goddess to those who looked at her.

Mayreon could have calmed a beast with her look. Even as she was still shying away she was awed at the moment. The queen herself was once seen in this way, but now a woman of far superior beauty had come into the sight of everyone. With nobles and royalty never paying attention to servants it was no wonder they were so captivated. Men described beauty and grace before but Mayreon surpassed every description ever told.

"Lyncade," Tamian called aloud, "Is this the woman you wish to call your own."

"Yes my king," Lyncade replied.

Tamian looked to Mayreon for several moments before he asked, "In what way will she service our people? As a noblewoman?"

"In a week I will sent her to the temple of Sygon. There she will be taught sorcery and magic to help protect her people," Lyncade explained.

Tamian rose from his throne and looked all around the throne room, "From this moment on all those who look at Lyncade and Mayreon will address them as if addressing Drizell and I. Their seeds will be considered royalty to our people and if blessed with a child their seed will breed with mine for the future of our people."

The throne room applauded at the statement as Tamian held out his hand to stop them.

"I am from this day forward will be soul ruler of Tamian with Drizell," Tamian replied, "Lyncade and Mayreon will be called King and Queen as well. In the next few days I will finally meet with the nobles in Boleadar and make peace over this matter that has us at a disagreement. I will have Lyncade and Mayreon rule Boleadar as their king and queen, and they will answer to me here in our great city."

The kingdom applauded again as Tamian walked forward and picked up Mayreon's hand. He kissed it gently as they looked at one another for several moments.

"My lord," Lyncade whispered, "Why so generous?"

"A union such as this requires a celebration of epic proportion," Tamian informed.

Lyncade and Mayreon slowly turned around as they began to slowly walk out of the throne room.

"How can I ever repay you?" Mayreon whispered.

"Love me all of your life," Lyncade whispered back.

"Always," Mayreon replied as she looked at him.

He looked back and smiled gently before he replied, "Look around you. One day you were a slave and the next you were a queen."

Mayreon just smiled as they walked out of the throne room.

Tamian made his way back to his chambers as he slowly walked in. Sitting on the bed angry was Drizell. She looked at him harshly as Tamian removed the cloak around him.

"I didn't even see you leave," Tamian replied.

"You wouldn't have," Drizell replied, "I saw the way you were looking at her."

Tamian just smiled as he hung the cloak up and walked over to Drizell.

"Is that so?" Tamian asked as he sat on the bed.

Drizell shifted away from him as she wiped the tears from her eyes, "Do not play games with me Tamian."

"What do you mean?" Tamian asked.

"The rumors of your infidelities are heard by me," Drizell assured.

"Don't you think they are just rumors by the nobles to get us to hate one another," Tamian replied.

"Do not look at me as if I'm a fool," Drizell yelled as she looked at him, "I am not blind."

Tamian didn't know what to say as he asked, "Than what do you want? Because in a heart beat I can have you on the streets doing what Mayreon was this morning."

"Do not threaten me," Drizell replied, "I have only wanted your heart and yet you go to others and love them the way you should love me."

"Like you have been a saint," Tamian said.

Angered, Drizell got up and looked at him heatedly, "To you it's all about power isn't it? Whatever woman you can have you get. The great Tamian and all powerful Royal Elf of this world. One day Tamian some time soon you will realize that the only reason those whores open their legs to you is because of what you are."

"And what about you my love?" Tamian asked in an uncaring tone as he looked at her, "Why are you with me?"

"For all the reasons I hate you," Drizell said, "You love someone for their faults, but I do not know how much more I can put up with it."

"Than by all means leave," Tamian replied as he rested back in the bed. He pointed at the entrance of the chambers and replied, "There's the door. You can easily be replaced."

Drizell went to her knees in front of him with tears falling from her eyes, "Do I mean so little to you?"

Tamian looked down at her as he got up without saying anything and made his way to the door. Closing the door behind him Drizell stayed on the floor and began to cry uncontrollable.

In Lyncade's chambers Lyncade and Mayreon stood in the middle of his room kissing heavily. Lyncade slowly began to remove his cloths as he went For Mayreon's dress.

"Wait," Mayreon replied as she broke from him. She stared at him and said, "Just give it a few moments."

"What do you mean?" Lyncade asked.

Mayreon smiled at him and said, "Maybe it's only because I've been royalty for a day but have you taken a look around."

Lyncade smiled as well.

"This dress is more expensive than the houses I lived in," Mayreon told.

"And you will have hundreds more," Lyncade replied as he kissed her.

She broke away and took a few steps back. Lyncade looked at her confused.

"What's the matter?" Lyncade asked.

Shyly she looked at the ground then back at him and said, "It is no secret the type of man Tamian is."

Lyncade kind on rolled his eyes as he looked at her and asked, "What does that mean?"

"In a moment's time he made you a king," Mayreon remembered, "Am I only here for your personal gain?"

"No," Lyncade replied, "I had no idea he was going to do that I swear."

Mayreon looked at him not seeing any deception in his face.

"Will I be the only one?" Mayreon asked.

Lyncade looked at her as if it was a stupid question, "Of course."

"Do not lie to me," Mayreon replied in a serious tone, "I will not stand for what I've heard."

"About Tamian?" Lyncade asked.

"How he goes around bedding all the nobles wives," Mayreon replied, "I've heard many tails."

Lyncade just looked at her as he walked up and stroked her face with his hand. Placing his forehead on hers he looked deeply into her eyes.

"I swear on the souls of my ancestors who died to make sure this kingdom was built that I will never hurt you," Lyncade said.

"You asked me that loving you was a way I could pay you back," Mayreon told, "The same goes for me."

"For all of your life," Lyncade assured.

With a gently kiss they agreed as slowly the kissing became more intense.

"Would you like to see what royalty does to expensive dresses," Lyncade whispered into her ears.

A moment later Mayreon felt the back of her dress rip as Lyncade used a dagger by his waist to cut threw it. With a flirtatious smile she looked at him and kissed him deeply again. Her dress fell to the floor as Lyncade picked her up and placed her on his bed.

In the southwest seas miles away from the shores of Racarn the land of Fadarth stood unnoticed by the eyes of the races in Tullian. Here the Great Humans lived. Great Humans lived longer than normal ones and were also known as Falmores. A Great Human at the age of ninety actually looked more like thirty in the eyes of regular humans. They were a savage type of human though. Practicing in the ways of lust and greed they used to enslave normal humans and use the woman as their slaves. They used to practice the dark arts chanting the names of the damned to try and bring them back into the world.

They stayed to themselves in the island and never caused any trouble in Tullian. Staying far away from trying to kill any normal humans they knew if they attacked they would have to deal with the Royal Elves. For hundreds of years they would breed and stay amongst their own people as the world of Tullian forgot they even existed.

The dark creature that stood on the balcony with Korack emerged just outside the gates of the dark city of Bylin. The dark city was named after its first king who ruled it fearlessly ages ago.

The Great Humans or Falmores as they were called by the gods; looked like normal ones. Usual they had long hair and would take the paint they made to cover their faces with war makeup. The land of Fadarth was a foggy one with barely any sun light. Their skin was milk white and their eyes were yellow. They were average in swordplay as well as archery. Each Great Human was a savage though. They lived their lives so recklessly and didn't care much for the god that created them. Most of them looked dirty and their pale skin always looked diseased somehow.

The dark creature looked as the gates of the city slowly began to open. As it opened completely thousands of Great Humans stood holding weapons and preparing to attack.

"I wish to speak to Artwore," The dark creature replied.

"Who are you?" One of the men asked.

"The Dark Lord," The figure replied.

The Dark Lord raised his hands to the sky as it crackled with lightning. The Great Humans backed off in fear as they quickly made way for him. The Dark Lord slowly began to make his way in as all the Great Humans walked out of his path quickly.

Coming to a large black castle The Dark Lord entered the main gates and was met by dozens of guards. Fearing him as well they moved out of the way as he entered the chamber of the king.

Artwore seemed to expect him as he lay on a large bed sideways looking at The Dark Lord as he entered. The human king was handsome by many standards. Unlike the people he ruled he was very clean and had his hair combed of any knots. His hair was pitch black and very long. His body was muscular and he looked like he could handle himself pretty well in battle. No scars were on his body though as if he had never even seen battle. Tattoos of tribal marks were all around his upper body and spread out to some parts of his arm.

Several small columns were in the kings chambers as on the left was a large tub. Filled to the top of this tub was a large pool of blood.

"The Dark Lord," The Falmore King replied, "So very nice to meet the god I've been worshipping."

"You do not seem surprised to see me," The Dark Lord replied in his inhuman tone.

Artwore rose quickly. Wearing a long black robe he walked over to The Dark Lord and kneeled before him.

"I've been told by my father of this day," Artwore replied, "The day when all the years of worship would pay off. You'd ask for my people to help you with a task."

The Dark Lord studied the Great Human as his glowing red eyes were seen looking at Artwore.

All of a sudden the pool of blood began to make waves as The Dark Lord looked over. A gorgeous woman emerged from it as she climbed out. The woman was completely naked as she grabbed a robe next to the tub.

"Sangrayus," The Dark Lord called.

"You know my wife," Artwore replied.

Sangrayus was a woman who had mastered dark magic in the beginning of her life. Blessed with abilities not of this world. Taught long ago to her by a woman she had grown up with in a village. She was an estimated four thousand years old. The many spells she had learned the ability to stop aging was one of them. She had married each of Artwore's ancestors and was in fact his mother.

She was as evil as she was beautiful. Her magic abilities let her stay at the peak of her beauty and she could enchant every man she came across. A human woman of her looks could even get stares from elves, which were usual not attracted to any woman of human race. Her milk white skin didn't have a scar on it. Her body was perfect and lusted by all those who looked at her. She had blood red lips and long red nails.

Sangrayus was a worshiper of The Dark Lord and had seen him several times in her life. She in fact was taught by him as well. She was by far the most powerful woman sorceress in all the world. Sangrayus covered her naked body with the black robed and tied the center of it. Blood dripped from her face and the rest of her body as it was even imbedded in her hair.

Being an unnatural people Artwore married his mother to keep the bloodline going. In years to come they would mate to have another son and she would do the same with that one.

"I told you he'd come," Artwore replied as she walked over to The Dark Lord.

"My greatest student," The Dark Lord called, "The years have been kind to you."

"Thanks to you my lord," Sangrayus replied as she took his hand with razor sharp nails and kissed it.

"My mother tells me you have a request for my people," Artwore replied.

"How many men do you command?" The Dark Lord asked.

"With Calvary, spearmen and my Dark Knights..." Artwore thought, "I could have a force of sixty thousand invade where ever you ask."

"You wish for us to attack the Royal Elves?" Sangrayus asked.

"When can it be done?" The Dark Lord asked.

Artwore looked over at Sangrayus with a glorious smile.

"When ever you wish," Sangrayus assured.

"How will we compete with them?" Artwore asked.

"I have that under control," The Dark Lord assured.

"Our people are ready to do your task when ever you like," Sangrayus assured.

"I will be calling you shortly," The Dark Lord informed as he seemed to vanish in front of them.

Artwore sat back on the bed as Sangrayus sat on his lap and placed her arms around him. The blood from her bath leaked onto him but he didn't seem to care. He just smiled as he looked up at her and embraced what had just happened.

"I knew he'd ask for us in due time," Sangrayus replied as she took her lips and brushed Artwore's face.

"He will be beside us when we go against the Royal Elves?" Artwore asked.

"Right beside us," Sangrayus assured.

"Does The Dark Lord know what we have?" A voice asked as a form emerged hidden in the room.

Artwore looked over to see what looked to be an elf walking toward him. Unlike normal Royal Elves or Forest Elves this one had dark pitch black hair. He was dressed in all black armor and wore a black cape that dragged on the ground as he walked. Written on his face were small ruins that were tattoos given to him by the god themselves. Tattoos on the faces of any living creator showed that they were blessed by the gods of every realm. This elf who hadn't seen the lands of Tullian for thousands of years bared these marks because of his age. Those who were there in the dawn of the creation of Tullian were given these marks as signs of how old they were. The elf had seen many battles in his life and was the most skilled warrior in all of the world.

He had received these tattoos from the others he was created with. He was the last remaining of the original six. The warrior known as Fayne, and the most feared warrior to ever walk the lands of Tullian. Much of his legend died when he vanished, but could quickly reemerge with the swipe of his sword.

"Fayne," Artwore realized, "You must keep your voice down."

"Why?" Fayne asked.

"The Dark Lord has ears in every corner of our world," Artwore reminded.

"You are in our kingdom to keep my son safe," Sangrayus reminded the elf, "Do not interfere with the plans of our people."

"I know my people well," Fayne told, "Your forces will not stand a chance against the Royal Elves."

"Leave the tactics of war to me," Artwore told, "You just do as my mother has asked of you."

"I shall," Fayne promised, "Matter of fact I thought I was doing that now. Do not go to war with these elves. You will be asking for nothing but trouble in these times."

"Fayne," Sangrayus called, "You are an ancient. Able to fight as many as two hundred elves on your own. If this war is what The Dark Lord wishes for then it will be done."

"Of course my lady," Fayne replied, "No matter your decision I shall be by his side."

"Then prepare to be called," Artwore told, "It is only a matter of time before The Dark Lord wishes us to go to war with him."

"Just remember my king," Fayne began to warn, "The Dark Lord always has other intentions."

"I know this better than anyone," Sangrayus assured, "What we have of his will always be protected by me."

"Be careful my lady," Fayne told, "In times to come if he knows what you have he will lash out against you."

"How will he find out?" Sangrayus asked.

"He is a god," Fayne, "When it comes to his powers he will know."

"The three rubies cannot be touched by him unless we touch them," Artwore reminded.

"I know his power," Fayne reminded, "He is after his ruby. If he finds it, he will destroy us no matter what we've done to help him."

"I was his student," Sangrayus reminded, "He will reward our kind for our service to him."

"I fought his orcs and goblins," Fayne replied, "I protected the Falmores for generations. I have assured its safety and that of all its children. I am to protect it because of who I am. Remember that."

"Your service to us is not overlooked," Artwore assured, "But we will handle it. We have The Dark Lords power and we can control him."

"You can never control him," Fayne assured, "And he holds no race of Warad in favor."

"We worship him," Sangrayus reminded.

"But you were still made by Warad my lady," Fayne reminded, "Keep that in mind and make sure you keep the ruby from his grasp. Do not let him know you have it."

Slightly bowing the elf turned and walked away.

"He has a point," Artwore replied.

"We are fine," Sangrayus assured, "Just keep an eye out and never let yourself drift when in The Dark Lords presence. He will know you are hiding something."

Chapter 4

Mayreon was being helped getting dressed as Lyncade leaned against the wall behind the maidens as they went to work. Mayreon looked at him angered short of as Lyncade just kept his eyes on his beautiful wife.

"I still don't understand why I must go," Mayreon replied.

"Learning from Sygon will be a great thing," Lyncade assured, "All of our children will become sorcerers as well. Tamian commanded it a few years back that all royalty will at least learn two hundred years worth of magic abilities."

"How much will I learn?" Mayreon asked.

"All of it," Lyncade told, "Once you are taught the basics. You will return to study the rest as an educated student."

Mayreon looked at him with a face of shock.

"I will be there for ages," Mayreon replied gasping.

"No you won't," Lyncade assured, "I will be permitted to see you once a month while you are training."

"Once a month," Mayreon replied saddened.

Lyncade snapped his fingers as the maidens walked away quickly. With her dress just about done Lyncade walked over to his bride and placed his arms around her shoulders as he looked at her in the mirror.

"Do you trust me?" Lyncade asked.

"Of course," Mayreon replied, "I don't understand this force of actions though."

"You must understand my love," Lyncade assured, "It is what needs to be done."

Mayreon saw the tears fall from her eyes as she nodded.

"Why sorcery?" Mayreon asked.

"Sorcery is done by speaking the language of the gods," Lyncade informed.

"Language of the gods?" Mayreon asked.

"It's the term used by the wizards and sorcerers," Lyncade informed, "There are many forms, used by the gods and you will study the ability to speak it. Only a select few are granted this, you should feel honored. Besides, Sygon is the best in the world."

"What types of things will I be able to do?" Mayreon asked.

"I don't know," Lyncade said as he looked at her.

"Can I be more seductive?" Mayreon asked with a playful smile.

"You don't need to cast a spell on me to be seductive," Lyncade replied with a smile, "You cast a spell on me in the temple when I saw you. I thought it fitting that you do it in real life."

Mayreon just smiled at his statement and couldn't help but blush.

A carriage was riding across the large territory of Endore. For days in went with Mayreon and Lyncade inside waiting to reach the gates of Sygon. Sygon was a temple placed in the middle of Arawon and Tamian. Each student that was chosen by the High Lords and Generals was sent there to learn magic abilities.

The ancient temple was seen in the horizon as they began to reach the center of the Tamian territory. The temple was massive and about the size of two of Tamian's castles. Thousands of Royal Elf students from Tamian and Arawon went there to train.

As the carriage reached the main stairway Lyncade opened the door for his wife as she slowly got out and looked at the thousands of steps to the top of the temple. Lyncade took her hand as they scaled the many stairs of the massive temple.

"I'm scared," Mayreon replied.

"Don't be," Lyncade said, "When you are done here you will have abilities the world has never seen."

"Why didn't Drizell go here?" Mayreon asked.

"She only wishes to look pretty and have the guards protect her from the evils outside our lands," Lyncade replied, "She is only a statue to our people. You on the other hand when Sygon is finished will be a queen of power. A queen able to protect us in battle as well."

The front of the temple had many large pillars in the center. Two towering statues stood on the sides of the great god Warad. The statues towered high into air as far as their eyes could see. Many colors were seen in the skies all along the temples grounds. It seemed far away, inside; many of the young sorcerers were training.

After what seemed like hours Lyncade and Mayreon reached the top as they began to see a blue bubble coming toward them. Catching them both off guard they stopped in their tracks. The bubble began to have lightning surging around it. As it stopped and vanished into the air an old elf stood in front of him.

Dressed in a white robe with blue strips around the cuffs the old Royal Elf looked at them oddly. He had a long white beard that touched the ground as well as long hair that stretched down to his lower back. His pointed ears stuck out of the snow white hair as he stud with a slouch. He had diminutive little eyes that looked as if he had trouble seeing. He stood with a staff in both his hands as he seemed to be leaning on it. The long white robe he wore touched the ground as well as parts of dirt could be seen on the edges.

He stroked his beard gently with his one hand as he replied, "General Lyncade. What do I owe this visit?"

Lyncade walked his wife to him as he replied, "This is my wife Mayreon."

Sygon looked at her for several moments as he replied, "A beauty not even a goddess could compare to."

"Thank you," Mayreon replied gently.

"Beauty will not help you here," Sygon assured, "Your mind is the only weapon you are allowed to use here."

"I send her as a favor to teach her all you know," Lyncade requested.

"No one can learn what I know," Sygon replied, "They aren't old enough to read the text of the gods."

"Of course," Lyncade replied as he bowed his head, "Teach her what you can. I will return once a month to see her progress."

Lyncade walked slowly down the stairs as Mayreon was left looking at the old wizard. As several moments passed she began to get uncomfortable and looked away.

"Look at me," Sygon demanded.

Mayreon did as the old man continued his stare.

"I've seen you before," Sygon was sure of.

"I've never met you," Mayreon replied.

Sygon looked at her again for several moments as he replied, "Follow me girl."

They both began to enter the temple as thousands of young Royal Elves were around her practicing their abilities. Many entrances to courtyard grounds were on either side of her. In each one hundreds of students were being trained their abilities. Bolts of colors emerged from many of them, explaining the lights she had seen when scaling the stairs.

"He told you that you would need to be trained for many years to become a master?" Sygon asked, "Some have spent their whole lives and still aren't skilled."

"Yes," Mayreon replied shyly.

"I think the first thing we must teach you is confidence," Sygon replied, "You are too shy for me."

"I'm sorry," Mayreon replied in a much louder tone.

"That's more like it," Sygon replied, "Your first lesson is to go to your chambers."

"Go to my chambers?" Mayreon asked.

Sygon walked her to a large building with many doors in the hallway. The hallways seemed endless as the doors on the wall never stopped. Sygon finally stopped in front of one and hit his staff to the ground. One door flew open and was just a small room with a desk in it. On the desk was a book with ancient writing all over it.

"There is the book of the gods," Sygon replied, "Collected by my father and his father before him in the caves all along the land of Tullian. Never say the words out loud. If you do you will be ripped apart pretty limb by pretty limb. You can only say them in your mind."

"How long will I stay in here?" Mayreon asked.

"As long as I feel necessary," Sygon replied as he looked at her, "Read the book front and back several times. Only when you can speak the words of the gods fluently will you be able to do the minor spells."

"What if they're major?" Mayreon asked.

Sygon laughed at the comment and replied, "Only I can read all the major spells. You need to be training for thousands of years before you can learn them. No one besides me is old enough in this world to say them."

"How can I read a book with a language not of my own?" Mayreon asked.

Sygon chuckled again and said, "Look at the words. If you are able to know what they mean then you will be allowed by the gods. That is the first test you will encounter here. If you cannot understand them, then you will no longer be in this temple."

Sygon just looked ahead at the room as many moments of silence past. Mayreon began to walk slowly into the room. She looked as if she was about to turn and ask another question. Quickly the door was shut behind her as she reached for the knob but couldn't open it.

She than made peace with the fact that she couldn't open the door as she went to the small desk and opened up the first page of the book of the gods. There she began to read about Shadow Magic, Fire Magic, Dark Magic, Light Magic, Death Magic, Life Magic (Water Magic), Plague Magic, Blood Magic, Magic of the gods (Warad Magic), Magic of the Dark Lord, Seduction Magic and Royal Magic.

Because she was a Royal Elf she was only permitted to learn that form of magic. All other forms she read would only help her when she first mastered Royal Magic. When she would master that she could learn Life Magic, Light Magic and of course Seduction Magic because she was a woman.

All other forms were forbidden for her kind to know. Because if was either the magic used by Warad and only powerful enough for a god or used by the evils of the world she had never heard of.

All of a sudden the door behind her opened. She looked to see Sygon walking in as the door closed behind him on its own.

"I see confusion in your eyes," Sygon replied.

"I read of evils," Mayreon informed.

"So you can read it," Sygon replied.

Mayreon then realized that she could see the text without any problem. She looked back at the book in shock.

"I guess I can," Mayreon replied.

"So you will stay," Sygon replied, "Now about those evils. You have never heard of The Dark Lord, Greco and Korack have you?"

She shook her head slightly looking at the old wizard.

"Warad the creator of this world made four guardians to protect us from ourselves, and the greed of others. In the beginning of time the only evils were the damned souls of those who chose to do evil to the rest of the living. They were banned from the afterlife and roamed this world trying to do evil to those who were still alive," Sygon explained, "When Warad gave us choice, some went against him, while others stayed faithful.

"Back then the guardians fought the evils away and would protect the living from them. They had kingdoms and ruled over all the races in every land. One of these Guardians who would later be called The Dark Lord thought himself to be more powerful than Warad. He convinced Greco and Korack his younger brothers to fight with him against Warad.

"They were easily defeated and cursed forever. The Dark Lord made his own land in The Dark Realm just off the shores of the west side of Tullian. He began to take all the damned souls and place them in the corpses of all those he had killed once he lashed out against Warad. These damned souls resurrected as orcs and goblins. They were raised in his land and sailed here to kill the races.

"By that time the race now had empires of their own. The humans, the Forest Elves, the dwarfs. Tamian was the first to built a kingdom and fight against them," Sygon explained.

"Greco and Korack resurrected damned souls of their own and did the same. For generations they have come to this land trying to kill all the races that live inside of it. Each attempt went meaningless because the gifts Warad gave the races."

Sygon's hand began to glow blue as he said, "The ability to do magic. The ability to use a sword against them. Each of these evil gods knows all the dark forms of magic you have just read about. Once they touch this land their powers of those forms of magic are taken from them. Their powers here are limited. As long as The Royal Elves and all other races have people doing sorcery than we can fight them."

"You said there were four guardians," Mayreon reminded.

"The fourth never turned his back from Warad," Sygon told, "It is said that the fourth Guardian will come to help protect us once the other three have built the armies they intend to destroy the world with.

"That army is an army no one has ever seen. A force of demons. Demons that haunt the nightmares of children as they grow. Demons that are relentless and are equal to even Elves with a sword. Orcs and goblins are not skilled like us and never will be."

"So me and many others will learn magic to protect us from these evil gods?" Mayreon asked.

"Yes," Sygon replied, "Keep reading."

The door opened again as Sygon walked out and the door shut quickly.

Getting back immediately Mayreon began to see the many texts that gave her the ability to do these forms of magic. She said them in her head trying to decipher them.

As the hours passed the candle lit next to her continued to shine. The wax of the candle melted slowly as a once high candle when she first started, diminished to a stub. It seemed like days she sat there reading over and over again. She had no idea how many hours or even days had passed that she sat in there reading away. She read the book dozens of times as she began to finally understand it.

The door opened once again as Sygon stood outside.

Mayreon looked at him and asked, "How long have I been in here?"

"Two weeks," Sygon informed, "Come now and wash up."

Mayreon followed him to a private room where a large tub was. Many blue sheets hung all around the small room to give her privacy. The room had marble blue floors and a table with many candles lit for them to see. There was a cloth next to the tub as Mayreon stroked the water with her hand.

"It is just how you like it," Sygon assured as he looked at her.

Sygon placed his hand over the water as bubbles began to form.

"I forgot you like a bubble bath," Sygon replied, "Forgive me."

"How did you know that?" Mayreon asked.

"Once you study that book long enough you will be able to know things no one else can," Sygon informed.

"I'm beginning to read it well," Mayreon told.

"Good to hear," Sygon replied in an uncaring tone.

Mayreon was about to remove her robe as she looked at Sygon. He didn't leave as he just looked at her. She signaled with her head for him to leave but the wizard stayed where he was.

"My lady I assure that the sight of you naked will not get me aroused," Sygon informed.

Sygon gently hit the end of his staff on the floor as her cloths were ripped from her body. Embarrassed Mayreon quickly went into the bath.

"How dare you," Mayreon replied offended.

"My lady," Sygon replied, "Here we do not get stimulated by the flesh of another. Celibacy is the only way you are able to learn the things from that book. I haven't been intimate with a woman in ages and I do not miss it at all."

Mayreon just looked at him as she dropped in the water and came back up. Pulling her long blonde hair away from her eyes she gently began to wash herself off.

"Clean up quickly," Sygon commanded as he walked out.

In the next several weeks of training Mayreon was only permitted to read the book as she sat in the courtyard surrounded by others learning the same things she was.

The beautiful courtyard was one of the many grounds inside the temple of Sygon. Green grass and beautiful flowers bloomed all around. Exotic fountains and many statues were also located in the center of this training ground.

In the center of the courtyard were hundreds of white pearls. A student Sygon was teaching was picking them up with his mind and hurling them at Sygon. Sygon would break them with his mind seconds before hitting him directly in the face. These white pearls were just a teaching tool so the students could learn how to pick things up with their minds. Dozens of them were thrown at Sygon as he broke each one seconds before hitting.

"Enough," Sygon replied to the student.

In back of Sygon a small explosion went off as one of his students was trying to learn a spell. Knowing immediately the spell was wrong Sygon walked over to the student.

"You are reading the text wrong," Sygon yelled at the student.

The student who had been throwing the pearls picked one up and hurled it toward Sygon with a small smirk on his face.

Sygon sensed the pearl as he turned. Just as he was ready to dispel the pearl broke in front of him. The student that threw the pearl was picked up and tossed into a wall. The student hit the ground and began to cough from the violent collision. Sygon looked all around him and same with the other students. When they realized it wasn't Sygon doing it they looked around in wonder as they all saw Mayreon with her hands glowing blue.

Sygon walked over to her slowly as Mayreon's hands went back to normal. Each student slowly followed Sygon as he stopped in front of Mayreon.

"What did you just do?" Sygon asked.

"Page four hundred and twelve," Mayreon replied, "Spell three of Life Magic."

Sygon gave her an odd look as he and the students looked at her in a state of shock.

The student she had thrown slowly got to his feet and shook the cobwebs. The student flew toward Sygon as Sygon's hand was glowing blue.

"When I say stop I mean it," Sygon yelled as the student dropped in front of him.

Sygon than looked at Mayreon again who didn't understand why he stared at her so.

"What?" Mayreon asked.

"Beginners luck," Sygon replied as he walked away.

The students all looked at her as Sygon walked away.

"How did you do that?" One asked.

Mayreon was still confused by their stare as she replied, "I just read the text."

In the same courtyard each student sat on the grass as Sygon looked over all of them. Mayreon and a few others were still sitting on stone benches only reading as apart of their first level of training.

"As I do every week," Sygon replied, "I will have a student perform a spell on another. The one who casts must throw everything they have. Because this week we will all learn dispelling."

The students all groaned with disappointment.

"What?" Sygon asked.

A male student raised his hand as Sygon pointed to him. He rose and said, "My lord we all know dispelling very well."

"Is that so Saybin?" Sygon asked.

"We can dispel each other," Saybin assured, "We can dispel everyone here but you."

Mayreon placed her hand in the air as Sygon looked over at her.

"Yes," Sygon replied.

"Can I try one?" Mayreon asked.

The students in front of Warad all laughed.

"She'll tar herself apart," Saybin replied, "She's only a level one she is only allowed to read."

"Silence," Sygon warned. He than looked at Mayreon and said, "Come over here."

Mayreon got up and placed the book down where she was once sitting.

"You forgot your book," Saybin called.

"I do not need it," Mayreon assured.

The students looked at one another with confused faces as she said that. Saybin just smiled confidently.

"You know if you mispronounce it you will die," Sygon reminded.

"I remember," Mayreon assured as she than placed herself in front of Saybin.

"You know what to do Saybin," Sygon replied, "When her blast comes at you dispel it at once."

Mayreon began to stare relentlessly at Saybin. Saybin still smirked as a blue type of mist came at him. It slowly drifted as Saybin looked at her curiously. The mist began to form all around him as Saybin began to try and dispel. The mist that Mayreon had cast went away as Saybin went toward her to try and kiss her. Mayreon backed away but Saybin began to force himself on her.

With a quick toss of his hand Sygon threw Saybin off of Mayreon. Saybin became incensed as he ran at her even after he was hit with a bolt by the great wizard. Mayreon's hand began to glow as she tossed a ball of blue light at Saybin and smacked him hard in the chest. When he landed and hit the ground he was knocked out cold.

Sygon once again directed his attention to Mayreon with an intriguing look.

Saybin was being pulled by four guards into a room as Sygon watched the door close and he began to scream for Mayreon. What ever Mayreon did to Saybin it completely made him infatuated with her. Sygon, as if in trance, looked at the door as if looking passed it.

Behind him with a distraught face was Mayreon.

"I didn't mean to," Mayreon assured, "He was suppose to dispel."

"I know," Sygon replied in a distant tone, "He tried. I could feel it."

"Then what happened?" Mayreon asked.

Sygon turned quickly and looked at her for several moments.

"Have you ever read the book I gave you when you first came here?" Sygon asked.

"No," Mayreon assured, "It was my first time."

Sygon just nodded as he walked passed her down the hallway of a thousand rooms.

Lyncade had made one of his monthly visits as him and Sygon walked down a large garden located in the temple. Mayreon was not far away just looking around at all the beautiful flowers.

"How is her progress?" Lyncade asked.

Sygon gave him a strange looked and asked, "Where did you find her?"

"She was a servant," Lyncade told, "There was something about her that made her..."

"Special," Sygon finished.

"Yeah," Lyncade replied, "She enchanted me with her beauty but it wasn't just that. Why do you ask?"

Sygon stopped and placed his staff in front of him as he used both hands to lean on it.

"She has learned more in a few weeks than anyone I have ever has in years," Sygon explained, "Last week she cast a spell on someone and I am still unable to release him from the trance."

"What did she do?" Lyncade asked.

"It seems your wife has mastered three types of spells in the book at a record pace," Sygon told, "She frightens me."

"Frightens you?" Lyncade asked.

"Thousands of years ago when the book of spells was created by my ancestors taking it off the walls of caves, my grandfather attempted to say them," Sygon told, "He was ripped apart by the wrath of the gods. When my father was many years older than my grandfather, he spoke the words. He recited them and was fine.

"We all then believed that someone who was old and wise was only able to read these words. That theory stayed true for thousands of years before you dropped this girl off in front of my temple."

Lyncade gave him a peculiar look as if not understanding what he was saying.

"Imagine this," Sygon replied, "You still teach in the temple for warriors do you not?"

"When Tamian doesn't send me on a task," Lyncade replied.

"Imagine a student going to the temple for the first time, picking up a sword and besting you," Sygon told. Sygon than sat down on the stone in front of a fountain and looked at Lyncade, "That is what she has done here. Came in and read the book for weeks at a time. The spells echo in her memory and when she says them it is like second nature to her."

"Is there anyway you can explain this?" Lyncade asked.

"You know about the prophecies of the Guardian of Light," Sygon replied.

"Is she?" Lyncade asked.

"I dare not say," Sygon replied.

"How powerful has she become?" Lyncade asked.

"Put it this way general," Sygon began, "You wouldn't want to make her angry."

Lyncade looked over at Mayreon who was looking down on the ground of the temple. Lying on the ground was a dead bird. Mayreon placed her hand over it as a green light exited her hand and entered the bird. Moments later Mayreon picked the bird up in her hand and raised her hand in the air. The bird flew from her grasp now and headed toward the sky.

"That is the Magic of Warad," Sygon told as they witnessed it, "It took me thousands of years to master. It had only taken her a short time."

Lyncade looked over at her in amazement.

"There is a reason you found her," Sygon told, "When you looked at a beautiful servant girl you thought you found the love of your life. In fact it was her that found you. She has a power that I will never be able to explain."

"What should I do?" Lyncade asked as he looked back at Sygon slightly.

"Keep her well," Sygon replied.

"Is she powerful enough to defeat you?" Lyncade asked.

"I want to say no," Sygon replied as he rose, "The amount she has learned in a short time, if she continues her pace she will be the most powerful sorceress in all the world."

"More powerful than Greco, Korack and The Dark Lord?" Lyncade asked.

"She would put up a fight," Sygon assured.

Lyncade just studied his wife for several moments as she looked toward him with a large smile.

Lyncade slowly walked to her as she went and embraced him with a big hug.

"I missed you," Mayreon replied with a kiss to his lips.

Lyncade looked at her as her smile shined from her face.

"I've never seen you so happy," Lyncade replied.

"I love it here," Mayreon replied as he looked all around her still in his arms.

She broke away and began to walk through the garden still searching her surroundings with her eyes.

"A part of it seems to put me at peace," Mayreon told.

Lyncade looked toward the ground and walked toward her as he replied, "Sygon has said that you do not need to be here much longer."

Mayreon turned and looked at him as she asked, "Why?"

"He says the rest of your training you can do just reading the books in Tamian," Lyncade informed.

"I thought I had to spend years here?" Mayreon reminded.

"Those who haven't the amount of skill you required in a short time have to spend years here," Lyncade replied.

Mayreon looked down sadly and replied, "He told you about Saybin."

"Some what," Lyncade told as he studied her and asked, "Did you do that to me?"

She looked at him offended by the question and replied, "Of course not. I never read anything in those books until now."

Lyncade looked at her and finally went to her. He wrapped his arms around her in apology.

"I owe you so much," She replied, "Without you this isn't possible, I would have never taken advantage."

Lyncade kissed her gently on the forehead and looked into her enchanting eyes.

"I'll be back here soon to retrieve you," Lyncade told.

"I'll be waiting," Mayreon replied with a large smile.

"I like what this place has done to you," Lyncade told, "Before such a shy girl and now so full of life. It's as if you've become more beautiful as impossible as that sounds."

Mayreon reached forward and kissed him deeply.

The sound of someone clearing their throat was heard as they both shot their faces over to Sygon who looked as if he was standing there for sometime.

Lyncade broke from her quickly.

"Sorry master," Mayreon replied.

"She has lessons," Sygon replied to Lyncade.

"Sorry," Lyncade replied backing away from her.

"We'll see you later General Lyncade," Sygon replied as he motioned for Mayreon to follow him.

Lyncade just slowly walked away looking back at Mayreon. Mayreon did the same with a large smile on her face.

Chapter 5

Tamian was on his throne with several guards surrounding the entire room. General Nagarth approached with his armor dented and scratched and kneeled in front of him.

"Rise," Tamian commanded.

"My forces got rid of the threat my lord," Nagarth informed.

"How many lost?" Tamian asked.

"About half," Nagarth told, "We were gone for a year because the forces kept hitting the beach. We did the best we could but then became outmatched."

"Are there others coming?" Tamian asked.

"They are inside Cavell as we speak," Nagarth told, "A few thousand of them now."

Tamian looked around for several moments as he said, "Round up The Royal Guard."

"My lord," Nagarth called, "Give me more men I can handle them."

"When Lyncade returns from the temple of Sygon he and I will take care of the threat personally," Tamian told as he rose.

Nagarth watched his king walk toward the east exit as he angrily walked out the entrance of the throne room.

Quickly exiting the city on horseback Nagarth went to the river a few miles away and rode to try and release his anger. Quickly dropping from the horse as the river came into view he walked toward in and kneeled. Placing his hands in the slow flowing river he began to toss the water in his face.

"He seems to not trust you," A voice replied.

At the sound of the first word Nagarth jumped to his feet and pulled out his blade. There standing on the water was a creature he had never seen before. It's whole body was red and filled with boils and large warts. The creature had razor sharp teeth and a large nose like a witches. The creature was very muscular and was wearing all silver attire. The armor around his chest could be seen wrapping around to his back. His arms were free and naked but the weapons of this world couldn't harm him. His silver case had a large sword in it then when released began to glow a bright green. It could penetrate the armor of this world like a knife threw butter and instantly kill the enemy he swung it at. His loins were covered with a red sash and silver armor on it as well. The sash dropped just below his knees where the top half of his silver shin guards started. A silver cape dropped to the water flowing behind him with a red lining inside of it.

"You won't need that," The creature replied pointing at the sword, "To give you a full warning it will have little effect."

"Everything I have ever hit with it has never gotten up," Nagarth told.

The creature laughed as it walked on the water toward the shore where Nagarth was. Nagarth backed away with his blade still in hand. The creature got to the shore still staring at the frightened Royal Elf.

"I know you," Nagarth replied, "Greco."

The creature laughed and bowed his head slightly, "Indeed."

"You are not allowed on these lands," Nagarth told preparing to swing. As he came forward and swung his blade down on Greco he felt nothing but air. Where Greco once was, was now nothing.

"What did I tell you?" A voice asked in back of him.

Nagarth turned and saw Greco in back of him now.

"How did you…" Nagarth began.

"I am a god," Greco reminded, "You are nothing compared to me."

"What do you want?" Nagarth asked as his blade lowered.

Greco seemed to study The Royal Elf as he replied, "I see anger in you."

"Anger for my king," Nagarth replied, "But that doesn't mean I will betray him."

"Never," Greco agreed deceitfully, "But he obviously doesn't trust you."

"I kept your forces away from my land," Nagarth told.

"That you did," Greco replied, "Which is why I am asking you to join my forces."

Nagarth looked at him and replied, "Never."

Greco just smiled and said, "As you wish. Maybe I'll come to you in another time, when you change your mind."

With that Nagarth watch Greco disappear in a black mist. Nagarth placed his blade away and quickly went to his horse. He studied the river once again as he directed his horse back to the city.

Lyncade and a small force of Royal Guard that had escorted him to The Temple of Sygon began to see the city. Behind them they heard a horse as Lyncade turned and saw Nagarth.

"General," Lyncade greeted, "How long have you been home?"

Nagarth rode up side by side with him and shook his hand forearm to forearm.

"A year by the shore is a vacation to me," Nagarth replied.

"How many did you kill?" Lyncade asked.

"Legions," Nagarth told, "So instead of coming back and getting more forces Tamian and you will go to fight off the orcs and goblins."

Lyncade looked at him in shock.

"My wife returns in a few weeks," Lyncade told, "I have no time to fight orcs and goblins."

"It's his orders," Nagarth told, "I offered to get more men but he insisted that you and him go."

Lyncade got a face of disguised on as he replied, "I'll speak with him when I get inside."

Lyncade quickly made it to the castle as he began to walk toward the throne room.

"My lord," A voice called.

Lyncade turned to see Drizell in the hall.

"My queen," Lyncade replied as he bowed his head.

"The king is in the main courtyard," Drizell told.

Lyncade nodded as he quickly changed directions and walked toward the courtyard. In the center of the castle was a large garden where statues of warriors in Elfish history stood. Back in the days of the clans and tribes, several men called themselves king and out of respect Tamian made statues in their honor.

Lyncade went into the courtyard as he heard sword fighting going on. He then looked several hundred feet down to see a large circle surrounding a couple of Elves. When he got closer he realized that Tamian was practicing. Each Royal Elf he was fighting was a captain in the Royal Guard. Tamian was holding them off well and seemed not to have a problem facing them. Tamian quickly disarmed all of them and kicked them away.

The rest of the men cheered as Lyncade walked up. All the men looked over at Lyncade as they seemed to smile a little bit. The men then looked at Tamian as Tamian smiled and directed the men he had fought to back away. He held his blade up and directed Lyncade to come toward him.

Lyncade had a serious face on as he slowly removed his blade. As it did all the men roared with cheer. Lyncade quickly got in the circle as him and Tamian circled each other.

Tamian seemed to tease the general as he'd jump at him faking an attack. Lyncade never bit as he just waited for the real one. It came as Tamian hurled toward him and threw his blade at Lyncade. Lyncade moved away from the swipe and threw out his leg hitting Tamian in his shin. Tamian flew in the air and landed hard on the ground.

Tamian got up quickly and brushed himself off as Lyncade carelessly held his blade lowered toward the ground. Tamian came at him once again as this time their blades clashed. Swipe after swipe the two attacked and countered. Each man never giving up or making a mistake. Lyncade finally came in with an attack as Tamian tied him up with his own blade and threw his elbow hitting Lyncade in the mouth. Backing off Lyncade felt his mouth as he had cut the inside of his lip.

Just shaking it off Lyncade once again lazily held his blade toward the ground but surprised Tamian with a vicious attack. Tamian blocked each time almost coming within inches of a cut. Tamian finally taking a few steps back and recovering blocked a swipe as he spun Lyncade's blade and disarmed it from him. The blade quickly went in the air and landed in Tamian's hand as he caught it and stood in front of Lyncade.

The crowd cheered as Tamian handed Lyncade back his blade.

"You test me every time general," Tamian replied.

"We need to talk," Lyncade told.

The two were walking through the castle standing side by side with two dozens guards not far behind.

"Why are we going for the shores?" Lyncade asked.

"Our regiments are the fiercest in all the world," Tamian reminded, "If Korack, Greco and The Dark Lord and coming to our shores we must send a message that they will be dealt with by the leaders of these lands."

"Maybe that's what they want," Lyncade suggested.

"They will never show themselves in this land," Tamian was sure of, "You and I together will wipe out all of their forces and send what ever remains back to The Dark Realm with a message to their masters."

"You can not underestimate them," Lyncade replied, "They are gods."

"Gods that have no power on this land," Tamian told.

"How can you be so sure?" Lyncade asked.

"Follow me," Tamian commanded.

The two of them walked into a part of the castle that Lyncade had never seen before. Tamian walked up to a room where no guards could be seen. The guards that were following behind them earlier had disappeared. It seemed they had already known they were not allowed in these parts. It was a very high tower as Lyncade looked out the small windows thousands of feet in the air.

Tamian opened the two large doors and pushed them forward with all his strength. Inside were a small fountain and a statue of the god Warad. All along the walls were writings that seemed ages old.

"What is this?" Lyncade asked.

"The word of the gods," Tamian said, "Not spells just warnings."

"Warnings?" Lyncade asked.

Tamian walked over to one part as he stood in front of it proudly.

"Do you know why I was chosen as king?" Tamian asked.

"Because you united all the tribes," Lyncade replied, "You were their best warrior and a born leader."

"Very true," Tamian agreed not one to not compliment himself, "But because I was chosen by Warad."

"How so?" Lyncade asked.

"Before you were a warrior in this army and just a boy Warad came to me and the generals," Tamian told, "Placed me down on my knees and made me king of all the Elves in the northern lands. He did the same for Rakar in the south regions of Tullian. The next time you visit your wife ask Sygon. He was there."

"So what do these words tell?" Lyncade asked, "All I see is a language not aloud to be read by us."

"At the dawn of Warad's chosen people. The rise of their first king will reign for ages in time. The king will be the protector of all that Warad had created and the other races. The building of this kingdom will result in millions of great warriors.

"As long as the king reigns supreme and lives until Warad asks him to the afterlife. The evil gods Greco, Korack and The Dark Lord will never be able to walk the land in Tullian with powers. They will only use illusion to try and cloud the minds of the people. If the king ever falls they will only be granted half their powers on Warad's sacred land."

"So as long as you live they have no power," Lyncade replied.

"Yes," Tamian said, "I was written about ages before my time. In the time of our ancestors Lyncade. Back when they were tribes and clans," Tamian replied, "I was chosen even before I was born for this purpose and as a king I gladly take it as a responsibility."

"What if you fall?" Lyncade asked.

"There is still hope," Tamian assured, "Half their powers is worse but not as bad as their full powers."

"How can they obtain that?" Lyncade asked.

"When Warad defeated them he took their powers on this land and made them into ruby's," Tamian explained, "These ruby's are hidden somewhere in our world."

As Lyncade looked around the room he soon saw a painting of an elf warrior.

"Who is this warrior?" Lyncade asked.

"The greatest fear of all," Tamian told, "Fayne."

"Fayne?" Lyncade asked.

"He was one of the first," Tamian said, "An elf warrior. One of the first elf warriors. He is blessed by every god in all the realms."

"He lives?" Lyncade asked.

"Somewhere inside the world," Tamian told, "He is the greatest threat to our people outside The Dark Lord, Korack and Greco."

"He is evil?" Lyncade asked.

"Once he was defender of Tullian," Lyncade told, "When the elves were just tribes he constantly went on missions defending those in need. Every race in fact. He was so skilled as a warrior in his younger years and it is only assumed that he is even greater now."

"Why did he turn?" Lyncade asked.

"It is believed that Fayne defended all but what he loved," Tamian told, "One night in an attempt to kill Fayne orcs and goblins of Korack attacked his home and killed his wife and children. Driven mad by what had happened he cursed the gods that had once blessed him with all his abilities. Begging Warad to let him see his wife, he was rejected. Warad told him he must defend the world for many mores years before he could see her. Angered he turned his back on Warad and never returned to the world of Tullian again.

"He later joined forces with The Dark Lord and was going to fight under him. What he didn't know was that once he left Tullian he was cursed to never be able to set foot on it again, until he killed the king of all the elves."

"You," Lyncade knew, "So as long as you never leave these lands you cannot be killed buy him."

Tamian short of laughed as he said, "I find no reason to fight The Dark Lord on any other land then Tullian itself. We have defeated him many times and will continue in ages to come."

"Do you ever think you will fight Fayne one day?" Lyncade asked.

Tamian looked at him and said, "I know I will."

"Will you win?" Lyncade asked.

"I have to," Tamian told, "If I do not then he will return to Tullian and do the opposite of what he once did, just to get back at Warad. He is capable of killing ranks by himself."

The two stared at the paintings of the warrior as they just stood there in silence. Lyncade taking in all that he was told finally said what was on his mind.

"My wife returns in a few weeks. I wish to be here when she returns so I can greet her," Lyncade replied.

Tamian nodded and said, "A reasonable request but you will join me in this mission."

"A mission that could require only Nagarth," Lyncade replied.

"I told you your purpose in this," Tamian said, "You will join me as a command from your king."

"I have never said no to you," Lyncade reminded, "This is though the only time I will and I beg of you to let me stay."

"No," Tamian replied quickly.

Lyncade just nodded angrily as if accepting his answer. Lyncade quickly turned around and left the king alone in the room.

Not far away into the land of Cavell the forces of the orcs and goblins stood as if awaiting their next command. The forces began to stretch into the horizons and seemed endless. The shear look of them intimidated the bravest of men.

Orcs and goblins were very scary creatures but they were reckless. With no remorse or care in their body they didn't have anything to really fight for. They lived off anarchy and destruction with their tortures souls being enslaved by Korack, Greco or The Dark Lord.

Banned from the afterlife by Warad for things they had done in their lives, they resurrected as these vile ugly creations to destroy all those who now lived in the world. Their advantage was numbers. Crowd their opponent and outnumber them at least five to one in every battle. That was the only way they'd be successful in warfare.

Goblins who were shorter than orcs always were on the front line. Holding spears to charge with and once in hand to hand pull the swords wrapped around their waist.

Orcs were the generals and commanders but also had fierce regiments of their own. Their reckless fighting could throw off the average elf and their uncaring for their own well being, gave them the advantage against an elf who was worried about seeing his family after the battle was over.

A dark mist began to appear on horseback as Korack began to form on a horse. He stood now in front of two general who were marching the large force.

"What's the count?" Korack asked.

"A few thousand," The orc general told.

"Hold your forces until you get more," Korack commanded, "With General Nagarth going home I'm sure he has told Tamian. They will have a force marching this way. Make sure the forces have an overwhelming advantage in numbers."

"Yes my lord," The orc general replied.

"I will meet with Greco to see where his forces will come from," Korack told as he slowly vanished in front of them.

In the forest of Cavell not far away from the traveling forces three elf brothers looked on at the large force. These men were rouge elves who didn't wish to live under the rule of Tamian. There were many like them, far away from where they were and in hiding for years. They didn't try to make themselves known to anyone they encountered. Even Royal Elves who lived in villages outside of the great city were much different from them.

The three of them stood ready for any encounter. All armed with bows strapped to their backs as well as arrows in a case on their backs. On the belts around their waist was knifes and large daggers. Next to those small tools was a case for their swords. All of them had their swords placed away but they knew it wasn't far from their grasp. Several hundred feet away from the army in front of them they knew they wouldn't need to draw their weapons. They all had fur on their backs as well from the days they had spent hunting.

Being hunters the three brothers were well skilled in the ways of warfare. Being brought up and living in a forest made them one with their surroundings. They were able to hide well if an enemy came toward them and could outrun any force who didn't know the forest trails like they did. Although not living in the city of Tamian or part of their forces they looked just like Royal Elves. They had long blonde hair that at the moments was dirty along with their faces. They only wore light armor and didn't carry a shield so they could be more agile. Their faces were covered in a green type of war makeup so they could be camouflaged in their surroundings.

The oldest brother Cloron was known by his face. Much older than the two young elves beside him. He had several tattoos on his neck and cheeks. These were made by his own doing. They were marks of Warad or Words of the Gods. His parents probable drew them on him when he was first born. These markings were to protect him in his life and so far they had done him well.

The other two just wore the green type of makeup. The middle brother, Hecorus who seemed to be the sharp shooter out of them carried two crossbows that were strapped to his back. Any elf wearing these could have them in his hands in a flash. The crossbows he had was a bolt throwing crossbow. Each time it fired it had a small chamber that would reload the arrow in seconds to ready another shot. The rounds or smaller arrows for this type of weapon were on a case strapped to his back under the cloak he wore.

The third brother Halouse was the sword master. He had double the amount of knives and daggers then his brothers and his sword was much larger. Unlike his brothers who wore a brown cloak, his was black. Easier to pick him out but his speed and sword ability was unmatched in these parts. He had a claw mark on the side of his neck that had been tattooed in by his older brother. Four small red slashes that represented a clan of elves called Lycans. It was a mark giving to him in recognition of his character. He was fierce and when you met him in combat, like a wound that left a scar, you never forgot him. Around his neck was a gold necklace with a small star as the charm. It was given to him by a young girl many years earlier. The day she gave it to him, he never took it off as a reminder of what happened to the village he once called home. As well as always remembering the young girl that captivated him when he was just a boy.

"Looks to be the largest orc and goblin force I've seen in these lands for some time," Cloron informed.

"Why so many?" Hecorus asked.

"All out warfare with Tamian," Cloron informed, "Korack or Greco who ever made this force wants to try and wipe out all the Elves with that force."

"Why are they waiting?" Halouse asked.

"For more forces," Cloron told.

"More?" Hecorus asked, "They have a legion there that can destroy hundreds of villages across the plains."

"They don't wish to go after villages," Cloron told, "Besides their numbers aren't what they seem. They are pathetic with a blade and the three of us could kill three of their regiments before we got overrun."

"So their building a massive force to take on Tamian's Royal Elves?" Hecorus asked.

"Yes and by the looks of it, if Tamian isn't informed by the number, than he can be in serious danger," Cloron informed.

"What do you suggest?" Hecorus asked.

Cloron just looked at the others as they read his mind. To the north they began to travel. With the army far behind and not moving they could reach the great city in the matter of a few days.

Nagarth sat silently in the main courtyard of the city as most of the forces began to get rounded up. Him and his regiments would stay behind and await the return of the forces that seemed moments away from leaving.

Lyncade soon sat next to him dressed in heavy armor and ready for warfare. With his war helmet in his hand he rested it beside him and looked at his friend.

"All I would have needed was a force of a thousand," Nagarth replied.

"Tamian is ignorant," Lyncade replied, "With such a small force of orcs and goblins he wants to take them out with himself in the battlefield. It makes himself look good in the eyes of the people."

"And you?" Nagarth asked, "You don't fight for the glory?"

"The glory is secondary to me," Lyncade assured, "The protection of my people and now the protection of my bride is at stake."

"Tamian makes you royalty and you have become one with lies," Nagarth joked.

Lyncade laughed and said, "Politics my friend. You must learn how important they are to the nobles and other generals. They care for the power but claim they do it for the people. It's only to further themselves within our people. One day you'll understand that."

"Hope not," Nagarth assured, "I never want to be twisted by greed and power."

"Every man wants more," Lyncade assured, "Even Tamian. He's king to his people and the most powerful race in the world. His constant affairs with other noble's wives while he has one of the most beautiful women as his bride proves he wants more. Since the beginning of our time those who walked before us are immortal in the stories and tails told of their lives. The battles they fought, the woman they loved and the evils they stopped so we could survive.

"Tamian is only a victim of history and the wealth of fame. He means you with no disrespect. You and I both know that you and a force of a thousand could handle what lies ahead. Tamian sits in an office or a throne room talking about laws and late night travels to houses of woman where their husbands have been sent off to fight in a battle he commanded. He feels the people will lose him if he stays inside this city forever. A king is supposed to be untouchable to his people.

"Let him have his glory Nagarth as you and I will always know who really wins those battles. The warriors in the front lines and the generals like you and I who would die to protect him and his people."

Nagarth took in all that the wise general said as he looked at him than away at the soldiers preparing for battle.

"I do not understand why you show such respect to a king such as him," Nagarth replied.

"Because he had done something that no one did in the ages of time," Lyncade replied, "United the elves as one. Brought them together as a kingdom and what have you and I and all these other men done? Made the world and this land safe from all the evils that dwell it. Greco, Korack and The Dark Lord will never stand a chance as long as we are one."

"He separates us with his antics," Nagarth told, "You don't think those nobles wives he runs around with keep it a secret? You think those same nobles don't know what he's doing with their wives? Do you think for a moment he cares for you and I?"

"My legions would leave here if I asked them," Lyncade assured, "They fought with me for my purpose at my commands."

"Do you think those same men would walk away with you with all the things Tamian could do for them?" Nagarth asked, "His arrogance and cockiness upsets the nobles as well as the other generals."

"They can do nothing," Lyncade assured, "He is a man blessed by Warad."

"So are you and I," Nagarth assured, "He pulls you and I away from our glories and every victory that came at the end of our blade he bathed in and took all the credit."

"General," Lyncade replied with a warning, "Discuss this another time when I've returned."

Nagarth looked at Lyncade as Lyncade rose and walked away. Nagarth picked himself off and began to leave the courtyard.

Tamian walked out of the castle dressed in clean armor. The type that looked as if it hadn't seen a war in ages. If his warriors and regiments had their way the armor he wore wouldn't get a scratch on it. Tamian took out his sword and raised it in the air as all the regiments roared. Lyncade mounted his horse as his captain rode next to him.

Next to Lyncade was his captain. A warrior by many standards good enough to be a general himself. He and Lyncade had fought for so long that he couldn't ride into battle without him.

"Raven," Lyncade called.

"Yes my lord," Raven replied.

"Ride out," Lyncade said, "Lead the men."

"Where will you be?" Raven asked.

"Escorting the king," Lyncade told.

"As you wish," Raven replied.

The gates of Tamian began to open as each regiment began to slowly make their way toward the empty horizon ahead of them. Just as they began to march a captain in Tamian's regiments walked up to him.

"My king," The captain called.

"Yes," Tamian replied.

"We've received word from The Forest Elves," The captain told him.

Lyncade and Tamian stopped their march a Lyncade looked at his king.

"What is it?" Tamian asked the captain.

"He sends word that he is on his way here," The captain told.

Lyncade looked at Tamian and asked, "What would he want here?"

"I don't know," Tamian replied as he looked at Lyncade, "Go ahead of me."

"What?" Lyncade asked in disbelief.

"Lead all the forces," Tamian told, "I must stay and await Rakar."
Lyncade looked at him as if he was joking.

"You heard me," Tamian said noticing his stare.
Lyncade began to ride ahead as the large force of Royal Elves began
to make their way toward Cavell.

"What was the meaning of that?" Raven asked as he approached
Lyncade.

"I don't know," Lyncade replied, "He got word from Rakar that he
is headed this way."

"Rakar?" Raven asked, "The Forest Elf King?"

"The same," Lyncade confirmed.

"What could that mean?" Raven asked.

"Who knows," Lyncade replied, "Keep the men on the same pace.
We'll fight this battle on our own."

As Tamian began to make his way back to the city two heavily
armed guards road next to him. One was the captain that gave him
the message about Rakar.

"My lord," The captain called, "What was the purpose of that?
Rakar sent you that message days ago."

Tamian just looked at his captain and replied, "I have my reasons."

The second captain moved away from them moments later and
dismounted as a servant took his horse. The helm he wore covered up
most of his face and only the eyes of the warrior was seen. The captain
walked into the crowded city and removed his war helmet. Nagarth
dropped the war helmet to the ground as he made his way toward a
tavern.

Mayreon kneeled silently in front of Sygon. On the top of the main
temple she kneeled with her head down as the wizard looked toward
the mountains in the distance. Behind her were thousands of stairs
leading to the main temple ground. They were alone and by
themselves as Sygon turned and faced her.

"You have been here for some time," Sygon began, "Most of my
pupils train under me for years and then are sent back to Tamian with
the book to study on their own. You have made fast pace, a pace that
I will tell in years to come as an impossible rate. You have a gift that
you were given the moment you were born. Able to read the words
of the gods with no punishment to yourself. No god seems angered

when you speak them. Most elves, me to be more clear, had to wait many years to be able to get permission by the gods to read it.

"Everyone dreams of having the gifts that Warad has given you. Everything in the book that you will study is now up to you to learn. Wizards, sorcerers, witches, warlocks, what ever you want to call them have the ability that no warrior with a sword will ever have. The ability to wield magic that Warad created for us to use. You can strike down legions of very skilled warriors with just a mutter of words. You can protect yourself with just a word from every weapon in this world.

"You though Mayreon have been given another curse. Beauty. Beauty in all my years of living that has been unmatched. With the powers you have been able to get through permission of the gods; both of them together is an excellent combination. There is no doubt that because who you are married to you will be a noblewoman among your people. The amount of wars your husband has won and his leadership will make him a great king. With you beside him that will make you a queen. You will have thousands that will adore you and love you.

"With everything you have been given here, if it is used improperly, can prove tragic. It is not coincidence that tragic rhymes with magic. It can turn quickly into it if lead astray. When you read these words each time The Dark Lord, Greco and Korack; each gods will know the words you speak and will soon know you."

Sygon took from behind him a blue ruby. It was on a cloth that he placed around her forehead and tied to the back of her head.

"This is the ruby of the elves. Protecting all of your thoughts from them. This ruby was blessed by Warad himself and each one I give to my students. With this around you, you are safe from the temptation of evil. Carry it always when casting and when in desperate need. This ruby shall give you a closer relationship with Warad himself. Walk with it proudly."

Sygon requested for her to rise and she did slowly.

"I pronounce you a master of sorcery," Sygon replied, "You are not yet a sorceress. Only in ages to come will you earn that title on your own. Go my student. Be careful with the things you have learned and travel well."

Mayreon kneeled slightly before she turned and began to walk down the stairs. Sygon turned back around and looked to the mighty mountains miles away. At this height it was easy to see them.

"She scares even me," A voice replied.

Sygon looked to his right as a large man stood beside him. He was in an all blue robe that dragged on the ground behind him. A larger staff rested in his hands griped by old and wrinkled skin. A long gray beard that almost touched the ground grew on his old crippled face. He was also wearing a large blue pointed hat. Behind the hat long hair went down his back. Looking like a feeble and helpless old man, he seemed harmless. When he spoke, the tone was that of light grunt. It was as if he had something caught in his throat and seemed to take every ounce of strength just to say simple words. His looks were certainly deceiving. This crippled looking man could do more with his staff than anyone else.

It was the god Warad himself. In the form he wished his creations to see him in.

"Her powers and ability is nothing that I've ever seen," Sygon told.

"I have," Warad told.

"Is what I think the reason?" Sygon asked.

"Do not dare say it," Warad warned, "She needs protection. She is not to know what she is and any word muttered will excess them to who she is. She will not know her purpose until ages from now."

"If the words I have read are true than she will go through a great deal of pain," Sygon informed, "Turn against the races you have created."

"All things happen for a reason," Warad told, "Do not dare interfere."

Sygon just looked ahead as he replied, "I feel a connection with her. Nothing I have ever felt before."

"She is beautiful," Warad said.

"Not that," Sygon assured, "I haven't felt the slightest attraction to anyone in ages. She has a quality to her that I cannot place."

"You look upon her like you would your own child," Warad said.

"I have spent a great deal of time with her," Sygon reminded, "I have grown to know her not just as a student, but a woman."

Warad nodded and said, "And you do not understand why she will become what she must become."

"I see no hatred in her," Sygon said, "No form of anger or rage at all. She is as pure as she is beautiful. What will make her get so twisted?"

"Many things," Warad told, "You and I both know that this world can destroy those who have even the purist of hearts."

"A creation like her should not be subject to her fate," Sygon told, "She is meant for something better. The way you created her, she could do more good than evil."

"All things have their purpose Sygon," Warad reminded, "Your care for her can be felt in just your words. Do not let it get too personal."

"I can't help it," Sygon told.

"I know," Warad replied, "It's the way I made her that draws you to her."

Sygon seemed to nod as he looked off into the distance with the god.

"In have felt something," Sygon told, "An old form."

"Fayne," Warad replied knowing Sygon's thoughts.

"Where is he?" Sygon asked.

"With the Falmores," Warad told.

"He has been off these lands for quite sometime," Sygon replied.

"And he will be until his death," Warad assured, "There is only one way he can return."

"How is that?" Sygon asked.

"He must kill the king of the Royal Elves," Warad told.

"Can he?" Sygon asked.

Warad looked at Sygon and replied, "Easily."

Chapter 6

In the territory of Tamian, many snow flakes began to fall in the cold forest. Mayreon was being escorted by dozens of Royal Elf Guards. Lyncade had sent word that he was unable to escort her himself. On horseback Mayreon rode as all the guards walked in front of her. They were to stay aware at all times. Evils were said to come out of this forest when ever they wished. Each man knowing of these legends kept a careful eye on Mayreon.

There were several guards in front of her and in back. One guard guided her horse through the deep snow as she rode atop and looked at the enchanting forest in wonder. Her eyes looked to the beautiful snow flakes as they floated down and touched her face. She seemed trapped in her own world as she was guided through the woods. With no care for what ever evils dwelled in these forests she was so happy with her progress in the temple.

The guards in the front quickly came to a stop as they saw a dark figure with a robe standing on a cliff in front of them. Two guards quickly aimed their bows and fired. The arrows flew toward the figure but as they were seconds from hitting, the figure vanished.

Mayreon looked to the cliff as the guards fired. The figure soon appeared again in the same place. Four guards pulled out their swords and rushed toward it.

"Hold your ground," The guard with Mayreon's horse yelled, "I command you to hold your ground."

The guards didn't seem to listen as they disappeared around the rocky bend.

"Where are they going?" Mayreon asked the guard guiding her horse.

An arrow flew into the guards neck as he was about to answer.

"Protect Mayreon," The other guards yelled as they went to her.

All around, Mayreon began to see arrows flying at the guards as they were killed quickly. Mayreon fearing her life began to look all around her as she began to shake. A guard that ran away earlier began to come from the bend.

"Thank Warad," Mayreon replied in relief.

The guard quickly fell to the ground on his stomach. With a large sword stabbed in his back the dark creature walked toward the fallen guard and removed the blade. Mayreon still in shock looked at the creature as it looked toward her. He was wearing all black attire with a hood over his head and mask covering his face. The deep red eyes of the creature could be seen.

Moments later several of these creatures came from the sides of the forest and began to make their way toward her. Mayreon began to chant something in her mind. As a few dozen of these creatures emerged several of them began to get blasted with a blue light firing from Mayreon's hands. The creatures began to back off as the one in her path held out his blade stopping the others.

His forearms could be seen as well exposing the gray pail skin he had. Removing his mask it seemed the creature had no face. Nothing but rotted flesh and the teeth of a skeleton.

"Give us the ruby," The creature replied as he pointed the blade to the blue ruby on her head.

"Who are you?" Mayreon asked.

"Give us the ruby," The creature said without hearing her statement.

Out of the forest a small bolted arrow flew into the creature's neck. He screamed an unnatural scream that made the others do the same. From the forest an ax flew toward one and slammed into it's face. Mayreon watched as Cloron, Hecorus and Halouse came from the forest with their blades ready. They swiped at the creatures as they began to fall around them. One of the creatures free from battle grabbed Mayreon's horse. The horse went crazy as it rose in the air and Mayreon was thrown back and fell hard on the ground. Dazed and seconds from passing out one of the creatures stood over her and raised it's blade. Halouse looked over and quickly tossed his sword as the blade flew into the creatures face. The being fell to the ground as its hand went limp and it didn't finish killing the dazed Mayreon. Halouse ran over and pulled his sword out. The creature began to roll toward the dazed Mayreon but Halouse kicked the creature away before it could. As he slid over her to protect her, another blade from a second creature was thrown down on him. He put the blade in front of his face as he blocked it and quickly stabbed the creature in the stomach. Jumping to his feet quickly he killed off several other creatures before they were all dead.

Mayreon came to as she saw Halouse over her. Halouse smiled gently at the sight of the beautiful woman. Thinking he was still a creature she kicked him hard between the legs. Caught off guard an obviously very hurt he bent over and fell backward.

Cloron and Hecorus began to laugh as Mayreon got up and realized what she had done.

"Is that the thanks your savior gets?" Cloron asked.

"My apologies," Mayreon assured to Halouse who was still hurt on the ground.

Halouse slowly got up limping from her kick still. He looked to her attire and studied it.

"Where did you come from?" Mayreon asked them.

"We took the Cavell Mountains to come to Tamian from the east," Cloron told, "We have come onto this land to see Tamian himself."

"Good thing we caught your trail a mile back," Hecorus replied, "These are cursed forest."

"How?" Mayreon asked.

"They have unnatural beings like the ones we just killed all over them," Cloron told.

"Who are you?" Mayreon asked, "You are elves from what I can tell."

"Cloron," Hecorus replied as he pointed at his brother. He than pointed at himself and said, "Hecorus."

"Halouse," Halouse introduced as he continued to study her, "You're royalty aren't you?"

"General Lyncade's wife," Mayreon informed as she studied Halouse and asked, "Your name is Halouse?"

"Yes," Halouse replied.

"I've heard of you before," Mayreon thought.

"I'm sure you haven't," Hecorus replied, "We don't know royalty."

Halouse looked to the ruby on her forehead and said, "Sorcerers ruby."

"Why did they want it?" Mayreon asked.

"For the power you have," Cloron told.

"No one knows what those beasts are," Halouse replied, "Some say they are demons from another god not of this world here to hurt Warad's creatures."

"But the ruby on my head…" Mayreon began.

"All the creatures of Warad will be killed if they said the words of the gods we know," Halouse replied, "They are not Warad's creatures like we said."

"Why are you going to the city?" Mayreon asked.

"Orc and goblin forces have gone into the thousands," Cloron told.

"Why does that affect you?" Mayreon asked.

"We are hunters," Cloron told, "Orcs and goblins destroy forest. That is our home."

"So you're Forest Elves?" Mayreon asked.

"We are Elves," Halouse assured, "Not of any type that Rakar and Tamian made. We are renegades and live under our own laws."

Mayreon began to look at all the fallen guards around her.

"These men died for me," Mayreon replied.

"These men were stupid," Halouse said.

"How dare you," Mayreon replied as she snapped her head toward him.

"They should have known not to come into these forests my lady," Cloron replied.

Mayreon still looked at Halouse evilly as she said, "Still doesn't mean you should speak so horrible of men that died to protect me."

"His apologies my lady," Hecorus replied for his brother, "He meant no disrespect."

Halouse just looked at Mayreon for a few moments than began to inspect the dead bodies of the Royal Elves. Halouse and Hecorus grabbed as many arrows as they could and placed them in the cases in back of them.

"We will be happy to escort you to the city my lady," Cloron replied, "It would be our honor."

"I thank you," Mayreon replied to him softly, "You came to my safety and saved me. You will surely be awarded for what you've done."

Packing up all they could Hecorus, Halouse and Cloron began to exit the cold forest with Mayreon between them. They went through it slowly as they soon came to the exit and open terrain in front of them. In the distance several towering mountains could be seen in an endless row.

Halouse took the lead position as he traveled several hundred feet ahead of Hecorus, Cloron and Mayreon.

"What is he doing?" Mayreon asked Cloron.

"Front position," Cloron told, "He makes sure there are no dangers ahead of us. If there are, he will warn us."

"So why is it that three hunters wish to live outside of the greatest empire known to this world," Mayreon asked.

"My father knew Tamian," Cloron informed.

"Are you all related?" Mayreon asked.

"Yes," Cloron confirmed, "I have a different mother than Hecorus and Halouse."

"Your father was a tribesman?" Mayreon asked.

"A very wise one at that," Hecorus claimed.

"Why did he branch away?" Mayreon asked.

"In the uniting of the tribes our father got into a disagreement with Tamian," Cloron told, "After the argument they never spoke again. It was a short meeting between the two of them but Tamian heard of my father's reputation. He knew he was a gifted warrior and wanted him as nobleman when the empire was first built. My father said no and Tamian shortly went out seeking my father. A warrior named Dalian told Tamian my father had died and we never heard from Tamian again."

"How many of you are their?" Mayreon asked.

"Enough," Cloron informed, "The three of us hunt for fur in these parts and many others."

"You can just buy them from the villages," Mayreon informed.

"That requires gold my lady," Hecorus reminded, "Gold in which we do not have."

"For many years we all lived separate," Cloron told, "Until many of our homes were attacked. I used to have a family of my own until creatures like the ones you just encountered attack my home."

"How many died?" Mayreon asked.

"Fifty or so," Cloron told, "Me, Hecorus and Halouse managed to get away. We avenged them in the next few days and lived off the forest from then on. The others have safety back in our home."

"Your home?" Mayreon asked.

Hecorus looked at Cloron and gave him a harsh look. Cloron just nodded as if telling him he would be silent.

Mayreon looked away as her horse rode further into the territory.

"If so alone why don't you join Tamian?" Mayreon asked.

"Our father never trusted him," Cloron informed, "We stay to that same vow."

"He may not be one to trust but he is a great king," Mayreon told.

"That's what you think," Cloron replied, "You aren't in the places we are my lady. You don't see the deaths of hundreds of your people as orcs and goblin's roam the villages of others and kill them. A few weeks go by before they are even avenged. The hundreds and thousands who wish to live off the land and not get involved with your king are just trying to live their own life. They are not made slaves and have to serve for thousands of years. Out here in these forests they just are; they never have to go under anyone's command."

"I guess I could understand," Mayreon replied, "But you said there are thousands like you."

"All over the place," Cloron told, "Humans, Elves of every hair color and eyes. They don't wish to live under Tamian or Rakar."

"How do you survive?" Mayreon asked.

"Humans will pay a decent amount for fur and meat that they can't catch," Cloron told, "We hunt all day and sell what we don't need. That is the way Warad intended."

"You said you had a home though," Mayreon reminded.

"Had," Hecorus jumped in, "Our home was destroyed."

Mayreon looked at him and knew he was lying. The many days of training were paying off and she could see the deceit in his eyes. She didn't want to bother them or annoy her saviors.

Mayreon just looked ahead as she saw Halouse's figure looking toward them on a large hill. He seemed to be waiting for them to catch up a little. He kept his eyes on Mayreon the whole time. Besotted with her every movement he stared for what seemed like years to him. She looked back not being able to control her stare as well. Halouse hadn't been affected by a glance like that since he was a boy. He felt the charm around the necklace he wore as he looked at her.

As soon as they were close enough he began to take off again. Sprinting in the open terrain in front of him as if he was flying. In the distance of the mountains thousands of trees were seen as he knew they'd run into another forest.

Mayreon still rode still burning the image of her savior in her mind. Standing over her seconds after he had saved her life. She was angry for not thanking him properly. She wondered about his stare and what effect it would have on her.

Artwore stood on the docks of Fadarth as thousands of the Great Humans began to place supplies in the mighty ships they'd sail on to hit the shores of Cavell. Sangrayus dressed in a pitch black robe stud next to him. On the crown she wore was a red shining ruby. This ruby was like the one Mayreon had except it used all the powers of Dark Magic.

"I can't fight these Elves," Artwore replied, "They are too skilled for me."

"You will not need skill my love," Sangrayus informed.

"How so?" Artwore asked.

"The Dark Lord will see you again," Sangrayus assured, "He will give you all you need."

Artwore looked once again to the thousands preparing the hundreds of ships.

"What reward will we receive after we defeat the Royal Elves?" Artwore asked.

"The protection of our people," Sangrayus told, "The Dark Lord will forever look to our kind as the chosen people in his eyes. Much like the way Warad looks at the Elves."

"Blessings not of this world," Artwore knew.

"Each general in the Royal Elf army as well as Tamian himself have been blessed. If Warad allows them to be, they will life forever. After one hundred thousands years they will be considered ancients. Ancients have powers that no one of this world will know of. Ability to be reborn, heal, and immortality," Sangrayus told, "Tamian is close to these gifts. When The Dark Lord has his way, Tamian will be nothing but a memory to his people."

"He will never become an ancient," Artwore assured, "Not if I am given these gifts you speak of."

Sangrayus looked at him and assured, "You shall."

Fayne walked up to Artwore in his black armor but this time he wasn't wearing his cape.

"I told you I cannot protect you in those lands," Fayne reminded.

"I will not need you," Artwore assured, "I will return I promise."

"When you do all those who died under your blade will be avenged," Fayne knew, "I will be here to protect you from them when you return."

"I know," Artwore replied.

"I envy you my lord," Fayne replied, "You will be able to kill many elves."

"Why do you hate your people so much?" Artwore asked.

Fayne just looked at him and replied, "Just make sure there will be thousands coming this way."

The savage Great Human army began to slowly board. The thousands set shall just before sun down and would reach Tullian in two days. Ready for warfare and destruction the land of Tullian had never seen. With The Dark Lord guiding them it would be the perfect sneak attack on the Royal Elves.

Halouse saw the large city of Tamian in the distance. He then slowly turned and saw the forms of Cloron, Hecorus and Mayreon not far behind. As he looked to the city again he saw the guards on the walls looking toward him. In a matter of moments a few dozen Royal Guards in heavy armor rode toward him atop their horses.

Halouse raised his hands in the air as they approached to assure he meant no harm. Cloron and Hecorus did the same as they reached their brother. Quickly Mayreon got in front of them on her horse to make sure nothing happened to them.

"My lady," The leader of the Calvary called, "Who are these men?"

"Hunters," Mayreon told, "Came to my rescue in the Cold Forest as my escorts were slaughtered. I am in their debt."

The captain nodded as he replied, "It is good to know you are safe. The king will be pleased to hear. Come, we will escort you and these men to Tamian at once."

Mayreon looked in back of her at them. They all began to walk slowly as Mayreon rode next to them.

The gates of the city were opened as hundreds of villagers crowded the streets to see Mayreon enter. They all seemed shady around Cloron, Hecorus and Halouse. Looking like Royal Elves but in different clothing had everyone giving them peculiar looks. Mayreon dismounted as Hecorus helped her down. Halouse seemed distant but managed to give her a look again. He seemed to be fighting whatever he was feeling inside when he looked at her.

"Follow me," Mayreon replied as she looked to the three of them.

The three hunters looked around them in fascination of the large and gorgeous city. Slowly though they did as she asked as they followed her into the main castle. Through several halls they walked before the main doors of the throne room were opened. Tamian sat on his throne, and then quickly rose in admiration at the sight of Mayreon. He quickly walked down from the throne platform and met her halfway.

"My lady," Tamian called, "I trust it was a safe journey."

Mayreon gave him a saddened look as she shook her head.

Tamian looked in back of her at Cloron, Hecorus and Halouse.

"Who are these men?" Tamian asked her.

"The dark races of the Cold Forest killed your men," Cloron replied, "Almost killed your noblewoman here."

"She is considered a queen," Tamian told them.

"They came to my rescue my lord," Mayreon told, "Escorted me here safely. It is because if them that I am alive now. I owe them my life."

Tamian looked at her than back at them.

"Drizell," Tamian called.

Drizell rose from her throne and slowly walked toward him.

"Take Mayreon and get her cleaned up," Tamian replied.

With a small smile Drizell took Mayreon as they began to walk toward the east exit of the throne room. Tamian signaled for the three brothers to follow as he made his way back to his throne.

The hundreds of guards in there kept their eyes locked on the strangers.

Cloron was the first to walk up the stairs halfway and kneel in front of Tamian. Hecorus and Halouse did the same as they followed their brother.

"Rise," Tamian replied, "Tell me how it was you three that were able to save the wife of General Lyncade."

"We came to give you news," Cloron replied as he rubbed sweat from his eyes, "Legions of orcs and goblins are in the territory of Cavell. A force that I haven't seen for ages. Since the Elves were tribes. They looked prepared for an attack."

"I had a general there with his forces," Tamian told, "I was informed that there were only a few thousand."

"There is more than that," Halouse told, "Legions being built and more on their way from the shore."

"Are you sure?" Tamian asked.

"We would never come to you and lie," Cloron assured, "You are a king among our people whether we live in your city or not, we knew we should tell you."

Tamian with a look of shock looked toward his captain.

"Rally the men," Tamian commanded, "We leave in the morning."

"Yes my lord," The captain replied as he kneeled and rose quickly running toward the west exit.

Tamian looked at them and replied, "Help yourself to anything in this castle. Food, wine, clothing, what ever you need it will be given with no question. General Lyncade is with his men taking care of what I thought was a small force of orcs and goblins. Now it seems an even larger force will need to be sent."

"Thank you for your hospitality. We will take what we need and leave," Cloron replied as he kneeled and was seconds from walking away.

"Gentlemen," Tamian called.

They stopped and looked at the king.

"Feel free to stay as long as you like," Tamian told, "You will be given chambers in my castle."

"We thank you but..." Cloron began.

"I insist," Tamian replied interrupting him before he could decline, "Your service will be repaid by me and when Lyncade returns he will thank you himself. I'm sure your honor will keep you here so he could show his gratitude."

Cloron looked at his brothers as they didn't seem to mind.

"We shall stay as long as you permit us," Cloron told.

"I thank you," Tamian replied.

All of them bowing slightly they began to walk away.

Mayreon sat in a bubble bath as she gently began to wash off her arms. Drizell sat on the side of tub looking toward her.

"Rough journey huh?" Drizell asked.

"I thought I was going to die," Mayreon replied as she rested her head back.

"Who were those men?" Drizell asked.

"Hunters from Cavell," Mayreon told, "Traveling to Tamian from the mountains."

"Can't imagine what you had to go through," Drizell replied.

Mayreon looked over at her and began to look her over.

"There is something different about you," Mayreon replied, "Is their something wrong?"

"No," Drizell replied as she rose slowly.

"You have a glow about you," Mayreon told.

"Must be your imagination," Drizell replied, "Your constant studying maybe has you seeing things that aren't there."

Mayreon looked at her and sat forward in shock.

"You're carrying," Mayreon replied.

Drizell looked over at her in astonishment as she asked, "What?"

"A child," Mayreon replied.

Drizell seemed seconds from walking away.

"Don't," Mayreon called.

Drizell looked back at her.

"Don't go," Mayreon said gently, "Stay with me."

Drizell walked back over and sat next to the tub. Saddened by Mayreon's discovery she had tears in her eyes.

"Why are you so upset?" Mayreon asked.

"He doesn't know," Drizell replied as she looked at her, "He has no idea."

"How long have you known?" Mayreon asked.

"A few months," Drizell told, "I've been wearing baggy dresses to hide it."

"Why hide it?" Mayreon asked.

"Back when our people were tribes the men used to kill the women if their first child wasn't a son," Drizell told, "Some of the nobles have believed in the old ways. Tamian and I have discussed children but he never told me what could happen if I didn't give him a son the first time."

"He loves you," Mayreon told.

"Nonsense," Drizell replied as she rose, "You think I don't know about the things he has done with the noble's wives?"

Mayreon couldn't reply to her response. She was only trying to make Drizell feel better.

Mayreon slowly rose from the tub as Drizell quickly wrapped a robe around her. Tying the robe she quickly began to walk into her bedroom. Drizell followed her as several maidens awaited Mayreon in front of a large mirror. Mayreon took the robe off quickly as the maidens began to dress her for the night.

"What will you do?" Mayreon asked Drizell as she looked at Drizell in the mirror.

"I don't know," Drizell replied, "I don't know how he'll take the news."

"He'll be delighted," Mayreon assured.

Drizell seemed to get an idea in her head as she looked at Mayreon.

"Is there anyway you can find out?" Drizell asked.

Mayreon looked at her in the mirror once again and replied, "As soon as I'm dressed I'll see."

A few moments later Drizell laid on a couch inside Mayreon's chambers as Mayreon came out dressed in a royal blue dress. The dress complimented her bust and showed off her sleek gorgeous body enough to leave little to the imagination of those who looked at her.

She took out her spell book and began to go through it as she sat next to Drizell.

"I haven't looked much into any Light Magic," Mayreon admitted, "I have to say I like some of the Seduction more than others."

"Seduction?" Drizell asked, "You don't need any spells for that."

Mayreon looked at her and gently smiled at her comment.

"You don't either," Mayreon assured.

"You do not need to say things just to be kind," Drizell assured.

Mayreon looked at her confused as she asked, "Does his infidelities make you think less of yourself?"

"What would it make you feel like?" Drizell asked.

Mayreon gave her a curious look and began to ask, "Does Lyncade..."

"Oh no," Drizell quickly replied, "The months you were gone you were all he could talk about. From what I can tell it's no. Than again he is a High Lord and they are allowed as many women as they want."

"But us?" Mayreon asked.

"If we are caught with another man or even looking at another man the wrong way, you and the man you are with will be executed within seconds," Drizell told, "That used to be the way of the tribes. Back when our people were savages."

Mayreon just flipped through her book as if trying to get off the subject.

"Here we are," Mayreon replied, "Trying to see that which is unseen."

"Be careful," Drizell warned, "If the words are spoken wrong..."

"I know," Mayreon assured, "I'm trying to see if there is anything in here."

Mayreon went through the text with her finger. She came to one spell and quickly closed the book. She stood up and looked toward Drizell.

"What?" Drizell asked.

"Lay back," Mayreon commanded.

"Aren't you going to read it?" Drizell asked.

"I've memorized most of the book," Mayreon replied, "As soon as I saw it I remembered."

"Will it hurt the baby?" Drizell asked.

"Of course not," Mayreon replied.

"What will it do?" Drizell asked as she slowly laid back.

"I can't explain," Mayreon replied, "Just lay back."

Drizell did as she was told as Mayreon began to whisper to herself. Her hands began to glow green as Drizell looked at her concerned. Mayreon placed her glowing hands on Drizell's womb.

Mayreon seemed to get transported to a place she couldn't explain. A valiant warrior was in a battlefield as he began to slice away at orcs and goblins around him. He seemed invincible as he saw the blades of his enemies even from in back of him. The type of style he fought with was near flawless. It was poetic in the way he fought, matching each strike and block with precision and the perfect amount of strength. Each kill as vicious and vivid as the first. The warrior always seemed to have the right strike for each enemy that came toward him. As the many bodies fell thousands of warriors in the field began to chant his name as he was fighting. The warrior slowly removed his mask as the face of a charming handsome man was seen.

Being shot back to the real world Mayreon jumped back. Drizell got to her feet in alarm as she looked toward her.

"Are you alright?" Drizell asked.

"Endore," Mayreon replied.

Drizell in bewilderment looked at her and asked, "How did you know what I was going to name him?"

"I saw him in my mind," Mayreon told, "He will be a great king passed the days of Tamian. He will be a warrior in which this kingdom has never seen. I see him fighting in a war of wars. One that our world has never seen."

Drizell went over to Mayreon and asked, "So it is a boy?"

Mayreon smiled at her as she rose and gently hugged her, "Yes."

"Thank Warad," Drizell said.

In the distance several of the guards began to see a small unit approach. Dozens of horses with spearmen began to come toward the city of Tamian. The flag of The Forest Elves was soon seen as the Royal Elves knew they were only there to speak with Tamian.

The gates were quickly opened as the king of the Forest Elves dismounted a few feet in front of Tamian. Dressed in forest green and brown exotic fabric with heavy armor protecting his chest he slowly walked toward Tamian with many guards around him.

Forest Elves were descendants of the same Elves that Royal Elves were. Because of the amount of time Forest Elves spent in the forest they began to change though. There once blonde hair turning brown and the same with their eyes. Their skin was a copper color allowing them to blend in well with their wooden surroundings.

Rakar was much younger than Tamian. He was a boy compared to Tamian but was still respected by even him. If Rakar were human he'd look only about twenty or so.

Tamian had guards of his own around him as both kings bowed their heads slightly to the other.

"How was your journey?" Tamian asked.

"Many weeks have passed since I've seen my kingdom," Rakar told, "Many. It has been long and dreary."

"My hospitality then will make up for the despondent voyage," Tamian assured.

"We have many things to discuss," Rakar told.

Tamian nodded as both kings walked toward Tamian's castle side by side. With all of their guards on the sides of them the people of the Royal Elves seemed to look at them in awe.

Entering the castle they slowly walked toward the throne room. On the side of the throne room both kings sat at both ends of a long table. With food and wine awaiting them there, they both sat and looked across at the other.

Rakar ate a meal given to him by the Royal Elf servants as he wasn't yet finished. Tamian sat back with a goblet of wine and just looked over at Rakar. Rakar looked up at him noticing his stare.

"What are you staring at?" Rakar asked.

"I'm just wondering," Tamian informed.

"Yes?" Rakar asked as he sat back in his chair and wiped his mouth with a napkin.

"Why didn't you join me when I combined the tribes all those years ago?" Tamian asked, "All you did was go to Cagore and make an empire of your own. You said you didn't want to be ruled by a king, yet you go away from the rest of us and make a kingdom of your own?"

"Some of us do not believe in your ways," Rakar informed as he took his goblet in his hand, "My people do not need large castles and great cities. We live in the world Warad provided."

"In your city of trees," Tamian knew, "How is your empire?"

"Good," Rakar replied, "Maykar still visits from time to time."

"Maykar the Black Ax," Tamian said with a small smile on his face, "How is the old Dwarf King?"

"Mad at you," Rakar informed.

"That's to be expected," Tamian replied.

Rakar just studied Tamian as the Royal Elf king seemed to drift into his own mind.

"What is going on with you and Boleadar?" Rakar asked.

Tamian just looked at him as his distant stare went away.

"What do you know of it?" Tamian asked.

"I know he has quit a distain for you," Rakar informed.

Tamian just nodded and replied, "Arawon wants the throne."

"Arawon?" Rakar asked, "I was speaking of Boleadar."

"Arawon is Boleadar," Tamian told, "Boleadar may live in the city but Arawon runs Boleadar much like he runs the city named after him."

"He seems to be king more then you are," Rakar told.

Tamian didn't like the comment too much but ignored it.

"Why do you let him get away with so much?" Rakar asked, "None of my lords have this much power over me."

"Our kingdom and yours are very different," Tamian reminded, "Arawon stood next to me as this city was built. He took control of all the main trades in our known world while I ruled it. He became rich and eventual wanted more like most of us do."

"His reputation makes you look like a bad king," Rakar told, "He must be dealt with."

Tamian looked across at Rakar and knew he was right.

"You ever hear of his general?" Tamian asked.

"Xanafear," Rakar replied, "I know of him."

"He's a legend," Tamian told, "Has never lost a battle he's gone into, and has never been wounded by another warrior. Arawon and many others think he is the Agein, or even the Guardian of Light."

"So many have claimed that," Rakar reminded, "He is mortal like us. He can die if a sword pierces him."

"Arawon has many of the nobles in even my city against me," Tamian informed, "If I go after him about this hunting thing in Celladom he will turn many of them against me."

"Maxus?" Rakar asked.

Tamian nodded, "He is good friends with Arawon and has the same distain toward me. They think we should be ruling over the other races."

"Try it Royal Elf," Rakar joked.

Tamian chuckled but didn't seem so amused.

"You can't kill him?" Rakar asked.

Tamian just shook his head, "He has too many allies. If there is foul play his followers will know."

"So this is what's been bothering you?" Rakar asked, "This and everything else going on."

Tamian looked to Rakar and asked, "How are the humans with all of this?"

"They hate you as well," Rakar informed, "Everything Arawon does he does in your name. You are the king, much like many of my men, when they do things it will be thought of as my command."

Tamian nodded and replied, "He won't help me with this war either. He wishes me to be destroyed."

"I've heard troubling news," Rakar began, "Thousands march toward your city."

"How is it that you are so knowledgeable about these things?" Tamian asked.

"The blonde hair Elves in Cavell, the hunters came to me many moons ago," Rakar informed, "Many of them seem to have a problem with you."

"Is that so?" Tamian asked.

"They see you as a hypocritical leader," Rakar informed, "Speaking as if you only care for those inside these city gates and the city gates of Arawon. The villagers, hunters and farmers seem to think you reject them."

"So you have come to my gates to tell me how to rule my people?" Tamian asked.

"No," Rakar assured, "I am only informing you of the mutiny of your actions."

"My actions are to protect the people," Tamian assured.

"The one's that are so far away have no protection but the warriors that live there," Rakar reminded, "With a legion of thousands, hundreds of farmers do not stand a chance."

"Do you wish to help them then?" Tamian asked, "Coming here to my kingdom and downgrading my rule? Perhaps you have sent ranks to go and meet them."

"I haven't," Rakar assured.

Tamian just looked at Rakar angered and replied, "Then you and your force here are more than welcome to come with me tomorrow."

"Where?" Rakar asked.

"To meet with the orcs and goblins," Tamian told, "General Lyncade and many ranks head to Cavell to confront them. I have just received word from three very loyal hunters from Cavell that there is more orcs and goblins on their way to meet them. Because of this news I will head out in the morning to go and meet with them myself."

"How many men will you take?" Rakar asked.

"Thousands," Tamian simply replied.

"I apologies then," Rakar said, "I only came here to know the reasons why you leave thousands of our people unguarded. Now I know you are doing all you could to help them."

"You came this far for that?" Tamian asked.

"And of course Arawon," Rakar replied, "I assured Maykar and the human leaders that I would speak to you about it."

Nagarth quickly came in and walked over to Tamian. Whispering in his ear Tamian nodded.

"I'm afraid I can not speak about much more," Tamian replied.

Rakar looked at him angered and asked, "Why not?"

"There are still some things I need to take care of before I leave tonight," Tamian told, "You can expect me to drop everything for you. I told you my hospitality will make up for your long journey and it will. If you wish to stay you will be treated just as I would by my people. You are more than welcome to join us."

"You insult me with this," Rakar admitted.

"Then let me make it up to you," Tamian replied, "I will meet with you in your kingdom. When ever you call when I don't have this army coming toward my kingdom I will be more then happy to travel to yours."

Rakar still looked angered but quickly nodded.

"You must understand that my anger is only because of my journey here," Rakar assured.

"I know," Tamian replied.

Tamian quickly got up as Rakar stayed where he was. Walking away the king walked outside the throne room and walked toward his chambers. Drizell was in the hall as she seemed to be walking out of the castle.

"Where are you going?" Tamian asked as he greeted her.

"To the temple," Drizell told with a kiss, "I need to pray."

Tamian just nodded as he kissed his wife gently and walked passed her. Dozens of guards followed both Tamian and Drizell as they went in separate directions.

Tamian looked in back of him at his guards and replied, "I will not need to be escorted."

They all nodded slightly and began to walk away from their king. Tamian came to Lyncade's chambers and slowly walked in. On the bed was Mayreon dressed in her night gown. Looking at him in surprise she held her spell book out. It looked as if she was studying.

"Where are your maidens?" Tamian asked.

"I told them to leave for the night," Mayreon informed still surprised by his sudden visit, "What are you doing here?"

Tamian slowly made his way toward her as he sat down. He looked to the ruby on her head and gently touched it.

"I came to congratulate you on your accomplishment," Tamian replied as his gaze quickly went to her eyes.

"Thank you," Mayreon replied trying to stop herself from looking at him but was unable.

Mayreon would be lying if she said she wasn't attracted to the powerful king. He had this affect on even the most loyal women. His charm and youthful look that made him ages younger than his actual time enchanted every woman he'd look at. It seemed his stare had even gotten to her.

Catching herself becoming infatuated with him she jumped up. "What are you doing?" Mayreon asked.

"Admiring your achievement," Tamian replied.

"My achievement or me?" Mayreon asked as she turned and looked at him.

Tamian smiled almost evilly and replied, "A little of both."

Mayreon became angered as she said, "I think you should leave."

"You wish to hide what you are feeling now?" Tamian asked.

"I assure you king that what ever you see is for my husband," Mayreon replied infuriated, "Who by the way is hundreds of miles away protecting your kingdom."

"I join him in the morning," Tamian replied.

"What will I say to him about his king making a pass at his wife?" Mayreon replied.

Tamian angered by her comment went over to her and grabbed her by her chin.

"Listen here," Tamian began in a horrible tone, "With one snap of my finger I will have you back in the temple cleaning floors. Far away from Lyncade's eye and he will be told that his beautiful wife was caught laying with three nobleman in his absence."

In shock Mayreon tried to get away but Tamian grabbed her and threw her up against the wall.

Staring at her Mayreon tried to fight his charm. Tamian slowly began to make his face get closer, Mayreon tried to fight it off but couldn't. Moments later she had fell into his trap. A type of spell he had that not even the Gods could mimic. As he kissed her she returned the embrace drunk from his appeal.

Not long after, Mayreon was in a state of shock as the king was placing his attire on. Naked and under the covers she had a tear falling from her eyes.

"What have you done to me?" Mayreon asked.

"The same thing you have done to me," Tamian replied as he was facing away from her, "No worry Mayreon. He will never know about this time or the others that are to come."

In a state of anger, something Mayreon had never felt before, the ruby on her head began to glow. Shooting a blue blast at Tamian the king was hit as he spun violently toward her.

"There will be no other time," Mayreon screamed, "If I so much as see you look at me the wrong way I will tar you limb from limb."

Hurting by her spell Tamian tried to fight it but began to yell in pain. He was tossed violently away from her as he landed on the ground. Getting up quickly Tamian looked at her in fear. Mayreon got up from the bed and held out her hand as it began to glow.

"Leave this chamber and my life at once," Mayreon replied.

Her eyes began to glow a deep red as in fear Tamian got up slowly. With a worried smile he tried to hide his fear and began to make his way toward the door.

"If you tell him he will hate you more than he hates me," Tamian assured.

With a small flick of her hand a blast flew toward him. Hitting him hard in the chest he was thrown through the closed doors. Mayreon used her mind to close them as her enraged sense seemed to leave her. Finally realizing what had happened she dropped to her knees crying. Unable to contain the tears she soon realized what betrayal she had given the man that gave her this life. Unable to forgive herself at the moment she got in the bed and covered herself. Screaming in emotional pain she hugged her knees and tried not to think about what she had done.

Chapter 7

Hundreds of miles away the regiments Lyncade were marching began to come to a large mountain inside the lands of Cavell. It was simply known as the Cavell Peak. Several hundred feet below them were miles of land reaching the shores just to the west. Where they stood they could see far into the land of Cavell. They were about a mile above the force of orcs and goblins below. If he looked enough he could see the shores. All he saw was thousands of regiments and legions of orcs and goblins spread across the land.

"My lord," Captain Raven called, "We are outmatched."

"No we're not," Lyncade assured, "Spread the men all across the peak. They have to come up this way if they wish to reach Tamian. We have the high ground."

"Will we wait for them?" Raven asked.

"Yes," Lyncade informed, "Send a scout back to the city and inform them that there are thousands here."

"Yes my lord," Raven replied.

Raven nodded to a Calvary rider as he nodded and took off.

"Raven," Lyncade called.

"Yes my lord," Raven replied.

"Gather a small force," Lyncade commanded.

"For what purpose my lord?" Raven asked.

Lyncade looked back at him. Raven quickly just nodded.

"Dismount," Lyncade yelled.

Lyncade stood on the edge of the cliff as he looked down. The peak was very steep and a legion of forces would have to take their time to climb it.

"Have the spearmen line up at once," Lyncade commanded.

The hundreds of spearmen surrounded two miles of the peak and held up their spears. A full line of twelve of them to a group and six lines back. The spearmen had their blades to their waist ready to use if any orc or goblin reached them.

The thousands of orcs and goblins could sense the elves as they began to charge from miles away. They could all see the flags of the Royal Elves hanging high on the peak.

General Bagaris of the orcs looked on while riding his horse.

"They got the peak," Bagaris replied.

The form of Korack began to form around him as he now was on a horse next to him.

"Shift the ranks," Korack commanded, "Flank them. Charge the peak then have the others charge a few miles away. They won't be able to shift that little of men every time."

"Yes my lord," Bagaris replied.

Lyncade began to take off his cloak and tossed it to one of his men. Raven followed as Lyncade was now just in his armor. Heavily armored in his chest only. His arms were free from restraints and the leather sash around his waist would do little for protection. He took the shield from around his horse and tossed it around his back. He pulled out his sword as Raven gave him a second one.

"What are you planning?" Raven asked.

"I'm taking a small forces down the peak," Lyncade told, "They'll try to flank us in secret and I'll be ready for them."

"Shouldn't you take a larger force?" Raven asked.

"I'll be fine," Lyncade assured.

A few foot soldiers from his unit began to follow as he quickly sprinted along the peak and away from the army.

Raven raised his sword high in the air and yelled, "Archers."

With the land covered in orcs and goblins every archer would hit a target. Land couldn't be seen at all below the peak. The archers aimed high in the air and quickly fired. Each time the fired they quickly went for another arrow in incredible speed and fired again. The sky was alive with arrows as it descended on the orc and goblin forces.

The goblins that were smaller and much more agile began to get up the peak quickly. The spearmen hurled their weapons toward them as they began to get slain quickly. Each spearmen backing off and letting the man in back of him throw next. The Royal Elves would quickly run to the back of the line and get another spear from a carriage filled with hundreds of them.

As the thousands of orcs and goblins began to scale the peak several units began to shift to try and flank the Elves. Quickly the Elves caught on as they began to shift as well. With the archers still firing over and over they quickly grabbed their arrows and moved to the edge of the peak. Without command they fired down of the charging orc and goblin forces. Orcs and goblins that were slain by the arrows or spears fell to the ground and rolled down the steep rocky hill. Their numbers wouldn't be damaged too much but the Royal Elves knew they could take on many with this tactic.

Thousands of feet down the peak several units of the orcs and goblins thought they had traveled far enough to reach the peak without a problem. As they began to climb up it Lyncade came from no where and slammed his blade in an orcs chest. Quickly removing it he ran down the steep hill and quickly stabbed any orc or goblin near him. The regiment he was with was quick to move as well. Each of them killing off dozens of orcs and goblins on their own. The unit Lyncade was with was a skirmish unit that was spread out all across the peak. Instead of fighting side by side these warriors were able to swing more freely without fear of hitting the man beside them. With the mighty general leading them they began to hit the ground floor below the peak. With thousands of orcs and goblins charging Lyncade moved through them swinging wildly but proficiently.

His unit was doing the same but many of them began to get overrun by the thousands that were on the ground. Lyncade quickly looked up at the peak as he began to see the orcs and goblins pass his unit and begin to scale the peak. The frontline of spearmen and archers were getting outnumbered. There weren't enough archers and not enough spearmen to handle the amount of orcs and goblins.

Raven and many of the warriors in the frontlines took out many but were soon overrun. Hundreds past Raven as he sliced any orc or goblin near him. The orc and goblin forces went deeper into the Royal Elf lines and engaged in the massive battle. The numbers of the orc and goblin force seemed endless. Never in all the years of fighting did Lyncade see this many. Even below on the land they still stretched across the large territory. There didn't seem to be an end in sight of the amount of carnage that was going on all around him.

Lyncade was still with his small unit as he sliced through orcs quickly. The High General smashed his blade into anything that came near him that didn't look anything like an elf. His speed was amazing as each time he looked moments from death but managed to stop the blade and counter with a killing blow. Dozens of his own men were behind him but began to get killed by the quick running goblins.

Now all alone surrounded by several units Lyncade reached the peak and began to swing all around. Anything that came near him was killed quickly as he wasted no time with wounding shots. Each stab or slice was to kill the orc quickly and not have to worry about them again. Each time he jumped away from a blade he was surrounded by so many orcs they accidentally stabbed another orc near him.

The brave general was in over his head though as he was finally sliced in chest. Falling to the ground he began to roll down the hill toward the charging orcs and goblins. Getting up slowly he stabbed any charging orc as a dark horse rode up to him quickly. Mounted on it was the Cobra King Korack.

The orcs and goblins seemed to run passed him as if they didn't want to fight him. He couldn't understand it as he looked up at the peak and saw the legions of orcs and goblins get further into the land. The Cobra King dismounted and pulled out his blade. Lyncade held up his not even knowing what he was up against.

Raven and the forces of Elves began to see that they were outmatched. Quickly giving the signal the hundreds of men that remained began to retreat. Just before they did though the Royal Elves took hundreds of carriages that were on fire and tossed them down the peak. The carriages claimed hundreds of orcs and goblins as the Royal Elves began to retreat away from the charging army. The flaming carriages would give those who survived plenty of time to take cover from the charging forces.

The Cobra King stared at the general as Lyncade prepared. With two quick swipes Lyncade knocked Korack's blade away and slammed his into his chest. Korack just looked at the wound then back up at Lyncade with a wicked smile.

"You think I can be killed by a blade from this world?" Korack asked.

Korack back handed the general as Lyncade went flying through the air. As he landed he looked up at Korack as Korack pulled out the blade from his chest. A red glow went around the wound as it began to heal. Korack just smiled evilly as he tossed Lyncade's blade away.

Lyncade began to crawl backward trying to get away from him but Korack quickly made it to Lyncade. He aimed his sword toward the ground and adjusted his grasp so he could stab downward on Lyncade. As he raised a quick black mist formed as a blade blocked Korack.

Lyncade looked up at the form of The Dark Lord as he stopped Korack from killing Lyncade.

"What is the meaning of this?" Korack asked angrily.

The Dark Lord turned as his red glowing eyes shot from the dark shadow in front of his face.

"Let him go," The Dark Lord commanded.

"His death with give us a great advantage," Korack reminded.

"Him alive and with his fate will give us a greater advantage," The Dark Lord assured.

The Dark Lord looked down at the Royal Elf Lord and slowly began to walk away. Korack angered looked at Lyncade as well and commanded him to rise with his hand.

"This will not be the last time you see me," Korack assured.

Korack vanished right in front of Lyncade as Lyncade found his blade and attacked any orc or goblin that came near him. He was all alone in the field, each orc and goblin didn't seem interested in fighting him though. They ran past him as if he wasn't even there. Lyncade couldn't make sense of it. The Dark Lord spared him and Korack wouldn't fight him. The orcs and goblins seemed to get this command in their head as they went deeper up the peak to get further into the lands.

Lyncade quickly made his way toward the retreating Royal Elves who had managed to find refuge in the forest not far away. The units he with him weren't able to withstand the awesome strength of the orc and goblin forces. There were thousands dead but it didn't seem to diminish their numbers. Lyncade knew this massive army would need to be stopped, but didn't know if it could.

With Lyncade's forces crippled the orcs and goblins wasted no time charging further into the land of Tullian and ever closer to the city of Tamian.

Inside the city of Tamian the largest home on the west wall was heavily guarded by the Royal Guard. It was the home of one of the most powerful nobles in the Royal Elf army. The home was filled with servant girls and many personal body guards for an Elf named Maxus. Lord Maxus was without a doubt the most threat inside the Royal Elf kingdom to Tamian's throne. He had the most influence on the other nobles and was as old as the city of Tamian itself.

He had a secret distain toward the king that no one knew about except him a select few of the nobles who shared his hatred. He assured any rumors to those in contact with Tamian that he didn't but the king knew better, He commanded several ranks of the Royal Elf guard and was no stranger to battle. The heads of orcs and goblins as well as other creature hung all along his hallways as trophies for every visitor to see. Because of his influence on the nobles Tamian always tried his best to keep him satisfied. He was granted everything he wanted even the choice whether or not he wanted to join in warfare with anyone who threatened the Royal Elf people.

Tamian began to make his way toward the chamber as hundreds of Maxus' guards moved out of the way for him. The doors were quickly opened as Tamian walked through and was witness to the trophies hanging on the walls. Each Royal Elf guard he passed kneeled before him as Tamian was escorted by his own guards to Maxus' chambers.

The doors were quickly opened as dozens of young servant girls walked passed him slightly kneeling and quickly walking away. Tamian walked in and held out his hands to his guards stopping them from following.

"King Tamian," Maxus' voice called hidden somewhere in the large bedroom, "What do I owe this unexpected visit?"

"Troubles," Tamian replied looking all around to see if he could figure out where the noble was.

"So I've heard," Maxus replied, "How is General Lyncade doing?"

"Word hasn't reached us yet," Tamian informed.

"I hear a rumor that it is thousands," Maxus replied finally coming from a side room and walking in front of the king.

Maxus threw on a robe at the moment. He seemed like he was just getting changed as he was wearing light armor and royal blue pants. He long blonde hair was tied back with two braided strands hanging in front of his face from both the left and right side of his forehead. He had an eye patch around his eye covering a wound he had sustained in a past battle. The eye patch though didn't cover the scar running down his right eye. A nasty gash to his handsome face but none the less not making him hideous. He was wearing a suit of light armor that was just for show with the large emblem of the Royal Elves. Every noble had this symbol telling those around the city who they were.

"They make their way here soon and I am going to meet them in the field," Tamian told.

"So you should," Maxus agreed.

"Do you wish to join me?" Tamian asked.

Maxus looked at the king for several moments as if studying him and replied, "Don't you think it best that someone of power stay behind? Just in case they pass your forces."

"They will not," Tamian assured.

"I admire your courage," Maxus replied, "But you must make sure there is a powerful enough force here to stop them."

"Nagarth will be the one commanding them," Tamian told.

"Nagarth," Maxus said with a small laugh, "A brave general I agree but a leader? The nobles see me as their greatest voice if I command them their men will fight under me and follow me to the death."

"They would with me as well," Tamian assured, "I think to win this battle I need you along side with me."

Maxus just looked at him as he slowly rested himself in a chair. With a wave of his hand a servant emerged with a drink and handed it to him. He took a sip and with his free hand commanded the servant to leave.

"You leave in the morning?" Maxus asked.

"Yes," Tamian told.

"I'll think about it," Maxus assured.

Tamian angered began to walk away as Maxus sat back ignoring the king's noticeable disappointment.

"If you're not careful he will know your hatred for him," A woman's voice replied knowing when Tamian was out of range of hearing.

Maxus seemed to know who it was as he didn't jump in fright. He stayed relaxed as he sipped on his wine.

"Take into consideration that this could be my time to get rid of him," Maxus replied.

"The people also have a love for Lyncade," The voice reminded, "How will you know that they do not wish him to be king if Tamian is killed?"

"The nobles and generals make the vote," Maxus reminded, "I am ruler of the nobles and there are more nobles then generals. With Arawon as an ally the other cities will not have a problem with it."

"You must go to war with him," The voice replied.

"And why is that?" Maxus asked.

"Kill him in the battlefield and take the throne," The voice suggested, "Let the orcs and goblins swarm his forces."

"He will have thousands protecting him," Maxus reminded.

"You will be by his side," The voice reminded, "Formulate an ill-advised attack and as the orcs and goblins swarm the forces kill him."

Maxus absorbed the possibility and began to go through it in his head. He took a large sip of wine and placed the empty goblet in front of him.

"It's something to think about," Maxus knew.

The woman's voice seemed to echo as she asked, "Do you think Arawon will give you the throne? How do you know he will take it for himself?"

Maxus just smiled lightly and said, "I'll worry about that once Tamian is out of the way."

Halouse, Cloron and Hecorus were escorted to Mayreon's chambers as the guards disarmed them and let them enter her room. They looked around at the expensive room in marvel. The many statues that had been created in respects to the gods along with the expensive marble tiling and beautiful columns set up all around the room. Dressed in an expensive gown Mayreon sat on her bed surrounded by several of her maidens as they were braiding a few strands of her hair.

She looked at the servants and nodded as they all walked away from her. Cloron, Halouse and Hecorus walked up to her as Cloron kneeled slightly. Hecorus and Halouse followed what he did then quickly got to their feet.

"You sent for us?" Cloron asked.

"I wanted to thank you personally," Mayreon began, "For helping me when I needed protection the most. The times I spent here I was surrounded by guards and even in that forest I was. Those men who died to protect me will be honored as warriors but I still found myself venerable and in danger."

"It was our honor," Halouse assured.

Mayreon looked at him and smiled slightly as she replied, "I trust you've been treated well."

"We had a good meal compliments of your king," Cloron told.

"It will be morning soon I wonder what your plans are," Mayreon asked.

"We have done our duty," Cloron told, "Warned Tamian of the army that approaches."

"Yes you have," Mayreon replied as she delayed trying to think of something to say, "You are more than welcome to stay as long as you like as my guest."

Cloron nodded and replied, "We would be honored and will think about your offer."

Mayreon just nodded as the hunters kneeled before her and began to walk away. Halouse stopped at the door and looked back at her. Noticing his stare she returned his look with a smile. He tried to leave but kept looking at her for several moments. Finally smirking he turned his eyes away from her.

Halouse walked out as Cloron replied, "We leave soon."

Halouse looked at his brother in shocked eyes and replied, "But you told her…"

"I told her what I did so I wasn't disrespecting her request," Cloron told as he looked at his brother.

Lyncade stood outside his tent with the remains of his crippled army. They had camped for the night far away from the marching orc and goblin forces. Several scouts were running through the night trying to get a position of the dark forces. Standing beside him was Raven as they both looked on at several wounded and others with a shattered morale.

"What do we do now?" Raven asked.

"There is nothing we can do," Lyncade replied angered, "That is the largest force I have ever seen. Tamian doesn't even know how large. He will march and not even know the vast forces that make their way toward our kingdom."

"There has to be a way we can stop them," Raven replied, "Or tell Tamian."

"Hopefully the scout we sent is close to home," Lyncade replied, "Maybe he'll be able to inform Tamian of the troubles that are making their way ever closer to our home."

Lyncade began to walk away from the camp and made his way toward a river. There he just took out his pouch and placed it in the cool stream. He than took the pouch and raised it to his mouth as he began to drink. He began to feel something, something he had never felt before. Something he couldn't explain began to call to him as he slowly walked downstream. He soon came to a small waterfall and felt as if he needed to stop.

"General," A voice called.

As Lyncade turned, in front of him stood a shining form. One that he had never seen before. Dressed in a white and gold robe that blinded him as he stared was a very attractive woman. A woman with such beauty it sent chills down his spine and made him almost not even want to look at her. Her striking presence didn't just make him admire her, but it made him fear her as well. It was a weird sensation he got mostly in his heart as he looked to her. It seemed she has just appeared there and the glow around her form soon vanished. It was hard to tell what race she was if any. He couldn't get a good enough look at her to even speculate. Her golden hair flowed freely behind her as it was somewhat curled. She was so beautiful it seemed to hurt his vision as he finally looked down.

"Who are you?" Lyncade asked.

"Talius," The woman replied in a voice that seemed to echo in his ears, "Goddess of the fourth realm."

"Fourth realm?" Lyncade asked.

"There are many realms of worlds," Talius told, "Six that the gods know of?"

"What gods?" Lyncade asked.

"Warad," Talius began, "God of Tullian and this world is the god of the first realm. He is my brother as you would call it."

"As we would call it?" Lyncade asked.

"Your world," Talius replied, "Your kind could say that we are brother and sister. It is too overwhelming for your fragile mind to understand."

"What do you want?" Lyncade asked.

"I am here to give you a warning," Talius replied, "A warning that only I can give you."

"Why is it that you are telling me and not Warad?" Lyncade asked.

"Warad can not interfere with his own world. The same rules apply to me and mine and the other gods and their world," Talius explained, "We though are aloud to interfere with the other worlds but never cause them harm. Your world is covered with evils that the other realms have never heard of."

"In what way?" Lyncade asked.

"Some worlds are all considered evil. Of course there the word evil is good and good is evil," Talius explained, "But like I said it's too much for you to understand. When Warad created his sons like all the gods did to protect their worlds his sons turned on him."

"The Dark Lord, Greco and Korack," Lyncade knew.

"Yes," Talius replied, "No other sons of gods had done that. In my realm or any other realm at that. Your world is split between so many entities."

"What can a goddess do to help me then?" Lyncade asked.

Talius placed out her hands and a blinding orange light began to emerge. As the light stopped a sword came to her as she handed it to him.

Lyncade finally got a look at her face. So flawless and beautiful that once again he had to look down. She though, unlike any other being, had purple crystal eyes that brought out her exquisite face. No statue in all the world, or painting that he ever came across, could ever match her beautiful presence.

"This sword has the ability to kill every enemy you come in contact with," Talius told.

"Even Korack?" Lyncade asked.

"Even Korack," Talius assured, "If used properly you can mortally wound any opponent to the point it kills his soul and not his body."

"What do you mean?" Lyncade asked.

"You can kill a man without an ounce of his blood being shed," Talius told, "The blade is called Soul Stealer. When the blade glows it steals the soul of your enemy."

"Orcs and goblins do not have a soul," Lyncade reminded.

"That's when the blade will be used as normal," Talius told, "The blade glows when the soul of an opponent is felt."

Lyncade pulled out his blade and grabbed Soul Stealer. His blade was quickly tossed away as Talius took it from his grasp and threw it in the river.

"With that blade the blessings of me are all over you," Talius told, "The moment your men watch you slay the enemy in the field they will instantly regain their morale and fight with a passion never before felt in warfare."

Lyncade looked at the blade in amazement as he looked at the goddess.

"Go now general," Talius told, "Leave and restore your morale."

Lyncade watched as the goddess vanished before him. He continued to study the sword as he walked slowly back to his camp. He placed the sword away and made his way toward Raven. With a face of shock still over him Raven looked at his General.

"What is it?" Raven asked.

Lyncade looked at him and replied, "The mountains."

"What?" Raven asked not hearing the soft reply.

"The mountains," Lyncade said regaining himself, "We'll attack from the mountains. Use the forest and the high ground as protection. Attack them from the sides but not charge them. Pick at them."

"That is suicide," Raven assured.

Lyncade looked at his captain and said, "We have to try. We have to do something to try and stop them."

Hecorus stood on the outside walls above the great city of Tamian. Looking down at the daily events he saw several guards close by keeping an eye out for him. He posed no threat to them but they still look at him curiously. Far away from their ears Halouse joined his brother and kneeled down next to him looking on at the city below.

"I have to admit I have never seen such a sight," Hecorus replied, "This place they built makes the gods jealous."

"Better than anything I have ever seen," Halouse agreed.

Hecorus studied his brother and asked, "You plan to disobey Cloron don't you?"

Halouse looked at his brother and said, "I have a reason to stay."

"That reason wouldn't happen to be married to General Lyncade?" Hecorus asked.

"That's more of a reason then anything in the forests of Cavell," Halouse told.

"She is married Halouse," Hecorus reminded, "Do you know what type of trouble you could be in if she even returns your feelings. Penalty of that here can get you killed. It isn't like the forest and the rules our people have."

"The way you describe the city before," Halouse began, "That's the way I look at her. A beauty that makes the gods envious."

"A woman like that will get you killed," Hecorus assured, "That I promise you. If your intentions are even heard about Lyncade's followers will come for you. He is very respected here among all the people."

"She gives me a reason for living," Halouse told, "What will we do next? Go back to the forest, hunt deer and bear just to get furs for the winter? Trade them to the humans just to survive?"

"That has been our life," Hecorus reminded.

"I see a different life with her," Halouse told.

They both just looked at the city several hundred feet ahead of them as they kneeled on the high wall.

"Why didn't our father join Tamian all those ages ago?" Halouse asked.

"Our father believed in a union with only the world," Hecorus told, "You and I do not owe an allegiance to any man. What makes Tamian so powerful that he is called a King? He bleeds like we do and can be killed just like you and I. Why is it that he can dress in expensive robes, wear a crown of jewels and be worshipped as if he were a god?

"He makes himself out to be a god among his people, Warad will strike down such ignorance. Maybe that's what this dark army is. A message to all those who will come after Tamian. Never disrespect the gods by passing yourself off as one."

"He made our people one," Halouse reminded, "Aren't we better as one than separated? We can fight every evil if we were among this army."

"A man is judged on his actions in battle in my eyes," Hecorus told, "Not by the crown on his head or how many bow before him."

"Perhaps we met her for a reason," Halouse told.

"What do you mean?" Hecorus asked looking at his brother.

"Perhaps our meeting with her was Warad's way of telling us what path we must take," Halouse suggested, "This battle has been out in front of us and not by chance. It is a sign brother. Finding her was our way of seeing our fate. We must fight in this war. If the Royal Elves lose and are destroyed they will come for us and our people next."

Hecorus looked back toward the city below.

"Are we planning without me?" Cloron asked from in back of them.

They both turned to see their older brother looking at them. As they rose from their kneeled positions they went to him.

"He has a point," Hecorus told Cloron.

"Are you sure this isn't the lust you have for Mayreon talking?" Cloron asked.

"Our safety is what I'm concerned about," Halouse assured.

"As well as hers," Cloron knew, "But perhaps you are right brother. Maybe this is a message from the gods for us to fight."

"If our people are told of this war then we can surround them," Hecorus knew.

"That's if father even speaks to us," Cloron reminded.

"He'll speak with us," Halouse assured, "We haven't been gone that long."

"We've been gone for years," Cloron reminded.

"It was your idea to try and live outside the Valley," Hecorus reminded, "Some plan that was to live away from the others."

"The Lycans and Murkildens do not see what is happening out the Valley," Halouse reminded, "Thousands of our people are going to war while they stay safely hidden away."

"That is the way our father intended," Cloron reminded, "He wanted Tamian to live in his city and not have to live under his rule."

"Some rule," Hecorus stressed, "I can't lay my head down from now on is we leave now. We have to help if we can. There are too many orcs and not enough warriors to fight them off."

Cloron just nodded as he looked to his brothers and then back to the beautiful city. They didn't want to go home it seemed. This sight was nothing they had ever seen before coming up the lands of Tamian to the great city. They wondered how many other sights were far from their view, awaiting them to see.

Chapter 8

Cloron, Hecorus and Halouse had past the news to Tamian as he was in the courtyard of the main castle getting his regiments ready to march. The thousands had gathered there to prepare for warfare. Drizell and Mayreon stood close to the discussion as they looked on in inquisitiveness.

"Sounds like a plan," Tamian replied to their news, "How many of your people can you get?"

Cloron looked at his brothers than back at Tamian as he replied, "Thousands."

"You're dreaming," Drizell replied, "The only other elf forces that reach the thousands are the Forest Elves of Cagore."

"Their king was here earlier," Tamian told, "He is aware of our problems but doesn't seem to want to join us."

"There are thousands highness," Hecorus replied to Drizell, "The native tribes of Cavell that didn't join Tamian so many years ago have grown. With our influence we can persuade them."

"What cost to me?" Tamian asked.

The brothers looked at one another.

"That is for them to decide when we meet with them," Cloron told.

"They will need something from you," Halouse knew.

Silence engulfed them for several moments.

"I will go," Mayreon replied.

Tamian looked at her in shock.

"What about Lyncade?" Tamian asked.

"My body will not be a gift," Mayreon replied clearing the air, "My presence as a queen will be a great gesture to assure them of your loyalty to them."

"It is a great gesture," Halouse replied.

Hecorus and Cloron looked at him in anger.

"That would be a gesture of our loyalty," Tamian replied as he looked at the brothers and asked, "What about her safety?"

"These are the men that saved my life and helped me when I was in need," Mayreon reminded, "I will be safe with them."

"I am trusting you with a queen of our people," Tamian said to them, "If harm comes to her..."

"Speak no more," Cloron replied, "It will not happen."

As the day went on as normal for the people of Tamian: Their king marched one of the largest armies toward the territory known as Cavell. With the amount of orcs and goblins finally being given to Tamian the force that would meet them was far more prepared than Lyncade's forces.

Cloron, Hecorus, Halouse and Mayreon took a different trail along the mountain sides to be able to march around any large force ahead of them. From the cliffs they watched the marching Royal Elf army go in the same direction they were. After several hours they began to get more ground because of their small number and see the Royal Elf fleet disappear in the horizon.

Hecorus took the front position as he was several hundred feet in front of Cloron, Halouse and Mayreon. He would be able to spot trouble and inform them in time to get away from it. Aware at all times he walked through the mountain cliffs almost expecting trouble.

Halouse dragged the horse carrying Mayreon as Cloron walked in front of them.

"How long until we reach your people?" Mayreon asked.

"Many days my queen," Halouse replied.

"I suggest you get some rest while you are being escorted," Cloron replied.

"The camp could take several days to find if we go off trail," Halouse informed.

"I thought you knew where it was?" Mayreon asked.

"The sorcerers make sure the trail is changed," Halouse informed, "To stop orcs and goblins or even humans from entering it. They change the prospective of the environment even from its own people."

"And you say thousands live there?" Mayreon asked.

"Are you always asking so many questions?" Cloron asked as he walked a few feet in front of them.

"Just curious," Mayreon replied to Cloron.

"Your questions will be answered in a few days," Cloron told, "There are more natives in the woods than Royal Elves."

"Really?" Mayreon asked.

Halouse looked at her and shook his head, "There are many but not as much as the Royal Elves."

"If the city of Tamian is full of Royal Elves and Rakar rules the Forest Elves. What do the elves in Cavell call themselves?" Mayreon asked.

"Elves," Cloron replied as if the question was stupid, "Some still go by the tribe name but we do not consider ourselves that anymore. We are the descendants of the same elves you and the Royal Elves are. We do not need royalty or cities."

"The Forest Elves have the same belief," Mayreon told.

Cloron laughed as he said, "This is coming from the people who have a king. We do not need a king."

Mayreon just looked at Halouse as he gently smiled than looked away. She knew what his glances meant and tried not to think about what feelings she might have had for him. She didn't even let it cross her mind.

Camp was set up that night in the mountains. The cold chilling air swept threw the small camp as Cloron and Hecorus were covered up in a large fur they had strapped to the horse Mayreon was riding on.

Halouse as well had a fur around him as he took watch over the camp not far from where the small fire was around his brothers. With his sword by his side he turned slowly to see Mayreon standing in back of him. Her presence startled him for a moment but he quickly acted as if he knew she had been there the whole time.

"Did I scare you?" Mayreon whispered as she wrapped a fur around herself.

"You should be sleeping," Halouse whispered to her.

"I can't," Mayreon gently replied.

Halouse and her looked at each other for several seconds before Halouse looked back toward the forest ahead of them.

"How do you know if anything is even out there?" Mayreon asked.

Halouse looked out to the dark forest ahead of them.

"You lived in the city most of your life correct?" Halouse asked.

"From what I remember yes," Mayreon told.

"I've lived in these forests for ages," Halouse told, "I was born in them. Once you've been living in this type of terrain you become one with it. You can feel things that no one else can. See things in the night without really seeing them."

"What do you mean?" Mayreon asked.

Halouse closed his eyes for several seconds then replied, "Fifty feet away from us is a deer. Female, coming out to find some berries off the bushes in front of us. About one hundred and sixty feet away from us is a wolf. He's hunting the deer and has just picked up her trail. He's hiding from it and hoping it crosses his path. It a few moments you will hear a chase and soon you will hear nothing."

Just as he finished snapping branches and the sound of running was heard. A small yelp was heard in the distance and a loud thud. Mayreon looked out in horror at the event she couldn't see.

"The deer didn't survive," Halouse told.

"Remarkable," Mayreon simply replied.

Halouse seemed to relax as he sat against a tree and looked toward Mayreon slightly.

"You worried about your husband aren't you?" Halouse asked.

"He's alive," Mayreon said with confidence, "I can feel him."

Halouse looked away and asked, "Do you love him?"

"Why would I marry someone I didn't love?" Mayreon asked.

"It's just a question I meant no offense," Halouse assured, "The way of this world is a man chooses. Some women where I am from have no choice."

"I was a slave when he met me," Mayreon told, "A servant."

"You a servant?" Halouse asked in disbelief, "You carry yourself as if you've always been royalty."

"What does that mean?" Mayreon asked with a sharp tone.

"You just look as if you've always been a queen," Halouse replied.

"You're just saying that," Mayreon said.

"No," Halouse replied.

"I see the way you look at me," Mayreon informed, "Your infatuation."

Halouse looked at her in discomfiture.

"I apologies if I offended you with my glance," Halouse replied.

"No," Mayreon replied, "I find it soothing."

"Is that so?" Halouse asked kind of happy she said that.

"I can barely remember anything when I was a child," Mayreon told, "Maybe I blocked it out for some reason."

Halouse looked at her and asked, "What made you say that?"

Mayreon looked over at him and saw his curious glance.

"There was a boy in a village I think," Mayreon tried to remember, "He looked at me the same way you did."

Halouse was in a state of shock as he leaned forward. Mayreon looked at him as Halouse took the charm of the necklace and held it out to her. Her eyes grew wide as she looked at it, then at Halouse.

They didn't know what to say to one another. Many moments had past as they couldn't believe this incredible discovery.

"I knew I'd see you again," Halouse replied finally.

"You kept it all these years?" Mayreon asked.

"I kept it in my heart," Halouse told her, "Thought of you everyday."

Mayreon just looked to him still with a state of shock. It seemed almost ridiculous as they thought about it more and more.

"I remember the huts burning," Mayreon began, "The villagers screaming as they came in. My father was next to me and before I knew it one came and killed him. My brothers and sisters were slaughtered as well and all I could do was stand next to my father and beg him to get up."

Tears came to her eyes as she finally remembered that horrible night.

"I didn't know what death was," Mayreon continued, "He always used to play this game with me when I'd find him, he'd fall and pretend to be dead. He would awake when I'd kiss him on the cheek. I did several times, over and over again and he never woke up."

Mayreon looked at Halouse as the tears continued to fall. Halouse just took his fingers and wiped one as it fell from her eyes. He stared at her for many moments as he searched her mind for some short of feeling. She cried but the event didn't bring back any feelings to her of anger or hatred.

"I forgot about that day," Mayreon remembered, "Went with my uncle to the city. That's when he sold me to be a slave to Farian."

She looked forward relieved at her discovery as she couldn't believe she had forgotten about it.

"I remember you killing a goblin just as it came near me," Mayreon replied softly, "Then another boy..."

"It was Hecorus," Halouse informed.

"He fired arrows at them," Mayreon told, "Kept them away from us for a long time. There were many women and children around us getting killed. They didn't stand a chance."

More tears fell as she spoke of the horrible night just as it flashed before her.

"You held me in your arms and hid my face from the carnage," Mayreon remembered, "You even laid on me when the orc was ready to strike us down to try and protect me."

Mayreon looked at him as he looked back not knowing how to react to her sadness.

"I wanted to protect you," Halouse told, "When I saw you as I came in from the fields I fell in love with you. We were just children but I knew what it was the moment I saw you."

"And I loved you," Mayreon remembered, "Loved you for saving my life and didn't want to leave your side even when my uncle tried to take me away."

"That's when you handed me this necklace," Halouse reminded, "Took it from around your neck and gave it to me."

Halouse reached in back of his neck and took it off.

"No," Mayreon began.

Halouse leaned back as she tried to stop him and he shook his head.

"This is yours," Halouse said as he placed it into her hand.

"I gave it to you to remember me by," Mayreon reminded.

"I don't have to remember you," Halouse told, "You're right here."

"For how much longer?" Mayreon asked, "I am married to a man I love."

"You are aware of how I feel about you," Halouse said, "I can no longer fight it."

Mayreon looked at him this time she became uncomfortable. The long awaited blocked out memory seemed tom do something to her as Halouse said that. There were too many things going on now. She didn't know how to feel or what to do.

"I'm..." Halouse began as if ready to apologies.

Mayreon quickly got up and stormed away as she walked back to the fire. Halouse saw her quickly lay down where her blankets were as kicked a tree in front of him out of anger.

The large fleet of Falmores landed on the south shores of Cavell. Artwore riding proudly on his horse as his mighty ship landed on the sand. The horse walked down the plank and to the beach as he quickly waited to round up his ranks.

A dark mist quickly formed around him as Korack appeared on horse back.

"You will march for many nights then set up camp near the great mountains," Korack commanded, "The Dark Lord will than give you your orders."

"As he wishes," Artwore replied, "I am ready to kill in his name."

"The presence of your army will surly upset the balance of the land," Korack informed, "The humans and natives will surly know you are here."

"It is not them we are concerned with," Artwore reminded.

"True," Korack replied, "But they may still attack if they are provoked. You must save as many forces as possible in order to take on Tamian and his army. The orcs and goblins will only do so much once Tamian arrives with his forces."

"I know," Artwore assured, "Leave the fighting to me Korack. Stick to your games of sorcery."

"Careful with your tone human," Korack warned, "May I remind you that it is only because of The Dark Lord's respect for you that I hold you in such favor."

"After Tamian and the Royal Elves are killed by my hand it will not be because of The Dark Lord that you will show respect," Artwore assured.

Korack short of laughed as he vanished in front on Artwore.

The large orc and goblin force continued their march through the valley's between the great mountains. When they finally left the large canyon they'd be halfway into the Royal Elf territory. Marching forward with a purpose they didn't pay any attention to the cliffs a few hundred feet above them. A few small rocks and dust fell from above and hit a regiment as they looked up. Just as several of them did an arrow flew down and hit and orc in the head. Hundreds more began to pore from the cliffs above as the surviving elves from the previous battle took the high ground as their advantage.

The arrows seemed endless as the orcs and goblins knew they'd have no hope of fighting back. Lyncade followed by several of his men slid down the cliffs in back of the large army as he removed his sword. With Raven by his side they went to the back line of the orc and goblin force and began to engage. With the valley not being so wide Lyncade and his small force could fight side by side and not fear any attack from in back, or to the sides of them. An elf next to Lyncade took a horn tied around his neck and blew on it hard.

That was a signal to the others in the cliffs as dozens of explosion began to go off in the cliffs above. Tumbling down the mountainsides below was hundreds of large rocks crushing the orcs and goblins quickly. Instead of trying to fight the small force in back of them the orcs and goblins ran forward trying to escape the canyon as quickly as possible. With hundreds of rocks still falling from the mountain sides many of them couldn't make their way out.

A larger explosion went off near the back line as rocks fell to the ground and cut off the back line of the orc and goblin forces from the others ahead. Their were still hundreds of them as the Royal Elves from above began to make their way to help General Lyncade. The large force ahead would need to be left alone with no way of being able to stop them. The Royal Elves had been crippled to just over a thousand as tens of thousands marched on in front of the battle they had cleverly blocked off.

Lyncade was in the front of all his men as he sliced through all the orcs and goblins in front of him. Royal Elves from the cliffs jumped from the highest points and crashed on the orcs and goblins below. With an accurate connection every time Lyncade swung as all he saw in front of him was blood poring from the wounds of his enemies.

With no mercy Raven and the others quickly followed their general as they kept up with his quick pace killing the nearest orc. Tireless moments past as no orc or goblin put up much of a fight. As the final one was slain by the hands of Lyncade he looked at the army in back of him and held his blade high. They roared in victory as the smoke from the falling rocks lifted into the air.

"Bagaris must have been in the frontlines," Raven replied as he reached his general.

"He will soon meet the fate of the regiments he left behind," Lyncade replied.

"What do we do now?" Raven asked, "Our forces are too small to take on the army that has escaped us."

"We must try," Lyncade replied, "there is still miles of the great mountains before it parts into open land. We travel up the cliffs and do it again. A thousand times if we have to. Until there isn't a breath in any of our bodies."

With that as his final statement the small force of just over a thousand did as their general commanded. Running back up the cliffs and running hard forward to try and meet with the largest orc and goblin force the land had ever seen. With every ounce of energy in their body their running never broke stride as they could see the back line of the army ahead of them in the horizon.

As Lyncade ran endlessly and arrow flew into his shoulder as he fell forward. The end of the arrow snapped the end he hit the ground. He yelled in pain as the men in back of him slowed down to go to their leader. Ahead of them hundreds of goblins had climbed the cliffs to meet them. Royal Elves stopped as they held up their bows and returned fore quickly killing them. Hundreds more were charging forward with their weapons ready to meet with the Elves.

Lyncade quickly got to his feet and he roared. His men did as well as they met with the force of goblins. The losers of each swordfight were mortally wounded or killed as they fell to the ground hundreds of feet below. Most of the elves used the height of the cliff as an advantage as they engaged with a goblin then kicked a second over the ledge. The goblins flew to the ground hundreds of feet below and were crushed by the rocks and the impact of the devastating fall. Lyncade once again became enraged in the battle and seemed flawless with each goblin that approached. It was only seconds that went by before the goblin was killed and tossed away from his path.

The back line of the orcs and goblin force had stopped below as they fired hundreds of arrows up at the cliffs. With no regard even goblins were being killed. Royal Elves fell victim to the arrows as well as Lyncade watched his forces get weaker and weaker by the second. The arrows flew up at them at an alarming rate as they hit the rocks just to the sides of them and flew above their heads as they missed their intended target.

Raven was still beside Lyncade keeping up with his general. Just as Lyncade turned and killed a goblin he quickly threw out his hand and caught an arrow flying toward his captain. With a state of shock and awe Raven looked at Lyncade and smiled. He went back to the fight quickly not trying to get caught off guard.

Lyncade stopped battling as he looked to the cliffs on the other side to see his forces their being killed off one by one as well. With damaged morale he tried with all he had left to keep fighting as the goblins fell before him or fell below to the ground. As he looked forward it seemed thousands awaited ahead as he saw and endless amount of them charging. Lyncade finally made it to a large hill that the goblins were using to climb and meet with his forces as they began to emerge all around him. Only a few hundred of his own men remained as they fought fearlessly. Each Royal Elf taking out five goblins before they themselves fell to the ground dead. Despite killing more the goblins still outnumbered his men. Each Elf would have needed to kill fifty goblins in order to even survive this confrontation. Lyncade now covered in blood continued to fight as he looked down to the ground to see a pathway leading into a different mountain valley. With no hope of surviving if he stayed there he pointed his blade toward the path.

"Retreat," Lyncade yelled.

The Royal Elves that remained did as he commanded. Hundreds of them still engaged in battle were unable to even do as he commanded. They were quickly overwhelmed as they fell dead before the goblins. As Lyncade and Raven ran down the path the orcs were soon joining the battle in trying to wipe out the Royal Elf force. Lyncade and Raven ran quickly down the path as Lyncade watched the men following quickly fall around him. As he ran he kept having to fight as he swung his blade killing an orc without breaking pace. As they continued their long run Lyncade quickly tripped over a branch and began to stumble down a long hill. Raven quickly followed his general as he ran after on foot. Stumbling to the bottom Lyncade was dazed as he finally got up. Raven was quick to his side as the orcs and goblins lost sight of their enemy. The others were surly being overwhelmed and killed as Raven only thought of his commander.

"You okay my lord?" Raven quickly asked as he helped Lyncade up.

Before Lyncade could answer Raven was knocked in the side of the head by the butt of a sword. With instinct quickly kicking the sword Lyncade swung his own at the shadowed figure that knocked out Raven. Lyncade battled his shadowy foe for quite sometime. Trying everything to damage the shadowed figure but nothing seemed to work. The shadow's intuition seemed to be as good as Lyncade's. Lyncade was forced to block a heavy blow as he reached forward with his elbow and knocked the shadow in the head. Lyncade quickly heard a woman's cry as he stopped in his tracks. The shadowed figure was soon given light by the full moon.

A beautiful elf woman stood in front of him holding the side of her head that Lyncade elbowed. He almost felt bad at the moment before his sight went black.

A second shadowed warrior in back of Lyncade emerged with his sword drawn. He had knocked out Lyncade with the end of his sword.

"You okay my lady?" The warrior asked.

Without answering she replied, "Take them to the Valley of Talius at once."

"Of course," The warrior quickly replied as more shadowed warriors began to emerge from the woods.

"The orcs and goblins haven't seen us yet," The woman replied, "We must hurry."

In the frontline an orc captain quickly approached Bagaris.

"Their ranks have been destroyed," The captain told.

"How many of ours did we lose?" Bagaris asked.

"My lord our numbers do not matter," The captain assured, "Lyncade has fallen."

"I want his body," Bagaris told.

"General the others have assured…" The captain began.

"Do you wish for me to assure The Dark Lord that Lyncade has fallen with no proof or blood to give?" Bagaris angrily asked.

The captain hesitated for several seconds before he replied, "I will send a small party to look for the remains."

Bagaris just watched the captain leave his side.

"Is there a problem," A voice asked as a dark mist formed in front of Bagaris.

Korack began to ride side by side with the General.

"My ranks have told me the Royal Elf force has been destroyed as I promised," Bagaris informed.

"An even larger more powerful one marches toward you," Korack informed.

"How do you know this?" Bagaris asked.

"I have eyes that can see as far as the Blazar Mountains," Korack told, "The king will be with them."

"His blood will rest on the end of my sword," Bagaris replied, "I will give it to you as a gift."

"Give it to The Dark Lord as a gift," Korack told, "Be careful with your army in these parts. Talius is said to roam here when she is not in her own realm."

"She cannot interfere," Bagaris reminded.

"Her influence will encourage those she meets," Korack informed, "You will have many days ahead of you before you will meet with Endore. Remember what I have told you."

"As you wish my lord," Bagaris replied.

Taking slim and hidden trails only known by Cloron the three brothers who escorted Mayreon began to get closer to the camp of the Native Elves. Mayreon still being pulled by Halouse as they continued down a strange and dark path. Hecorus was still several hundred feet ahead making sure no trouble was in front of them.

Halouse stayed quiet never looking back at Mayreon as he pulled her horse along. Cloron was several feet in front of them but very close to make sure they didn't lag behind.

"Why do we take such gloomy roads?" Mayreon asked.

"Do you prefer the main roads where renegade orcs and goblins are, as well as the largest orc and goblin army ever seen by mortal eyes?" Cloron asked.

"These trees seem to have eyes," Mayreon replied.

"Many of them do," Cloron told, "There are many creatures that lurk these forests that not even we have seen."

"What type?" Mayreon asked.

"Many of them have no names," Cloron told.

"Surly they do," Mayreon replied she looked to Halouse and asked, "Have you seen any Halouse?"

"If I haven't he hasn't," Cloron told.

Mayreon noticed that not even with her call did Halouse look at her. Just as they were silent an arrow hit a tree next to Cloron. Halouse was quick to begin to pull his sword.

"What was that?" Mayreon asked.

"Hecorus is warning us ahead," Cloron informed, "Come but be quiet."

Halouse reached for Mayreon and helped her down. Without looking at her for even a moment he pulled his sword and kept her close to him. The three made it to a large rock where Hecorus was crouching behind. He signaled for them to be silent then called to them with his hand. They all stayed low as they began to get closer to him.

"What is it?" Cloron asked.

"Menaceus," Hecorus replied.

"What's a Menaceus?" Mayreon whispered.

"They are creatures," Cloron told silently, "Ones the Native Elves talk about in legend. They are black skinned. Their flesh is very thick almost like leather. They do not speak and are very vicious."

Mayreon looked below to see these dark creatures surrounding a fallen deer. They stood on two legs and looked very human. They only wore furred loincloths and their faces were very ugly. With yellow glowing eyes looking out into the empty woods in front of them it was the only thing that could be seen. Their shadowed figures moved quickly as they surrounded the fallen prey and ripped the flesh from the fallen animal like savages. They all had four small horns coming from the top of their heads that they often used when provoked.

Before Mayreon could look any further Hecorus pulled her down.

"Stay down," Hecorus warned, "They only attack if they see you. Hopefully they'll eat the deer and leave."

"Why not go around them?" Mayreon asked.

"They have very good eye sight and a perceptive cunning to spot anything that moves," Hecorus explained in a whisper.

"Can you kill them?" Mayreon asked.

"We were hoping not to do that?" Cloron told.

"We don't want anything to know we are here," Hecorus told, "Any sign that we passed, anything that roams these forest that is in league with The Dark Lord will know where we are going."

The Menaceus' made horrible sounds as they tore their meal apart. One of them began to sniff the air. It seemed a different sense hit the air as he looked around in curiosity. Cloron heard this as he looked to the others.

"I think they know we are here," Cloron warned.

Hecorus pulled his crossbow strapped to his back as Cloron and Halouse silently readied their swords. The Menaceus got up as he looked in the opposite direction of them and began to run. The others were quick to follow as the skeleton of the deer was all that remained of their once presence.

"They're gone," Hecorus told.

"That quickly?" Mayreon asked.

"They move five times faster then we do," Cloron told.

Hecorus and Halouse quickly went down to the dead deer but stayed ready. They looked all around them before they quickly put their weapons away. Cloron and Mayreon came down as well.

"Do you smell that?" Hecorus asked Cloron.

Cloron put his nose to the air and smiled.

"What?" Mayreon asked.

"Ogres," Hecorus told.

"They're scared of Ogres?" Mayreon asked.

"Yeah," Cloron told, "And we should be too."

"Are they close?" Mayreon asked.

"A few miles or so," Cloron told.

"We should keep moving," Hecorus replied to Cloron.

"Halouse," Cloron called.

Halouse quickly looked to his brother.

"Take the front position and give Hecorus a break," Cloron replied.

Halouse nodded as he quickly began to go forward.

"Hecorus get her horse," Cloron commanded.

Halouse and Cloron stayed close to Mayreon as Hecorus dragged the horse along. The night sky above them made everything pitch black to Mayreon but the two natives beside her were used to this type of darkness and could see perfectly. It seemed the silence had lasted years as Mayreon looked all around her as best as she could.

"Cloron," Halouse yelled from ahead.

Grabbing Mayreon quickly Hecorus placed her down as Cloron ran toward the voice of his brother. Hecorus was not far behind as he didn't wait up for Mayreon. They all soon came to the hundreds of bodies that remained of the battle between Lyncade's men and the orcs and goblins. As Mayreon approached she soon almost lost herself at the amount of Royal Elves dead in front of her.

"My Warad," Mayreon replied.

"They were slaughtered," Cloron added as he looked at the carnage around him.

Halouse was looking at trails as Hecorus joined him.

"Anything?" Hecorus asked.

"There were hundreds of ranks," Halouse told, "They never stood a chance."

"Because they weren't warned," Cloron replied, "They had no idea how many they were up against."

Mayreon's state of shock soon faded as she began to look around at all the bodies.

"My queen," Hecorus called as Mayreon began to sprint out of sight.

"Where are you going?" Cloron called.

In a blind state Mayreon began to look at the faces of all the Royal Elves. Hecorus finally reached her as he grabbed her and spun her around.

"What is it?" Hecorus asked.

Mayreon began to cry uncontrollable.

"This was Lyncade's force," Halouse replied as he caught up with them.

Mayreon tried to rip Hecorus off her.

"My queen if you wonder only Warad knows what's in these woods," Hecorus warned.

Mayreon pushed him softly away and still searched.

"Stay with her," Cloron replied.

Hecorus stayed closely to Mayreon as Cloron went to his brother. Halouse crouched over a fallen Royal Elf as he looked over the body.

"He has six different points of attacks," Halouse told, "That means six different orcs or goblins were stabbing him at once."

"Why would they fight this battle?" Cloron asked.

"Their pride got in the way," Halouse told, "I'll need to study the trails a little better."

A loud scream was heard as Cloron and Halouse quickly went to the yell. Mayreon stood kneeling in front of a shield as Hecorus was in back of her.

"What is it?" Cloron asked.

"Lyncade's shield," Hecorus told as Cloron approached.

"No body?" Cloron asked.

"They won't leave his body," Mayreon replied crying.

"His head would be used as a gift to The Dark Lord," Halouse told.

"Same with the hands," Cloron added, "To show what he used to kill so many of The Dark Lord's forces with."

"Doesn't mean he is dead," Halouse replied.

Mayreon looked in back of her at Halouse.

"How can you be so sure?" Mayreon asked.

Halouse looked at Cloron and Hecorus.

"Search for any wounded and I'll look over the trails," Halouse replied.

"We have no time," Cloron reminded.

"For her sake," Halouse replied, "She has a right to know."

Halouse quickly walked away as Cloron and Hecorus looked toward Mayreon.

The morning sky was soon beginning to rise as it could be seen in the horizon. Halouse finally returned as Hecorus and Cloron looked to him.

"By the mountains they were attacking," Halouse told, "Simple tactics trying to stay out of any major confrontation. The goblins and orcs began to scale the walls of the mountain and met them. They than overwhelmed and chased the remaining forces here. This is where many of them had their final moments."

"They should have just marched home for more men," Cloron replied.

"And disappoint Tamian?" Halouse asked, "They wouldn't do that."

"They'd still be alive if they did," Hecorus reminded.

Halouse approached Mayreon who was sitting on a rock trying to hold in her emotions.

"My queen I found a trail where two men had fought off several orcs. One of them tripped and fell all the way down a small hill. Their trail ends there because someone dragged the bodies away," Halouse told.

Mayreon's face began to get red as she started to cry again.

"I didn't find any blood," Halouse quickly told, "He could still be alive."

"They took him then," Mayreon said, "They would want his body."

"I will find him," Halouse replied.

"We have no time Halouse," Cloron told from where he was.

Halouse looked toward his brother and said, "Then go on without me if you must."

Cloron and Hecorus looked at one another.

"At least wait until we have reached the Valley," Cloron replied, "We can send a whole party if we must."

"Stay with our current journey," Mayreon replied to Halouse, "Then do as you said."

Halouse nodded as he helped Mayreon up.

"Even if they did capture him we will know in time if something happened," Mayreon assured, "If he is alive I know how fierce he is."

Chapter 9

The Dark Lord sat silently in a throne room in The Dark Realm. Surrounded by silence and darkness, two black mists formed in front of him. His brothers Greco and Korack were there as they looked to him.

"Artwore and his humans are on a great pace," Korack told, "When the Royal Elves meet the orcs and goblins they will not be far behind."

"Tell Artwore to send his forces back," The Dark Lord quickly replied.

Korack and Greco quickly looked at each other in shock.

"But Master..." Greco began.

"Silence," The Dark Lord quickly said.

"Do you not understand what preparations we have gone through to plan this invasion?" Korack asked.

"I know what needs to be done," The Dark Lord assured as he rose, "Tamian will never be killed but one of us or our forces. He must be killed by one of his own."

"What do you mean?" Greco asked.

"Tamian is the first king of The Elves," The Dark Lord reminded, "Blessed by Warad to never fall in battle with our kind."

"Leave him to me," Greco replied.

"Don't be foolish Greco," The Dark Lord warned, "We can not fight in this battle."

"So what do we do?" Korack asked.

"Have Artwore set up a camp and I will meet with him," The Dark Lord told.

"What about the orcs and goblins?" Korack asked.

"They will be used as a distraction to get what we want," The Dark Lord told, "Talius is not communicating with Warad's people very well. By the time she informs Tamian of what our plans are we will have what we want."

"What do we want?" Greco asked.

"I will inform you as well as Artwore," The Dark Lord told, "Go now and tell him what I requested."

"As you wish," Greco replied as he began to leave.

Korack stayed and looked at The Dark Lord.

"What is it?" The Dark Lord asked.

"How many of my forces will be sacrificed so you can get what you want?" Korack asked.

"The orc and goblin forces aren't strong enough to fight all of Tamian's ranks," The Dark Lord told, "They will all be destroyed by Tamian's power."

"So all the forces I had commanded for an invasion are only a diversion?" Korack asked in anger, "All the forces in my power to summon so you could get what you wanted."

The Dark Lord looked toward his younger brother as he approached. Towering over the Cobra King he asked, "Do you challenge me brother?"

"I only wished to be informed of what was to be, earlier," Korack told, "Now knowing that my forces will be wiped from the earth upsets me."

"Our time is not now Korack," The Dark Lord told.

"When is our time?" Korack asked.

"Soon my brother," The Dark Lord assured, "Do you really think we can destroy all the races of this world with orcs and goblins?"

Korack studied the dark hood of his brother. Not able to see his face Korack looked away and began to leave. The Dark Lord slowly went back to his throne.

"When the time comes Korack you will be the first one I tell," The Dark Lord assured.

Korack stopped and looked at The Dark Lord and nodded.

"Do not look so disappointed brother," The Dark Lord replied, "I will ride with you in battle once the time comes. Certain things need to fall into place."

"Is that what we are doing now?" Korack asked.

"Of course," The Dark Lord replied.

Back at the once battle zone of Lyncade's Royal Elf force, Halouse searched as much as he could through the bodies of the fallen Royal Elves. Cloron and Hecorus stayed close to Mayreon as they searched as well. Hecorus stopped at one body and began to take a spear from the fallen warrior.

"What are you doing?" Mayreon asked.

"I could use this," Hecorus told.

"So could he," Mayreon replied.

"Where?" Hecorus asked, "He's dead."

"The Royal Elves believe what ever a man falls with he goes to the afterlife with," Mayreon told.

"If he's in the afterlife my lady I don't think there is anything there he needs to fight," Hecorus assured.

Mayreon just walked away as Hecorus looked at Cloron.

"She's very upset to see all her people fallen it's no way to disrespect her with your ways," Cloron replied.

"We take weapons all the time," Hecorus reminded.

"Not in front of her," Cloron told.

An arrow at incredible speed flew through the air at Mayreon. As if using instinct she held out her hand as it stopped a few inches from her face. The ruby atop her head began to glow as the arrow snapped. Swarms of orcs began to emerge as Hecorus and Cloron pulled their swords.

"Halouse," Cloron yelled.

The orcs began to surround them with their swords as they hissed at the Elves. Mayreon's ruby began to glow as she began to pick up stones and toss them toward the orcs. Nailing them flush in the face the orcs soon attacked. Hecorus and Cloron quickly engaged killing the orcs with every swipe. Dozens more began to emerge as Cloron and Hecorus began to get overwhelmed.

Mayreon began to pick up orcs with her mind and toss them against trees just as they began to get closer to her. The powerful force made them hit the trees as the sounds of their bones snapping was heard. They went lifeless at the collision as Mayreon continued her spells toward them.

As Hecorus killed two orcs he saw one charge Mayreon from her blind side. Hecorus picked up the spear he had taken and tossed it toward the orc. Seconds from killing Mayreon the spear hit the orc right in the chest.

Mayreon turned and saw the fallen orc as she looked at Hecorus. Hecorus kind of smiled as he pulled out his crossbow and began to fire at all the orcs coming toward him.

Halouse jumped from a cliff above them and crashed on top of two orcs as he killed them quickly. His blade went wild in every direction as the large beasts were cut through by his blade. Engaging the rest with his brothers it was only moments before all the orcs were killed.

Hecorus went to the dead orc and pulled the spear.

"She my lady," Hecorus called, "Your fallen warrior knew we'd need this in this world."

Mayreon's ruby began to glow as she ripped it from his grasp and tossed it in back of Hecorus. Hecorus turned and saw it nail an orc running toward him.

Hecorus looked at Mayreon in shock.

"Perhaps you're right," Mayreon replied.

Cloron smiled at Hecorus as Halouse was checking the bodies of the orcs to make sure they were dead.

"Where were you?" Cloron asked looking at Halouse.

"I was searching for the passage way," Halouse told.

"You were supposed to be looking for Lyncade," Cloron reminded.

"Anything?" Mayreon asked Halouse.

"No," Halouse simple replied as he walked passed her without even looking at her.

"I think we should get out of here," Hecorus suggested, "This was a small war party that must have went off track. Who knows how many more of them there are."

"The passage is no where in this area," Cloron assured as he looked at Lyncade.

"They were here though," Halouse informed.

"Who?" Hecorus asked.

"The others," Halouse told, "I got tracks from an unknown source a few hundred feet ahead. They aren't Royal Elf tracks."

"How do you know that?" Hecorus asked.

"They're Elf tracks that disappear into the forest," Halouse told, "No Royal Elf is capable of that."

"Then the passage is close," Cloron replied.

"No," Halouse said, "There were only about ten or so. They're hunting for the winter. They must have caught a trail of the battle and came to check it out."

"So what do we do?" Mayreon asked.

"Keep looking for the passage," Cloron commanded.

"What about Lyncade?" Mayreon asked as Cloron began to leave.

"He is not our problem my lady," Cloron told, "We must press forward."

"You go," Halouse replied to his brother.

"What?" Hecorus asked in disbelief as he stood next to Cloron.

"It's important to her to find him and I gave her my word," Halouse replied.

Cloron and Hecorus looked at one another.

"It's important that we reach the valley soon Halouse," Cloron replied.

"Go without me," Halouse replied.

Mayreon looked at Halouse then to Cloron and said, "Go without us."

"You are Tamian's gift to our people to insure his word," Cloron reminded.

Mayreon began to untie the ruby on her head as she handed it to Cloron.

"Let that be the gift if you find the passage," Mayreon replied.

Cloron took it in his hand and looked at her.

"Sorceresses are to never take this from their brawl," Cloron reminded.

"That will insure Tamian's word," Mayreon replied.

Cloron looked at her and nodded as Hecorus rushed off.

"If we reach the passage Halouse I will send men to find the both of you," Cloron told, "Remember that I gave Tamian my word that nothing would happen to her.

Halouse nodded as Cloron quickly took off.

Tamian and the large Royal Elf army were in an open field just inside the territory of Tamian. He held up his hand as the hundreds of ranks behind him stopped. With the flag of The Royal Elves in the hands of the front man of every rank the colors of their people showed brightly. Tamian rode his horse a few feet in front of his army as a general followed. They both stopped as Tamian looked to the land around him. A large hill and mountain side rested a few hundred feet to his right as the path to the great river was to his left. It was an open terrain that was fit for the battle that was only days away.

"My lord why do we stop?" The general asked.

"This is where we make our stand," Tamian told.

"But my lord if we press forward we can take the high ground," The general informed.

"No," Tamian commanded, "We do not hide from our enemy we take them on."

"Do you know how many ranks we could lose?" The general reminded.

The army began to move as a warrior in decorative armor rode ahead and met with Tamian and the general.

"Lord Maxus," Tamian replied as he saw him, "Where were you marching?"

"In back of you," Maxus replied looking ahead and not at his king, "What seems to be the problem?"

"I think we should go forward and take the high ground," The general told.

"General," Maxus called, "Tamian and I are leaders here and you shall do as we command."

"Of course my lord," The general replied to Maxus. The general looked at Tamian and said, "I will do as you command even if it means I lose my life my king."

"Fall back," Tamian replied, "Leave me and Maxus alone."

"Of course my lord," The general replied as he rode back to the ranks.

The two leaders sat silently as Tamian still looked around.

"He has a point," Maxus replied to Tamian.

"In the pages of our history in thousands of years from now it will read that we took on Korack's forces head on and not hiding in trees," Tamian replied.

"You are fierce Tamian none of the men have ever denied that," Maxus said, "We will have more forces if we take the high ground in the end."

"My men fight besides me," Tamian replied, "I will not have them all killed for nothing. I will wait for this orc army and wipe it from the earth as Warad as my witness."

Tamian got off his horse and looked to the large hill to his right.

"Take your Calvary over that hill at once," Tamian commanded, "Set up a camp and wait for the orc and goblin forces. When they come the ranks will meet them in the field, then you will charge and flank them."

"Where will you be?" Maxus asked.

"In the front lines beside the peasants as well as the nobles," Tamian told, "Right that in the history of our people as well. Tamian the first king of The Royal Elves didn't sit back and watch his army. He fought beside them unlike the leaders and so called kings of the past."

The general rode up at that moment and replied, "My lord the men are getting restless. They wish to get your commands."

"Set up camp," Tamian immediately said, "We wait for our enemy and fight them here just as I told you before."

"Should I set up your camp above the mountains in back of us?" The general asked, "There is a passage above where you can see the whole battlefield."

"No," Tamian replied, "I will sleep tonight in a tent next to the poorest of warriors. So he knows that his king does not look down on him in these times."

The general looked at Maxus.

"You heard your king," Maxus replied. The general began to ride away as Maxus said, "If you do not know what you are doing the only thing that will be written in the pages of our people is the foolish king that slept next to the peasants at night and died next to them in the battlefield."

"Why worry Maxus?" Tamian asked as he looked at him, "If I die it is you that takes the throne is it not?"

Maxus smiled as he rode back to his ranks.

The Falmores had set up a camp as the thousands stood ready for their leader's word. Artwore along with his mother Sangrayus awaited in their tent restlessly for word from The Dark Lord. A black mist was soon formed as Korack appeared in front of them. Another black mist formed not far away from Korack as Greco appeared. The two leaders looked to the opening of the tent as a large black mist came and The Dark Lord stood.

"My lord," Artwore replied as he rose from his seat and kneeled in front of The Dark Lord.

"Rise," The Dark Lord replied.

Sangrayus stayed where she was never looking to kneel before The Dark Lord.

"Why do you show such disrespect?" Greco asked.

"It's alright Greco," The Dark Lord assured, "I'm sure she has already sensed why I have stopped the army from marching."

"We will not turn back," Sangrayus told, "Not when our enemy is at its weakest."

"Dark Lord," Artwore called before he could answer, "Our forces are strong and with the orcs and goblins we can destroy Tamian's men."

"That is not our purpose," The Dark Lord replied.

"Why send us just to have us return to our homes?" Sangrayus asked, "Each warrior has come to soak his sword in the blood of The Royal Elves. You will send them back with their blades still signing? You will send them back to our kingdom with no hair to brag to the others, no wounds to show the future warriors in times to come?"

"Brave words sorceress," The Dark Lord replied, "But my purpose is for the future. What to do to Tamian and his people to make them weak for later on. They are too strong and when they unite with the Natives not even your army will be able to fight against them."

"The Natives are only a myth," Artwore reminded.

"Will you go against what I know Artwore?" The Dark Lord asked, "You do not know what I do. You are nothing more then a mortal and you dare defy a god."

"I meant it with no disrespect Dark Lord," Artwore assured, "I only wish to know what you command of me."

The Dark Lord looked at Artwore then at Sangrayus as he said, "Have you felt a presence Sangrayus?"

"What kind?" Sangrayus asked.

"The kind that haunts your dreams," The Dark Lord told, "If not then your powers will be no match for what lies ahead."

Sangrayus looked at him with a concerned look as she begged, "Tell me."

The Dark Lord looked at her and said, "The Royal Elves have a sorceress of their own. Sygon's student."

"Sygon is nothing compared to you," Artwore reminded, "How can a student of his be powerful."

"She has a gift like nothing I have ever felt before. Such a gift that it's called to me thousands of miles away," The Dark Lord told.

"Tell us who she is and we will destroy her," Sangrayus promised.

"No," The Dark Lord said gently, "Her abilities can be used to our advantage as well as help our cause."

"Who is she?" Artwore asked.

"The name Mayreon came to me in my slumber," The Dark Lord told, "She travels now with one Native Elf. He was with two others that will go to the army of the Natives. She is wife to General Lyncade as well as a mistress to Tamian."

"You want her captured?" Artwore asked.

"She is no good to me dead," The Dark Lord told, "And if she does die I will be very upset."

"Where is she now?" Sangrayus asked.

"With one called Halouse," The Dark Lord told, "By the time you search for her she will be with the Natives in The Valley of Talius."

"Then why tell us now?" Artwore asked.

"This is why I will not need your army," The Dark Lord told, "You will find this valley with my help and attack the Natives. Make sure all of your men are told to leave Mayreon alone once they find her. Capture her and bring her back to Fadarth with you."

"It is rumored that there are thousands of Natives," Artwore reminded.

"This is true," The Dark Lord told.

"How many thousands?" Artwore asked.

"A kingdoms worth of warriors," The Dark Lord told.

"I can not fight a kingdom," Artwore replied.

"You won't have to," The Dark Lord assured, "Once they leave to meet with Tamian in Tamian's lands you will strike then."

"Just a diversion until we have Mayreon?" Sangrayus asked.

"Yes," The Dark Lord replied.

"Consider it done," Artwore replied.

The Dark Lord looked at Korack. Korack then looked at Greco. Greco approached Artwore and looked at him.

"Kneel," Greco commanded.

Artwore looked at his mother as she nodded softly. Artwore slowly did as his head looked to the ground. Greco placed his hands around Artwore's head as a yellow light emerged around his temple. Second later a gold helmet rested on his head as Artwore looked up at Greco.

"This helmet will protect you from the blades of all enemies," Greco replied as he took a step back.

Korack stepped forward as the armor around Artwore was ripped quickly from his body and crushed by Korack's mind. A light then emerged around Artwore's chest as gold armor was placed on him by the power of Korack.

"This armor will protect you from all your enemies," Korack replied.

The Dark Lord then moved Korack away from Artwore and held out both his hands. A yellow light connected both his hands as a sword soon emerged. He lowered it to Artwore as Artwore took it and rose.

"With these weapons and protection given to you by us, you will be able to complete the mission we have given you," The Dark Lord told, "No enemy that stands in front of you will survive. These weapons will give you a power and skill you never thought you possessed."

The night soon became cold in the forest of Cavell. The winter was only months away but the chill at night gave a sign of weather to come. Halouse grabbed the fur he had tied to his back and began to wrap himself in it as he looked to the great lake in front of his eyes. Buried and hidden in a small passage inside the forest he and

Mayreon took cover for the night. Halouse looked in back of him as Mayreon was in front of logs.

"I'll light that in a moment," Halouse called.

"No need," Mayreon replied as she placed her hand over the logs and a burst of fire went in the air.

"It's good to feel wanted," Halouse sarcastically replied.

"I'm sorry would you like me to put it out so you can do it and feel more like a man?" Mayreon asked.

Halouse smiled as he began to take off his things and place them near the fire. Mayreon went over to her horse and took out a white fur as she wrapped it around herself.

"You'll need to sleep with that tonight," Halouse told, "These nights get colder especially in these parts."

Mayreon laid down next to the fire as she placed her blankets down and she stared across at Halouse who seemed to be looking around at the forest in front of them. Halouse looked for several moments before he finally realized Mayreon was starring.

"Is there a reason for your look?" Halouse asked.

"What is that mark on your neck?" Mayreon asked referring to the four claw marks he had as a tattoo.

"It represents my personality according to my father," Halouse told.

"What does it mean?" Mayreon asked.

"Do you know what a Lycan is?" Halouse asked.

"I've heard of them," Mayreon told.

"Lycans are wolves that are said to walk like a man," Halouse told, "After stories of them turned out to be false some of the natives even in the time of the tribes and clans used to call themselves the Lycans. To try and strike fear in all those who opposed them. Some of them still do even to this day.

"When I was younger my father watched me mimic him and Cloron as Cloron was being taught the ways of fighting. He said I was fierce and would never back down from anyone. As fearless as the legendary Lycans. The four claws represent their mark."

"Is your father still alive?" Mayreon asked.

"He's a councilman among the circle," Halouse told.

"The circle?" Mayreon asked.

"You have Tamian to tell you what laws there are," Halouse replied, "With the Natives we have councilmen that tell us what our people are to do."

"So you do have leaders?" Mayreon said.

"The circle is a council of one hundred men that vote either for or against a proposal," Halouse told.

"Kind of like nobles," Mayreon replied.

"Yes."

"How are these men decided into power?" Mayreon asked.

"Tests," Halouse told, "Hecorus and I still have to do five tasks before being considered. Cloron is there but he must wait for one of the elders to die."

"Hecorus and you look a lot a like but Cloron seems much older and different," Mayreon replied.

"That's because he had a different mother then Hecorus and I," Halouse told, "My father and Cloron's mother had forty children. Cloron was the only one to remain when the orcs destroyed their clan. My father then met my mother and settled down with a clan called the Lycans."

"Hence your tattoo," Mayreon replied.

"Yes," Halouse replied. Halouse looked over at Mayreon and asked, "What about you?"

"What?" Mayreon asked.

"I'm sure you have a story," Halouse replied.

Mayreon looked at him suddenly as he remembered their last conversation.

"A different one," Halouse said gently.

"I wouldn't want to bore you," Mayreon told.

"That's impossible," Halouse replied as he got comfortable on his blanket.

"You're sweet," Mayreon replied as she blushed from his glance.

"Come on," Halouse replied, "I'm sure you have a great story of how you boss people around day in and day out."

"Is that what you think?" Mayreon asked.

"Well tell me what happened then?" Halouse asked, "Before what happened in the village that night I mean. Tell me about your father and mother. What were they like?"

Mayreon looked in front of her for a few moments almost searching for the words as she replied, "I don't remember them."

"Just like before huh?" Halouse asked, "You blocked everything out?"

Mayreon nodded and said, "Besides. The man who took me that night wasn't my real uncle. The man who died wasn't my real father."

"Really?" Halouse asked, "Who were your real parents?"

"I can't remember them," Mayreon told, "I was found when I was about one by a human family. At the time it was considered a crime for any human to raise an elf. They immediately brought me to the village we first met in and I was raised as one of their own. I always knew though that I wasn't their real daughter. He even told me right before the village was attacked. After..."

Mayreon stopped as she remembered what had happened.

"The next thing I knew I was traveling to the great city of Tamian," Mayreon quickly said, "My uncle sold me for gold. There I was bought and used as a servant for about two hundred years. Lyncade saw me in the temple one day and married me. I've not been royalty for that long. I was then sent to train with Sygon."

"Hence the ruby you gave my brother," Halouse replied.

"On my way back from the temple I was saved by three brothers," Mayreon replied with a small smile.

"You're welcome," Halouse said.

They enjoyed a small laugh as Mayreon looked down and asked, "Do you have a woman back where you live?"

"I don't live anywhere," Halouse reminded.

"In the Valley," Mayreon corrected.

Halouse thought for a moment then asked, "Would it make you jealous if I said yes?"

Mayreon smiled and replied, "Just answer."

"I told you I have to complete five more tasks before even being considered a councilman," Halouse told, "Only women and children live there the men hunt for food and fur because of the winter that is getting closer by the day. Besides most women do the same as the men where I'm from."

"They're allowed?" Mayreon asked.

"Some are warriors," Halouse told.

"Like the Forest Elves," Mayreon replied.

"Yes but they aren't forced to fight," Halouse told, "Our women and children are allowed to choose their life as long as it helps the people."

Mayreon sat back and looked to the stars above. The top of the branches cleared for a few feet allowing her to see the sky. Halouse picked up his sword and began to sharpen it with a tool he had in a pouch by his waist. She studied them for several moments enjoying the silence of the moment.

"Aren't they so beautiful?" Mayreon asked in a soft tone.

Halouse looked over toward her and to the sky as well as he said, "I've seen things with more grace."

Mayreon smiled as she looked to him and asked, "Do you really think I don't know what you're talking about?"

"I can't be so blunt with you. The last time I was you walked away from me," Halouse reminded.

"That was because of the story," Mayreon assured, "Not because of your feelings?"

"Do you feel the…" Halouse began.

"I owe you my life," Mayreon told, "Not just for saving me before but from when we were children."

Halouse knew she didn't want to answer as he looked at her for a moment stopping what he was doing. He just looked at her and nodded as he continued to sharpen his blade.

"Do you love him?" Halouse asked.

"You asked me that once," Mayreon reminded.

"I don't think you answered," Halouse replied.

"I said I wouldn't marry a man I didn't love," Mayreon reminded.

Halouse nodded remembering as he said, "Then I do have plenty of women back in the Valley awaiting me."

Mayreon smiled at him knowing he was only saying that to try to get some read off of her.

"You make me smile," Mayreon replied, "I don't think anyone has ever made me smile as much as you have."

"Maybe it's a sign of Warad," Halouse suggested.

"You need to burry the way you feel," Mayreon told, "If we find Lyncade he'll know the way you look at me. You'll need to hide it better."

"I am taught to always embrace how I feel," Halouse told.

"You won't be able to embrace it properly if I do not return your feelings," Mayreon.

"You said if," Halouse replied to her with a small smile.

Mayreon noticed the mistake as well. She sat up and looked at him as she wrapped the blanket around her tighter.

"Do you enjoy this?" Mayreon asked.

"If it makes you feel better and I must be honest…" Halouse began as he looked at her, "Yes."

"I can admire a man who tells the truth," Mayreon admitted, "But Lyncade is alive."

"You seem so sure," Halouse replied.

"I would have felt it if he died," Mayreon said.

Halouse placed his sword away and picked up his bow.

"Where are you going?" Mayreon asked.

"I'm hungry," Halouse told.

"You're going to leave me alone?" Mayreon asked.

"For only a short while I promise," Halouse replied as he placed his sword away and began to walk off.

"If you have such strong feelings for me your actions certainly don't back them up," Mayreon yelled to him as he disappeared.

Chapter 10

The morning breeze touched the faces of all who felt it. The dark night drifted and a blessing of a new day was upon the world of Tullian. The sun shined brightly in the skies above almost indicating a promising day. With dark armies far away from any real danger all the living creators roamed freely as the beautiful cloudless sky reigned down upon them.   Lyncade slowly began to come to as his blurred vision began to see a beautiful woman in front of him. As he rose he soon noticed he was chained to the bed he was in. He looked around him and saw he was in a small tent. With the amount of voices and actions going on outside he knew he must have been in a village of some short. With all his armor stripped he was only wearing a loincloth. All his armor and his sword were hung not far from the bed next to the woman.

She was an elf for sure. Her long beautiful blonde hair as well as pointed ears gave that away. Her eyes captured him like all elfish women's always did. Unlike women that he had seen in the past she was wearing a suit of armor that covered her chest. The cleavage of her breast could be seen as a cloak was wrapped around of her with it covering her shoulders and falling to the ground in front of her. A sword in its case rested as she had her hand close to it. With Lyncade chained she looked comfortable enough though to not draw it. She was wearing a leather skirt showing off her thighs but was wearing high knee boots. On her neck rested a tattoo of claw marks.

"Where am I?" Lyncade asked.

"Valley of Talius," The woman informed, "Home of the Native Elves."

"So rumor of your existence is true," Lyncade replied, "What is your name?"

"Salryn," The woman replied, "Sorry about the terrible headache you must have."

"I was merely taking it easy because I knew you were a woman," Lyncade assured.

"What ever makes you feel better," Salryn replied.

"Confident are we?" Lyncade asked.

"It was you that couldn't best me not the other way around," Salryn reminded.

"Where is Raven?" Lyncade asked.

"He is fine I assure you," Salryn replied.

"Why am I chained?" Lyncade asked.

"We've come into contact with your kind before," Salryn told as she rose, "The last rank we had to kill because they attempted to rape a few of our women."

"I'm not that type," Lyncade assured.

"Well then you understand the chains," Salryn.

"You can undo them," Lyncade replied.

"Do you really think I'm that dumb just to take your word?" Salryn asked.

"Do you know who I am?" Lyncade asked.

"A general obviously," Salryn knew, "Your ego gives you away. You're obviously a high lord as well."

"The greatest general in the Royal Elf army," Lyncade added.

"If your skills as a warrior tell me about how you run an army then I must say I'm not impressed," Salryn replied.

"Oh really?" Lyncade asked angrily.

"Running like women away from your enemy," Salryn replied.

"If I weren't chained…" Lyncade began.

"What? You'd teach me a lesson like you did before?" Salryn asked.

Lyncade kind of smiled but it was out of anger.

"Guards," Salryn called.

Two Native Elves entered with spears as Salryn looked at them and nodded. One of the guards entered and began to unlock Lyncade's chains.

"So you trust my word?" Lyncade asked.

"No," Salryn replied, "Reminding myself of the way you fight without chains, you pose no threat."

"You enjoy kicking me while I'm down?" Lyncade asked.

"Just meet me outside when you are done putting your things on," Salryn commanded.

"A woman where I'm from would be beaten for giving a man of my stature orders," Lyncade told.

"Women where you're from are nothing more then legs that you open when ever you feel like spawning," Salryn replied.

Lyncade just watched the beautiful warrior leave as he began to place on his armor.

Moments later as Lyncade opened the cloth and escaped the tent his breath seemed to be taken away. Around him were thousands of small tents hidden away between two of the largest mountains he had ever seen. The mountains stretched miles into the sky and the top had never been reached by any living creature. The large valley was blocked in by all the mountains as Lyncade couldn't see and entrance or an exit to it. Atop the mountains, hundreds of guards stood watch looking over the entire valley. As he searched the valley it stretched farther then his eyes could see. In the distance he saw dozens of large forts used by the elders that were heavily guarded. Hundreds of children stood around him some wearing armor and with swords by their side. Dozens of other warriors looked at him with such amazement. His look and cloths were so much different he stuck out to all those who passed him.

With many marks on the chest of the warriors around him, two were the most seen. The mark of the Lycan, which was four red slash marks, and the mark of the Murkilden, the dark red crescent moon.

Salryn looked at him as he admired the valley.

"It certainly deserves its name," Lyncade replied.

Salryn smiled at his look, she seemed to enjoy his expression like he enjoyed the surroundings. The smile quickly left her face.

"Calbrawn is expecting you," Salryn informed.

As they walked the hundreds and hundreds they passed soon made room for them. They seemed to be heading toward the largest fort as Lyncade looked to the mountain sides and watched the beautiful waterfalls run to the lakes below.

"How many do you have here?" Lyncade asked.

"The number of woman and children could be close to a million or so," Salryn informed.

"How many warriors?" Lyncade asked.

"About half that of the population," Salryn told.

"Who leads you?" Lyncade asked.

"We do not have a leader," Salryn informed.

"Then who is Calbrawn?" Lyncade asked.

"The eldest of the council," Salryn replied.

"The council?" Lyncade asked.

"We have a council who lead us," Salryn told, "Not one man."

Lyncade and Salryn made it to the front of the large fort. The guards slowly let them in. The fort was very slim like most of them and stood one hundred feet in the air. Calbrawn's fort was the tallest of them all as Lyncade entered. Climbing stairs that seemed to be endless they made it to the top. In a large open room four guards looked at Salryn as they began to walk away.

A coughing was heard as a shadowed figure stood behind a blanket. It seemed the figure was changing as a second shadow was helping it. After several moments of coughing the shadow finally placed on his rode and came out. A long bearded elf looked over at Lyncade. For an elf to have a beard it was a telling of his age. Only those who had lived for over seventy thousand years could grow one. This elves beard was long and white. His face wrinkled with age as his blue eyes looked to the Royal Elf General. Though very old Calbrawn still stood straight in front of him and didn't have a slouch. His long white hair hung freely in back of him as he placed on a cape and tossed it to his back. Lyncade knowing immediately how old Calbrawn was went to one knee out of respect.

A small laugh came from Calbrawn as he replied, "I was wrong about your kind."

"You may rise," Salryn told, "You do not need to show such respect."

"I admire your gesture General Lyncade," Calbrawn replied.

"You know my name?" Lyncade asked as he rose.

"I know more then you know," Calbrawn told, "Looking at me you finally realize that you are not immortal."

"What do you mean?" Lyncade asked.

"I am the first of our kind," Calbrawn told, "I was there in the beginning when Warad created all of us."

"You are one of the first?" Lyncade asked in disbelief.

"Before your king was even a thought in Warad's mind," Calbrawn told, "Only Elves of a certain age are able to grow beards."

"It almost seems atypical to see one," Lyncade told.

"Well you have seen Sygon," Calbrawn reminded.

"Of course but no matter how many times you see it, it never looks right," Lyncade replied.

The second shadow emerged as it was a dark haired elf who was a servant girl. Lyncade looked at her for several seconds. A few moments later Salryn elbowed him gentle in the arm noticing his stare. Lyncade looked at her.

"What is she?" Lyncade whispered.

"I am a half breed," The servant girl replied.

"I'm sorry," Lyncade replied as he noticed the servant girl heard him.

"It's alright," The girl replied.

"Her mother was a human," Calbrawn told, "Thus the dark hair."

"At first sight she seemed unnatural," Lyncade said as he looked at the servant girl and said, "My apologies."

"Leave us," Calbrawn replied to the servant girl.

The girl soon left as Calbrawn looked at Lyncade.

"An Elf raped a human woman not long ago," Calbrawn told, "He was executed for his crime and I took care of the woman when she was carrying. She died about a thousand years ago."

"How does she age?" Lyncade asked.

"Like we do," Calbrawn told, "The only difference is her hair and the way the males look at her."

"What do you mean?" Lyncade asked.

"Male Elves don't find her as attractive as a normal Elf," Salryn told.

Calbrawn pored a glass of wine and handed it to Lyncade.

"You must be tired," Calbrawn said as he handed it to him, "Please sit and speak with me."

Lyncade did as he was told as he sat on a chair. Calbrawn sat across from him as Salryn stayed standing next to Calbrawn.

"Where is Raven?" Lyncade asked.

"Safe I assure you," Salryn replied, "He awoke an hour or so before you and was very aggressive with our men."

"He only wishes to know my safety," Lyncade told.

"We know," Calbrawn replied, "That's all he kept raving about."

"Why have you captured me?" Lyncade asked.

"I thought we saved you," Calbrawn replied.

"Forgive me," Lyncade replied.

"I have brought you here to ask what you intend to do about the current war," Calbrawn told.

"Tamian isn't far behind me," Lyncade informed, "He has a larger force headed toward the orc and goblin forces."

Calbrawn looked at Salryn then back at Lyncade and said, "I'm not talking about the orcs and goblins."

"Then what are you talking about?" Lyncade asked, "That's the only army headed toward us."

"No," Calbrawn quickly told, "The Falmores."

"The what?" Lyncade asked.

"Great Humans," Salryn replied, "They landed in Cavell not too long ago and are headed for your city."

"Great Humans?" Lyncade asked.

"Do not tell me you've never heard of them," Calbrawn said.

Lyncade just shook his head slightly.

"They live in Fadarth," Salryn told, "Not much is known about their origin. They can live triple that of a normal human. So if their a hundred they look thirty three or so."

"If their only a little better then a human they still do not stand a chance against Royal Elves," Lyncade assured.

"Wrong," Calbrawn replied, "They have the protection of The Dark Lord."

"The Dark Lord," Lyncade said in disbelief.

"Their army draws near," Calbrawn told, "But they have a different purpose then what you would think."

"You are correct to think they aren't as strong but they are here for a woman," Salryn told.

"What woman?" Lyncade asked.

"A Sorceress," Calbrawn told, "One that is more advanced then anyone in the history of our world."

Lyncade looked at them for several seconds and replied, "Mayreon."

"You know her?" Salryn asked.

"She is my wife," Lyncade told.

"Where is she now?" Calbrawn asked.

"In Tamian," Lyncade told.

"So she is safe?" Calbrawn asked.

"Yes," Lyncade said.

"Are you sure?" Salryn asked.

"Positive why?" Lyncade asked.

Calbrawn and Salryn looked at one another.

"I have felt her near," Calbrawn told.

"That's who we were looking for when we found you," Salryn told.

"She travels now with one," Calbrawn informed, "She was with three but they have split up. Three brothers who come here often."

"One of them bares the same mark as I do," Salryn told pointing to her tattoo.

"I do not know of them," Lyncade told.

"They head this way," Calbrawn told.

"It is what The Dark Lord wants," Salryn told, "The closer she comes to us the more danger she is in."

"We must find her then," Lyncade replied as he rose.

"Salryn and a few of my best men will go with you," Calbrawn told, "Retrieve them at once and bring her here. If you find her it will not be safe to try and travel home. The armies will be after her. Bring her here and we will keep her safe."

Traveling swiftly across the river Hecorus and Cloron didn't slow down as they both knew they were close to the Valley. Several hundred feet from one another Hecorus could just make out his brother as he began to sense something. Hecorus quickly pulled out his crossbow and fired. Several moments later an arrow hit a tree next to Cloron. He turned and began to walk slowly toward Hecorus. Cloron met with him as Hecorus looked all around to the cliffs above them.

"Do you feel that?" Hecorus asked.

"What is it?" Cloron asked.

"An army," Hecorus replied.

Hecorus ran swiftly to a trail leading up the cliff as he climbed a steep rocky terrain. Finally making it to the top he heard Cloron in back of him. They moved through the forest quietly as they came to the other side of the cliff. Ahead of them miles away on the ground was the large army of the Falmores.

"What is this?" Hecorus asked.

"Falmores," Cloron told, "Thousands of them."

"An invasion?" Hecorus asked.

"What else would it be?" Cloron asked.

"They're here to back up the orcs and goblins aren't they?" Hecorus asked.

"The largest army of orcs and goblins is only a diversion," Cloron knew.

"That's a perfect diversion," Hecorus told.

"We need to make it to the Valley at once and warn the others," Cloron informed.

"They're not here for us," Hecorus knew.

"They're here to destroy all of Warad's creators," Cloron knew.

"What about Halouse?" Hecorus reminded.

Cloron looked at him and replied, "We must hurry and get a search party at once."

Tamian and his forces stood still in the open field awaiting their enemy. Awaiting the largest orc and goblin army anyone had ever seen all that was heard was horses whining as each Royal Guard member composed his stead. Tamian sat up front like he said he would as he began to look around the ranks at the scared faces of all his men. Not taking the high ground was a sign of certain doom. It seemed the king wanted his men to fail. Rumors around the ranks were that Korack, Greco and The Dark Lord would fight with the dark army.

As Tamian looked to the sky the sun was setting. In the distance not far from them, dark clouds began to ascend. The only reason for this was the dark army that approached. The darkness followed them where ever they went. Hellacious cries could be heard in the distance as the horses got more and more erratic. The spearmen in the frontline looked ahead with fear as the dark clouds got closer and closer to them.

Tamian quickly rode out a few feet in front of his large force and began to look around. Each man his glance passed, they all looked back wondering why their king was studying them so. Tamian pulled his blade from his case and held it lowered to the ground.

"Is this how you want to be remembered?" Tamian asked in a soft tone. The battlefield was so quiet everyman seemed to hear, "Scared of what enemy lies ahead? Shaken in your armor unable to contain your trepidation?"

"Permission to speak my king," A spearmen replied.

"There are no kings here," Tamian yelled.

"Why not take the high ground?" The spearman asked, "Why not get the advantage?"

"Do we fight to get an advantage?" Tamian asked, "Do we fight one battle for victory so our enemies know the only reason we did was so we could get the higher ground? What will our enemies say then? They will know the only reason we won was because of the high ground."

"My lord with all respect isn't that the point of battle?" Another spearman asked.

"Who said that?" Tamian demanded.

The ranks were silent.

"Do not fear me," Tamian assured, "Come forward at once."

The man did as he looked to his king.

"What will they say about the army that took on its enemy head first?" Tamian asked, "Send a message now and never make them think the only reason we won was because of our position. Strike at them on even terms with them knowing we will not fear them. Even if The Dark Lord, Korack and Greco rode with them."

"They are gods," A spearman told.

"Gods are not born," Tamian told, "Gods are made by the action they make. By the stories they tell with each swipe of their blade."

Tamian pointed at one spearman and asked, "What will they say about you when you are gone?" Tamian pointed at dozens more each time asking, "Or You? Or You?"

Each mans morale seemed to get better with each word exiting Tamian's mouth.

"I may be a king," Tamian told, "But at the end of this battle I will be the same as you. In this fight we are all the same. Each man before you or next to you is a warrior for our people. Each man that swings his blade is no better or worse than I.

"Will you die? Yes. Some of you will. Some of you will see your final day here in this field. How many of you though will pull your blade from at least six or seven orcs before you do? How many of you will yell so loud that the God Ward himself will loom down upon you and smile brightly. So when you are called to the afterlife he will greet you and bow before you," Tamian dropped from his horse and yelled, "Today I fight beside each of you. All of you that are soldiers, all of you that have fought in the frontlines before and watched each of your Royal Elf brothers fall to their death. Today I will fight beside each of you and I will die if I must next to each of you."

The ranks roared as they raised their blades in the air. The sky crackled but it was silent among the roars of the Royal Elves. Tamian hit his horse as it began to ride far away from the battlefield. The ranks of Royal Elves began to make their way to their king. They looked ahead at the hills as the first ranks of the orc and goblin forces were being seen. Their large Calvary of fierce and ugly orcs began to emerge. A black colored flag of the mark of Korack was hanging high as it waved next to heaviest armored orc.

Bagaris was that orc staring down at the Royal Elf army. As he slowly walked his horse closer and closer he saw the hundreds of spearmen in the frontlines. With a small evil smile he pulled his blade and threw it in the air. The orc and goblin army stopped marching as he slowly began to ride in front of it. He went out several hundred feet in front of his forces as he looked down at the ranks of the Royal Elves. A black mist soon formed around him as Korack rode on a horse next to him.

"They didn't take the high ground," Bagaris told.

"Let that be their demise," Korack replied.

"They obviously been here for quite sometime awaiting us," Bagaris told.

"Why let them wait any longer," Korack told.

Bagaris looked at his master as he nodded. Korack soon disappeared as Bagaris took another long look at the Royal Elves.

"General," Tamian yelled from where he was.

"Yes my lord," The general replied as he rode on his horse in front of Tamian.

"Hold the Calvary until you get my signal," Tamian told, "When they come close enough give the command to the archers. When we attack stop firing and wait for my signal."

"Yes my lord," The General replied, "May Warad be with you."

"He is," Tamian confidently replied.

Bagaris rode back to his rank as he looked to his captain.

"Send in the goblins," Bagaris commanded, "When they meet their foot soldiers I will strike with the Calvary."

"Yes my lord," The orc captain hissed.

The goblins quickly went to the front of the line as they began to walk slowly toward the Royal Elf army in the distance. As the thousands emerged they began to pick up pace. With a loud yell by one goblin in the front they all ran toward the Royal Elves. The entire land was filled with them as the large Royal Elf army looked on with no fear.

Tamian held up his blade high as a loud roar emerged from the ranks of the Royal Elves. Tamian threw up both his hands. In the cliffs behind them hundred of archers picked up their arrows and aimed toward the sky. A captain lowered his arm as each arrow flew toward the marching goblins. With each arrow shot another was quickly picked up and aimed. The arrows flew in five second bursts as they flew quickly toward the charging goblins. They flew quickly shrieking above the first wave of Royal Elves. Seconds later they hit the goblins as each one quickly placed their shield in front of their face. Many of them weren't lucky as an arrow hit them just as they were seconds from blocking it. As the charging ranks of the goblins got closer the archers in the cliffs stopped firing.

Tamian began to run at the charging goblins as thousands of his spearmen and foot soldiers followed. As the two opposing armies collided Tamian and his Royal Elves were fearless. With each reckless strike by Tamian it always hit his target perfectly killing a goblin with each strike. The spearmen quickly impaled their first goblin and removed their blades hidden in their cases. The battlefield began to flow with the blood of the goblins as the thousands of Royal Elves never gave up when another goblin came toward them.

Tamian like the legendary king he was slowly began to get covered in the blood of goblins but inexorably kept fighting. The adrenaline in his body kept flowing as each strike seemed effortless and without draining of his strength. As more and more goblins fell before him he stood alone as each one seemed to avoid him. The king stood watching the battle around him. Throughout the battlefield only the Royal Elves who were overwhelmed by six or so goblins fell to the ground dead. Each Royal Elf quickly killing five or so goblins in the matter of moments.

Tamian ripped the cape from in back of him and threw it away as he stared at Bagaris in the distance.

"Send in the orcs," Bagaris commanded.

"Yes my lord," his captain replied.

The ranks of the larger stronger orcs began to emerge as they quickly ran down the battlefield toward the Royal Elves. The archers in the cliffs began to fire once again. Unlike the goblins an orc could get hit with an arrow and never feel the pain unless they got hit several times or in a vital area. Without care the orcs hit the Royal Elves as hundreds of them were filled with many arrows around their body.

Tamian again seemed unstoppable as he blocked blows with his shield and quickly killed an orc as it challenged him. After fighting off six or so Tamian placed his sword in his case and began to run toward a large rank of his forces. He grabbed the flag from one of them and began to wave it over and over.

From the right Maxus emerged from the hills with the thousands of Royal Guards and nobles as they rode high on their mounts. Maxus pulled his blade as the large Calvary charged to flank the orcs and remaining goblin foot soldiers.

"All out attack," Bagaris yelled as he saw the flank.

The orc and goblin army left no force behind as they charged the battlefield. The Royal Elves who stayed behind did the same as the archers in the cliffs began to climb down to join the fight as well.

The dark clouds above kept out the sun as the battle raged on. At the pace of fighting the Royal Elves would lose a lot of forces by the reckless tactics they had. Although they were gaining the upper hand it would prove to be devastating to their ranks. Blood began to fly in the air hitting the faces of the warriors engaged in battle. Dirt from running soldiers kicked up in the air as the warriors of each army were covered in dried blood and wet mud. The battle raged on for endless hours as the sun was completely set. Only dark forms of each army remained as the battlefield began to flow with blood. So much was spilled the blood turned into puddles that splashed as warriors stepped upon them.

Tamian saw the large Calvary of orcs come his way as he prepared himself. The dark form of Bagaris surprised him as it jumped off a small hill. Bagaris' spear pierced Tamian in the shoulder as he was thrown to the ground. The impact of the blow forced Bagaris to jump from his horse. As he hit the ground he quickly got up and pulled out his blade.

Tamian removed the large spearhead from his wounded shoulder as he picked up his sword in pain. Tamian's shield was far away from his grasp as he prepared for the orc. Bagaris tried to take advantage of his wounded enemy quickly striking with thunderous blows. Tamian was caught off guard by the hard hitting strikes as he blocked each one. By the time the sixth strike hit he was tossed back as he blocked and tripped over his own feet. Bagaris stalked over Tamian as he threw his sword down trying to end the king's life. Tamian from the ground somehow blocked as he spun his blade and sliced the Orc General in the ankle.

Bagaris limped in pain as Tamian rose to his feet and swiped again slicing Bagaris in his chest. Tamian came forward knowing he wounded the orc but Bagaris blocked the next strike. With his sword tangled with Tamian's Bagaris threw his elbow forward and nailed Tamian in the face. Tamian backed away just as Bagaris tried to swipe at his head. The wind of the strike hit Tamian as he dodged the blade by inches. With an inattentive stab Bagaris came forward. Tamian used the armor on his shin to absorb the blow as the blade stabbed into the ground. Tamian used his blade to stab up as it pierced into the bottom of Bagaris jaw and spit out the top of his head.

Pulling out the blade quickly Tamian watched as the mighty Orc General fell to the ground dead. With no time for rest Tamian blocked on coming forces easily killing them as the orc and goblins were now without leadership. As Tamian continued to battle he began to see large arrows hit the orcs in the face with astonishing precision. As Orcs would ready for an attack on a Royal Elf they were hit with a large thick arrow in the face or head.

As if endless the arrows kept coming hitting their target every time. Tamian fought off orcs still but as he readied to kill them an arrow would hit his target every time. With the amount of orcs and goblins fading he looked to the left side of the battlefield and saw hundreds of archers standing side by side. The orcs that remained tried to attack them as well but it went with no positive outcome.

Sitting atop a horse in the middle of the ranks of archers was Rakar. The Forest Elves had responded to Tamian and came just in time to help the Royal Elves finish off their enemy. Tamian and the Royal Elves yelled with excitement as they continued to battle their enemy. Tamian tired of fighting could relax as his remaining ranks continued to fight courageously.

The shadowed figure of Maxus made it to Tamian as he held two swords in his hands. With minor wounds to his person he was covered in the blood of orcs and goblins as he smiled slightly at his king.

The battlefield was soon quiet. The flags of the Royal Elves once held proudly by a warrior lay on the ground next to dead hands. The blood of fallen warriors soaked into the sand and at times splashed as others tried to gather the wounded. An endless river of blood was all around as Tamian sat atop his horse looking out at the battlefield.

Maxus rode up to the king as he sat silently morning his fallen warriors.

"How many have we lost?" Tamian asked.

"About ten thousand and still rising by the hour," Maxus told. Maxus looked to the Forest Elves gathered by Rakar as Maxus said, "If they didn't come in and help we would have lost far more trying to destroy the remaining forces."

Tamian looked back at the ranks of the Forest Elves as Rakar seemed to be speaking to many of his captains. Tamian directed his horse toward Rakar and rode quickly.

The Forest Elves became quiet as the Royal Elf King approached. Out of respect they all lowered their heads slightly to him. Rakar looked at his captains and without word watched them ride away.

"I owe a great debt to you," Tamian told.

"You owe me nothing but your word," Rakar told.

"What word?" Tamian asked.

"That you will come to my aid when ever I call," Rakar requested.

"I do not need to think about it," Tamian told, "It is done."

Tamian's horse stood next to Rakar's as both kings looked out.

"How was it that you were so close?" Tamian asked.

"I followed you," Rakar told, "From a distance though. I came when I could."

"How were you able to get so many forces in a matter of days?" Tamian asked.

"We kings have our ways do we not?" Rakar asked.

Tamian nodded and said, "Your archers are very skilled. How did they not fear that they'd hit one of my men."

"I'm sure they did," Rakar told with a small smile.

Tamian looked at a fallen orc and dropped from his horse quickly. He ripped an arrow out of the orc and looked at it. The arrow that hit the orc was by a Forest Elf. It was twice the size of one his men's arrows and twice as thick.

"If you ask me your men fire spears not arrows," Tamian replied.

"The bigger the arrow the bigger impact it has on a bigger enemy," Rakar told.

"My lord," A Royal Elf captain called as he rode up to Tamian.

Tamian looked to him as so did Rakar.

"I think there is something you need to see," The captain told.

Both kings rode slowly with the captain as they reached a mystical trail. Dozens of lights fell from the sky slowly like snow flakes. They began to glow blue as they did and when they hit the ground they vanished quickly. Rakar was escorted by two of his most trusted guards as he rode behind Tamian. The captain dropped from his horse as he saw a trail.

"What is it?" Tamian asked.

174

"You and King Rakar must go there at once my lord," The captain said.

"Why him and I?" Rakar asked.

"Just do as I ask my lord," The captain said, "I am not allowed to say a word."

"By whose command?" Tamian asked angered.

"Please," The captain begged, "Once you see you will know."

Tamian and Rakar dropped from their horses as Rakar's guards did as well.

"No," Rakar told, "Tamian and I will go alone."

Both the kings walked down the trail as they came to a small waterfall. A small creek stood before them with an enchanting blue texture to the water. A sight that would take the breath away of the fiercest warrior. That though wasn't what the two kings looked at as they entered. Above the waterfall painted into the rocks was a picture of the two of them side by side on horses. Just as they were moments ago in the battlefield.

"What sorcery is this?" Rakar asked.

"Messages," A voice told.

The two kings turned to their right and saw a glowing light. The form of Talius emerged bright and beautiful before them. With not even a moment to react the two looked at her in awe. Never seeing the goddess before in their lives they already knew who she was.

"Talius," Tamian replied, "Goddess of beauty indeed."

The glowing light around the goddess soon vanished as she stood before them.

"You say it's a message?" Rakar asked as he slightly looked at the painting then back at the intoxicating goddess of beauty.

"The Guardian of Light," Talius told as her voice echoed in their ears, "Years before the first of your king's time. The Guardian of Light is giving you messages that it has seen before it would happen."

"What are we suppose to think after seeing this?" Tamian asked.

"Nothing," Talius told, "All that you will need to know I will tell you now."

"Our ears are listening," Rakar told.

"When The Dark Lord, Korack and Greco were defeated by Warad most of their powers were taken from them. The inability to fight against those of this world and to only watch was one of their many curses on the lands of Tullian. Their powers here are still stronger then any sorcerer in these lands accept one."

"Who?" Tamian asked.

"The one who goes by the name of Mayreon," Talius told.

"Mayreon," Tamian replied, "Lyncade's wife."

"Of course," Talius told, "It was Warad's will that she would infatuate him with her beauty and grace. She has a bigger purpose then the two of you can ever imagine. Her life is more important then any others in this world as we know it."

"She goes to the natives in Cavell," Tamian told.

"I know of her whereabouts," Talius told, "You must find her at once. If The Dark Lord finds her he will be able to regain his powers."

"How?" Rakar asked.

"Each of the three brothers when defeated had their powers transferred into rubies. Ruby's that were scattered along the lands of Tullian," Talius told, "Mayreon was born knowing where these rubies were. She though doesn't know she knows where they are. If The Dark Lord finds her he can search her mind and know where the rubies are."

"Why is it that we must do this task?" Tamian asked, "If Warad is the god of all things why can't he find them himself?"

"He is not allowed to interfere," Talius told, "Only guide and try to protect those who search for the rubies. The army you just fought was not an invasion."

"Then what was it?" Rakar asked.

"An illusion," Talius told, "They come in search for Mayreon. They have your forces tied here so by the time it was your fate to see this painting and find out the purpose of your meeting; they would be soon capable of capturing her."

"They can't interfere either," Rakar reminded.

"They're not," Talius told, "The Falmores are here to get her."

Tamian and Rakar quickly looked at each other.

"They landed many days ago and are searching for her as we speak," Talius told.

"She is being protected by Cloron, Hecorus and Halouse," Tamian told.

"No," Talius quickly replied, "Halouse is the only one with her. Cloron and Hecorus went in search of the Valley. Halouse and Mayreon are searching for Lyncade."

"They promised she wouldn't be hurt," Tamian said in anger.

"Trust me Tamian when I say Halouse will guard her with his life," Talius reassured, "He will not let a single soul hurt her."

"How are we supposed to retrieve these rubies?" Rakar asked.

"Two of them are in the Valley of Talius," Talius told, "In the hands of the third king of the elves."

"Him and I are the only kings," Tamian told.

"There is a third," Talius informed, "Calbrawn. He has no crown and he does not bare the title but in the eyes of Warad he is a king."

"Will he guide us to these rubies?" Tamian asked.

"Calbrawn knows where they are," Talius told, "He will carry out the orders to find them. Regain them and bring them to Celladom."

"Where is Celladom?" Rakar asked.

"The Stream of Eternal Light," Talius told, "Only all three rubies open the gateway to the Stream."

"Where is the third?" Rakar asked.

"That is why you must go after the Falmores," Talius told, "That ruby will be your task. Sangrayus has it."

"She is in league with him," Rakar told.

"She will never give it to The Dark Lord," Talius told, "She knows if those rubies are given to Korack, Greco and The Dark Lord; her people will be destroyed."

"How do we get it from her?" Tamian asked.

"You must kill her," Talius told.

"The most powerful sorceress in all the world?" Rakar asked in disbelief.

"You will find someone," Talius assured, "Leave this place at once."

The two kings bowed their head slightly as they began to walk back toward their men.

Chapter 11

The second night alone with each other started to settle in as Mayreon and Halouse were back at their camp. Halouse looking across at a large lake like before as he ripped apart a piece of meat that had been cooking on the fire. Mayreon just sat silently disturbed that they didn't find Lyncade all day. Halouse tossed the bone of the meat away as he took out his container of water and pored it on his greasy hands. He had his weapons close by knowing that animals and other evils could attack them in the middle of the night. His bow was to his back with a sack of arrows and his sword was tied around his waist. His many daggers around the belt he wore were ready for him to grab if he felt his life in danger.

"Feels like I haven't bathed in years," Halouse told.

"The lake isn't too far away," Mayreon reminded, "Perhaps you should go."

Halouse looked back at her slightly as he smirked a little.

"You must feel disgusted," Halouse replied, "A woman of your title stuck in the forest with no servants and no way of bathing yourself."

"I'm fine," Mayreon assured, "When I was a servant there were many days like this."

"Really?" Halouse asked.

"I went weeks without sleep," Mayreon told, "Washing this one or scrubbing the floors of the temple, or cleaning Tamian's robes."

"Must have been harsh," Halouse replied.

"It had its moments," Mayreon replied.

Halouse looked around for several moments before he replied, "That's what will make you a great queen."

"What do you mean?" Mayreon asked.

"You have lived your life on both sides," Halouse reminded, "Both as a slave and as a queen. As a queen now you will appreciated it more."

Mayreon looked at him and said, "Maybe you're right?"

"Of course I am," Halouse told with a small smile, "You won't throw your weight around as much as Drizell. She has always been royalty. I heard she once had a servant executed because she ruined a dress."

"That is true," Mayreon informed.

"I doubt you will ever have that done," Halouse replied, "Knowing the long hours a servant has to go through."

Mayreon thought to herself and asked, "Did you really think about me everyday?"

Halouse just glanced at her as he smiled and said, "Not a moment had past that I didn't."

"I doubt that," Mayreon replied.

Halouse looked ahead again and said, "I did everyday. Wondering where you were, what you were doing, what kind of woman you'd become."

"And?" Mayreon asked as she looked at him.

Halouse just kept his eyes forward and replied, "And it figures that when I finally found you again, that you were married to another."

Mayreon looked at him and as she gave a smile Halouse returned it. Just as they continued to look at one another an arrow flew right into Halouse's arm. In pain he dropped to the ground.

Mayreon jumped from her camp as Falmores began to swarm the camp. With their weapons drawn Mayreon went to action quickly. The fire in front of her began to blow toward two Falmores as they caught on fire.

Halouse quickly got up as he snapped the arrow that was inside of his arm. He pulled his blade out and ran at a Falmore. A few blows were exchanged as each warrior blocked. Halouse took no more time finally stabbing the Falmore in the chest and beheading him. Placing his sword away Halouse took out two daggers and awaited two more Falmores. As they attacked Halouse ducked each attack and stabbed them quickly in the throat with his daggers. When he stabbed the Falmores he left the blade in their throats as he quickly grabbed another and awaited his next opponent. Taking one quickly from his belt he hurled it toward a warrior close to Mayreon. Hitting his target he pulled out another and quickly killed a Falmore coming toward him.

Mayreon used her magic abilities to pick up one Falmore and toss him into three others coming toward her. Already occupied by one spell a Falmore from her blind side hurled his sword. Halouse jumped to the ground and rolled up placing his blade in the way just in time. Halouse quickly got to his feet and cut off the Felmores arm as he swiped again and cut him across his chest. Kicking the Falmore away he grabbed Mayreon by the hand.

"Come on," Halouse yelled.

Running as fast as they could through the dark forest they both heard the sounds of arrows flying above their heads. Halouse ducked as he dragged Mayreon along with him. In front of them Halouse could see a Falmore coming there way. Because of years in the dark forest he could make the Falmores out perfectly. It wasn't sight so much as it was radar he seemed to gain. Grabbing an arrow from a tree that flew passed them earlier Halouse met the Falmore as he stabbed him in the neck with the arrow. Mayreon gasped in fear as Halouse killed the Falmore.

Climbing to higher ground they were traveling on a trail just above the great lake Halouse was looking at earlier.

"Don't let go of my hand," Halouse demanded.

"I'm getting tired," Mayreon yelled to him out of breath.

"If we stop we're dead," Halouse told.

Standing on the trail in front of them was another Falmore as he could barely make out Halouse and Mayreon. He readied his bow as he fired at them. Halouse moved him and Mayreon from the arrow just in time. As the Falmore readied to fire again Halouse reached him and pushed him over the edge of the cliff. The Falmore fell over the cliff yelling all the way down. The echo of his screams would give away where Halouse and Mayreon were.

As they began to go down hill there was an endless trail in front of them. The trail seemed to go for miles and as far as their eyes could see. Halouse and her ran quickly as Halouse didn't hear the sounds of footsteps behind them. Halouse stopped and looked in back of him just as Mayreon did.

"What are we doing?" Mayreon whispered.

"There not far behind," Halouse told as he grabbed the bow behind his back.

"What are you doing?" Mayreon asked.

"Follow this trail until it doesn't go anymore," Halouse told.

"I'm not going anywhere without you," Mayreon told.

"My lady you must," Halouse told as he grabbed an arrow and fired.

A few hundred feet down a Falmore that was well ahead of the others was hit in the face.

"I don't know where I'm going," Mayreon told.

"You won't have to," Halouse told as he readied another arrow, "Follow this trail and it will take you to the Natives hunting ground."

"What if they think I'm an enemy?" Mayreon asked.

Halouse fired another arrow as he hit his target far away from them.

"They won't. By now Cloron and Hecorus have reached the camp and have a search party looking for the two of us," Halouse looked in back of him at Mayreon and said, "Go."

Mayreon looked at him with a begging look as she was scared for her protector. Mayreon walked slowly still looking at him.

"Go," Halouse yelled.

Mayreon turned and began to run as tears fell from her eyes. Halouse looked in front of him and aimed another arrow as he fired. Grabbing another arrow quickly he fired again. With his perfect eyes he could see his targets falling on the trail. Falmores fired arrows of their own but missed by several feet as they flew passed Halouse. As the dozens of them began to get closer, Halouse fired more and more. When Halouse reached for another arrow he realized there were none left. He pulled out his blade and awaited the others coming toward him.

Mayreon ran for what seemed like hours. The sound of fighting soon faded but she kept running like the Falmores were right behind her. Before Mayreon knew it the sun began to hit her face. She quickly stopped as she fell to the ground exhausted from her run. With no breath in her lungs she heard the sounds of a river not far away. This same river must have branched off from the great lake she and Halouse were once camped by. Dragging her tired body to the river she placed her hand in and began to scoop water into her mouth.

"The beautiful Mayreon," A voice replied.

In fear Mayreon backed away from the river as the form of Korack was soon on the water. In fear she dragged herself away and got up from the ground. Korack reached his hand toward her as Mayreon was frozen from movement. Mayreon knew she was cast under a spell as she yelled in fear.

"Do not run," Korack warned, "You can not escape me."

Mayreon was forced to turn around by Korack's powers as she was levitating in the air and began to get dragged toward Korack.

"You haven't learned this spell yet," Korack informed her, "It's a control spell that is way too advanced for you. There was talk of you being a great sorceress. I don't quite see it."

Mayreon some how managed to moved her hand as a vine ripped from the banks on the other side of the river and flew toward Korack. It wrapped around his neck as Korack choked. Releasing Mayreon she dropped into the river of the water and began to get dragged downstream. Several other vines began to rip from the ground as they wrapped themselves around Korack. Snapping the one from around his neck The Cobra King was able to breathe.

"I may have underestimated you," Korack replied as dozens of vines wrapped around him.

Mayreon drained from the spell Korack once had on her lost consciousness as she felt herself being dragged by the river.

Hours away from where Mayreon was Lyncade and a search party of Native Elves along with Salryn looked at the dozens of Falmore bodies around the trail Halouse once was.

"What happened here?" Lyncade asked.

"A small war party of Great Humans must have found Mayreon and Halouse," Salryn told.

"But there are dozens of them and no sign of Mayreon," Lyncade told.

"That is Halouse," Salryn said with a small smile.

"Is he a great warrior?" Lyncade asked.

"Calbrawn's son," Salryn told, "You figure it out."

"I'm already impressed," Lyncade told, "But we must follow this trail and find them."

The search party wasted little time as they all began to sprint down the trail. Nothing but the bodies of dozens of Falmores in front of them as each kill was just as vicious as the next.

Mayreon's body had drifted along the bank of a small creek as the river calmed. She was still knocked out and unable to do anything as her body laid on the sand near the bank. Three forms soon emerged as the three Menaceus' from days before found her. They circled around her slowly as if ready to attack. One of them went to her and poked at her for several moments. As nothing happened the same Menaceus picked up her arm and watched it drop. He jumped away from her just in case it woke her. Still laying still they seemed to know she was alive but were still fearful of her. Mayreon slowly began to come to as the Menaceus jumped away from her but still encircled her. As she cleared her eyes she soon realized where she was. She looked as if she hoped she was in a dream as the Menaceus swiped at her from several feet away. They didn't hit her but it was almost a warning to her. Scared and not knowing what to do Mayreon got up and began to run back into the creek.

A Menaceus quickly jumped high in the air and landed on her back. Using his razor sharp claws he scratched her in her back several times before taking her head and dumping it in the water. The other two stayed far behind yelling with excitement as he did. It seemed they wanted to drown her and then eat her. As Mayreon felt the air from her lungs leave her head she began to get dizzy.

One of the Menaceus on the bank had a sword stabbed into it as the blade of the sword shot out it's chest. The second was quick to jump away as Halouse kicked the dead Menaceus away. The second used it's incredible speed to encircle Halouse as it jumped into action. Jumping high in the air Halouse took a dagger from his belt and hurled it toward the attacking Menaceus. Imbedded in the creature's throat he fell from the air dead and splashed into the water of the creek. The third had heard what was going on as he turned and let go of Mayreon. Halouse saw as Mayreon's body was lifeless and she was floating in the water face down. The third Menaceus jumped at Halouse as it hit him in the chest and dug it's claws in Halouse's shoulders. Yelling in pain Halouse tried to stab the creature with his sword. The Menaceus clawed him several times in the face as Halouse finally grabbed the creature by the throat and threw him off. The Menaceus slashed around in the water for several seconds before it jumped at Halouse again. This time Halouse just pointed his blade out in front of him as the Menaceus impaled itself. Kicking the creature away from him quickly he grabbed Mayreon and pulled her from the water. Dragging her lifeless body to the sand he took both his hands and placed it on her chest. He began to push into her chest over and over again. He reached up and began to blow air into her mouth with his. Moments later Mayreon began to cough as the water in her lungs came out. Halouse held her as he looked down on her. Mayreon looked at him in shock as she had realized what he had done.

"You okay?" Halouse asked, "Say something."

Mayreon caught her breath as she replied, "I see you got your bath."

Laughing and in disbelief Halouse just cradled Mayreon in his arms.

"You survived?" Mayreon asked.

"Falmores are nothing," Halouse assured.

Halouse fell back exhausted as Mayreon kneeled beside him and looked down on him. Looking at the scratches all over his face and several slices across his arms from the fight with the Falmores.

"You're heavily wounded," Mayreon informed.

"Most of them are just scratches," Halouse assured as he looked at the broken arrow on his arm and said, "This one hurts the most."

Mayreon looked at it for several seconds. Halouse quickly sat up as he went back into the creek and began to wash the dried blood from his face. He winced in pain as he finished up. Fresh blood from his scratches pored from his wounds as he exited the stream. Grabbing Mayreon softly she let out a small cry. Halouse quickly turned her around and saw the wounds the Menaceus gave her on her back.

"He got you pretty good," Halouse told.

"How bad?" Mayreon asked.

"It's not deep," Halouse assured.

Mayreon looked deeply at Halouse.

"This is the third time you saved me," Mayreon told.

"I got lucky," Halouse assured, "If I would have slowed down I wouldn't have reached you in time."

"But you did," Mayreon told.

Halouse sat down on a log and tried to regain his strength.

"It's almost as if Warad made you find me," Mayreon told.

"Maybe," Halouse replied, "I came just in time."

"I'm not talking about just now," Mayreon informed.

Halouse looked at her for several moments. The two captivated by one another. Halouse hiding his true feelings just looked away as he rubbed his shoulder blade.

"I owe a great debt to you now," Mayreon told.

"No you don't," Halouse assured, "I did what any other man did."

Halouse got up and looked as if he was going to walk away. Mayreon quickly grabbed him and stopped him.

"Why are you hiding it now?" Mayreon asked.

"Because we have to my lady," Halouse told.

Staring at each other for seemed like ages the two finally heard the snapping of branches.

"Halouse," A voice called.

Halouse turned to see Cloron and Hecorus.

"I thought you went for the Valley?" Halouse asked.

"We turned back because of the Falmores," Hecorus told. Hecorus looked his brother over and asked, "What happened?"

"I ran into some of them," Halouse told.

"The trail isn't far," Cloron told.

Hecorus looked over at Mayreon and noticed her saddened face.

"You alright my lady?" Hecorus asked.

"Yes," Mayreon assured.

"She was attacked by the Menaceus," Halouse told, "She's just a little shaken."

"Come," Hecorus called to Mayreon, "We are close to home."

Below the high cliffs along a riverside the four traveled. The mountains beside them stood high in the air and were scary to even look at from the ground. The four quickly came to a small rock that when you crouched you were the same size as it. Cloron quickly picked up the rock along with Hecorus as they moved it out of the way. Cloron and Hecorus went first as they were followed by Halouse and Mayreon. Halouse took the rock from the side of the mountain and placed it back where it was. Moments later the four were in a dark cave that gradually got taller and wider. Before Mayreon realized she was blinded by the sun light as she entered The Valley of Talius.

Exiting the small cave they had entered the beautiful Valley as it captured her eyes. She stood in awe for several seconds as the hundreds of Natives watched the four enter. Many of them quickly came up to Cloron, Hecorus and Halouse welcoming them. Most were captivated by the stunning majesty of Mayreon.

"As unlikely as it sounds we found her in Tamian," Hecorus joked to the fellow warriors.

They walked through the large valley passing huts and small shops as they began to see the towers of the nobles in the distance.

"Your father is looking for you," A Native replied as he passed Cloron.

"These are your people?" Mayreon asked Halouse.

"They are just people," Halouse told, "The valley is just a safe haven for all those who live in Cavell. There are many tribes here. The ones that dominate are the Lycans and Murkildens. My father is only a counselor to the people if they ever wish to speak to him about advice."

"Do you have an army?" Mayreon asked.

"You're looking at them," Hecorus replied hearing her question.

Small children began to walk with Mayreon as they studied her with marvel. Halouse noticed this as he laughed softly.

"What?" Mayreon asked.

"You are so different in their eyes," Halouse told, "They have never seen your kind before."

Mayreon stopped and looked at the children. With her hands she cupped them closed and just as she opened them a flame came over her hands. She quickly made the flame a butterfly that began to flap it's wings. The children all laughed as Mayreon then made the flaming butterfly fly out of her hands and away. Mayreon touched the face of a small girl as she smiled gentle to her.

"I hope you have hundreds more of those," Cloron replied as he awaited her to join them again, "They'll want to see it again."

The four of them were quickly taken to Calbrawn's fort and they scaled the many stairs. As they reached the top Calbrawn sat in a chair with the half breed next to him.

"Father," Cloron called.

Calbrawn looked up as he saw his sons enter. His servant helped him up as he welcomed all his sons with a hug.

"Good to see you well," Calbrawn told each, "I trust your journey was safe."

"For some of us," Hecorus joked as he looked at Halouse.

"What happened?" Calbrawn asked.

"Menaceus'," Halouse told, "I am fine."

"What about the sword marks?" Calbrawn asked.

"Falmores," Cloron told.

"We know about them," Calbrawn told.

"Father," Halouse called as he moved out of the way of Mayreon, "This is the queen on the Royal Elves."

Mayreon took a step forward as Calbrawn's eyes became surprised at how beautiful she was.

"Do I see the goddess Talius herself?" Calbrawn asked.

"Nonsense," Mayreon replied, "I am just a messenger of Tamian."

"Queen of your people as well," Calbrawn corrected.

"One of the queens," Mayreon told.

"Tamian has two wives?" Calbrawn asked.

"No," Mayreon told, "I am wife to Lyncade."

Calbrawn looked at her in awe again as he said, "Mayreon."

"You know her?" Cloron asked.

Calbrawn looked at his eldest son and said, "You did the right thing bringer her here."

"It was her own idea," Cloron told.

"No," Calbrawn told, "It is the fate of Warad that brought her here."

Cloron quickly went in his sack tied behind his back and pulled out the blue ruby. He handed it back to Mayreon.

"Sorry," Cloron told, "Forgot I still had that."

Mayreon walked to Calbrawn and kneeled before him holding the ruby out.

"Consider this a gift from me to you," Mayreon replied, "To assure Tamian's allegiance to you."

"Your presence here Mayreon is all that I will need," Calbrawn assured, "So please rise. You owe me no veneration."

Mayreon got to her feet and said, "What ever rank you have to these three men in my request have them commemorated."

"It shall be done," Calbrawn assured, "A certain task will need to be done. They will carry it out."

"What task?" Halouse asked.

Calbrawn looked to his wounded son and replied, "Halouse. Go and get yourself cleaned up. I will meet with the council once Salryn and Lyncade have returned."

"Lyncade?" Mayreon asked with shocked eyes.

"We have him safe my lady," Calbrawn assured.

Hecorus looked at Halouse as a face of disappointment came over him. Halouse quickly left before Mayreon had a chance to see it.

"Cloron," Calbrawn called, "Have another party seek out Salryn and the others at once."

"Of course father," Cloron replied.

"Hecorus go with him," Calbrawn commanded.

Hecorus nodded and followed his brother out.

"Queen Mayreon," Calbrawn called, "Please sit and relax. Your journey to be among my people is over."

Mayreon did as Calbrawn saw the robes she wore were dirty and ripped from her long journey.

"May I offer you some new cloths?" Calbrawn asked.

"Nonsense," Mayreon said, "You have done enough for me so far."

"We must," Calbrawn said, "You are a queen and are to look presentable. May I ask you what your empire usual prefers?"

"White or blue," Mayreon told, "Those are the colors of my people."

Calbrawn nodded as he looked to his half breed servant. She nodded and walked out as Calbrawn took a pot of herbal tea and pored it into a cup.

"This will make you feel relaxed," Calbrawn told as he handed it to her.

"Thank you," Mayreon softly replied.

Calbrawn studied her for several moments as she sipped from her cup.

"Have we met before?" Calbrawn asked.

Mayreon looked at him and nodded, "When I was a little girl."

The flash of that horrible night went off in Calbrawn's mind as he remembered.

"Oh yes," Calbrawn said, "You are the little girl."

"Yes," Mayreon said with a gentle smile.

"A villager who lived among commoners and now you are a queen," Calbrawn said.

"I guess I have to thank you and your son Halouse for that," Mayreon said, "He has saved me two more times since I met him again."

"Is that so?" Calbrawn asked, "He had a liking toward you when you were children. How about now?"

Mayreon nodded as she said, "Things haven't changed."

"You cannot return his feelings even though you fight it," Calbrawn knew.

Mayreon looked at him shocked by his accuracy.

"Don't be so surprised," Calbrawn said, "I could tell that without the powers I posses. You are to stay true to your husband."

Mayreon just nodded as the old elf laughed.

"I was going to take you in as my own," Calbrawn remembered, "I wonder what our lives would have been like if I did."

"Makes you think doesn't it?" Mayreon asked.

They both sipped on their tea as Mayreon relaxed from her long journey. She was soon dressed in a white gown given to her by Calbrawn as his half breed servant helped prepare Mayreon from when ever her husband returned.

The Falmores camp site was still setup. The small war parties that were sent out to retrieve Mayreon had not returned and word of them getting killed was soon spread around. Each fire that burned dozens of angered Falmores stood around still wondering what their next move would be.

An angered Korack stormed through the camp as all the Falmores quickly got out of his way. He quickly went to the large tent setup for

Artwore as he moved the clothed entrance and entered. The Dark Lord and Greco were there along with Artwore and Sangrayus.

"You failed," The Dark Lord said.

"I had her," Korack assured.

"How was it that a simple Royal Elf was able to get away from your grasp?" Sangrayus asked, "And a women at that?"

Korack looked at her angered as a warning to never speak to him like that again. Sangrayus didn't change her expression as she awaited an answer.

"I had a domination spell on her," Korack told The Dark Lord, "Her hand was some how able to become free and she cast a spell on me."

Greco looked at The Dark Lord and asked, "Is that possible?"

"I warned you about her," The Dark Lord reminded Korack, "I guess you needed to see for yourself."

"Indeed," Korack replied still upset.

"She is powerful?" Greco asked.

"All powerful," Korack told, "Her abilities are unlike any I have ever felt."

"Better then mine?" Sangrayus asked.

Korack looked at the sorceress and said, "If she is as good I think she is. Then you don't stand a chance."

Sangrayus looked at Artwore offended and replied, "Lead me to her."

"Don't be a fool," The Dark Lord yelled, "Everything is going to plan as expected."

"Losing your orc and goblin forces was apart of your plan?" Artwore asked.

"By now Talius has informed Tamian and Rakar why we are here," The Dark Lord told, "By the time they come to try and save Mayreon she will be in our grasp and we will have the rubies."

"If they are taken to the Stream of Eternal Light than we are done for," Greco told.

"No we aren't the greed of man will come into play," The Dark Lord assured, "Besides with Mayreon in our grasp the whereabouts of the ruby's will be told to us."

"I hope you're right," Artwore replied, "I only wish to use the least amount of forces once we find the passage to the Valley of Talius."

"It will be in our grasp soon," The Dark Lord assured, "My eyes see all."

The three evil gods vanished at that moment and teleported back to Korack's castle in The Dark Realm. The Dark Lord sat silently on his brother's throne as Greco and Korack looked toward him.

"What purpose will we have for the Falmores?" Greco asked.

"I do not care if they are wiped from the earth," The Dark Lord told, "That is ultimately what will happen to them."

"If they go what forces will we have to fight Warad's creations?" Korack asked.

"Patience brothers," The Dark Lord said, "We will have our army in time. Certain things must fall into place before we can strike."

"The time is now," Greco assured, "Why wait?"

"If we fight now then all the Elves will join forces," The Dark Lord knew, "We want them separated not joined."

"How will you do that?" Korack asked.

"It is being worked on as we speak," The Dark Lord assured as he rose.

Greco and Korack watched as The Dark Lord walked out the balcony and looked to the dark lands.

"Brother," Korack called, "Who is this sorceress?"

"How is it that she has so many powers?" Greco asked.

"Is it our..." Korack began.

"No," The Dark Lord answered, "The Guardian of Light is a man. Warad erased it from our memories but I assure you that I remember a man."

"Then who is this woman?" Korack asked.

"A great force if we get her on our side," The Dark Lord told.

Greco and Korack looked at one another as they seemed to understand The Dark Lord's plan.

"Sangrayus has become hard to deal with," The Dark Lord said, "Her actions lately are starting to annoy me."

"Take her out and replace her with Mayreon," Korack knew.

"That will take some time," The Dark Lord told, "Certain things must fall. She is now Queen as well as Drizell. Once she wins the heart of the Natives like I know she will..."

"Then she will be their queen," Korack finished.

"And if something very unfortunate somehow happens to Mayreon," The Dark Lord began.

"Then she will turn against Tamian," Greco finished.

"And do just as we ask," The Dark Lord replied.

The three looked out into the lands of The Dark Realm all on the same page and understanding what they must do to make their plan work to perfection.

Chapter 12

Mayreon bathed privately inside Halouse's hut. Halouse was far away in the valley taking care of his wounds. Cloron entered the hut by himself as he heard the sounds of water. He stood just outside the entrance of the room Mayreon was bathing in.

"My lady," Cloron called.

Caught off guard Mayreon kind of jumped and replied, "Yes."

"Your husband is close," Cloron told, "Hecorus is bringing them here now."

Mayreon jumped from the tub and grabbed the gown given to her by Calbrawn as she quickly began to get ready. Cloron watched as Mayreon emerged from the room and looked at him. She was pulling her hair back as it was still wet from her bath.

"I will escort you," Cloron told.

Cloron walked Mayreon through the valley as the hundreds that passed still stared at her in amazement.

"I would have figured they'd be used to me by now," Mayreon replied.

"They see something in you that they haven't seen in others before," Cloron told, "They are enchanted by you."

"What clan are you?" Mayreon asked.

"I am Murkilden," Cloron told, "Hecorus is as well."

"Why is Halouse a Lycan?" Mayreon asked.

"Calbrawn wanted his influence in as many clans as he could," Cloron told, "To assure that he knew what was happening at all times."

Mayreon just nodded as she was brought to the entrance of the Valley. Halouse was standing on a cliff in the distance as he could see Cloron and Mayreon. Seconds later Hecorus walked in as Mayreon saw the form of her husband not far behind. With a glorious smile Mayreon went to him as they embraced. With a small kiss Mayreon wrapped herself around Lyncade as he held her tightly. She broke and grabbed his face.

"I thought I lost you," Mayreon told.

"Same here," Lyncade told.

With a distraught expression Halouse looked on. Hecorus noticed his brother standing far off and looking toward Mayreon. As Halouse saw Hecorus looking at him he quickly vanished. Salryn walked passed Hecorus with a smile as he returned her look.

"I'll see you later?" Salryn asked.

Hecorus just nodded.

Lyncade kissed Mayreon for several seconds as he stopped and looked at her, "You must take me to this man who looked after you."

"Of course," Mayreon told.

Lyncade saw the necklace around her neck and looked at it queerly.

"What is this?" Lyncade asked as he picked the charm up while it was still on her.

Mayreon kind of smiled as she said, "It was mine, when I was a little girl."

"What are you talking about?" Lyncade asked.

"It seems the man who saved me had done it many lifetimes ago as well," Mayreon informed.

Lyncade still had a confused look as Mayreon just reached in and kissed him, happy to finally see the man she loved.

Halouse sat alone at the bottom of a small hill near the mountains that kept the natives safe. He was picking up small rocks and tossing them inside the pool of water not far in front of him. Hecorus emerged on top of the hill as he slowly made his way toward his brother.

"Do they know where I am?" Halouse asked feeling his brother's presence.

"No," Hecorus told as he sat next to Halouse, "But they will soon."

"I do not wish to see him," Halouse told.

"You must," Hecorus said, "If you do not he'll be offended."

"So be it," Halouse replied, "Seeing him with her will only anger me."

"If you show your anger and he notices then you could be killed," Hecorus reminded, "You must hide your feelings brother."

"Easy for you to say," Halouse replied, "She has done something to me that I can not explain."

"Women of her beauty are known for that," Hecorus reminded.

"There are none with her beauty," Halouse assured, "Women that have torn men apart had no effect on me."

"If Warad wishes for you to be with her then you will," Hecorus told, "You must wait for his time."

"I have no patience for his time," Halouse told as he rose and turned away, "I've desired this since the moment I met her and I can barely contain it."

"Every warrior has a great task," Hecorus told as he turned and looked at his brother, "This is your great task. You must overcome it and fight how you feel in your soul. Every warrior has an eternal battle brother. You must defeat yourself."

Halouse turned slightly and looked at Hecorus. With those final words by his brother Halouse began to walk away. Halouse quickly went to his father courtiers and went to the top floor. There Calbrawn sat in a chair rocking away with a pipe in his mouth. Calbrawn took it from his lips and exhaled smoke as he placed it on a table in front of him. He saw his son's distant look as he could barely face his father.

"The worst feeling in the world my son is having something to say but never being able to say it," Calbrawn replied.

"How do you know what I feel?" Halouse asked.

"I saw the way you reacted when word that Lyncade was alive," Calbrawn replied, "Your heart almost broke at that moment."

"He's going to come up here and thank me," Halouse told, "I'm afraid I can't see him."

Calbrawn turned and looked at his son as he gestured for Halouse to sit. Halouse went to a chair in front of his father and sat.

"When I tell you what I'm about to tell you, you mustn't get angry," Calbrawn replied, "You mustn't walk out of here with anger or depression. You must fight how you feel and never look at her any differently."

"Of course father," Halouse told.

"She shares the same feelings that you do my son. She may hide it well from the world but she can not hide it from me," Calbrawn told, "But you mustn't act on that now that I've told you."

"Why?" Halouse asked.

"Besides the fact that she is married to a powerful man?" Calbrawn asked, "There are many reasons why you can not involve yourself with such a woman."

"Tell me then."

"Mayreon is cursed," Calbrawn told, "Cursed with something that not even the god Warad can change. I see an age of darkness in her eyes one which I will not be alive to see."

"Who will curse her?" Halouse asked.

"The Dark Lord," Calbrawn told, "She will endure a pain which you and I will never feel in a thousand lifetimes."

"Can I stop this fate?" Halouse asked.

Calbrawn leaned forward and replied, "My son. If you love this woman and she returns it, it will be the death of you. I have foreseen it."

"Why does every part of my soul say that what I feel is pure?" Halouse asked.

"Do you love her?" Calbrawn asked.

Halouse nodded.

"He makes her happy," Calbrawn said, "If you love her you will not interfere."

Halouse just nodded and said, "You're right father. If she goes with me she will be guilt stricken by her decision. I mustn't let her do that."

Halouse just looked at his father as moments later Lyncade entered with Mayreon.

"Halouse," Mayreon called.

Halouse got to his feet quickly as he saw the two.

"Lyncade this is the man you owe a great thanks," Mayreon told.

196

"Halouse," Lyncade replied as he approached, "I've never heard the name, but because of what you done I shall never forget it."

Halouse shook his hand as kept his eyes to the ground. Not being able to look at the man who was married to his love.

"I would do it again if I had to," Halouse replied as he quickly walked away from Lyncade and out the door.

Lyncade turned and looked at the door as Halouse exited with speculation.

"You must forgive my son," Calbrawn told, "He has had a long journey."

As Lyncade turned and looked at Calbrawn Mayreon still looked at the door Halouse walked out of in sadness. Hiding it quickly she looked forward at Calbrawn.

"There is a task that must be completed," Calbrawn told.

Located on a high cliff in the Valley the members of the Native Council met. One hundred seats all in line on the left and right of the open temple as every member took their seat. Calbrawn was the only one that was standing as all the rest sat. Mayreon and Lyncade stood next to Calbrawn as he walked in the middle of all the seats.

"My fellow Elves," Calbrawn began, "We all knew that this day would come. The ruby's given to us by Talius so many ages ago must be found. The Dark Lord, Greco and Korack are on our lands searching for them. If the one's we have are found then our people, and the people of Tullian will all be destroyed."

"Once they are found what will we do with them?" A Councilman asked.

"Bring them to Stream of Eternal Light," Calbrawn told, "It is in Celladom. Talius and Warad will lead us to them. Once all the ruby's are found they will open the gates to The Stream."

"We only have two," A Councilman reminded, "Where is the third?"

"The third ruby will be carried out by someone else," Calbrawn told, "Warad entrusted me to find the other two."

"How far away are they?" A Councilman asked.

"Not far," Calbrawn assured, "When I send out a party they will be brought back in no time."

"What happens once we have the rubies?" A Councilman asked.

Calbrawn looked all around and replied, "I will not lie to you. The Dark Lord is drawn to the rubies. It will give away our home to the enemy."

"Then this task can not be done," A Councilman replied.

"Then we will all die," Calbrawn told, "If we get the rubies then there is hope that The Dark Lord, Korack and Greco will not get their powers. I will not lie when I say many of us will die."

"Who will go on this task to retrieve them?" A Councilman asked.

"We will," A voice replied.

The entire council watched as Cloron walked up the staircase with Halouse, Hecorus, Salryn and the half breed servant of Calbrawn.

"I will go as well," Lyncade told.

"So will I," Raven said as he emerged in back of Cloron.

The warriors knew this journey might have been the last they ever embarked on. The quest ahead was sure to be filled with Falmores trying to take the rubies from their grasp as soon as they got them. The increasing evil could be felt throughout the air as each councilman looked at all of the warriors ready to die to defend their home. The warriors were from different parts of the world, different beliefs, different leaders, but they all knew what needed to be done to save their empires. This day was inevitable, and the warriors that stepped forward valiantly were seen in the highest respects but all who saw them.

"We will need more men," A Councilman said.

"No," Calbrawn replied, "A large force will make our presence known to our enemy. The smaller the party, the easier the rubies will be found without much attention."

"You must stay here and defend yours homes," Lyncade replied, "They may try to invade the Valley when we are gone. Our small force will do what ever it takes to make sure the ruby's are in our hands and not that of the Falmores."

"We have our party," Calbrawn replied, "Now all we need to do is have them get what we need."

The Valley began to go crazed with the movement of the people. Knowing that their home would be found once the ruby's was brought into the Valley; hundreds of villagers began to get their things in preparations to leave.

"Where should the women and children go?" Halouse asked Calbrawn as they walked through the valley.

"March them near the river," Calbrawn commanded, "The Falmores are camped and have stopped marching. They know they are close to our home. Make sure the women and children go north. Tamian will find them and give them shelter."

"How do you know this?" Halouse asked.

"Warad has told me," Calbrawn said, "Tamian will know what must happen."

"What will happen?" Halouse asked as he stopped.

Calbrawn did as well as he said, "The future my son is in your hands."

"How?" Halouse asked.

"Cloron, Hecorus and you are my descendants," Calbrawn told, "When the time comes you will know what we must do with our people."

Halouse watched his father walk away as Cloron and Hecorus caught up with him.

"We must meet with the others at once," Cloron told.

In a hut surrounded by hundreds more Cloron, Hecorus, Halouse, Salryn, Lyncade, Raven, Mayreon and the half breed known as Drayus all met.

"What should we do?" Lyncade asked.

"I'll take Hecorus and Halouse..." Cloron began.

"No," Halouse interrupted, "The three of us must split up."

"He's right," Hecorus agreed, "They don't know these parts."

"I'll take Lyncade and Raven," Cloron told.

"As well as me," Drayus told.

"What can she do?" Raven asked.

Drayus looked at him offended.

"She'll cover your ass better then most of your foot soldiers," Hecorus assured.

"Is that so?" Raven asked nodding his head, "What's your specialty?"

"A bow and arrow," Cloron told, "It will be needed."

"The Falmores will send search parties after us," Halouse knew, "Large ones at that."

"Who will I go with?" Mayreon asked.

They all looked at her in shock.

"My lady with all due respect you must stay," Cloron told, "You heard my father you are very important."

"Stay behind Mayreon," Lyncade commanded, "You will only make me worry if you go."

"So we have Lyncade, Raven, Drayus and Cloron on one?" Halouse asked.

"Yes," Cloron told, "Than you, Hecorus and Salryn."

"That's one man short of our party," Halouse reminded.

"We don't need anyone else," Hecorus assured, "We'll be fine."

"When do we leave?" Halouse asked.

"Gather your things," Cloron told, "We leave at nightfall."

"You know where the rubies are?" Lyncade asked.

"We will be guided by Talius," Cloron assured.

"We will be followed," Raven knew.

"The Falmores are not allowed to touch the rubies and neither can The Dark Lord, Greco or Korack," Cloron told.

"Once the rubies were placed where they were Warad made sure that only a soul of a pure heart could touch the rubies," Hecorus added.

"Once our hands remove the rubies from their rightful place the hands of others are able to take them," Halouse told.

"What makes Mayreon so important?" Lyncade asked.

"She will be able to tell The Dark Lord where the third ruby is," Hecorus told, "That is truly the only one he cares for because the third is his own."

"So the other two belong to Korack and Greco?" Lyncade asked.

Cloron nodded and said, "The Falmores will be waiting near the place of the rubies."

"Once you have it in your possession you will need to come here quickly," Hecorus told.

"Once one of them is retrieved by The Dark Lord he can easily take the others," Halouse added.

"It will be an all out attack when we return," Cloron knew.

"May Warad be with you all," Salryn told.

The parties all split knowing they wouldn't see each other again until their tasks were complete.

Hecorus was in his tent gathering his weapons that he'd need on his quest. As he readied his crossbow for his travels a form entered his tent. He looked to see Salryn already in armor and a cloak. A bow was behind her and her sword was in its case around her waist.

"You ready?" Salryn asked.

"As ready as I'll ever be," Hecorus told as he continued to get his other things.

"How much trouble do you think we'll run into?" Salryn asked.

"Hopefully a lot," Hecorus replied with a small smile.

"You're a glutton for warfare," Salryn told.

"I figured it was the best part of my personality," Hecorus replied.

Salryn walked up to him and tried to kiss him. Hecorus backed away and just looked at her.

"Have you told your father?" Hecorus asked.

"He wants me to settle with a Lycan," Salryn replied.

"So it would be alright if you settled with my brother but not me?" Hecorus asked, "We have the same blood."

"Halouse was welcomed into our clan by my father," Salryn reminded, "Calbrawn wanted you to stay with his."

"Then join mine," Hecorus replied.

"I am bond by my bloodline," Salryn told.

"So am I," Hecorus replied, "If you do not have the courage to tell your father your feelings for me then I must stop this affair before it gets too serious for the both of us."

"I've already fallen for you Hecorus," Salryn told.

"Then tell your father," Hecorus replied.

She grabbed his face and looked at him deeply as she replied, "If you complete this task then nothing will stop him from agreeing that we should be together. When we return with the ruby we will both tell him."

Hecorus looked down then back at his love as he asked, "You would do that?"

"I would do anything for you," Salryn told.

Hecorus reached forward and kissed her for several moments. The kisses began to get deeper as Hecorus drifted back on his bed. Salryn fell with him and they continued their embrace.

Halouse sat alone by the same stream he had once before. The darkness soon began to engulf the whole Valley. Nothing but the stars and bright moon gave light to the peaceful place Halouse had called a home. In the morning the women and children would march away and the thousands of warriors from every clan would prepare for the invasion that was almost certain. Halouse felt a presence in back of him but didn't have any idea who it was. Slowly looking back he saw the form of Lyncade. Halouse went to get up but Lyncade held out his hand.

"Do not rise on my occasion," Lyncade replied.

Halouse relaxed again trying to hold in his distain for Lyncade.

"It's almost time," Halouse replied.

"I am ready," Lyncade replied as he stood in back of Halouse.

"You will need to be," Halouse told.

"I've been in plenty of battles," Lyncade assured, "There is nothing on the quest that I haven't seen before."

"I'm sure," Halouse said uncaringly, "But you are traveling with my brother. I just want to make sure you know what you're up against so you don't slack and have him killed."

"He'll be fine with me," Lyncade assured.

"I noticed that when I saw your tracks, they were running away from orcs and goblins," Halouse replied.

Lyncade looked down at Halouse in anger as he put his hand to his sword.

"Pull that weapon," Halouse warned, "and I swear it will be the last time you go for it."

Lyncade just smiled impressed with Halouse's instincts.

"Must the two of us really fight over something this stupid when it is apparent what we really are fighting about?" Lyncade asked.

"I'm afraid I do not know what you mean," Halouse replied.

"Of course you do," Lyncade assured, "I see the way you look at her."

"Since when is it a law that I can't look at a beautiful woman?" Halouse asked.

"It is the intentions I see in your eyes that I worry about," Lyncade replied.

Halouse stood up and looked at Lyncade. The two stared at each other for several seconds as Halouse relaxed himself and looked down.

"My feelings for her will never be acted on," Halouse assured, "I will never disrespect your people for what you will ultimately do for mine. I give you my word as a Lycan and the word of the Native Elves that I will never go to her in that way. I will stand next to you and die with you if I must. I will protect Mayreon if I must die doing it. Her purpose is more important then ours right now. She is the key to The Dark Lord. She will tell him where the rubies are and we must protect her from him. Let us as men put our differences aside for now. I will never fight you for her. What she has told me about you, I look at you with nothing but the highest respect. You are by all means a king in the eyes of your people and a valiant warrior. I apologies for my insult to you earlier. I saw the amount of orcs and goblins your men killed."

Lyncade looked at Halouse with surprise for what he had said. Lyncade just nodded as he held out his hand. This time Halouse looked at him as they shook forearm to forearm.

"May Warad be with you on your quest," Halouse replied.

"Also with you," Lyncade said.

Each party set out. As the seven stood next to each other as they exited the cave they all spread out quickly. Each party quickly rushing to where they needed to go. The night would be their sanctuary to their trackless quest. With the night pitch and their tracks silent they couldn't be seen leaving the entrance to the valley. With no words said for several hours each member of the party followed the other without breaking stride.

Cloron didn't care for the whereabouts of those behind him. With a reckless pace he scaled rocky terrain and ran through trails as if knowing what was ahead of him before his eyes could see it. Lyncade, Raven and Drayus were quickly behind doing what their leader did. At times side by side they never let their journey end. No time for rest knowing time would be of the essence.

Hecorus, Halouse and Salryn did the same as they traveled to the opposite end of Cavell territory. Not knowing where the ruby was it seemed Warad himself was guiding them to their destination. Hecorus would stop every now and again to get a sense of where he was. Halouse and Salryn would stop never saying a word as Hecorus caught a feeling and went with it.

Soon the sun came as each party traveled on knowing they could be tracked easier in the daylight. War parties were scattered all across the Cavell territory and almost awaited any small party of Natives. The Dark Lord, Korack and Greco knew what they were searching for.

Back at the Falmore camp Artwore stood outside his tent as his army was camped very restless. All who were scattered across their camp site looked to him awaiting his command. He was only dressed in a robe showing off his naked chest. A small sash wrapped around his waist as he tied his long black hair back.

"My lord what are our commands?" A captain asked.

"We must await The Dark Lord's orders," Artwore told, "Only he can command us."

"What ever elves lie ahead they will surly be dealt with by us," The captain assured.

"Our men are fierce," Artwore agreed, "but The Dark Lord has eyes that see farther then ours. We must trust his patience."

"The more time we kill the closer they get to preparing for our forces," The Captain reminded.

"Patience," Sangrayus replied exiting the same tent, "Do not disrespect your king."

"My lady," The captain replied bowing his head, "I assure that my concern is only for the victory of our people and not the questioning of my king."

"You will make a great general for my forces one day," Artwore told, "But victory will be ours, and I will personal damage the morale of these Natives as well as Tamian's army."

"Some say Calbrawn can not be killed," The captain reminded.

"You leave myths and prophecies to me captain," Artwore replied, "For I will be the one to prove them wrong."

"Yes my lord," The captain replied as he rode off on his horse.

Sangrayus leaned on her son's shoulder and looked at him. Staring ahead he did seem to be a little frustrated by the patience of The Dark Lord himself.

"Don't worry my son," Sangrayus replied, "One day you will have all the world. It is I that hold the key."

"I await the day," Artwore told.

Chapter 13

The Valley of Talius was home to only one temple of Warad. In a wide open stone floor Mayreon approached the Native Elves version of the statue of Warad. Standing about fifty feet in the air she walked slowly. The blue ruby given to her wrapped around her head as her blonde curly hair flew freely in back of her. Her white gown sparkled with the glitter that was placed all around it. She kneeled slowly in front of Warad and looked up at him with begging eyes. Tears filling in her captivating glance as she could barely contain her sin.

"Warad," Mayreon called, "God of all things evil and good. I beg of you to help me with this burden I carry every moment of the day. The longing and lust to another that has saved me from certain death many times. For the man I am married to I also love and owe my entire existence to. I can not help but feel love for both of them and I beg of you to help me let go of the way I feel for Halouse.

"He is indeed one of the greatest men I will ever meet in my life. For now though my heart should only belong to Lyncade. Why have you cursed me with such a feeling for two men? Both of which are humble and honorable. If I could have had it my way I would have died the time Halouse, Cloron and Hecorus saved me. For the way I feel for Halouse eats at my soul and is tarring me apart."

Mayreon's eyes could no longer contain the tears built up as they began to pore from her eyes. She looked up to the statue in frustration.

"Why do you not call to me?" Mayreon asked, "Why do you not speak to me as my god and help me when I am in need of your guidance. Just please tell me whether or not you hear me."

"He hears you," A voice called.

Mayreon turned her head to her right still on her knees as Sygon emerged. In shock she slowly rose and looked at her master.

"How is it that you are here?" Mayreon asked in disbelief.

"I can go where ever I want," Sygon told, "With just a simple word I can go as far as the grasp of Warad himself. What ever his eyes see in time you will be able to travel in a matter of moments. And I can certainly go to the call of my greatest student. Your pain I can feel for miles away."

Mayreon's face went red as an uncontrollable gloom came over her. She paced herself as she let the tears out. Finally able to look at her master she stared with longing eyes hoping he could give her answers.

"Why does he not speak to me himself?" Mayreon asked.

"You asked for a sign," Sygon reminded, "I am that sign. He too cries for you and bares the same pain."

"Why do I feel as if I'm going through it alone?" Mayreon asked.

"You're not," Sygon assured.

"Help me," Mayreon begged, "The pain I have can barely be contained and I cannot go on like this."

"Everything has its purpose," Sygon assured.

"Becoming a whore?" Mayreon asked.

"What do you mean?" Sygon asked.

"Marrying Lyncade because I did love him," Mayreon told, "Being seduced by a king I saw as a friend but truly he only used deception to take advantage of me. Falling for another man even though Lyncade has never done anything to me to change my feelings for him."

"You are not what you claim to be," Sygon told, "Your feelings for both Lyncade and Halouse are pure and you haven't fallen subject to something that many other women haven't when in the presence of Tamian. He is blessed by Warad but his future is cursed for all that he has done in his life. His sin to you will only be another sin he needs to answer to once he reaches the afterlife."

"I carry his child," Mayreon yelled in anger.

Sygon searched the soul of Mayreon as he replied, "You must never tell Lyncade. If he finds out he will have you killed."

"How can I carry such a burden for the rest of my life?" Mayreon asked.

"The pain you have now will only be armor in future times," Sygon told, "You are a strong girl. You will be something this world has never seen and when you become of your prime these trivial pains will only be a distant memory."

Mayreon looked down in pain absorbing the things Sygon had told her.

"What can I do with these feelings I have for Halouse?" Mayreon asked.

"Burry them," Sygon told, "You will do what you will. Warad blessed you with the ability to choose. He must never be told the way you feel and you can never act on it."

Mayreon nodded as she looked at her master.

"This world of royalty is filled with more pain then it was when you were a slave isn't it?" Sygon asked with a small smile.

"I'd rather be in the temple scrubbing the floor," Mayreon replied some how smiling back.

Sygon came forward and hugged her as she wrapped her arms around him tightly.

"I feel so selfish," Mayreon said, "Crying to Warad about my unfaithful feelings when hundreds have died in the past week and hundreds more will be dieing in the days to come."

"Pray that those who are valiant enough make it home safely and all those with evil in their hearts find the afterlife before they are able to act on them," Sygon replied.

"Thank you master," Mayreon said still in his arms.

"I will always be there for my student," Sygon told, "Especially one that is as important as you are."

"One day when I'm not in such a state I will ask you about this purpose of mine," Mayreon replied.

"Another day," Sygon replied, "Another day indeed."

Miles away the party of Halouse, Hecorus and Salryn continued their journey as they scaled the steepest cliff and made it to the top. Never breaking stride Hecorus went down a large hill as the leafs of the forest fell around him. Crossing the great trail in record pace the three were closing in on their destination. As Hecorus was moments away from the mountain he was seeking he stopped suddenly and began to feel the world around him.

Halouse and Salryn running for several hours stopped in back of Hecorus and felt the world as well. Not tired at all they stood there silent and wondering what disturbance had stopped them.

"You feel that?" Hecorus asked.

Halouse and Salryn began to pull their weapons and put their bows in position to where they could reach them when they needed. Halouse pulled out two daggers and kept them at his side.

"How many?" Salryn asked.

"Enough for all of us," Hecorus assured with a smile.

"Salryn," Halouse called.

Salryn turned to see Halouse's sack of arrows getting tossed toward her. She quickly swung it around her back as she now had two full cases. Hecorus pulled out his crossbow as he quickly began to sprint toward their destination.

As Hecorus emerged from a hill several ranks of Falmores awaited. Hecorus fired over and over with his barreled crossbow. Each arrow hitting its mark as it retracted and quickly reloaded another.

As Salryn got to the top of the hill she quickly aimed with her bow and began to fire over and over. With incredible quickness and accuracy each target was hit between the eyes and fell dead. Any Falmore that began to come at her fell quickly with her arrow fired at a remarkable pace.

Halouse engaged with each Falmore as he dodged their swipe and quickly countered with his dagger stabbing his opponent in the throat or slicing their neck. As more engaged he was forced to throw his dagger at a Falmore and quickly pulled his sword just in time blocking a Falmores strike. Taking on as many as he could he stood his ground swiping away and killing any Falmores that came within the range of his sword.

Hecorus tossed his crossbow to his back as he began to scale the small mountain cliffs. Falmores seemed to come from no where as he pulled his sword and quickly pushed them away as they fell off the cliff. He either killed them quickly or struck their blades so hard they were forced to lose their balance and fall from the thin cliff trail.

Halouse awaited Salryn as he fought off Falmores allowing her to get to the trail without having to engage with the Falmore warriors Halouse held back. Halouse then began to follow behind as dozens of arrows flew over his head barely missing him. As he began to run on the cliff an arrow missing him flew forward and hit a Falmore in the neck in front of him. Halouse just pushed him out of the way as they began to turn a corner away from the Falmore ranks.

They all came to a small cave on the cliff as Hecorus hesitated.

"What are you waiting for?" Salryn asked as she caught up with him.

"Once we touch the ruby they will send their entire force," Hecorus reminded.

Halouse finally came around the bend as he replied, "There are none in back of me."

"They're waiting," Hecorus assured.

"We must find an alternate route," Halouse suggested.

"Can you two find one while I retrieve the ruby?" Hecorus asked.

"It shouldn't be hard," Salryn replied.

"But if the two of us are looking for a route you'll be all alone," Halouse reminded.

"I'll be fine," Hecorus assured with a small smirk.

Halouse and Salryn quickly began to press forward hoping to find a way out of where they were without traveling back to where the Falmores were.

Miles away Lyncade, Raven, Cloron and Drayus were walking through a dark forest as they began to look at the trees around them. Each of them was prepared for what ever was ahead of them. Taking their time walking down the trail Cloron and the others knew they weren't alone.

"The forests have eyes," Raven told.

"What are they waiting for?" Drayus asked.

"The right time to strike," Lyncade knew.

"They're waiting for us to fall into they're trap," Cloron said.

"How close are we?" Lyncade asked as he moved forward slowly.

"Only a few hundred yards," Cloron knew.

A Falmores jumped from the forest and into the trail in front of them. A second went by as an arrow from Drayus landed in the chest of the Falmore. Lyncade watched as a second emerged and fired an arrow toward him. Drayus fired one of her own that connected with the arrow in midair and stopped its path. Drayus reloaded and fired again in a matter of a second. The arrow hit the Falmore right in the head as he fell dead.

Lyncade looked over at Drayus in amazement.

"Told you she'd watch your back," Cloron replied.

"Not bad," Lyncade replied to Drayus.

"Next time I'll let him hit you," Drayus replied to his selfish remark.

Out from the sides of them dozens of Falmores began to attack.

"It's an ambush," Cloron yelled.

"Go to the ruby we'll handle them," Lyncade yelled.

Cloron looked back for only a second as he began to sprint forward.

Lyncade and Raven stood back to back as Drayus soon joined them firing arrow after arrow. Lyncade got his blade caught up with a Falmores as he sensed an arrow flying toward him. With his freehand he grasped it in the air and slammed it into the neck of the Falmore he was tied up with. A second later he pulled a dagger and tossed it underhand toward the Falmore that had fired the arrow. He hit his mark as he continued to fight several more that came his way. Drayus fired so many times with her bow that she soon ran out of arrows.

"Raven," Drayus yelled as she began to run toward a dead Falmore.

Raven went away from Lyncade as he began to kill Falmores charging toward Drayus. As she reached two sacks of arrows from fallen Falmores she quickly tossed them to her back and made her way back toward Lyncade as she fired. Raven backed off as well going back to his general. Before he reached an arrow hit him hard in the right breast. Yelling in pain he watched as Drayus killed the archer quickly.

"Forgive me," Drayus replied as she pulled the arrow from his chest and fired it at a Falmore charging toward them.

"Move forward," Lyncade yelled, "We must protect Cloron."

The three sprinted as quickly as they could as the Falmore forces began to follow not far behind.

Cloron ran into little resistance as he reached an old broken down temple. Dozens of pillars stood holding nothing as the remains of the temple were all over the ground. Cloron ran onto the entrance of the temple as Falmores came from the sides and tried to ambush him. The well experienced hunter was quick to react as he killed them quickly and pressed forward. A Falmore came from his blind side and sliced at him but the Falmore got nothing but air. Quickly he grabbed the hand of the Falmore and killed him instantly with the Falmores own sword. Cloron ripped the blade out of the Falmores hand. Spinning both blades in his hands he watched as five Falmores stood ready in front of him.

A sixth Falmore stood in the distance and loaded and arrow as he fired at Cloron. Cloron knocked the arrow out of midair as he engaged with the five warriors in front of him. Using his surroundings he ducked between the ruins of the temple and quickly stabbed at his opponents killing them instantly as his sense of surroundings was too much for the Falmores. As he beheaded the last warrior with one hand he tossed the blade of the Falmore he had killed earlier and watched it land in the chest of the Falmore Archer.

Cloron then felt an arrow land in his shoulder blade as he drifted back quickly. As he turned he watched the archer load another arrow. Before he could fire a blade beheaded the archer as he saw Lyncade running toward him.

"Cloron," Lyncade yelled.

Cloron turned to see a blade flying toward him. Wounded slightly he was able to pick his blade up in time and block. The Falmore used so much power it made Cloron fall back and hit the temple ground face first. Lyncade reached him before the Falmore could kill Cloron as Lyncade killed him quickly. Raven and Drayus soon ran to them as dozens of Falmores followed them. Drayus went to Cloron and pulled the arrow from his back as she aimed and fired at a Falmore coming at her.

"Forgive me," Drayus begged as she watched the arrow hit her target.

Drayus sensed something in the air as she reached her hand up and snatched an arrow before it could fly passed her. She aimed it on her bow and hit another Falmore only a couple feet from her.

Raven then charged the Falmores with Lyncade by his side as they were heavily outnumbered. Cloron was quick to his feet as he pulled his crossbow from behind his back and fired over and over as the barrel reloaded the next arrow.

Stuck picking up arrows from the ground or arrows from fallen victims earlier, Drayus spent little time resting as she fired every arrow she had in a matter of seconds. Only two Falmores remand as Lyncade and Raven quickly killed them.

The two Royal Elf Warriors dropped to their knees in fatigue. Cloron tried to lift his arm as he winced in pain from his arrow wound. Drayus didn't rest as she began to get together as many arrows as she could and place them in her sack.

Cloron walked to the middle of the temple as a table sat empty and filled with the words of the gods. Unable to read them in fear of what it might do he looked all around and saw several large ruins in the middle of the table.

"What are you reading?" Lyncade asked.

"I'm reading nothing in fear of what might happen to me," Cloron informed, "These are the words of the gods."

"So what must we do?" Lyncade asked as he approached.

Raven did as well as Drayus looked to the path to make sure no one was coming.

"What ever it is it better be soon," Drayus warned.

Cloron, Lyncade and Raven all turned to see hundreds of Falmores running their way.

"I don't know about the rest of you but I don't think we can handle anymore," Raven told.

"I agree," Cloron replied as he looked back at the table.

"What do you have to do?" Lyncade asked.

"Press down on one of these ruins and a passage opens," Cloron told.

"You don't remember which one?" Lyncade asked.

"It's the mark of Talius but I can't remember which one it is," Cloron told.

"She's goddess of beauty," Drayus reminded as she looked at the charging Falmores hundreds of feet away.

"At this point I'm ready to guess," Cloron told as he searched the bored.

"Watch out," Lyncade replied as he pulled his sword.

"What are you doing?" Cloron asked.

"I'll close my eyes and strike the table," Lyncade told, "Which ever ruin it hits that'll be the one we chose."

"Have you gone mad?" Cloron asked, "You strike the wrong ruin and you'll kill us all. To the fires of hell we will be cast that's the punishment for the wrong ruin."

"We have no other choice. May Warad guide my sword," Lyncade replied as he closed his eyes and swung down.

He struck one of the ruins in the middle as they all backed off. Drayus saw the Falmores get in her range as she took aim with her bow. They all heard the sound of the table moving as Cloron looked at Lyncade.

"Lucky shot," Cloron replied in relief.

"Don't ever do that again," Raven replied.

Cloron was the first to run down the hole as he was quickly followed by Lyncade.

"Drayus," Raven called.

The half breed turned and just as she ran to the hole was struck in the back with an arrow. The arrow came out just above her breast as she collapsed forward. Raven caught her as he dragged her in the hole. Seconds from reaching them the table was close as the Falmores yelled in anger.

Cloron and Lyncade picked up a torch hung on the wall as they began to walk through the passage. Raven wasn't far behind as he carried Drayus in his arms.

"What happened?" Cloron asked as he saw them.

"I got careless," Drayus told.

"Move forward," Lyncade told, "Who knows how long it will take until they open that door."

"I'm fine," Drayus told as she cringed in pain.

They walked for what seemed like miles before they reach an open room. No light was visible but there was none needed as the red light of the ruby lit up the room. Dozens of skeletons laid in front of the ruby as Lyncade searched the ground with his torch.

"Whose are these?" Lyncade asked.

"Fallen warriors who didn't have a pure heart to touch the rubies," Cloron told, "That is its other curse."

"Then who will take it?" Raven asked.

Lyncade and Cloron looked at each other.

"I am no saint," Lyncade told.

"Neither am I," Cloron told.

The two of them looked at Raven.

"My sins haven't been forgiven," Raven told, "Matter of fact if I get out of this alive that's what I'll ask Warad for."

"Drayus," Cloron called.

Drayus motioned for Raven to let her down as he did slowly. Drayus walked toward the ruby as she reached with both her hands. It took several moments but her hands touched the ruby and nothing happened.

"Here," Cloron called as he handed her a blanket, "Wrap it in that."

Once Drayus touched the ruby it stopped shinning. She wrapped it in the blanket and handed it to Cloron. Cloron yelled in fear but nothing happened.

"What is your problem?" Lyncade asked.

"It stops its curse once someone of a pure heart touches it remember?" Drayus asked.

"I forgot," Cloron replied.

The sounds of voices were heard from the passage they came from.

"Falmores," Raven warned.

"There is no way out," Cloron replied.

Lyncade looked at him in anger as he asked, "What?"

"The passage in is the only exit," Cloron told.

"That information would have been useful when we got in," Lyncade yelled, "Now how the hell are we going to leave here in one piece?"

"Gentlemen I suggest you save the fighting for another time," Raven replied, "We'll have company very soon."

In frustration, Lyncade leaned against the wall as his elbow hit a brick. All of a sudden a passage in the wall opened. Cloron and the others just looked at him in amazement.

"First the stone on the table and now this," Raven replied, "You're on a roll."

The four wasted no time as Lyncade took his torch and lit the way. Every time they seemed to gain ground they began to hear the Falmores behind them catching up.

"Where are we?" Lyncade asked.

"Inside the mountain," Cloron yelled, "Or below it, one or the other."

As they traveled they started to go up hill beginning to hear the sound of waves in front of them. Not long after Lyncade began to she light at the end of the tunnel as he rushed toward it. Just as he came to the exit he quickly stopped as he realized he was high in the air hundreds of feet over a river. The torch in his hand fell as he almost went over himself. Cloron quickly grabbed him before he could go over completely.

"Now what?" Lyncade asked.

"Can you swim?" Cloron asked as he dove below.

Raven held Drayus in his arms as he looked at Lyncade and said, "You've got to be kidding."

Lyncade quickly jumped as Raven heard the Falmores behind him.

"Forgive me my lady," Raven replied as he tossed her forward toward the river below.

Raven jumped as he fell slowly toward the raging water. As he drifted he caught up with Drayus and pulled her toward him. Gasping for breath as they floated down stream Raven had his free hand out as it was quickly grabbed. On a rock by the shore Cloron and Lyncade grabbed their companion and pulled him in as Raven held on tightly to Drayus.

Gasping for breath Drayus yelled, "I lost my bow."

"Mine too," Cloron told.

"We only have close range weapons," Raven yelled over the high sound of the raging water.

"We must move quickly then," Lyncade commanded, "If they know where we are we are done for."

The four quickly ran across the bank as Cloron took the lead knowing exactly where they were.

"We're not far," Cloron yelled.

"They're not either," Raven replied as he continued to carry the wounded Drayus.

"Put me down," Drayus commanded, "I can't let you die if you're carrying me to safety."

"My lady..." Raven began.

"Put me down," Drayus replied looking at him.

Raven did as he went to his waist and pulled out a small sword.

"Take this," Raven replied as he handed it to her, "Just in case."

"I don't know how to use one," Drayus told.

"Hit your enemy with the sharp end before he can hit you," Raven replied, "That's the only lesson we have time for."

"Would you two hurry," Lyncade demanded.

"I wonder how the others are doing," Cloron replied.

Hecorus walked through the dark cave using his perfect vision to get through it as the vibrations from his steps seemed to help him see what was ahead of him. Soon though he began to see a red light not far from him. Moments later on a shrine was the ruby he was searching for. He walked up to it and read what it said on the shrine.

"Only one who is pure at heart can remove the ruby from its place," Hecorus read to himself.

Moments later Hecorus exited the cave just as Halouse and Salryn came to him.

"We have a problem," Hecorus told.

The three stood in front of the shrine and read the inscription.

"What about you Salryn?" Halouse asked.

"I betrayed my family," Salryn told.

"How?" Halouse asked.

Salryn looked at Hecorus as he returned her glance.

"You two?" Halouse asked in disbelief.

"Sorry brother," Hecorus replied.

"What about you Halouse?" Salryn asked.

"He lusts for another man's wife," Hecorus told.

"Mayreon?" Salryn asked.

"I would have figured it was obvious by now," Hecorus told.

217

"Never mind that," Halouse said angrily, "What are we going to do?"

"We have to leave it here," Hecorus informed.

"And tell Calbrawn what?" Halouse asked.

"He should have informed us of the rules," Salryn told.

"Besides The Dark Lord cannot touch it and neither can any of his forces," Hecorus reminded.

"I've never failed a task," Halouse told.

"Then you go for it," Hecorus dared, "Pure of heart? Only Warad knows."

Halouse placed his sword away as Hecorus looked at him in disbelief.

"What are you doing?" Hecorus asked.

"You're right brother," Halouse replied, "Only Warad knows."

"Halouse I was joking," Hecorus assured, "You will surly die for lusting after another man's wife trying to grab the ruby."

"Have faith," Halouse replied.

Halouse slowly placed his hands near the ruby as he stopped himself several times from grabbing it.

"It really makes you question yourself doesn't it?" Salryn asked.

"Please be quiet," Halouse begged, "These could be my final moments."

Halouse closed his eyes and touched the ruby. He stood still for several seconds until he realized that he was still alive. He picked up the ruby as it stopped glowing.

"Lusting after another man's wife and Warad lets you live," Hecorus complained.

"It's not lust brother," Halouse assured, "It's completely pure."

Halouse wrapped the ruby in a blanket and strapped it to his back as they all exited the cave. Reading each others minds they all began to rush up the mountain hoping to find an alternate trail back home. They all knew that the Valley was far away and they would have to undergo more war parties in the near future.

Chapter 14

The village soon came alive with cheer as Cloron entered the Valley. With the others behind him Raven was still caring Drayus as he let her down.

"I figured Royal Elf men to be lazy," Drayus replied.

"I'd do it again if I had to," Raven informed.

"I'll keep that in mind," Drayus replied in a flirtatious tone.

Mayreon emerged from one of the hills and watched as Lyncade entered. With a large smile on his face he drifted toward his wife and hugged her as she came to him. Cloron watched as the two embraced. As he saw Mayreon's face as her head rested on Lyncade's shoulder; he noticed a face of disappointment. Lyncade looked at his wife as she quickly changed her feelings to a smile.

"I tire," Lyncade told, "Will you join me as I rest?"

"Of course," Mayreon said.

Cloron stood at the entrance as he looked to one of the warriors standing guard.

"Any word?" Cloron asked.

"None," The warrior told.

"If they do not make it by nightfall we search," Cloron replied.

Calbrawn sat silently on his chair in his fort as he heard footsteps. As Drayus entered he quickly looked over. She smiled gently at her adopted father as she rubbed her wound.

"What happened?" Calbrawn asked.

"Just a scratch," Drayus assured, "I got it wrapped up."

"Do you have it?" Calbrawn asked.

Drayus pulled the sack from around her back and unwrapped the ruby as she handed it to Calbrawn. He held it in his hands as he gazed at it for several moments.

"I haven't seen this for ages," Calbrawn told.

"It wasn't an easy task," Drayus assured.

"I'm sure it wasn't," Calbrawn told, "Are you the first ones back?"

"Yes," Drayus told, "The others shouldn't be long behind."

Calbrawn looked at Drayus and asked, "Who took it from its place?"

"She did," Cloron informed as he entered.

"Where is Lyncade and Raven?" Calbrawn asked.

"Resting," Cloron told.

"I guess most of us will need rest as well," Calbrawn knew, "The invasion isn't far away."

"Father I recommend a search for Halouse and them if they aren't here by nightfall," Cloron told.

Calbrawn looked up at his son and nodded.

"What is our next mission?" Drayus asked as she sat across from Calbrawn.

"These rubies must be placed into hands that are safe," Calbrawn told, "I know just the place."

Mayreon and Lyncade rested near a small waterfall away from the huts inside the Valley. Next to them was the large mountain protecting the Valley from being seen by the outside. Mayreon just stroked her hand through the water as Lyncade laid in front of her facing her.

"Did you miss me?" Lyncade asked.

Mayreon looked at him with a smile and replied, "I can't hide anything from you can I?"

Lyncade kissed her softly then asked, "Are you hiding something?"

Mayreon looked at him for a few moments and asked, "Like what?"

"You seem like a girl with a secret," Lyncade told.

"It's nothing," Mayreon assured as she looked at the water, "I just have a great amount on my mind."

"Like what?" Lyncade asked.

"What will happen," Mayreon told, "How many will die and knowing that one of those reasons is because of me."

"How can you say that?" Lyncade asked.

"Have you heard Calbrawn?" Mayreon asked, "Talking about how I am the key to the rubies."

"I will not let them harm you," Lyncade assured.

"I know you mean that and you truly believe it Lyncade," Mayreon replied, "It's just that this is The Dark Lord. The creature and evil god that haunts our nightmares and swears death to all of Warad's creatures. How is it that I am in connection with him, Korack and Greco?"

"Our purpose sometimes is never understood," Lyncade told.

Mayreon looked down for a moment and said, "Do you know lately I've been wishing you never found me."

Lyncade just looked at her and asked, "Why?"

Mayreon looked back and said, "If something were to ever happen to you because of me I don't know what I'll do. Because of some purpose I had in connection with The Dark Lord."

"I will never regret ever finding you even if this war means I'll die," Lyncade told.

"Don't say that," Mayreon begged, "My heart screams even thinking about you hurt."

"Nothing will happen to me while I'll love you," Lyncade assured, "Warad wanted me to find you and why do that if he was just going to tar me away from you?"

"Sometimes that's just how life works," Mayreon told.

"Not in our case," Lyncade replied, "I will never leave your side in a thousands lifetimes."

Mayreon just looked at the water again as she smiled gentle.

"What?" Lyncade asked.

Mayreon looked at him and replied, "I'm pregnant."

Lyncade with a face of shock took a little while before he smiled at her.

"How long?" Lyncade asked.

"Our wedding night," Mayreon replied.

"What do you feel?" Lyncade asked.

"A boy," Mayreon said.

"Really?" Lyncade asked as he ran his fingers through her hair.

"Call it a feeling," Mayreon replied as she looked at him shyly then away.

Lyncade reached forward and kissed her gently. Never wanting to stop he kissed her several more times before looking at her.

"You are my life," Lyncade told, "And now more then ever I will never die without making sure I see him."

Mayreon kissed him at the statement as she broke and stared into his eyes.

"Have you thought of any names?" Lyncade asked.

Mayreon looked down as if thinking then said, "Nabian."

"Nabian?" Lyncade asked thinking about it, "Why that?"

"Sounds fierce and brave," Mayreon replied, "It's the only great name I could think of for a future warrior of our people besides Lyncade."

Lyncade smiled and replied, "I like it."

"You better have because I had my heart set on it," Mayreon told.

Lyncade kind of laughed and replied, "I'll never forget this moment in this place."

"What do you mean?" Mayreon asked.

"Being the only time we'll ever be here I will always remember it as the place you told me you were pregnant," Lyncade told.

"What do you mean last time?" Mayreon asked.

"Once we have these rubies and defeat the Falmores we are going home," Lyncade replied, "I thought you knew that?"

"But never coming here again?" Mayreon asked.

"These people are not like us," Lyncade told, "They believe in different things then we do."

"Tamian promised them by me coming here that they had his allegiance," Mayreon reminded.

"And they do," Lyncade assured, "But you will never be here again."

"I like it here," Mayreon told.

"It's not your home," Lyncade reminded, "After what almost happened to you I will never want you to leave the city again."

"How can you do that?" Mayreon asked as she rose.

"Mayreon it's always been the way," Lyncade told as he slowly got up, "Drizell has never left the city since she married Tamian. Kings and generals go to war not queens. After this I will not let you leave the city unless I'm beside you."

Mayreon looked around upset at his statement as he looked at her confused by her anger.

"I thought you knew that?" Lyncade asked.

Mayreon stood there as she rubbed her head with her hand and replied, "You're right. I just never wanted to accept it I guess."

"Besides once you're back in the city you'll be rained with gifts by me and the nobles just to kiss my ass," Lyncade replied as he wrapped his arms around her, "Besides what do you have here?"

Mayreon looked at him and said, "Friends."

"Hecorus, Halouse and Cloron?" Lyncade asked, "You'll forget about them before you know it."

"They saved my life Lyncade I will never forget them," Mayreon told, "Besides what they have done for me in something that no one in this lifetime besides you will do. Halouse nearly died trying to save me when we were looking for you."

"Halouse," Lyncade complained as he broke from her and turned away.

"What?" Mayreon asked.

Lyncade looked at her for a moment and asked, "If I ask you something will you tell me the truth?"

"Of course," Mayreon said with no hesitation.

"Do you care for him?" Lyncade asked.

"Yes," Mayreon admitted, "But nothing that will ever go passed my friendship with him."

"You are aware of the way he feels about you?" Lyncade asked.

"Yes," Mayreon said, "He's admitted several times."

"And yet you wish to see him again after all this?" Lyncade asked, "What am I suppose to think?"

"If there was something to hide why admit to what he said?" Mayreon asked, "Look at me."

Lyncade did.

"Nothing has ever happened between Halouse and I," Mayreon told.

Lyncade just nodded as he reach his hand out, "Come here."

Mayreon went to him as he kissed her gently on the forehead.

"I am only angry because I was blessed with a beautiful wife that will without a doubt have many admirers," Lyncade replied.

"I told you what my feelings were for you," Mayreon informed, "And if it makes a difference we will never be here again like you said. So Halouse and I will never see each other."

Lyncade nodded as Mayreon and him kissed gently.

Hecorus, Halouse and Salryn walked toward the rock that hid the cave to the Valley. With the night finally falling, the reflection of the moon on the water acted as the only light the party had. After running into several more war parties they were tired of fighting and filled with slash marks all over their arms. Carrying the ruby on his back Halouse watched as Hecorus and Salryn entered the cave. Halouse slowly entered and placed the rock in front of the secret passage.

Moments later a Falmore form walked out to the small river and looked at the rock. The face of Artwore was soon seen as the moonlight entered his face. Sangrayus stood next to him as they both had a small smile on their face. A black mist soon formed as Korack stood next to them as well.

"When do we attack?" Artwore asked.

"You don't," Korack told.

"What?" Sangrayus asked in anger.

"Only Mayreon is important," Korack replied, "Once we get her it won't matter where they hide the rubies. We'll choke it out of her if we must."

"So what do you command?" Artwore asked.

"Go in at night and get her," Korack commanded.

"What about our war?" Sangrayus asked.

Korack looked at her with a smile and replied, "Trust me sorceress. There will be blood."

"I'll go back to the camp and have our forces prepare to go home," Artwore told Sangrayus, "When I give them the command I will stay with only fifty or so men and wait for you."

"Of course my lord," Sangrayus told, "Give us a few hours to get to the top of this mountain."

"Hurry," Korack told, "By the time you reach the top it will only be a half hour or so before the sun rises."

The Valley began to roar as the second party returned just before Cloron was going to send a party to find them. Cloron laughed as he approached both his brothers and greeted them with a hug. Halouse looked all around before he saw Mayreon standing on a small hill in the distance. As far away as she was he felt the warmth of the smile that came across her face. Many warriors began to surround Halouse as they celebrated with him. As he pushed them out of his way he looked to the hill and saw that she was gone.

"Halouse," Cloron called from all the cheering, "The council waits."

Cloron and Hecorus walked up the stairs to the floor of the councilmen. Calbrawn was the only one standing as the ruby Cloron gave him was held in his hand and resting against his body. Halouse took the sack from behind his back and unwrapped the second. He slowly approached his father as he handed it to him. Calbrawn took the second ruby with his freehand and rest it against his body like he did the first.

"Your deed has only one reward," Calbrawn told, "But before I tell you what that is I must ask which one of you removed the ruby from its place?"

Halouse looked down for a moment then looked at his father and replied, "I did."

Calbrawn smiled a bit as he replied, "Then let me be the first to welcome the three of you to the council of the Natives."

Calbrawn held out his hand as three empty seats stood across from him.

"Are you serious?" Halouse asked in disbelief.

"You have earned your place," A councilman told.

The three brothers approached as they turned and sat slowly across from their father. Next to them many members of the council smiled proudly. Calbrawn took his seat as well as all one hundred and three of the council opened the floor.

"Our next task it to retrieve the third from the sorceress Sangrayus," Calbrawn replied.

"How will we do that?" Cloron asked.

"When they invade the Valley," Calbrawn said, "We must go after her at once."

"But she is the most powerful sorceress in all the world," A councilman reminded.

"Warad will not let us fail," Calbrawn assured, "We must prepare for war at once."

The city was alive again with action as all the warriors of every clan began to gather their things. All the women and children were placed on the far end of the Valley where there was no entrance or exit. If the Falmores attacked they'd need to pass the thousands of warriors in the Valley to reach them. The huts were now used as a stay for the warriors as they rested. Those who were awake would sleep when their sift was over. Each warrior lay in his hut with his weapon close to his side just in case the sound of the war horn echoed throughout the Valley.

At the far end of the Valley inside his chambers, Calbrawn met with Cloron, Hecorus, Halouse, Lyncade, Salryn, Drayus, Raven and Mayreon. They all stood around the eldest elf in the world as Drayus placed a robe around him.

"Cloron, Hecorus and Halouse you all must rest," Calbrawn told, "For tomorrow night you will watch with your ranks just in case the Falmores attack."

"Of course father," Cloron knew.

"Lyncade and Raven," Calbrawn called, "I am not your king so I can not give you commands…"

"We are yours to serve," Lyncade replied interrupting.

"If that is so then you can watch tonight," Calbrawn informed, "Lyncade tonight and Raven tomorrow night. With you two in the field you may be able to help our warriors with tactics."

"Well if I can make a suggestion now," Lyncade replied.

"Go ahead," Calbrawn assured.

"I do not think it wise to leave the back end of the Valley completely defenseless," Lyncade began, "Couldn't they somehow get in?"

"No," Calbrawn told, "There is no way in the Valley from the back end. You'd have the climb the mountains and it would be far too much for an army of warriors. They'd freeze to death or lose most of their force if they ever tried."

"Of course," Lyncade replied, "Just something I wanted to put on the table."

"Good to know you are thinking about our weakest points," Calbrawn told, "But I assure that no army will come in that way."

"If that cave is the only way in why would they attack?" Raven asked, "They'd be slaughtered the moment they entered. It's too slim and they could never overrun us with that small of an entrance."

"That will be our advantage," Calbrawn knew, "They will stop at nothing to get the rubies as well as Mayreon."

"Where will I be?" Mayreon asked.

"Where you are now," Calbrawn told, "Make sure you do not go where the army has set up. Stay away from the confrontation once it starts."

"Our forces will wipe them from the earth," Cloron assured.

"Enough talking," Calbrawn replied, "They will attack soon."

They all left quickly as Lyncade went toward the front of the Valley to keep watch. Halouse watched as Mayreon walked away to her hut located as far back as possible. He walked away from the huts and planned to stay up trying to clear his head.

Hecorus walked to his tent and kept his eyes on Salryn. She smiled gently as Hecorus entered his hut. Looking around for several seconds Salryn ran to his hut making sure no one could see her. He quickly greeted her as she entered kissing him deeply. Salryn was quick to remove her weapons from around her waist as she kissed Hecorus. Hecorus tossed his weapons away recklessly as he began to untie her armor. Moments later the lovers went to the bed as Hecorus blew the candles out in his hut.

Cloron was half asleep in his bed as his adopted sister laid in a bed across the hut. She was awake sitting up changing the cloth on her arrow wound. Wincing in pain she quickly wrapped it up as tried to lay back and go to sleep.

Halouse sat silently by a fountain built by the natives. The water flew freely out of a statue as he stared at it not even knowing what was in front of him. The haunting feelings he had for Mayreon would never allow him to sleep. Crazed thoughts tried to make sense of how he was allowed to touch the ruby knowing only a person with purity could remove it. How could a man who lusted over another man's wife have purity in his heart?

Mayreon's form emerged over the hill as she looked down at Halouse. Wrapped in a fur she walked slowly toward him. He was kneeled trapped in his mind as he could almost sense her walking toward him.

"Can't sleep either?" Halouse asked.

"Like you I'm haunted," Mayreon told.

"What are you haunted with?" Halouse asked.

"Of what will be after I leave here," Mayreon told.

Halouse rose as he still looked at the fountain.

"Beautiful isn't it?" Halouse asked.

As he turned and walked in front of Mayreon the crystal blue water of the fountain covered her face. Her beautiful eyes shined through the darkness as she stared at him. Halouse just studied her as the cool breeze waved her long blonde hair.

"Do not look at me so," Mayreon begged.

"If you didn't want me to look at you this way how come you came to me?" Halouse asked.

"I owe you my life there is no question about that," Mayreon told, "But know that when this war is over no matter the outcome you will never see me again."

Halouse just nodded hiding his sudden heartbreak.

"Is that what you want?" Halouse asked.

"It doesn't matter what I want," Mayreon informed.

Still mesmerized by her sight Halouse just stared and replied, "I wish you could see yourself now. I wish you could see what you do to me and the way you look right now."

Mayreon lowered her head not returning his stare anymore.

"Ignore it if you like," Halouse replied.

"I have to," Mayreon said angrily.

"So be it," Halouse said in an uncaring tone, "But there is no need for anger, but I don't think it's I that you have such fury with."

"This is what I chose," Mayreon replied, "Once I leave here, once I'm gone that is it for this."

"Okay," Halouse replied in an uncaring tone as he turned from her, "Then I suggest you leave."

"Is that all I get?" Mayreon asked.

Halouse turned to her in frustration as he asked, "What is this? Angered good byes from you but when I turn uncaring you are offended?"

"You're right," Mayreon said annoyed, "It would be better to leave it this way wouldn't it?"

"Do what you will queen," Halouse snapped, "Leaving this world behind forgetting what I've done for you."

"I will never forget," Mayreon yelled, "Not in any lifetime I assure."

"So quick to leave us behind and forget," Halouse told still turned away.

"Don't you understand that this is what I must do?" Mayreon yelled.

"Then do it," Halouse said, "Go now and never forget me and remember that this was the last time you saw me."

Mayreon turned and began to walk away but quickly stopped herself. Trying once again she only took a step as the tears began to leave her eyes. She walked for a couple of feet before quickly going to Halouse. She turned him around and kissed him deeply. He returned her embrace as he held her in his arms. For several moments they stood in front of the fountain unable to break away from one another. Before it could go any further though Mayreon broke from him and looked into his eyes.

"This will never happen again," Mayreon replied as the tears fell from her eyes, "Goodbye."

Halouse just looked at her as she continued to stare deeply at him. As he made himself nod Mayreon ripped herself away from him and ran off quickly. Halouse just touched his lips trying to embrace the way she felt. With frustration he looked to the heavens and shook his head at his god.

From the tops of the mountains surrounding the Valley a few shadows began to run around. No warriors could see them because they were all guarding the entrance. It was only a small force as they climbed down the cliffs and made it to the ground. The shadowed figures quickly moved around the hunts trying not to get into the light of the moon. The saddened Mayreon soon passed as a shadowed figure grabbed her by the arm. Relying on instinct she began to yell Halouse's name. She only got into the middle of it before a hand was placed over her mouth. As she tried to cast a spell to get the creatures of her she soon realized she was being dispelled. She turned to see Sangrayus looking at her with an evil smile.

"Sorry sorceress," Sangrayus falsely replied, "You are no match for me."

Halouse not far away could almost feel something wrong. He quickly began to walk toward where Mayreon had gone. Quick walking turned into running as he began to see the shadow's scaling the cliffs. Halouse was too far away to catch as he pulled out his sword.

"Hecorus," Halouse yelled and then screamed, "Cloron."

The two brothers jumped quickly from their beds as they heard their brothers cry.

"They have her," Halouse yelled as he began to scale the cliffs.

Hecorus jumped up and quickly gathered his things as he placed on his cloths. Salryn did the same knowing something was going on. Hecorus had no time to wait for her as he grabbed his sword and left his hut. There he saw Cloron half dressed as well.

"What has happened?" Hecorus asked.

"You heard Halouse," Cloron whispered, "They have her."

They both saw their brother scaling the high cliffs as they began to as well.

Salryn was tying her armor as she saw Drayus leaving her tent.

"Cloron just left," Drayus told.

"There is something wrong," Salryn knew, "Hecorus did the same."

"Should I warn the others?" Drayus asked.

"Yes," Salryn told, "But I do not know what the problem is."

Drayus quickly began to run toward Calbrawn's courtiers as Salryn sprinted toward Hecorus and Cloron.

Halouse began to see the sun beginning to rise as he reached the top of the mountain. Cold winds passed his face as the snow on the ground was hard to move in. He quickly followed the tracks of the Falmores but soon the tracks just vanished.

Sangrayus using a magic bubble levitated her, the rank of Falmores and Mayreon to the ground below far away from the top of the mountain. Knowing she was being followed she grabbed Mayreon as the forces stood all around her. Mayreon screamed as her cried echoed throughout the land.

Halouse quickly heard her screams and followed them as he sprinted down the rocky terrain.

A Falmore took his sword and knocked Mayreon in the back of her head knocking her out.

"Hurry," Sangrayus commanded, "Artwore waits for us."

One warrior picked Mayreon up and placed her on his shoulders as he ran as quickly as he could with the extra weight. Sangrayus could almost feel Halouse as they began to go back to where Artwore awaited them.

Calbrawn and several other councilmen as well as warriors walked through the back end of the Valley.

"What happened?" Calbrawn asked as Drayus was next to him.

"There was some commotion," Drayus told, "Hecorus, Halouse, Cloron and Salryn left. They scaled the cliffs to get to the top of the mountain."

"They could have sent small ranks to try and trick us into thinking they were invading from here," A Councilmen suggested.

"Just a trick to try and get us to leave the front gates unguarded," Calbrawn thought, "Cloron and them probable went to kill them."

"I don't think so," Drayus said, "They would have been back by now."

"Check the huts," Calbrawn commanded, "I want to make sure they didn't kill any women or children."

Lyncade ran up at that moment as well as Raven.

"What's going on?" Lyncade asked.

"A small party of Falmores must have scaled the mountain and came in," Calbrawn told.

"Just as he thought," Raven replied pointing at Lyncade.

"It doesn't make sense," Calbrawn said in anger, "Why come in knowing you were going to be seen with such a small force."

"Maybe they didn't come to attack," Lyncade replied as he quickly realized it at that moment, "They came for Mayreon."

"Check her tent," Calbrawn quickly yelled to his soldiers.

Moments later they ran to it as they saw it empty. Lyncade yelled in anger as he began to walk to the front gate.

"What are you doing?" Calbrawn asked, "They want you to leave. If you walk out that cave they'll ambush you."

Lyncade ignored Calbrawn as he quickly ran to the front entrance. Raven not far behind as he didn't have on any chest armor. He just had his sword strapped to his back as they ran quickly to the front of the Valley. Running passed all the guards they knocked the rock out of the way to see no one around.

"Where could they go?" Raven asked.

Lyncade looked high to the mountain as he began to see where it touched the ground. Miles away from them they began to see the high mountain gradually touch the ground.

"This way," Lyncade commanded.

With the mountain farther then they could see they knew they were hours behind if they went through the cliffs. No time to turn around and try to scale from the inside because that would take much longer.

Salryn well behind the rest didn't go down the mountain as she reached the top. Instead she figured she'd stay on the high terrain and try to cut off the party. Sprinting quickly she realized the only way the Falmores could leave is if further ahead they got back on the mountain.

Cloron and Hecorus thousands of feet behind their brother just followed his tracks as they ran as quickly as they could. Knowing his infatuation could get him killed they tried to reach him before any harm could come to him.

Halouse had to stop where he was, looking all around and seeing there was several different routes the party could have went. He began to have tears come to his face in frustration. Calming himself quickly he placed his hands on his face and quickly ran in the direction he felt was right.

As Cloron and Hecorus came to the same fork they both looked at one another.

"This is going to make it harder," Hecorus replied.

"You think this was going to be easy?" Cloron asked, "Choose."

"Split up," Hecorus suggested.

"We can't," Cloron told.

"We have to," Hecorus replied.

Cloron looked at Hecorus knowing he was right. The two brothers took two different valleys between the large mountains above. The mountain ranges stretched for several miles as they both knew the Falmores and Halouse had to have taken these paths.

Salryn still atop the mighty mountains scaled as if knowing every path in front of her. She soon looked out over the mountain as she saw a large party of Falmores in the distance. Where she was at the moment she knew it would take some time to reach them. Not wasting time she quickly pressed forward trying to reach the party. Her leg slipped as she grabbed the mountain before she could fall over. At any moment she could have fallen to her death. She would need to be careful but knew she had no time to be patient.

Sangrayus and her small rank of Falmores caught up with Artwore as he waited with several more ranks. Artwore smiled as he saw one of his warriors carrying Mayreon.

"We must hurry and travel south to the ships," Artwore commanded, "They know she is gone by now and will send their forces."

Artwore and his forces began to climb the mountain knowing it was the quickest route to the shore in the south. The party couldn't run giving Cloron, Hecorus, Halouse and Salryn plenty of time to catch up.

Halouse finally realizing he was far off the path began to scale the mountain quickly trying to reach the top. Not having any trouble it was a matter of moments before he finally got there.

Salryn saw Halouse on the mountain range she was on. He was too far to call but she knew now that she wouldn't be far behind if Halouse met with the Falmores. She quickly pressed forward tired of running as she ignored her strained legs.

Hecorus not far behind the Falmores ran up the mountain range they were traveling on as he scaled a steep slope. He could see the tracks of the Falmores as he began to get hope of finally catching them.

As the ranks of Falmores traveled on a narrow path along the cliffs any wrong step could have been their last. Miles ahead of them was the shore as they could almost sense the water. Traveling slowly they didn't expect nothing more then a large army to march toward them. They figured at their pace the army of Natives would never reach in time.

Halouse could see the back of the ranks below him as he slowly climbed down to the same trail they were traveling on. He could no longer climb up because of the angle of the mountain.

A Falmore in the back of the ranks heard the sound of running as he turned slowly. He saw Halouse running toward him as he stopped a few of his companions. The Falmores took out their bows and took aim. One by one they fired as each arrow just missed Halouse. As Halouse began to get closer as an arrow from an unknown source was fired hitting Halouse dead in the chest. Halouse fell back from the impact and lost his footing. He fell off the cliff and began to feel the wind hit his face. The Falmores lost sight of him just as they heard a crunch sound. They looked to see Sangrayus holding a bow.

"That takes care of that," Sangrayus replied, "Move forward."

As they did Salryn from the top of the mountain began to climb down not knowing what had happened to Halouse. As she scaled she realized she would drop right in the middle of the Falmore forces. Taking her time she stopped and awaited help.

Hecorus quickly ran out of the passage jumping on the cliffs and going forward. He pulled his crossbow forward as he ran with every last breath in his lungs. The back of the Falmores heard the running again as they turned. Preparing to fire Halouse quickly aimed and fired with his crossbow as he ran. Hitting his target he kept his crossbow in front of him and continued to run.

Cloron emerged from the passage as well as he could see the dead bodies of the Falmores. He quickly pulled out his blade as he ran across the trail on the high cliff.

Salryn saw the Falmores stop as they realized there was someone following them. She used that as her reason to drop as she slowly did. Landing on a rock just above the cliff trail she swung at an unsuspecting Falmore. Killing him instantly she swung at a second beheading him. She ran across the high rock and swung down cutting into the face of another. As a Falmore came forward and swung at her feet she flipped over him and landed on the cliff trail. As she landed and turned she sliced into the back of the Falmore.

Many more came at her as she pushed them out of her way and saw Mayreon being held by a Falmore.

Artwore was beside the warrior as he saw Salryn run to him. He pulled out his blade and blocked a strike just as Salryn came at him. She threw everything she had at the Falmore King but he blocked each strike with perfection. As she continued her attack she was caught off guard when Artwore countered and sliced her in her thigh. Yelling in pain she dropped to her knees as she pulled her sword back to swing. A Falmore in back of her hit the blade as it fell from her hands. The sword dropped and hit the ground as it bounced over the cliff. Artwore kneed her in the face as she was defenseless and dazed by the hit. Artwore grabbed her by the back of her head and put his blade to her throat.

Hecorus fighting with nothing but pure rage saw this as he killed the Falmores in front of him. Artwore turned his head as Hecorus leaped toward him. Artwore let Salryn go as he swung at Hecorus. Hecorus ducked as he swung his blade in back of him as he passed Artwore. Artwore was prepared as he blocked it. Hecorus turned as he tried a combination that usual put his opponent down. Artwore blocked each strike as he caught Hecorus with a slash to the chest. The Falmores in back of Hecorus went to go at him but Artwore held out his hand stopping them. Hecorus attacked again as Artwore blocked the strike and stabbed him in the thigh. Hecorus fell to his knees as Artwore removed the blade and chopped down on Hecorus' head. Hecorus blocked the strike but left his chest open as Artwore quickly sliced it. Hecorus weak and wounded went to strike at Artwore but Artwore grabbed the hand and stabbed Hecorus in the ribs. Artwore then ripped the sword from Hecorus and tossed it over the cliff. Artwore grabbed the wounded Salryn and placed her up again. Hecorus with tears in his eyes looked at Salryn for the last time. Artwore placed his blade to her neck and sliced her throat. Chocking violently she placed her hands to the wound. Artwore grabbed her by the hair and tossed her over the cliff as her body fell hundreds of feet below. Hecorus heart broken and not able to retaliate stayed kneeled as Artwore raised his blade.

Hundreds of feet away on the same path Cloron watched as Artwore cut of Hecorus' head and kick his body over the cliff. Cloron watched as his brothers lifeless body fell against the rocks violently and to the ground below.

Artwore ordered his men to go forward as they did. Sangrayus in the front of the line just watched her son as she didn't interfere. The party of Falmores walked off as if nothing happened but Cloron was still running from in back of them. Cloron caught up quickly as he hurled his blade at the Falmore in the back of the line. It hit him square in the back as he fell to the ground. Cloron pulled his blade from the Falmore and picked up the dead warriors blade as he went forward.

The slim cliff opened up as the rank of Falmores didn't have to worry about falling over. Just as they thought it was over they heard the sounds of swords again. Artwore looked to his mother who was by the warrior who carried Mayreon. He signaled for her to go forward as him and the remaining twenty Falmores stayed where they were. Several of them took out their bows as they prepared for Cloron. As Cloron came out of the narrow cliff arrows flew toward him. Two missed but one hit him flush in the shoulder. Ignoring the pain he quickly killed the archers and went at the warriors with their blade out. Fighting recklessly he was sliced several times by the Falmores but continued to fight as he quickly used both the swords he had to chop at them. As he swung his blades wildly at the Falmores and successfully killed them as he approached Artwore. With two blades to one he swung. The skilled Artwore backed away and blocked with his sword as Cloron came at him. Not able to get away from one the blade sliced him across the top of his head. Artwore backed off holding his face as Cloron went to finish him. From in back of him a Falmore took his ax and chopped it into the back of Cloron's leg. Cloron yelled in pain as he took his sword and stabbed it in the Falmores neck. The blood pored from the wound as the Falmore dropped dead. As Cloron was caught off guard Artwore swung at the other blade knocking it out of his hands. The other Falmores backed off as Artwore continued his battle. As Cloron raised his blade Artwore went in and sliced Cloron in the ribs. Cloron tried to turn and face Artwore as he passed but when he did Artwore's blade came down and chopped into Cloron's shoulder. Cloron reacted quickly and stabbed the Falmore King in the ribs. Artwore yelled as he removed his blade and stabbed Cloron in the neck.

He kept his blade there as he forced it further into Cloron. Cloron's eyes began to roll in his head as every ounce of live that remained began to fade. Cloron's intense face went to calm as his very soul began to leave his body. Placing his foot on Cloron's face he kicked him away as his blade exited Cloron's neck. Cloron fell to the ground dead and unable to avenge his brother.

Artwore placed his sword away as if it was a normal thing he walked toward where he mother had traveled to get to the shore. The other Falmores followed as the body of Cloron continued to pore with blood from his wounds.

Chapter 15

An hour or so later Lyncade and Raven made it to the sight of the battle. They followed the trail of dead Falmores before they came to a large pool of blood where Hecorus was killed. Raven kneeled and touched the blood as he looked at Lyncade.

"Elf blood and it's dry," Raven told, "We are too late."

Lyncade quickly went forward seeing the bodies of more Falmores. That is when the two made a gruesome discovery. Laying face down surrounded in his own blood was the body of Cloron.

"My Warad," Lyncade replied.

Raven saw as well as he looked around, "Where are the others?"

Lyncade looked below as he could just make out the bodies of several Falmores. The two quickly looked for a way down as they found it. Just below they walked further and further back. Stopping suddenly Raven saw the smashed body of Salryn. He began to walk slowly as around a rocky bend he stopped in horror to see the beheaded Hecorus. Lyncade was soon there as he noticed it too. Raven walked around in anger as he tried to hold back his emotions.

"Halouse," Lyncade said softly as he ran down the bottom of the mountain. As the cliff above began to get lower they soon came to a large bush. On the bush was a body as Lyncade rushed to it. Seconds later Lyncade pulled Halouse away as he could see his chest moving.

"Halouse," Raven called trying to revive him.

The bush saved him indeed but he was still full of pain as he slowly came to. He tried to get up but the pain from the fall was too much. The arrow stuck out of his breast as he sat up and looked at them.

"Mayreon?" Halouse asked.

"They still have her," Lyncade told.

"I shouldn't have gone after her alone," Halouse said softly.

Raven went to him and helped him up.

Lyncade didn't say anything as he finally replied, "You weren't alone."

Halouse looked up at him with a look of shock as he slowly tried to get up. Wincing in pain Raven tried to help him but Halouse pushed him away and went forward. After seeing many Falmores smashed into the rocks below he made his discovery. He saw the bodies of Hecorus and Salryn as he placed his hand in front of his face. The sight was too horrible to look at as tears fell from his eyes. Crying uncontrollable he ran his fingers through his hair not able to look anymore. He gained control of himself as he walked away and began to scale the cliff. As he reached the top in pain he came to the opening where the body of Cloron was. Once again taken over by his tears he dropped in front of his brother. Lyncade and Raven watched as Halouse stared into the dead eyes of his brother. He reached forward and closed them as he stroked the face of his older sibling.

"They only died because I was too reckless," Halouse replied, "I should have taken my time and then they could have caught up with me."

"Do not blame yourself," Lyncade replied.

Halouse turned and looked at Lyncade as he got up slowly.

"They have her," Halouse told, "I must go after them."

"You're mad," Raven replied.

"They will pay," Halouse yelled.

"We must go with an army," Lyncade told.

"They have Mayreon and they killed my brothers," Halouse yelled.

"Halouse," Lyncade said as he walked toward him, "They will not kill Mayreon they need her. We must go back and get the forces."

"We'll go to Fadarth at nightfall," Raven promised, "Do not go without us."

"I can't face my father," Halouse told them, "I can't even look at him. I must avenge them and then see him."

"Going alone is imprudent," Lyncade said.

"I'm all I have," Halouse told, "I will go alone."

Lyncade tried to stop him as Halouse turned around. Quickly Halouse turned and punched Lyncade hard in the face. Lyncade fell back as Raven caught him.

Shaking his hand Halouse replied, "I know it will kill you for me to say this but she is all I have. If something happens to her I will have no reason to go on. I will go forward and I will make sure I kill that bastard Artwore and watch him bleed in front of me."

"They won't kill her," Lyncade yelled, "They need her."

"Go back to the Valley," Halouse commanded ignoring Lyncade, "It was a trap and tell them I will see them in Fadarth."

Lyncade went to go after Halouse again but Raven stopped him.

"No my lord," Raven replied, "This is something he feels he must do alone."

Lyncade didn't fight as he quickly turned around to go back to the Valley of Talius. Raven watched as Halouse went off and bent down to pick up Cloron's blade.

Resting on his seat amongst the council Calbrawn sat quietly as well as the others. A deep pain haunted him as he looked down. It was as if he had already known as he placed his hands to his face and rubbed his mouth. He stopped as he looked to the staircase. There standing with a look of anguish was Lyncade. Raven was only a few feet behind as he approached the Native Elf leader. With his own sword away in its case Raven held two blades as he walked toward Calbrawn.

The council just exhaled as they knew the swords Raven carried. Raven approached and kneeled in front of Calbrawn as he then rose slowly.

"Their blades are soaked in the blood of their enemies," Raven replied, "They fought fearlessly and never gave up even when they neared their doom."

Raven held out both the blades in front of Calbrawn and kneeled once again. The broken leader just rose as he took them from Raven's grasp. Calbrawn looked at Lyncade as a tear rolled down his eye.

"They took her and retreated," Lyncade told.

"The cowards," A councilman replied.

Calbrawn held out his hands for silence from the man. Calbrawn walked toward Lyncade as he stood face to face with him.

"Halouse?" Calbrawn asked.

"He went after them," Lyncade told unable to look into the eyes of Calbrawn, "He said he couldn't see you again unless he got his vengeance."

"A vow promised the moment I made them proud hunters and warriors of our people," Calbrawn told.

"My lord," A Native warrior yelled from below.

Calbrawn and Lyncade looked down as the warrior pointed to the entrance of the Valley and said, "Royal Elves."

Lyncade quickly jumped from the staircase to the ground below as he sprinted toward the front of the Valley. Raven wasn't far behind as Calbrawn slowly went and sat on the cold ground. He looked to the heavens looking for answers as he still absorbed the news of his sons.

Lyncade and Raven left the Valley through the secret rock as they began to see the Royal Elf forces marching toward them on the river.

"Tamian," Lyncade yelled.

The Royal Elf King rode side by side with Rakar as they quickly rode ahead to the calling Lyncade.

"Lyncade," Tamian said in disbelief as he dropped from his horse.

The two met up quickly as Tamian seemed shocked to see his general.

"You're alive," Tamian said in shock.

"Barely," Lyncade told, "Raven and I were the only one's left from the battle with the orcs and goblins."

"That many forces lost?" Tamian asked.

"Who's with you?" Raven asked.

"Rakar and the Forest Elves," Tamian told, "They came to our aid when we wiped out the orcs and goblins."

"They join you on your quest?" Lyncade asked.

"As well as Maxus," Tamian informed, "Tell me. Where is the Falmore army now?"

Lyncade and Raven just looked at him not answering.

"What is it?" Tamian asked.

"They have Mayreon," Lyncade told, "They took their forces back to Fadarth."

"Do you know where the Natives are?" Tamian asked.

Lyncade just smiled slightly as he said, "Follow us."

Commanding his army to stop marching Tamian followed the two with Rakar and Maxus behind him. The three walked into the Valley as it quickly took their breath away.

"My Warad," Tamian replied, "I would have never guessed."

"I did not know so many were still here after our kingdoms were created," Rakar told.

"Cloron and Hecorus were right," Tamian said.

"My lord," Lyncade called, "Do no speak those names."

"Why not?" Tamian asked.

"Follow me," Lyncade replied, "You will meet their leader."

Tamian began to walk through the Valley as every warrior of the Native Elves of all the tribes looked at him in amazement. It was the king of all the elves. The mighty warrior who had battled The Dark Lord, Korack and Greco several times with his forces. He had never been slain and had never lost a victory in all the years he had ruled.

Lyncade walked up the stairway to the councilmen as Tamian stopped him and was the first to the top.

Lyncade grabbed him and whispered, "Their leader has lost both his sons."

The council looked at Tamian already hearing the many stories of the great king and all the battles he had fought.

Calbrawn still mourning the loss of his sons did as well. Seconds later he rose looking at the great Royal Elf King. Tamian looked at Calbrawn in amazement as he slowly walked over to him. Calbrawn despite his lose smiled as he approached Tamian.

"Calbrawn?" Tamian asked.

"Your father would have been proud this day," Calbrawn replied, "Coming to the aid of your people when they are at their weakest."

Lyncade and Raven looked at each other as the same with Maxus and Rakar.

"You are their leader?" Tamian asked.

"Have been since you started your kingdom," Calbrawn told.

"Why have you never come to me?" Tamian asked in disbelief.

"Because our people do not need to have anyone protect us," Calbrawn told, "We have our own ways."

"They know each other?" Maxus muttered.

"Seems so," Lyncade whispered to him.

"Come," Calbrawn called, "We must speak among your warlords."

Calbrawn, Tamian, Rakar, Lyncade, Raven and Maxus all stood in Calbrawn's courtiers. Drayus entered and handed Calbrawn a cup of tea as he sat in front of his guests. Drayus looked at Raven with a small smile as he just watched her walk out of the room.

"What has happened?" Tamian asked.

Taking a long sip of his tea Calbrawn placed it down in front of him and said, "Today I lost two of my sons. Out of the many I had with both my wives I have buried them all but one."

"Which ones did you have to burry?" Tamian asked.

"Cloron and Hecorus," Calbrawn told, "Actually your captain, Raven brought their swords back to me."

Tamian looked at Raven.

"When Mayreon was captured Halouse went after them," Raven explained, "Salryn, Cloron and Hecorus followed."

"By the time Raven and I tried to catch up the battle was already over," Lyncade added.

"Your queen is now in their hands and both my sons are dead," Calbrawn told.

"They will not harm her," Rakar reminded, "Talius told us."

Tamian looked at Rakar then to Calbrawn and asked, "Did you get them?"

"The rubies?" Calbrawn asked, "It was the last task Cloron and Hecorus did successfully."

"We must get the third," Rakar replied.

"You plan to invade?" Calbrawn asked.

"They have our queen," Tamian reminded, "Do you not want vengeance for your sons."

"Warad will grant me my vengeance," Calbrawn assured.

"Warad is not in this fight," Tamian said frustrated, "Calbrawn it is time for action."

Calbrawn just looked at Tamian as he asked, "What will you have me do?"

Tamian looked at him confused and replied, "Go to war. Invade with me what ever it takes."

"My sons are dead Tamian," Calbrawn reminded.

"Halouse?" Tamian asked Lyncade.

"Went to Fadarth alone," Lyncade told.

"He must get his revenge before he can see me again," Calbrawn told, "He can not look at me until that time comes."

"Then you must have forces go with me," Tamian replied.

Calbrawn looked at Tamian and said, "You and I both know that I am too old to have anymore children. He is the last of my seeds. I request that you make sure he stays alive. With Cloron and Hecorus dead he will fight recklessly to get his revenge."

"Why will you not go?" Tamian asked.

Calbrawn looked at all the others in the room. Tamian looked in back of him and signaled them all to leave. Quickly they did his request without him having to even say the words.

"Sit," Calbrawn invited.

Tamian did as he was told as he sat across from Calbrawn and leaned toward him. Tamian and the old elf looked at each other for several moments as Tamian tried to think of what he could say to start the conversation.

"Dalian said you were dead," Tamian finally began.

"He told you what I said to tell you," Calbrawn informed.

"So he did find you," Tamian replied.

"He fought with me when the village I lived in was attacked by orcs and goblins," Calbrawn told.

"That's why I formed the empire," Tamian reminded.

"I never wanted part of your empire because of what happened to *her*," Calbrawn reminded.

"She would have been safe if she were with me," Tamian told.

"You banished her and cursed her name when you found out we were married," Calbrawn reminded.

"You were an outside clansman," Tamian reminded, "She was suppose to marry within our tribe."

"To a man that didn't love her?" Calbrawn asked, "A man who wanted to get favor from you?"

"She was my sister," Tamian yelled reminding the old elf of the fact, "Do not speak as if I didn't care for her."

"Your care drove her away from what you wanted," Calbrawn reminded.

"And into your arms where she died," Tamian painfully reminded.

Calbrawn was wounded emotionally as he heard that. He seemed to bring back all the sadness he had buried ages before.

"You and I never saw eye to eye," Calbrawn remembered, "You wanted kingdoms with castles as far as the eyes could see in the sky and large kingdoms that spread across the lands. I look around me here Tamian and I see my kingdoms. The stones built by Warad with his own two hands.

"I never wanted to have royalty anywhere near me because it was surrounded with politics and betrayal even by your own blood. In the world before elves when it was just humans. It was all that happened. The kings before us when Warad destroyed his own world was filled with greed and suffering."

"What world?" Tamian asked.

"Many years ago before we were even a thought in Warad's mind he had a world of just humans," Calbrawn told, "Scattered across the land of Tullian they all built large cities and castles just like you did. There were dozens who claimed themselves king. They went to war with one another and eventually ended up destroying themselves. It is said in legend between the first Elves Warad created that we would never do such a thing. We were people of the land and Warad's true chosen guardians of his world. You chose to combine the two. High castles with the many ranks of skilled warriors. I on the other hand swore my oath to Warad when I was first created."

"Do you not understand that there is no peace with these people?" Tamian asked, "Killing both your sons in battle and kidnapping a queen of our people. *Our* people Calbrawn not mine and not yours. We all are Elves. We all are the chosen people of Warad. If they killed your sons and you do not want blood what must they do?"

Calbrawn looked at him and asked, "Do you remember when we were all tribes? Every elf divided by the land and village they grew up in?"

"Of course," Tamian remembered.

"All we did then was fight," Calbrawn told, "I am tired of fighting Tamian. That is why I didn't go to your empire when you called for me. Not just because she died, but because my sword had seen enough blood."

Tamian saw the agony inside the eyes of the old elf as he could almost feel his pain.

"What do you want me to do?" Tamian asked.

Calbrawn just looked at him and asked, "When you get to Fadarth take care of my son. Welcome him among your people in Tamian once this war is over. Make him marry a beautiful woman of purity and make sure my seed is never wiped from the earth by the evils that have taken Cloron and Hecorus from me."

"What will you do?" Tamian asked.

"This is my home," Calbrawn told, "My age is catching up with me and all the Lycans and Murkildens want is peace."

"They have discovered your Valley," Tamian reminded, "It won't be long before one of those evil gods sends their forces to kill you."

"Let them come," Calbrawn told, "We have Warad to protect us."

Tamian shook his head and replied, "You put too much faith in a god that only watches and never helps."

Tamian rose as he began to walk out.

"Tamian," Calbrawn called.

Tamian turned and looked at his brother.

"Halouse was a Lycan," Calbrawn told, "Cloron and Hecorus were Murkilden. Go to the warriors and see if they will go to war with you. I'm sure they wish to have revenge for their fallen brothers."

Tamian heard what Calbrawn said as he just walked out.

"How did it go?" Maxus asked as Tamian walked down the stairs of the fort.

"He is still heartbroken over the loss of his sons," Tamian told, "He wishes no part in our invasion but does insist we ask the Lycans and Murkildens."

"King Tamian," A voice called.

Rakar, Maxus, Tamian, Lyncade and Raven turned as Drayus began to walk from atop a hill. As she began to get closer a large force began to come over the hill as well. Hundreds of them were baring the mark of the Lycan and the mark of the Murkilden.

"The Native forces await," Drayus replied as she came to them.

Tamian looked at the others and smiled.

"Who will they be commanded by?" Tamian asked.

"You until they find their lord," Drayus told.

"Their lord?" Tamian asked.

"Halouse," Lyncade told.

"How many of them are there?" Tamian asked.

"Thousands," Drayus simple replied.

"Another large amount of ranks added to your already powerful army," Maxus replied.

"We will need them," Tamian knew, "Who knows how many Falmores there are in Fadarth."

Lyncade removed his blade and threw it air in the air as he yelled, "For Cloron and Hecorus."

The army roared as it echoed throughout the Valley.

Chapter 16

Mayreon slowly began to awake from her coma as she looked all around her. By the rocky world around her she knew she was on some short of ship. She tried to get up but then noticed she was chained to the bed she was on. The room she was in was dark as she slowly began to recite a spell. The candles that were in the room lit up but the nasty Korack sat in front of her. Out of fear she screamed as she went to the head of the bed trying to get as far away from him as she possible could.

He smiled evilly at her as his cobra tongue shot in and out of his mouth. He studied her for as long as he could, making the silence uncomfortable for the young queen.

"Did you know that some of the humans don't believe Warad exists?" Korack asked.

Mayreon just looked at him confused by the statement as she softly asked, "What?"

"It's true," Korack assured as he leaned forward, "In the villages all around Tullian. Mostly in Cavell where the humans live the fiercest of their warriors and leaders don't even believe their own creator exists."

"I'm not sure why you would tell me that," Mayreon replied.

"Simple," The Cobra King said, "Looking at you now how could no one believe in the existence of a higher power. Near mortals couldn't just mate and create such a sight as yourself."

Any creature besides Korack, The Dark Lord or Greco could have said that and Mayreon would have blushed. Because though it was Korack the feared Cobra King and evil god of the Dark Realm, it kind of scared her.

"Don't worry," Korack told, "I haven't the tools to even contemplate ravaging you."

Mayreon just nodded still in fear of his presence.

"Killing you is not an option either," Korack told, "The Dark Lord has something bigger planned for you."

"Like what?" Mayreon asked.

Korack laughed and asked, "What and ruin the surprise?"

"They'll come for me," Mayreon warned.

"Oh I hope they do," Korack replied, "That is our plan."

"I know why you need me," Mayreon told.

"Why?" Korack asked.

"The ruby," Mayreon said, "We have the other two but I'm the only one that can tell you where the third is."

Korack nodded and said, "Very good. I see Calbrawn told you after all."

"But I don't know where it is," Mayreon assured.

"You think you don't know but you do," Korack replied.

"How is that possible?" Mayreon asked.

"Who are your parents?" Korack asked.

"I don't remember," Mayreon assured.

"You see?" Korack asked, "There are many things you don't know but are somewhere in that mind of yours."

"When Halouse informs the natives..." Mayreon began.

"Threats?" Korack asked, "I think it's too late for that. Besides your little love slave is dead along with Hecorus and Cloron. Artwore did the deed himself. Well Sangrayus killed Halouse; Artwore ripped the other two in half along with the woman warrior...what's her name?"

"Salryn," Mayreon replied as she began to feel something she hadn't before. A sudden pain in the pit of her stomach.

"You feel that?" Korack asked, "That sadness that has just hit you. I truly live for these moments."

Mayreon looked at him as her eyes filled with tears.

"I may not be able to kill you now but I assure one day I will tar you apart," Mayreon threatened.

"Simple threats do not bother me Mayreon," Korack assured, "Besides I can kill you any moment."

Halfway through the statement he held out his hand as Mayreon began to choke. As he made his fingers close further she choked more. Letting her go she quickly began to cough violently gasping for breath.

Korack rose slowly as he said, "Rest queen of the Royal Elves. You will need it."

Korack walked out as Mayreon began to look all around her in worry.

The Falmore army soon began to hit the shores of Fadarth as Fayne stood awaiting the arrival of his master. Artwore was the first to dock his large ship and walk off with Sangrayus behind him.

"My queen," Fayne replied to Sangrayus.

"Fayne," Artwore called as he approached, "Prepare your sword."

"Why?" Fayne asked.

"There are two elf kings on their way to rescue their queen," Artwore told.

With a large smile of his face Fayne watched as Mayreon was pulled off the boat surrounded by dozens of guards.

"Stop," Fayne replied to the guards as he was only a few feet from Mayreon.

Mayreon looked intimidated at the sight of Fayne as he stared at her.

"An Elf?" Mayreon asked in disbelief, "With black hair?"

Fayne just smiled as he told the guards to walk. He walked beside Mayreon as they began to go to the castle in just in the sight before the mountains.

Picking up her hair Fayne studied Mayreon and said, "I've seen you before. In my dreams I think."

"Is that so?" Mayreon asked.

"Queen of the Royal Elves," Fayne replied, "So nice to finally meet you."

"I am only the second queen," Mayreon told.

Fayne looked at her as he asked, "Second queen or first it does not matter. Your presence here will draw many to come to try and rescue you."

"What's in it for you?" Mayreon asked.

"My freedom," Fayne told, "Revenge on the god that created me."

"What revenge do you need?" Mayreon asked, "Betraying your people."

"My people?" Fayne asked, "I was one of the first. You do not even know what pains I have went through so that our kind could continue to spawn. I have shed more blood and killed more men then ranks of your finest warriors."

"Is that so?" Mayreon asked, "If you're so great why is it that you are taking commands from a human?"

Fayne stopped the guards and looked at Mayreon as he replied, "We all have our own agendas my queen. Once your king comes here with his forces to rescue you, the ruby will be found and I will slay your king freeing me from the curse Warad has placed on me. All along your people thought it was an invasion. In fact, all it was only a diversion from stopping Tamian from reaching you in time to save you."

"Capture me and find the ruby," Mayreon realized, "Draw in Tamian to slay him."

"You have the idea," Fayne replied as he began to walk again.

With Mayreon forced to walk by the guards she looked at Fayne and asked, "What will they do with me once they get what they want?"

Fayne glanced over at her for a moment then replied, "Probable kill you."

Mayreon just glanced on the ground as she walked concerned about her safety.

"You do have a choice," Fayne added, "Join us and you will live."

"What good what that do me?" Mayreon asked.

"You are a sorceress are you not?" Fayne asked.

"Yes."

"The Dark Lord, Korack and Greco can teach you things that aren't in the text of the book you read," Fayne told, "You can learn every ability in the known world and unlike The Dark Lord, Korack and Greco you can use it anywhere."

"But I will watch the people I love die," Mayreon replied.

"You will live," Fayne reminded, "Fighting for the side that will ultimately win."

"How do you know that Tamian will not kill you?" Mayreon asked.

Fayne smiled a bit as he replied, "That is what I miss about my kind. The false hope we always have for the good to always beat the evil."

"That's all I have," Mayreon told.

"It's in our soul," Fayne told, "To think that there is always a chance to win."

Mayreon looked over at Fayne and asked, "It will be you that goes to Tullian to kill all our people?"

Fayne smiled and replied, "Of course. I will have vengeance finally and will be able to live in peace."

"There is no peace if The Dark Lord wins," Mayreon assured, "He will surly kill you as well."

Fayne still had his smile on his face as if thinking Mayreon was stupid.

"Have you seen me?" Fayne asked, "These ruins that are tattooed onto me are blessings from each god of every realm. No god of this world or the next can kill me. Only the descendant of one of the original six."

"And there is none in this world?" Mayreon asked.

"I haven't met one yet," Fayne told.

"I assure defender," Mayreon began, "That in a few days I will watch you fall."

Fayne just smiled at Mayreon as they began to get closer to the city. Thousands of Falmores prepared as they waited outside the gates. Camped all around they were the first line of defense against the Elf armies that headed their way.

Tamian and all of his forces marched in back of him as he rode next to Rakar, Maxus, Lyncade and Raven. Strapped to his horse hung two sacks that carried two of the ruby's that contained the powers of the evil gods. The forces stretched long behind him as they walked in a valley headed toward the shores of Southern Cavell. They soon began to get closer to open terrain as the fields in front of them were filled with high grass and the smell of the ocean was in the air.

"My lord," Lyncade called, "How are we going to get all the forces over to Fadarth."

Tamian seemed not to hear the question traveling as he stared dead ahead. Lyncade looked at him for several moments before he just faced forward and knew Tamian didn't want to be disturbed.

"Humans," Tamian informed.

"Excuse me?" Lyncade asked.

"The humans have ships at their ports in Cavell," Tamian informed.

"How will we pay them?" Lyncade asked.

Tamian continued to look forward once again ignoring Lyncade's question.

"My lord?" Lyncade asked noticing his distant look.

"We're about to find out," Tamian told.

Lyncade looked forward as in the distance a lone warrior sat atop a horse.

"Company prepare," Raven yelled to the Calvary behind him.

"Hold on," Tamian yelled.

"It's only a lone warrior," Maxus reminded Raven.

"Could be a trap," Raven reminded.

"Smells like one," Tamian agreed, "Ride forward. Lyncade, Maxus, come with me."

Tamian, Lyncade and Maxus began to pick up pace as they got closer to the lone warrior on horse back. As they approached they slowed down as the warrior didn't seem to move.

The warrior was definitely human. Only wearing a war helmet with the face of a vicious creature his human feature remained hidden behind it. Not wearing any type of armor the warrior's fat stomach hung out around his waist. The warrior held a large ax in his hands pointed toward the ground as his other arm held a shield lazily to the side of his horse. A large sword was in a case around the saddle of his mount. Around his stomach and arms were several tattoos all around his fattening chest and stomach.

"Why do your armies come this way?" The warrior asked through the intimidating mask he wore.

"We're going to Fadarth," Tamian informed, "I am King Tamian of the Royal Elves."

The warrior looked at him for a few moments then replied, "I don't really give a rat's ass."

In shock Lyncade and Maxus looked at the warrior as if he were crazy.

"Do you not know who you are speaking with?" Lyncade asked.

"No king of elves comes this way unless it's to claim the lands of my fathers people," The warrior informed.

"I assure that your fathers lands are no desire to me," Tamian replied, "And with a force as large as the one in back of me I'd watch your tongue."

"My father was never scared of your kind and neither am I," The warrior told.

"Remove your mask," Maxus requested, "Let us see the brave face of this stupid warrior."

The warriors head seemed to sift toward Maxus as he studied him for several seconds.

"Who are these two with you king of elves?" The warrior asked.

"General Lyncade and High Lord of the Royal Elves," Lyncade informed.

"General Maxus and Highest Lord of the Royal Elves," Maxus replied as well.

Tamian held out his hand toward his marching army as they stopped. Tamian took one look at the warrior and asked, "And your name?"

The warrior quickly placed his ax in a case around his saddle and removed his mask. A bald long bearded human stared directly at them as he held his helmet tucked under his arm.

"My name is Tazzill," The warrior told, "Champion of my village located just east of here."

"Tazzill," Tamian announced as he bowed his head, "I hold your people with the highest of respects. We mean your village and your lands no harm."

"We go to fight with your mortal enemies," Lyncade added, "The Falmores."

"The Falmores haven't been on Tullian in ages," Tazzill claimed.

"Then I guess your blind," Maxus replied.

Tamian looked at him sharply warning him of his tone.

"How so?" Tazzill asked.

"A large army landed on the shores of Cavell many weeks ago," Lyncade told, "Captured a queen of our people and retreated home."

Tazzill looked at them for several seconds then raised his arm in the air. In back of the warrior several hundred humans arouse hiding in the tall grass. They all looked forward at the large Elf army marching their way.

"You were going to fight us with a rank of only a few hundred?" Maxus asked.

"I had the element of surprise," Tazzill told.

"Your army of three hundred or more was going to surprise a force of thousands?" Maxus asked.

"We would have taken more with our surprise attack," Tazzill told.

"A surprise that we would have seen only a few moments after it happened," Maxus said in an irritated tone, "It's not as if you out number us."

"We all would have been killed to tell your forces that we have no regard for our lives if your kind came to attack," Tazzill told, "We would have died with honor."

"Slaughtered," Maxus replied.

"Enough Maxus," Tamian commanded as he looked at Tazzill and asked, "Do you have any ships?"

"Several hundred," Tazzill told, "Able to fit about two hundred warriors on each. Why?"

"We would wish to use them for our journey," Tamian told, "Our ships are north of Tullian all the way in our lands."

"It's too late to go and get them now," Lyncade added, "My wife the queen is in grave danger."

"She's your wife?" Tazzill asked as he pointed at Tamian and said, "But he's the king."

"The Royal Elf people have two queens," Tamian told, "Her beauty and grace could only be called that of a queen."

Tazzill studied them as he asked, "Can I bring the three of you to my village to talk about this further?"

"We have no time," Maxus claimed.

"For what reason?" Tamian asked ignoring Maxus' comment.

"If I am to give you ships I will need something in return," Tazzill told.

"Lands?" Tamian asked.

Tazzill shook his head.

"Gold?" Tamian asked.

Tazzill once again shook his head.

"Then what?" Tamian asked.

"Come with me and I will show you," Tazzill told.

Tamian looked at Lyncade then replied, "Allow me time to give my commands to my forces."

"Of course," Tazzill replied.

Not long after Maxus, Lyncade, Rakar and Tamian all began to ride toward a large village where Tazzill was from. It was filled with a lot of women, children and the men that remained all seemed to be simple farmers. Tazzill's forces all marched in back of them as they began to come into town.

"There are not many warriors," Maxus replied.

"Most were killed protecting the village from The Dark Lord and his forces," Tazzill replied riding a few feet in front of them, "The warriors that are in back of us are all trained by me and will fight to the death to protect their people."

"Such a small number," Rakar replied.

"I can raise more if I wish," Tazzill assured.

"How?" Tamian asked.

"There are several more villages not far from here," Tazzill told, "We fish near the shore and trade it for fur with some of the Native Elves just north of here."

"Some of them march with us," Tamian told.

"The Murkildens and the Lycans," Lyncade informed.

"They are fierce," Tazzill replied, "The largest of the tribes among the Native Elves."

"You are all so open here," Rakar noticed, "How is it that you haven't been wiped out yet?"

"That's what I wish to talk to you about," Tazzill informed.

They came to a small hut as Tazzill got off his horse and tied it to a post outside the hut. Tamian, Rakar, Maxus and Lyncade dismounted as well. Tazzill looked at Tamian then pointed. In front of them was a small Valley in the distance as they all began to see sails and large ships at the end of a large dock.

"There they are," Tazzill told, "Just under a thousand of them all across the shore."

In the distance thousands of humans were soon unloading fish from their daily catch. They all worked hard to try and keep the fish fresh to get to the other villages near by.

"How many of you are there?" Tamian asked.

"A few hundred villages," Tazzill told, "All of them with mostly women and children. The men are all farmers and never wish to get involved with the evil that come to our land. In the last few months we lost about twenty ships to raiding orc and goblin forces."

"You don't have an exact count?" Rakar asked.

"If I wished and if all the humans of Cavell were in danger I could raise a force of over three hundred thousand. One third of that being skilled in warfare and no match to your forces if we outnumbered you three to one," Tazzill informed.

"If you are so vulnerable why stay?" Lyncade asked.

"It's the only thing that keeps us in line with the rest of the world," Tazzill told, "The dwarfs come and trade with us every so often. We only see them twice every five years though. They barely come out of the caves of the Blazar Mountains. The thing is if we leave these parts we will not be able to find any food or water."

"What do you ask of us?" Tamian asked.

Tazzill looked at him with a small smile and replied, "High walls."

"A city?" Lyncade asked.

Tazzill nodded and said, "Your city is the greatest in all the world. You have never lost it because of your high walls. We wish to have a city of our own to protect our people."

"Our help in building the humans a city and you will give us those ships in return?" Tamian asked.

"That's madness," Maxus replied.

Tamian held up his hand to Maxus as he said to Tazzill, "Agreed."

With a small smile Tazzill said, "I must speak with you and Lyncade alone."

"For what purpose?" Rakar asked.

"To help you understand what you are fighting in Fadarth," Tazzill replied.

"Falmores we know that," Maxus said annoyed.

"No," Tazzill told, "Fayne."

Lyncade and Tamian looked at one another as Tamian looked up at Rakar and said, "Stay here. We will return soon."

By a large mountain Tazzill lead the two Royal Elves to a large rock like bridge. As he walked across it Tamian and Lyncade looked down to see they were several hundred feet in the air. With the large bridge very wide they made sure to stay in the middle of it as they walked. They entered a cave with the entrance of it a few hundred feet in the air. As they entered a torch was on the side of the cave as Tazzill grabbed it. The cave was massive and the high walls stood hundreds of feet in the air. Several rocks all over enabled the willing man to climb up if they wished. At the end of the large cave as Tazzill lead them was a large painting that looked to be thousands of years old.

"What is this?" Lyncade asked.

Tazzill threw the torch on a large bowl as the whole bowl lit in flames lighting up everything around them. He turned and looked at the two elves.

"Do you now why elves were created?" Tazzill asked.

"To protect humans," Lyncade replied, "In the begging that's all there were was humans."

"Many kingdoms as well," Tazzill added, "Many kings claiming to be rulers of the world. When they began to get greedy and destroy one another Warad created elves. In fact he created six of them."

"Six?" Lyncade asked.

"They were to protect the humans from the evils of the world including protecting them from themselves," Tazzill told, "When all the humans of the world killed each other Warad knew he needed to create balance. The six elves that he created all went there different ways but were commanded by Warad when he wished to protect all the world and all the creations of Tullian from every evil that threatened it.

"Warad went and created women for every elf he first created. They all began to spawn and Warad in time created more elves. When they rose into the thousands he stopped knowing they would all spawn with one another and create the greatest army in all the world. A race that didn't age, a race that would never reach its prime in fighting and would only get better. His chosen people. The Elves.

"The six that were the first were all blessed by each god of each realm. Fayne was champion of our realm and Warad's greatest warrior. In fact he was believed to be The Guardian of Light himself. The other five were blessed by the other gods including one blessed by Talius.

"Now rulers of there own tribes they lead into battle killing the tribes of their own people. Each elf running into the other in the battlefield. When it was all over Fayne, the last of the first elves was the winner. In return he had received each blessing by each god. As he killed his equals the blessings tattooed on their flesh went to him. Each time making him more powerful and indestructible."

"We know the rest," Lyncade told, "The Dark Lord tricking him and so on."

"What does this have to do with us?" Tamian asked.

"Lyncade is the spawn of one of these six elves," Tazzill told, "The elf blessed by Talius. The elf known as Fyncade."

One of the six paintings seemed to catch Lyncade's eye as he knew it was the painting of his father.

"Impossible," Lyncade replied.

"It's true," Tazzill assured, "Told to me by my father and his before him and so on. You will meet Fayne in Fadarth. The only one who is capable of killing him is Lyncade. He is the seed of Fyncade."

"Is it true?" Tamian asked.

Lyncade looked at the painting and replied, "I never knew who he was."

"The curse on Fayne for the sins he committed against Warad and his people will be lifted if Fayne kills you Tamian," Tazzill told, "Only the bloodline of the other five elves can kill Fayne."

Tamian looked at his general as Lyncade looked at Tazzill and replied, "It will be done."

"It must be done," Tazzill told, "If Fayne kills the king of the elves then my people will be the first he destroys once he lands on Tullian."

"Give us the ships," Lyncade told, "And I will give you his head on my lance."

Tazzill smiled and replied, "No. You will have my ax in battle. I will go with you to battle the Falmores."

259

"Then let us not waste anymore time," Lyncade replied as he looked at Tazzill, "We must rescue my bride and make sure Fayne is never lifted from his curse."

Chapter 17

Thousands of Falmores began to camp outside their city as they prepared for the elf invasion. Inside the city thousands more protected the castle as Artwore and Sangrayus kept their prisoner stuffed in a dungeon away from any embrace from the sun.

In the darkness Mayreon's hands were cuffed to the chains on the wall. Barely able to reach the chains she was forced to stand on the balls of her feet as her heals rose in the air. Dirty from the nasty dust and mud surrounding the dungeon her still beautiful face looked all around her cold atmosphere.

A form was heard coming her way as she looked to the dim light to see a woman's shape coming toward her. A red gem on the head of the woman began to glow as the cold face of Sangrayus was seen.

"It is time queen of the elves," Sangrayus replied, "The Dark Lord awaits you."

"He won't have time," Mayreon assured, "I can feel them."

"Feel them all you want," Sangrayus told, "We will only need a few moments."

"I will escort her," A voice replied as the shape of Fayne emerged in back of the evil sorceress.

Sangrayus turned to see him as she soon slowly walked passed him. Several Falmore guards stood in back of him as one unlocked the dungeon. Two walked over to Mayreon and began to unlock her chains. One of the guards smiled at the other as he began to run his hands down Mayreon's body. Sickened Mayreon turned away as the guard grabbed her breast. The sound of a sword was heard and a loud slice. Mayreon opened her eyes to see the guard looking right at her. Soon the sign of life exited his eyes as he fell dead. Fayne had blood on the end of his sword as he quickly placed it away and looked at the other guards.

"Let that be a lesson to the rest of you," Fayne replied.

As Mayreon was let down she stood next to Fayne as they walked up the stairs of the dungeon.

"My apologies," Fayne replied.

"It's alright," Mayreon assured, "You didn't have to kill him."

Fayne looked at her and said, "He disrespected a pure woman. He deserved to die."

"I believe in forgiveness," Mayreon told.

"I do not," Fayne replied.

"Maybe that is why you are cursed," Mayreon said.

Fayne looked at her as they walked and then forward as he said, "Perhaps. But my curse will be over soon. That I assure."

"And then what?" Mayreon asked, "Kill all those in Tullian?"

"That's the plan," Fayne replied, "Nothing will give me more pleasure."

"Over a love you lost?" Mayreon asked.

Fayne looked at her and asked, "Do you love?"

Mayreon looked down and said, "Yes."

"What would you do if you lost them?" Fayne asked, "Not just lost them but were the reason they died. I was the one who slammed my blade into my loves chest and watched her die before my eyes."

"I can never imagine your pain," Mayreon told, "But there must be a way you can forgive your maker."

"Never," Fayne said quickly, "I do not want his forgiveness. I want him to have the same look on his face as I destroy every one of his creations."

"Not even you can take on an army," Mayreon reminded.

"I will have an army of my own," Fayne assured.

"Falmores?" Mayreon asked.

"When Tamian is killed by me I will be able to send the blessings I have onto anyone I wish," Fayne told, "And you know what that means. An Army of Falmores blessed by the first warrior of Warad. Warad's champion who took the lives of all the other god's champions. Their blessings are written on my body. Not even they can take away what I've won in the battlefield."

"Do you remember the first humans?" Mayreon asked.

"Yes," Fayne replied, "I was there when they destroyed each other."

"What killed them?" Mayreon asked.

"Greed," Fayne said.

"That is all I have to say," Mayreon replied.

Fayne looked at her as she continued to get escorted to where ever she was going.

"I know this love of yours," Fayne said.

"You do?" Mayreon asked.

"Lyncade," Fayne said.

"Yes," Mayreon said in disbelief.

"I remember his father," Fayne told.

"How?" Mayreon asked.

"Fyncade was Talius' champion," Fayne remembered.

"Lyncade is the son of one of the first elves?" Mayreon asked.

"Yes," Fayne confirmed, "And weak like his father. It's a shame that he hasn't been informed of his true fate. He has no idea who he truly is either."

They soon came to a large hallway as the doors opened slowly. Mayreon was escorted in by Fayne as the guards stayed outside the doors. The doors closed as Mayreon walked through a large throne room where Artwore sat next to his mother. As they walked Mayreon saw a platform on the side of the throne. Unable to do anything Mayreon watched as Sangrayus held out her hand and lifted Mayreon in the air. Mayreon tried to dispel but Sangrayus was too powerful. She lifted Mayreon over to the platform and placed her on it. Seconds later a red cage made from Sangrayus' magic surrounded Mayreon and made her unable to move.

Artwore pulled out his blade and walked to the bottom of the stairs leading up to the throne. He slammed the blade into the ground as the ground itself began to shake. Seconds later three forms of black mist came out in front of them as The Dark Lord, Greco and Korack appeared.

Artwore and Sangrayus quickly kneeled in front of The Dark Lord as he gestured for them to rise. They did as The Dark Lord stared at the imprisoned Mayreon.

"What do you command?" Artwore asked.

"Prepare your ranks," The Dark Lord commanded, "Greco and Korack will help you and fight beside you as they invade. Make sure Fayne is in the frontlines. Once he and Tamian meet in the battlefield do what ever you can to keep them alone. Lyncade must be killed before he has a chance to get near Fayne."

"What about me?" Sangrayus asked.

The Dark Lord looked at his student and replied, "Your powers are strong here. The Elves set sail not too long ago. Make sure they lose many forces before they come near your lands."

Sangrayus smiled as she said, "Of course."

"So you will be left alone with this sorceress?" Greco asked.

The Dark Lord held out his hand as the force field around Mayreon vanished.

"What are you doing?" Korack asked.

"Leave her to me," The Dark Lord commanded, "Go at once."

Korack and Greco looked at each other puzzled for several moments before walking with Artwore and Sangrayus toward the exit. Fayne stood in back of The Dark Lord as he studied Mayreon.

"I've seen her before," Fayne told.

"Impossible," The Dark Lord said, "I believe you have a war to fight."

Fayne just bowed his head slightly to The Dark Lord's back and walked away.

The Dark Lord quickly began to look at Mayreon as she stayed on the platform in fear. The Dark Lord held out his hand as Mayreon tensed in fear. Mayreon slowly began to get lifted in the air as she was placed in front of the massive demon creature.

"You are intoxicating," The Dark Lord complimented, "No doubt the definition of beauty and purity itself."

Mayreon looked at him in fear and slowly asked, "What will you do with me."

The Dark Lord began to pace in front of her as he said, "The choice is really up to you."

"What do you mean?" Mayreon asked.

The Dark Lord short of smiled as Mayreon could just make out his mouth hidden in the hood as he did.

"I am aware of the life you have inside of you," The Dark Lord said.

"Please don't hurt him," Mayreon begged.

"Tell me what I wish to know," The Dark Lord commanded.

"I don't know where they are," Mayreon assured.

"Sure you do," The Dark Lord replied, "You were born with the knowledge. Born with it somewhere in your mind."

"Warad must have erased it from my mind," Mayreon replied, "I swear to you now that I have no idea where it is."

The Dark Lord studied her and then replied, "I see no deception in your eyes, but I must search your mind."

"You will harm the child inside of me doing that," Mayreon knew.

"Do you really think I care for the life of Tamian's child?" The Dark Lord asked.

"How do you know?" Mayreon asked.

"I know many things," The Dark Lord assured, "You reek of infidelity."

"I was powerless against him," Mayreon assured saddened.

"And a love for another," The Dark Lord saw.

Mayreon tried to hide it as the form of Halouse went through her head. Blocking him out it seemed The Dark Lord was inside her mind as he soon came to her thoughts.

A small laugh came from The Dark Lord as he replied, "The son of Calbrawn."

Breaking out in tears Mayreon knew she couldn't hide anything from him. She took a few steps back almost tripping over the first stair to the throne. The Dark Lord laughed as it seemed he was getting off on her fear for him.

"I can give you a choice," The Dark Lord told.

"What do you mean?" Mayreon asked.

"Join me," The Dark Lord requested, "Fight beside me against Warad and all of his creations. I can help you with your training. Finish it if you wish. Teach you things that not even Sygon knows."

"I cannot betray my people," Mayreon assured.

Holding up his hand Mayreon began to choke.

"You do not have much of a choice," The Dark Lord replied as he loosened his grip.

Outside Sangrayus stood on the highest cliff as she stared out into the ocean in front of her. She began to chant the word of the gods as the clouds above her began to turn black and gray. With her hands electrified with red lighting the clouds soon began to fly toward the land of Tullian and the hundreds of ships that were sailing toward her home. The whole world around her turned black as well as the warriors camped in front of the city began to take cover in the small tents they made.

In the open sea Lyncade stood at the front of the ship as he looked toward the horizon ahead. It would only be a few more hours before the land of Fadarth was seen. He soon felt the wind pick up as it began to get intense. The hundreds of warriors rested on the deck of the ship as they too began to feel the severe breeze.

"My lord," Raven called to him, "What is it?"

Lyncade looked in back of him at Raven and replied, "It is surly the tactics of The Dark Lord. He wished us death even before we land."

"He has no power," Raven reminded, "He cannot raise such a storm."

In the distance Lyncade began to see the black and gray clouds as they quickly rushed toward them. The hundreds of ships in the water all began to feel the intense waves as the storm was seconds away from hitting them.

"Brace yourselves," Lyncade yelled.

All across the water the ships dealt with heavy waves. Each wave that hit shocked the boat as warriors who were too close to the sides were tossed off and thrown into the deadly sea. Lyncade stood on the front of the ship still looking ahead. He watched as ships in the water in front of him were broken in half by the powerful waves. Hundreds of Royal Elves drowning as the others were unable to do anything about it.

Mayreon still frightened by The Dark Lord in front of her feared for the life she carried and her own. His request was thought about for several moments as she looked at him.

"It isn't a hard choice," The Dark Lord assured, "Sangrayus is becoming a bit of a nuisance. She is in fact only human and unable to acquire the many skills I can give her."

"I can not go against Warad," Mayreon assured, "I will surly be killed."

"No," The Dark Lord replied, "Unlike gods your kind is capable of going beyond your own expectations. You are able to take in the knowledge the other gods instilled into the world and use them to your advantage. Korack, Greco and I are cursed. Unable to use the powers we were once given."

"And you will be forever," Mayreon assured.

"You are so imprudent," The Dark Lord said, "Unable to see the whole of everything. The location of all the rubies is within you. Why would Warad give you that wisdom unless he knew you were powerful enough to defend it from me?"

"I am not powerful," Mayreon assured.

"Not yet," The Dark Lord replied, "But you will be soon. I see it I you now. The powers you can have if you only let me teach you."

"I can't," Mayreon yelled, "I will not."

"Your mind will soon change," The Dark Lord assured.

With what she knew Mayreon saw a spear hanging on the wall as she used her mind to pick it up. As it levitated in the air she tossed it toward The Dark Lord. With little effort the spear stopped several feet in front of him as he grabbed Mayreon with his powers. Using a control spell Mayreon was lifted in the air as the spear was now thrown toward her. Holding out her hands slightly the spear stopped in front of her. The two now battled for control of it as it was several feet from Mayreon. Still levitating Mayreon was squeezed as The Dark Lord closed his hand. Mayreon was forced to let go of the spear with her powers as The Dark Lord made the end of the spear go to Mayreon's neck.

"I see we are going to have to do this the hard way," The Dark Lord replied.

A ball of green light was thrown from his hands as it covered Mayreon's head. Dropping to her knees her eyes rolled in the back of her head. All the hatred The Dark Lord had began to go into the mind of Mayreon. The unbearable hatred began to surge throughout her body as it entered into the child she was carrying.

Back on the open sea there were several ships that had fell victim to the spell Sangrayus was casting. Lyncade was now on the deck keeping all the soldiers away from the edges of the boats. The waves got more and more intense as he watched ships get crushed in front of him. The wreckage of each ship came toward them as it smacked into the front of the boat. The ship was tossed high in the air as several warriors were thrown from the ship and were lost to the sea. The ship then narrowly missed more peaces as Lyncade got up and looked at the gigantic waves in front of him. Just as Lyncade thought the storm was becoming too much he heard a loud thunder as a blue light was fired to the sky above. In the matter of seconds the powerful storm seemed to fade as the water and wind went back to normal. Lyncade in shock and soaked in seawater looked to the top of the ship to see Sygon.

"I think you are in need of some assistance," Sygon replied.

Smiling in relief Lyncade fell to the deck in exhaustion. The other ships around them soon saw Sygon standing on the top of the ship as they roared in cheer. The wizard just looked ahead as Fadarth would be in their sight very soon.

Washed up on the shores of Fadarth was a small boat as five Falmore guards slowly walked up to it. It was ashore on the opposite end of the city and who ever sailed it made sure they couldn't be seen by the masses. Walking over to it slowly the guards pulled out their blades and quickly inspected the boat. Finding nothing they quickly looked to the beach and saw footprints leading to the forest near by. They quickly took off after the footsteps as the fifth guard went back in the direction he came to make sure he went back and informed the kingdom what they had found.

As they ran toward the direction of the footprints the sound of a hurling weapon was heard. The first Falmore in the front was hit in the forehead quickly by an ax as he died instantly. Halouse emerged from the forest with a bow an arrow as he aimed two arrows at once. Firing he hit one Falmore in the head and a second in the chest.

Quickly pulling his blade he finished the Falmore he wounded with the arrow and chopped into the chest of the last one as it came at him. Removing his blade from the dead Falmore he quickly went in the direction of the Falmore running home to warn the others. He picked up pace quickly as he was only a twenty feet in back of the Falmore. Unsuspecting of Halouse the Falmore slowed down. As the Falmore caught his breath he heard the sound of running. Just as he turned he saw a blade coming right for him. Stabbing him viciously in the eye Halouse kicked the Falmore away. Halouse walked over to the wounded guard and swung his blade down on him over and over. As the blood flew from the wound it began to get all over Halouse's face as he gained control of himself. Not bothering to remove the blood he just went in the direction of the city and placed his blade in his case around his back.

Sangrayus entered her personal chambers to see her son Artwore awaiting her. She just looked at him as he sat lazily in a chair with his hand covering his face.

"Are you waiting for something?" Sangrayus asked.

"War," Artwore told.

"You shall have it in a matter of moments," Sangrayus told as she walked over to a bowl of blood and placed her hand over it, "It is only a matter of moments before the elves hit our shores."

"Our army outnumbers them," Artwore replied as he sat forward, "And with the weapons I was given they do not stand a chance."

"As soon as The Dark Lord finds what he is looking for inside the mind of Mayreon their army will be destroyed in a matter of seconds," Sangrayus added.

"With Fayne as well it's over," Artwore knew.

Sangrayus began to see a form as she looked into the bowl of blood.

"There is a problem," Sangrayus told.

Jumping up Artwore went to his mother's side.

"What is it?" Artwore asked.

"The elves you killed," Sangrayus began, "Their bloodline is here."

"In the ships headed to shore?" Artwore asked.

"No," Sangrayus quickly yelled, "He is on our lands right now."

Artwore jumped to his feet as he began to walk out of the room.

"He is headed our way from the northeast," Sangrayus yelled.

As quick as Artwore could command, a force of one hundred men began to go out and search for Halouse. Fayne stood next to Artwore as they watched the party quickly go mounted on horseback.

"You should have sent me," Fayne told.

"I need you here," Artwore told, "Who knows how close Tamian and his forces are."

"I wouldn't have taken me long," Fayne assured.

"Let my forces handle it," Artwore replied.

"What if they fail?" Fayne asked.

"What will he do?" Artwore yelled in anger, "Storm the city surrounded by thousands of our guards?"

The loud sound of a war horn went off as Artwore and Fayne looked to the sea. There in the distance hundreds of ships began to come into view. Artwore seemed to smile as the forces around him began to scatter to prepare for the war.

"Here is your time to lift your curse," Artwore told.

Fayne looked to a Falmore guard and yelled, "Get my armor and things at once."

The guard quickly took off as Artwore could almost feel the presence of Tamian.

Tamian looked out from the front of his boat at the army of Falmores preparing for them on the beach. Rakar stood next to him on the ship as they began to see the army closer.

"They'll have thousands on the beach and thousands more in front of the city," Rakar told, "We can't afford to lose our men."

"We won't," Tamian assured, "Maxus has my command for the archers. As soon as their in range they'll take out hundreds before we even hit the shores."

"We are taking on a whole civilization," Rakar reminded.

"We are elves," Tamian reminded, "One of our men is ten of theirs."

"Fayne is with them," Rakar reminded, "If he finds you in the field he will kill you."

Tamian looked back at the Forest Elf King and said, "I have that under control."

Lyncade and Raven were side by side on their boat as they began to get closer to the shore. With arrows flying passed them Lyncade hung over the front of the boat a little as he was anxious to go to battle. The beaches became overrun with Falmores as they stood only a few feet where the water washed ashore. Each warrior inside his ship crowded in back of him as they stared down the thousand awaiting at the beach. Lyncade's ship was in the front of the rest by only a few feet but he would surly be the first to step foot on the land of Fadarth.

"Men," Lyncade called as he still looked forward, "My wife is in grave danger. I will walk through hell to get her back and there is no other rank I'd rather fight beside then you."

From the top deck of the ship Sygon raised his hand high in the air as lighting began to go off in the heavens. Lighting struck down on his hands as they began to glow a deep blue. Throwing his hands toward the shore lighting bolts began to hit the first few ranks of Falmores that awaited. Sand blasted into the air as each bolt hit its target killing every Falmore as it struck.

Lyncade was in throwing distance of the Falmores as he held his hand out to Raven. Raven quickly handed him a spear as he held one of his own. Lyncade, Raven and all the others in the front of the boat hurled their spears. Lyncade's hit his target as a Falmore was thrown back from the force of the impact. Lyncade once again held out his hand as Raven handed him another. With arrows flying passed him at an incredible rate he hurled a second killing another Falmore. Removing his blade Lyncade felt the boat hit the sand below as he jumped from the top and landed into a foot of water. Just as his feet hit his sword was immediately throw outward killing a Falmore as it charged. Soul Stealer then began to glow as he swiped recklessly at every Falmore that came. Each blade that struck was shattered into hundreds of peaces at Lyncade began to took on swarms without a problem. Raven and the others in his rank stood by his side as they too had no problem with the army of Falmores that awaited. With each ship landing many ranks of elves began to land quickly taking out the ranks of Falmores that stood in their way.

Landing further away from the battle Tazzill was aboard the ship Tamian was on. Running with a purpose he kept his sword away in its case and held his mighty ax with one hand. Like the brute he was he swung with the power of a god chopping Falmores in half with each attack. Tamian and his ranks began to get together as the ships containing the Forest Elves began to land. Staying back to get his forces Rakar awaited them as he watched Tamian's ranks flank the Falmores on the beach.

From the city wall in the highest tower Sangrayus watched the battle with Artwore beside her. Korack and Greco soon appeared as they too watched from a distance. The battle was about a mile or so away but because of the height of the tower it could just be seen by all of them.

"I'll unleash my men," Artwore replied.

"No," Korack quickly replied, "Have them retreat at once and take cover inside the city."

"I will not run," Artwore replied angered.

"You must," Greco jumped in, "If you retreat now you will have thousands remaining to protect your high walls. With the high ground you stand a chance."

Artwore looked to a guard standing behind them and nodded his head. The guard quickly blew on his war horn as the thousands on the beach soon began to retreat.

"They will wait for the rest of their army to land before they can do anything," Korack assured, "Prepare the walls and gather your men."

The rank of one hundred Falmores could hear the sounds of the horn but ignored it. Knowing their city was under attack their quest was to seek out the elf that Sangrayus had seen in her bowl of blood. Searching endlessly for tracks of the experienced elf every track seemed to vanish as they continued their vigorous search. As they swiped at every bush and stabbed into every peace of tall grass that might have been a safe haven for the elf; a pair of eyes looked down on them from the highest tree. The tired warrior was hidden inside a large bird nest that was abandoned by the resent wildlife that used it to raise their young. Filled with mud and dirt that stuck to him from his wet clothing it was the perfect concealment from the Falmore warriors that hunted him. Tired and weary from traveling on a boat to the island the warrior was emotional and psychically drained. The loss of his two brothers wounded him deeply. Though there was no blood shedding from his skin the emotional torture of losing the only family he had was a stab to the heart that only he could heal.

Halouse couldn't face his father after what had happened unless he avenged his brother's deaths. His eyes stayed over the nest very carefully as he watched the large regiment continue to try and get a sense of where he was. Warfare was in the air even as he tried to hide. He knew his fellow men were on the beaches giving the Falmore army all they had. His quest was not to kill the Falmores, but to kill their king. Avenge his brothers and save the only woman he ever loved. Her love was with another and this was also another burden on his mind as he tried to balance each pain as he laid there.

The sense of no hope went through his mind constantly as he rested in the nest looking up at the beautiful blue sky. The sounds of the warriors below seemed muted as he tried to lose himself in the moment of the elegant heavens. Even that seemed to remind him of Mayreon as the sky seemed to be a mirror image of her eyes piercing through him like a cold knife in the dead of winter. The emptiness in his stomach increased as once again he tried to find a way to not think about her.

As flashes of her went through his subconscious he felt himself fade. The constant thinking and endless traveling seemed to finally catch up to the warrior. With his sword resting tightly in his hand he could almost feel himself letting it go as he drifted asleep. Short moans of emotional pain came from his mouth as he saw the bodies of his brothers at their final moments. The embrace him and Mayreon shared seemed to be a disturbing tattoo forever in his mind. A moment he feared he would never get to share with her ever again even if he succeeded. The sounds from below faded as Halouse knew his mind was carrying him far away from where he was.

Halouse arouse what seemed to be seconds later. Instead of a tree he was in a comfortable bed inside an open temple. Large pillars held up the massive roof of the temple he laid so peacefully in. Instead of doors there were white curtains all around gusting toward him as the wind passed through them. All around him were candles and the dark night plagued the outside world. This place was so alive though with color and embrace as he got up from the bed and looked around.

"I like it," A voice called as it startled him.

Halouse went for his weapon but realized it wasn't there. He looked over to see Warad walking toward him as the flames from the candles seemed to go toward him. Never seeing or ever being in his presence before, Halouse knew immediately who it was. Rising slowly he seemed in awe of the god as he stared at him in wonder.

"Most people when they get away pick waterfalls or rivers," Warad replied to him as he looked around the temple, "I like the touch you put into this place."

Still in awe Halouse shook his head and asked, "Excuse me?"

Warad looked at him and replied, "You created this place inside your mind. A way to escape where you were to try and drive away the demons that lurk inside your fragile mind."

"How did I make this?" Halouse asked with his hands out to his sides.

"You made it with your mind," Ward told.

"So it's a dream?" Halouse asked.

"Call it what you want," Warad said, "But I assure that I am no false image in this dream you are having. I am the real thing."

"Why did I come here?" Halouse asked.

"To escape," Warad told, "When you awake you will figure out what it is you must do."

"And what is that?" Halouse asked.

"Only you know," Warad replied as he sat in a chair and leaned forward.

The feeble wizard seemed to moan in pain as he slowly sat. Halouse knew that the weak look of the god was only a mirage to those who challenged him. With just a flick of his finger he knew the mighty god could cripple him and not even think twice about it. Those old wise eyes had many things behind it that Halouse couldn't even begin to understand. Warad knew it all; the meaning of life, his fate, and the fate of the world around him at that very moment. He couldn't even begin to understand the ultimate purpose Warad wanted for him. He skipped the usual questions that he thought were asked to the god as he just continued to stare at him.

"You're mad at me," Warad knew.

"I have every right," Halouse told.

"Do you?" The god asked just looking forward.

"Why do this to me?" Halouse asked.

"Your brothers died with honor," Warad told, "They died for a cause they believed in."

"And I have prayed to you in every moment since to help me avenge them." Halouse told, "But why so much at once?"

"There are many things I will instill on you that you will not understand until later on in your life," Warad told.

"I must know now," Halouse yelled, "They were all I had."

Warad looked over at him and replied, "There is someone else in which your soul calls to."

"And she is married to another," Halouse reminded angrily.

"Love is very complicated," The god replied softly.

"She loves him," Halouse replied, "It's not as if it was a marriage she never wanted. I see the look in her eyes when she is around him."

"And I see the way you look at her," Warad replied, "Your intentions are pure you proved that when you picked up the ruby."

"Then what?" Halouse yelled, "Try to be with her while she is with another? You have cursed me when all I have done is serve you and your people faithfully."

"And you have," Warad replied as he rose, "I am forever in debt to you for that."

"Then why curse me?" Halouse yelled, "I feel like I can't breathe every moment I'm not with her. Like I'm drowning in a river struggling to try to reach the surface. Even if I kill this man and save her what will it do?"

"It will prove what I knew you always were," Warad explained, "What I wanted you to be since you were born."

"The valiant warrior who wins but never gets the benefit?" Halouse asked, "The man who gets to watch the woman he loves be with another? You had our paths cross too late."

"It was perfect timing," Warad yelled as a gust of powerful wind flew toward the elf.

In fear Halouse backed away from the blast as he was forced to sit on the bed. The candles went out as Warad realized he had frightened the mortal warrior. With just a lift of his hand the candles lit up once again.

"Come," Warad called.

Halouse slowly got up and followed the god to a small bowl. Warad stood in front of the bowl as Halouse looked at it.

"To you this is just a bowl," Warad replied, "but it will help you with what you need to know."

"What is it a magic eye?" Halouse asked.

"No it's just a bowl," Warad replied frustrated.

Halouse looked to the ground in humiliation as Warad put his finger in the bowl and began to stir it slowly. He stopped as he waited for it to settle once again. Warad squeezed his hand together as a blue light took over his hand. He opened his palm to reveal a small pebble.

"Take it," Warad demanded.

Halouse slowly took the pebble from his maker and looked at it for several moments.

"That is your key," Warad told.

"Is it a magic..." Halouse began.

"If you say magic stone I will hit you," Warad replied.

"I'm sorry," Halouse assured.

"It's simple Halouse," Warad told, "Pretend this bowl is your existence. Your world as it is now. Each event was cause by a tiny pebble."

"How?" Halouse asked.

"Drop the pebble in the bowl," Warad told.

As Halouse did he saw all the small ripples in the water.

"Each event has a ripple effect," Warad told, "One simple thing can change the outcome of a world. If you cast that tiny stone into a large lake you would see the same result. The ripples that begin to affect everything around it. The center of it all was the moment you met Mayreon. From that point forward the fate of the world began to spread. All things that stand it that way will fall if this world wishes it to. Your brothers were your life but weren't in the future of what was to be. They were with you so they came to the end of their life like they were supposed to. To drive you to do what you needed for the rest of the ripples to happen. Your fate, your purpose will never be clear maybe not even after you leave this place behind.

"I needed you to find Mayreon, Halouse. To fall in love with her so you will end up doing what needs to be done. You can hate me now, never fight for my cause every again after this battle but in the end you must understand that everything has its reasons. Do not let the heartbreak of never be able to call her your own cloud what you must do. You are the only thing right now that will decide the outcome of this world. You may not except it now or understand but I swear to you that you it will be repaid. Take everything your father and brothers have taught you and use it to claim your prize."

"My prize is her," Halouse told.

"Your prize is to avenge your father's bloodline," Warad assured, "All other things may come in time. You must place your faith in knowing that when it is all done; like I promised you will have what you seek."

"Do not lie to me," Halouse begged, "You have no idea the pain I go through."

"I feel it every moment," Warad assured, "Every pain of every creation I have ever made. Never forget that I am your maker and I hate the things I must place in front of you for the world you know to be saved. I do not like to be the one that must place these afflictions on you but it must be done."

Halouse staring at his maker slowly nodded. Warad did the same as Halouse felt himself fading away. Wondering what was going on he looked to Warad for help. The god just watched him vanish as Halouse seemed to jump up.

Back to his normal existence Halouse fell from the tree he was in and shored toward the ground. Holding out his hand he grasped a branch but it snapped. He fell to the ground hard as all the wind inside of him was knocked out. Realizing it was nightfall now the stars he looked out began to get blurry. Moments later he saw the forms of Falmores above him.

"Should we kill him?" A Falmore asked.

"Bring him to Artwore at once," The leader of the Falmores replied, "He is a lord of the natives. He could be used for something."

Tamian didn't press the fight any further as he commanded to set up camp near the beach. More ships began to come in by the seconds scattering all across the Fadarth shores. He walked slowly along the beach as more of the forces landed followed by Lyncade, Rakar and Maxus. Behind them were ranks of the Royal Guard closely protecting their king.

"Why do we not attack?" Rakar asked.

"We gather the rest of our forces first," Tamian informed, "They outnumber us. Their whole race against just a fraction of my forces."

"My wife is in there," Lyncade reminded.

"No harm is coming to her," Tamian assured, "Warad wouldn't let that happen."

"You must stop putting all your hopes into a god that may or may not want her alive," Maxus reminded.

"He wants her alive," Tamian assured, "He came to me and told me."

"When?" Maxus asked.

"He came to the both of us," Rakar jumped in, "The Dark Lord needs her."

"What of the natives?" Tamian asked Lyncade.

"They landed fine as we hoped," Lyncade told, "They fight under your command."

"Good," Tamian replied, "Make sure they do just as I request when I need them."

"They are under orders from Calbrawn," Lyncade reminded, "They will not disobey you."

"My lord," Raven called as he approached and stood before Tamian. With a quick kneel he rose and replied, "A small ship was spotted not far from here from a few of our scouts."

"What does it mean?" Tamian asked.

"Believed to be the ship Halouse used to land," Raven told.

"How does it look?" Lyncade asked his captain.

"The tracks aren't old at all," Raven told, "He landed just before we did."

Tamian looked to the castle ahead and asked, "Would he go without us?"

"His infatuation with my wife is strong as well as the thirst to get vengeance for the death of his brothers," Lyncade admitted, "It may even get him killed."

"May Warad be with him," Tamian replied.

"My lord," Raven called once again.

"Yes," Tamian replied as he turned to him.

"We lost three ships with our horses aboard them," Raven informed, "Our Calvary is big but not as intimidated as it should be."

"How many ships of ranks did we lose?" Tamian asked.

"About five or so," Raven told.

"It will have to do," Tamian replied as he looked at the city again, "I want that city burning to the ground for the disrespect Artwore has given my people and its queen."

"I will give you his head," Lyncade promised.

"Leave him to me," Maxus jumped in.

"He is right," Tamian told Lyncade, "You know who your fight is with."

Just as Tamian said that in the distance Lyncade could see a black armored warrior staring at them. With the shadow of a sword peeking out of his back the cold eyes of Fayne watched Lyncade as he looked back. They would soon meet in battle and the two awaited their fate to cross paths.

"He will come for only you," Rakar told Tamian as they all seemed to see Fayne awaiting them.

"Get my armor ready," Tamian replied to one of his servants.

Lyncade quickly grabbed the servant and looked at his king.

"What?" Tamian asked.

"I think I have a plan," Lyncade replied.

The others just looked at Lyncade curiously as he made the statement.

Chapter 18

Fayne entered Artwore's chambers in an angered mood as he grabbed a table and flipped it over. Sangrayus watched from the corner at his rage as she didn't seem upset or fearful of it. Artwore sat in a chair with his hand over his mouth as he didn't seem to flinch at Fayne's actions either.

"This battle should be over," Fayne yelled, "Why hold me back?"

"It is the command of The Dark Lord," Artwore told still staring blankly ahead, "He wishes to have more personal time with the sorceress and queen, Mayreon."

"He is wasting time," Fayne yelled, "They gather outside your city as we speak moments away from attacking. They have the blessing of Warad on their hearts but I have it scratched into my flesh since the day I was made."

"You took those marks from the five others that were made the same time you were," Artwore replied frustrated.

"I earned them by slaying them by my own hand," Fayne replied so angered he spit from his mouth.

"How many of my sons will you preach this same argument with?" Sangrayus asked as she walked toward the warrior.

"As many as I need to until I get what I want," Fayne yelled, "I will go to the field with no one in back of me and take what is mine."

"Tamian will not die quickly," Artwore assured, "He is blessed to never be killed by his enemies."

"But he is cursed to die by the hand of a member of his own race," Fayne reminded, "That member is me."

"Do not confuse yourself with silly legends," Sangrayus warned.

"Legends is all we have to predict what will happen," Fayne told.

"What *can* happen," Sangrayus stressed, "It is not assured."

"It will be assured by my hand," Fayne told, "Like all things I have went to battle for."

They watched the elf walk away as they looked at one another. Artwore continued to stare blankly ahead as his mother studied him.

"What bothers you?" Sangrayus asked.

"How long it is taking them to crack a simple sorceress," Artwore replied, "I want my commands at once."

"Demand them," Sangrayus replied.

Back in the throne room The Dark Lord continued his torture to Mayreon for many hours. The surge of his hatred and rage went through her and the child she carried inside of her. She fought back everything as it hit her. Many things couldn't be stopped as she lay on the ground getting blasted over and over again. He continued his spell on Mayreon as the blast he threw at her continued to surge through her whole body. Yelling in pain Mayreon begged with every scream to stop what he was doing. She didn't fear for her life but for the life that was inside of her. She had no idea what affect it would have on her child. Pure evil seemed to be the motive of the spell but because of what she was she was unable to be harmed by it mortally. It tore at her soul but wasn't killing her body or causing any long term harm. The Dark Lord stopped his spell as Mayreon's entire body smoked from the after affect. The clothes she was wearing was starting to burn off as her naked body began to get exposed.

"How many nobles and kings would wish to see this moment," The Dark Lord replied evilly as he stalked over the young sorceress.

Trying to move, her wounded body reached out to The Dark Lord in an attempt to cast a spell of her own.

Laughing evilly The Dark Lord replied, "You lack the strength."

"Warad is my strength," Mayreon assured softly.

"He watches as I torture you slowly," The Dark Lord reminded, "Does that sound like a god that cares at all for you?"

"He is giving me strength in other forms not of attacking," Mayreon assured.

The Dark Lord continued to walk around her as he replied, "You only fear for the life inside of you. Why not that of your own life?"

"It is my duty now to not care about me but to care of him," Mayreon told.

"Him?" The Dark Lord asked, "You feel a son?"

"A warrior that will have my courage as a brave warrior," Mayreon told.

"You seem so certain," The Dark Lord replied.

"It is he that will destroy you and all your evils," Mayreon assured.

A statement that would usual make The Dark Lord laugh had him silenced. He looked at her his face still hidden by the hood worn over his massive head. He seemed to tilt his head as her statement seemed to echo inside of his mind. Mayreon noticed the silence and quickly looked over at him. With fear in her eyes she slowly tried to get up. With a quick blast the most intense ray struck the young sorceress in her chest as she lifted into the air. The brief surge entered her body as the hatred of a thousand lifetimes entered her and affected her whole body. It was a blast that would definitely kill her if the blast continued. As The Dark Lord watched her body raise into the air as a result of the hit it was soon countered by a blast in back of him. Mayreon was tossed away and knocked out cold from the impact.

The Dark Lord turned and soon saw the feeble form of his father standing at the entrance of the throne room. The Dark Lord looked down at him as he slowly began to approach.

"What is this that I feel father?" The Dark Lord asked, "Searching for one answer and getting another. What she said is true isn't it? Trying to hide her from me because she holds the key to your ultimate plan."

"Do you have any idea what will happen here?" Warad asked as he then began to walk slowly toward his son.

"Thousands will die," The Dark Lord knew, "The Falmores wiped from the earth just as soon as I get what I want. The answers that lie within that sorceress you tried so hard to keep from me."

"Killing her now out of frustration will only delay your search for your ruby," Warad assured.

"It will stop the son that is inside of her from being able to be born and stop me," The Dark Lord told.

"You kill her now," Warad began, "You will never have what you want."

"Fayne will kill Tamian and return to Tullian as my champion," The Dark Lord told.

"You really think he can kill Tamian?" Warad asked.

The two finally stood only a few feet from the other. The large Dark Lord standing massively over his creator.

"Tamian will be killed by a member of his own race," The Dark Lord reminded.

"Then it is settled," Warad replied.

"What?" The Dark Lord asked confused.

"If Fayne should kill Tamian I will give you your ruby," Warad told as he slightly looked up at his son.

"You lie," The Dark Lord said as he paced in front of his father, "You only protect the sorceress that I am trying to get answers from."

"Forget her," Warad replied, "I will give you every answer you need if and when Tamian falls. Call it a small wager between two gods that will settle their fate among the mortals that have been created."

"I do not put my fate into the hands of mortals," The Dark Lord told.

"But you seem so sure," Warad replied, "You guarantee the death of Tamian by the hands of Fayne and now you wish not to place that into the hands of my champion?"

Greco and Korack emerged in back of The Dark Lord at that moment. The three of them together still couldn't defeat the god that had created them. The battle had been waged ages ago when they were at full strength. Now with half their powers taken and placed inside the ruby's that The Dark Lord wanted they could easily be killed by him. Warad though was unable to attack them, he could only fight them if they tried to attack him first. Knowing this The Dark Lord just looked at his father as well as Greco and Korack.

"What is this wager?" Korack asked.

"Here are the other two," Warad replied as he noticed them, "If you gain your ruby like I promise if Tamian falls you can regain theirs.

Raise the army of hell and come into my lands with all your powers. All that needs to happen is what you promised."

"Take it," Greco replied.

"It is written in legend," Korack added.

The Dark Lord just studied his father as he asked, "What care do you have for this sorceress that you have never had for any other?"

"The answers you seek from her she does not have at this moment," Warad reminded, "Let her live. Let her son be born and then you can fight him. He is no threat to you now and won't be if you gain your ruby. You and I both know that if you kill her the knowledge of where your ruby is will never be known. Get passed that now."

"Fayne wins I get the ruby," The Dark Lord said.

"Fayne loses you return to The Dark Realm for five hundred years," Warad replied, "And leave the world of Tullian in peace for all that time."

The Dark Lord looked at Warad for several moments before he turned around and replied, "Prepare to get my ruby."

The Dark Lord, Greco and Korack all vanished as Warad leaned on his staff and vanished himself.

Moments later Artwore and Sangrayus entered as they looked all around.

"What has happened?" Artwore asked.

"I feel the presence of The Dark Lord far away from here," Sangrayus told.

"Why has he left?" Artwore asked.

"I do not know," Sangrayus replied confused.

Just as she began to say that sentence the Falmore guards rushed in dragging Halouse all the way to where they were. They dropped him in front of Artwore as Halouse ached in pain.

"What is this?" Artwore asked.

"We found him in the forest," A Falmore told, "He is the warrior our queen had seen in her vision."

Halouse didn't pay any attention to Artwore or Sangrayus as he saw the body of Mayreon lying unconscious. Sangrayus and Artwore noticed this as they turned and looked at Mayreon as well.

"So if it isn't the brother," Artwore replied as he sifted his head toward Halouse, "Come to get vengeance for the death of his brothers."

"He is here for the sorceress as well," Sangrayus told.

"I shall give her back to him," Artwore told, "In peaces."

Halouse sword was dropped a few feet in front of Artwore as Halouse looked at it quickly. Mayreon slowly began to come to as she looked at Halouse. Her eyes widened as he looked at her. A small smirk came to his face as knew she was safe. She seemed to feel the same as she looked at him. Halouse seemed to talk to her with his eyes.

"Leave us," Artwore commanded to his men, "You will need to be on the walls as the elf army attacks."

"Yes my lord," A Falmore replied as the rest of them began to leave.

Artwore kept his hand on his sword as he kicked Halouse's toward him. Halouse looked on cautiously as he reached a little and watched as Artwore paced in front of him.

"You must kill him," Sangrayus told, "Do not play games with him."

"It'll be quick," Artwore told, "Take care of the sorceress."

Sangrayus turned to try and kill the unconscious Mayreon but she had vanished behind them.

Outside the city the elf army began to get in their ranks. The thousands were ready as the form of their king rode on horseback. Covered completely in armor and unable to see his face the army roared at the sight of the armor worn by their valiant king.

On the walls of the city the archers of the Falmores prepared as they crowded every inch of the wall. Below the entrance of the city was slowly being opened. The form of Tamian looked on in shock as he saw only one man on horseback begin to ride out. In all black armor the warrior Fayne slowly rode out until he stood outside of the gates alone. With a large spear in his hands he stabbed it to the ground below and pulled his blade from his case.

The form of Tamian commanded a rank to go to him as two hundred warriors soon began to run toward the champion. Standing in the frontlines were Lyncade, Rakar, Maxus and Tazzill.

"When he kills the last warrior it's a full out attack," Lyncade told, "*Tamian* will charge and fight him alone. He will ignore all the other ranks just to kill the king."

Fayne dropped from his horse removing his blade and killing each Royal Elf warrior that came near him. The other Royal Elves watched as the champion Fayne killed many of their most skilled warriors as if they were nothing. His blade swung freely through the air and hit vital parts of the Royal Guards bodies. The strikes dropped them quickly and didn't give them a chance to get back up. Many were wounded mortally as his sword dripped with the blood of the warriors he soon killed.

Tamian's form dropped from his horse and removed his sword as he began to walk toward Fayne. Fayne prepared holding his blade ready in his grasp. As the form of Tamian attacked the Elf army ran toward the city. Fayne ignored all the warriors passing him as he stared down the form of Tamian. All he could see was the eyes of the warrior trapped behind Tamian's war helmet.

The city walls stood high in the air as the Elves quickly charged. With no way of getting over the walls the elf warriors used their steel blades to chip away at the wall as arrows rained down upon them. The first hundred or so men slowly began to die as arrows flew into their flesh not covered with armor. The thick walls would take several attempts to break through but each rank was fierce in striking it.

In the back lines of the large army charging the city Sygon stood with his arms raised in the air. With the clouds above circling him a mighty bolt of lighting flew toward the front gates. A massive explosion even killed the first few elves up front as the wall exploded open. Falmores by the hundreds began to run out engaging with the elf army. Tazzill the only human warrior fighting for the elves swung his large ax effortlessly as the double bladed weapon pierced through Falmores even when they put up their shields to block. His ax was razor sharp and easily cut through their shields and armor with little resistance. He stood unaffected buy the many arrows that had penetrated his unarmored chest and body. Most of the arrows weren't in a place he needed to worry about at the moment.

The ranks of Royal Elves on foot fighting in the trenches of the battle soon began to clear a path. On horseback Maxus, Rakar, Lyncade and several other warriors on horseback rode into the massive hole and into the city. Surrounded by hundreds of Falmores they dodged arrows and swung down on every Falmore within their reach. The massive Calvary had little resistance getting through as hundreds of Royal Elf warriors on horseback raided the inside of the Falmore city.

Outside Fayne swung at the form of Tamian over and over as more and more elf warriors of every race passed him to get to the inside of the city. The form of Tamian seemed to be blocking and never engaging as Fayne became frustrated with the warrior. Almost chasing him in the battlefield Fayne swung recklessly as the form of Tamian blocked and jumped back from the impact of Fayne's swipes.

"Fight me," Fayne yelled in anger.

The form of Tamian stayed back still blocking and never countering the reckless strikes of Fayne. Fayne finally came in leaving himself open for a strike. The form of Tamian blocked Fayne's ill-advised attack and elbowed Fayne in the chin. Fayne swipe his blade up as he slashed the form of Tamian across the chest. The form of Tamian fell back and hit the ground hard as Tamian's war helmet fell from the warriors head. As the warrior sat up Raven stared directly at Fayne as he grasp his wound. Fayne's look of intensity turned to shock as he turned and watched the thousands of elf warriors charge the Falmore City. Ignoring Raven he turned and walked toward the city quickly as he angrily swiped at every elf warrior near him killing them instantly.

Inside the city a warrior on horseback removed the helmet he was wearing exposing the face of Tamian. He had switched armor with Raven and charged passed Fayne as Fayne fought what he thought was Tamian. Jumping from his horse he killed dozens of Falmores that faced him. Lyncade dropped from his horse as well standing side by side with The Royal Elf King. Rakar still on horseback rode up to them as Tamian looked to him.

"Burn their temples and safe houses at once," Tamian commanded, "I want all their warriors dead before my feet. Until we get Mayreon we show no mercy."

Rakar nodded as he quickly rode away giving his commands to every Forest Elf that was inside the city walls. Lyncade and Tamian

begin to walk toward the large castle as they killed every passing
Falmore quickly charging toward the front gates.

"Once we get inside the castle be aware of Sangrayus," Tamian
warned.

Hundreds of elf warriors were behind them charging along side
their leaders as they made their way toward the castle. Even on the
insides of the city the thousands of Falmores didn't stand a chance
against the better skilled elves. It would take some time but at the
pace it was going every elf was killing at least ten Falmores before
falling themselves. Lyncade and Tamian quickly saw thousands of
Falmores coming toward them as Tamian looked at Lyncade.

"Go without me," Tamian called, "Save your wife."

Inside the throne room Sangrayus searched endlessly for
Mayreon as in an angered trace she began to flip every chair and table
with her mind looking all around for the sorceress.

Halouse grabbed his blade just as Artwore removed his and struck
down on Halouse. Halouse blocked and countered quickly engaging
back but Artwore was well advanced and blocked every counter.

Falmores soon began to overrun the throne room as the battle
continued. Artwore walked away from Halouse to try and get inside
of his head as Halouse was forced to fight off each Falmore as he
watched Artwore go toward the side exit of the throne room. Seconds
later the throne room burst open as Sygon walked in with no one
beside him. Quickly feeling his presence Sangrayus turned as her
eyes began to glow red. The ruby atop her forehead did as well as she
looked down at the wizard. Quickly helping Halouse the Falmores
inside the throne room were all picked up by Sygon with his mind
and tossed toward Sangrayus. Never expecting them to come toward
her Sangrayus was overwhelmed by the men and hit with several of
them as she fell back. All the Falmore warriors were piled on top of
her as Sygon looked over at Halouse.

"Leave this place," Sygon commanded, "You will not want to stay
to see what happens."

Halouse quickly ran toward the door Artwore exited as he left the
wizard alone as he commanded.

Tamian was fighting hundreds of Falmores all along a high wall as he attempted to get closer to the castle. Many of his fellow guards were beside him as he fought the Falmores off. Ahead of him Tamian watched as a Falmore was stabbed in the back and the blade came out his chest. As the Falmore was tossed away a warrior hidden behind a mask that looked like a dragon stood in front of the Royal Elf King. Tamian swung his blade around and engaged with the warrior. Thinking it was a human Tamian did his best combination but was surprised as the warrior blocked and countered with a slice to Tamian's forearm. In surprise Tamian backed away and looked at the warrior. Holding his blade in front of him quickly he readied for the warrior to strike again. This time Tamian was prepared for the skilled warrior never underestimating him.

Fayne continued to slice away at every elf warrior angrily trying to get to Tamian. He watched as the elves were easily killing every Falmore warrior inside the gates but continued his quest to find the king of the Royal Elves. Watching in the distance he could see several thousand feet away Tamian fighting with the mysterious Dragon Warrior. Staring forward he swung accurately at every elf to the side of him as he effortlessly began to make his way toward the king.

As the war waged on all the rock throwing machines used by the Falmores soon got overwhelmed by the forces of the elves. The ranks of Royal Elves soon took the large machines and began to turn them around as they fired large boulders at the high towers and buildings inside the Falmore City. Trying to destroy the entire city they also began to pore tar on the boulders and set them on fire. All around the city with no regard for their own kind the elves threw the large boulders as they crashed into the buildings of the Falmore City. Each boulder that was on fire quickly began to burn the huts and shops the Falmores had all along the main roads.

Arrows still flew everywhere from the Falmores this time inaccurate and getting some of their own people. Tazzill attacking with a regiment of elves began to charge all along the city walls slaughtering the archers as they passed them. Each archer aimed at the charging elves as they saw them but they soon met their fate.

Lyncade searched the castle quickly never finding any signs of Mayreon being there. As he went threw a hallway he heard the sound of footsteps in back of him. As he turned he briefly saw the form of

Artwore going into a different hallway. As he gave chase he saw Halouse running after Artwore and began to follow him. Artwore exited the castle on a high wall as he jumped from it and landed on a large building next to the castle. Halouse was out of the castle as well as he jumped to the large building too. Artwore wasted no time as he dropped to the ground as the battle raged on below. Lyncade made it to the wall outside as well as he soon jumped to the building and began to follow Halouse.

As Tamian fought endlessly with the mysterious warrior he came in with a flurry of strikes and finally slashed the warrior across the shoulders. Grasping his wound the warrior backed off holding it to prevent it from bleeding. Tamian used that as his opportunity and charged. The warrior was quick to block as he countered and struck Tamian's blade so hard Tamian lost it from his grasp. Tamian reached for the blade but the mysterious warrior sliced him down his back. Tamian fell to his knees in pain as the warrior raised his blade. Fayne came in at that moment and kicked the warrior in the chest.

"He is mine," Fayne yelled to the warrior as he then raised his blade.

Lyncade followed Halouse as he soon sensed something. Looking on top of a wall he saw his king on his knees seconds away from dieing. Thinking quickly he grabbed an elf next to him holding a bow as he grabbed an arrow from his sack in lighting speed and fired. The arrow flew into Fayne's right hand as he dropped his blade. Tamian jumped forward with all the strength he had and threw his shoulder into Fayne. Fayne fell below to the ground as Tamian was then surrounded by all his guards. Massively protecting the king Tamian laid in pain as he reached for the wound on his back. Lyncade ran to where Fayne had fell as he soon didn't see him laying there. He heard the sound of yelling as he turned to block a strike from Fayne. Two more strikes came as Lyncade blocked and backed away. Shaking his hand Fayne realized that using his right hand to strike put an intolerable amount of pain on his hand. Looking at Lyncade in anger Fayne then switched his stance to a southpaw and readied for Lyncade to attack. Lyncade knew now that he stood a chance as he quickly struck at the wounded champion.

Sygon awaited Sangrayus to get up in the throne room but the moment never came. Sygon then walked impatiently over to the bodies he had thrown at her as with his mind they began to get tossed from the pile. Seconds later as all the bodies were picked up nothing was in the place of where he assumed she was. A ball of red light quickly struck Sygon in the back of he was caught of guard. Never feeling her presence he was beginning to get defeated as each second of the blast drained him of his power. Not a moment too soon and a blue light struck Sangrayus' red one as Sygon fell to the ground. Sangrayus looked over as a half naked Mayreon stood with her hands glowing. Sangrayus smiled evilly as she looked over at the inexperienced sorceress.

"Okay Mayreon," Sangrayus began, "Let us see how powerful you truly are."

With a red bolt of light Mayreon levitated in the air as the blast Sangrayus threw hit the ground. The floor exploded as Sangrayus used her other hand to throw a spell at Mayreon in the air. A green shield emerged around Mayreon as the blast seemed to bounce off it. Mayreon stopped the spell as she shifted away from the light blast and fired a blue one of her own. Sangrayus was struck in her chest as she fell back in surprise at Mayreon's quick casting. Sangrayus smiled as she rose unaffected by the force of the blast. She quickly began to make hundreds of small lights around her. Each light soon turned into a deadly weapon as she created swords, spears and axes out of the light. With just a flick of her head they were tossed in Mayreon's direction. Thinking quickly Mayreon ran out of the way of each weapon just as it missed her. An ax hurled toward her in incredible speed as Mayreon was trapped in the corner of the wall. She stopped and muttered a few words. The ax stopped inches from her forehead as Sangrayus couldn't believe what she had just seen. Mayreon sifted the ax and tossed it back at her. Because Sangrayus created the spell she quickly waved her had as the ax vanished before her.

"Impossible," Sangrayus replied in shock.

Mayreon quickly began to toss fire balls as she softly spoke the words of the gods. Her words though seemed to echo even as they were said slowly. An orange glow emerged in her hand as she fired each ball of fire at the evil sorceress. Sangrayus used her own abilities to make each ball of fire shift away from her. They hit into the walls burning them for a few moments before they vanished. To counter her onslaught of fire balls Sangrayus made her hand glow green as she created a magic whip. The whip was glowing a blood red as she threw it at Mayreon and it wrapped around her neck. Burning and choking her at the same time Mayreon tried to grab the whip out of instinct and both her hands caught on fire. Screaming in pain Mayreon dropped to her knees and began to think quickly. The earth below Sangrayus feet cracked as the earth cracked and began to move. Mayreon made the center of where Sangrayus was standing open up as a bottomless abyss was now below her.

Catching her off guard Mayreon managed to unwrap herself from the whip as a burning black mark was now around her throat. Mayreon held both hands toward Sangrayus and fired as a wave of water went at the evil sorceress. Covering her Sangrayus just looked at Mayreon wondered why she threw that particular spell. Mayreon then threw out her right hand as a bolt of lighting struck Sangrayus and her body began to get electrified. The blasts came in endlessly as the evil sorceress winced in pain as each hit her. Sangrayus thought quickly as a red bolt of fire flew from both her palms and hit Mayreon in the chest. The bolt burned what Mayreon was wearing as he flesh burned as well. Sangrayus walked toward Mayreon angrily as she held out her hand. From several feet away Mayreon's body began to tighten. The control spell Sangrayus was casting would put an end to this battle quickly. Mayreon felt as if a large hand was grabbing her entire body and squeezing.

Mayreon rose up and faced Sangrayus knowing it was the evil sorceress that made her do so. With a face of shock Mayreon could almost feel every bone in her boy tighten up as if ready to snap. Her hand began to glow as Sangrayus felt her dispel. Mayreon's feeling of being squeezed slowly began to go away as she managed to dispel it slowly. Sangrayus with a look of outrage gazed at her as she tried her spell with more conviction in her eyes. Mayreon's dispel was so powerful though that the evil sorceress couldn't believe it. She used her other hand to make the whip again as she threw it and wrapped it around Mayreon's neck again. Mayreon fought it off as she still held her hand to dispel.

Mayreon fought the choking sensation as she knew if she stopped her dispel that Sangrayus would shatter every bone in her body. Her vision began to fade as she was losing air to her brain. The magic whip burned tightly around her throat as she could feel blood coming from it. If the spell went in any deeper it could cut her throat mortally. Mayreon's hand began to fade as her consciousness did as well. She tried to scream but couldn't as the whip seemed to get tighter and tighter. Her other hand began to glow and unlike the other that was blue, this one was red. A sign of evil spells that she couldn't have known. Her face got intense and filled with rage as she was finally able to yell.

Mayreon's screams soon turned to pure anger. The spell The Dark Lord put on her earlier began to come over her as her eyes began to glow a deep red as well. Red colored lighting began to surge around her as she soon became immune to the spell Sangrayus had on her. The whip was unwrapped and Sangrayus' control spell was broken as the light around her hand shattered. Mayreon began to levitate in the air with the red lightning surging around her. Sangrayus began to throw everything she had at Mayreon but it bounced off effortlessly. Mayreon created a magic sword in her hand and hurled it at Sangrayus. The sword covered in fire flew at Sangrayus as she attempted to stop it. The sword implanted perfectly in Sangrayus chest as blood began to poor from her mouth. From the ashes of the abyss a large hand grabbed Sangrayus and began to squeeze her. Screaming in fear Sangrayus was being crush by the hand of an evil she had never felt before. Mayreon dropped to the ground and lay unconscious.

Sygon awoke from the aftereffect of his battle to hear Sangrayus screaming uncontrollable. The scream made him tremble with fear as he himself almost felt sympathy for the evil sorceress. Tears emerged from her eyes as he watched the second hand of the monster rip her in half. The crack in the earth soon closed as the evil spell Mayreon created faded away. As Sygon rose to his feet a black mist soon began to form in front of him. A moment or so later the massive form of The Dark Lord was seen.

Knowing his people were going to lose the battle Artwore then began to run back toward his castle in attempt to find a safe haven. Halouse still followed killing Falmores that surrounded him. They quickly went to their king's side as Halouse was beginning to get overwhelmed by them. As warriors to his blindside seemed seconds from killing him he heard arrows. Each arrow fired hit a Falmore just

IDIUS KANE

as they were about to kill Halouse. When all the Falmores fell Halouse looked over to see Drayus dressed in the armor of a foot soldier holding a bow an arrow. She softly nodded as Halouse followed Artwore up the large staircase. Many more of Artwore's personal body guards began to emerge as they ran passed there king on the staircase and charged at Halouse. Running up the stairs Halouse swung at their ankles quickly slicing the Falmores and watching them roll all the way down the stairs mortally wounded. Halouse seemed possessed as he continued his chase of the Falmore King. In back of him large amounts of elves began to give chase as well. The large city of the Falmores was beginning to get completely taken over as all the elves seemed to follow Halouse into the castle.

Far away from any major confrontation Lyncade was barely keeping pace with the much more skilled Fayne. Fayne was fighting with his opposite hand which gave Lyncade a chance but he was still more skilled then the Royal Elf General. Several massive strikes by the champion forced Lyncade to his knees as Fayne struck moved in as they were tangled with their blades and elbowed Lyncade in the face. Lyncade fell to the ground as Fayne raised his blade. Quickly turning over Fayne struck the shield strapped around Lyncade's back as Lyncade lifted himself up so his back was to Fayne. Thinking quickly Lyncade threw out his elbow returning the favor. Fayne backed away from the impact as Lyncade turned swiped and sliced him across his heavily tattooed face. Fayne reached to his face and touched the wound.

"It's been ages since I've seen my own blood," Fayne told.

"I assure you shall see more," Lyncade told.

With a small laugh Fayne picked up his sword and struck again. Each accurate throw of his blade if not blocked would sure end the life of the Royal Elf General. Lyncade was swift and precise with his blocks keeping the champion away taking small steps backward as Fayne came forward. As the blessed champion came in further he blocked away Lyncade's sword and swiped hard smashing into his armor. The slash completely devastated his heavy armor as Lyncade back away and Fayne relaxed. Lyncade tried to move but the amount of damage done to the armor it would be too uncomfortable. It seemed Fayne was giving him permission to remove it as Lyncade stabbed the sword into the ground and removed his armor. A

294

moment or so later Lyncade quickly grabbed his blade as Fayne came in with a strike. With a quick block Lyncade saw the look of happiness on Fayne's face almost showing Lyncade he was playing with him. A sadistic smile as he engaged every time knowing he was better than the Royal Elf General. With a flurry of quick strikes Fayne hit away Lyncade's blade and sliced him across the chest. As he tried to move in for the kill Lyncade tied him up and kicked him square in the chest. Falling back but able to catch his balance Fayne watched as Lyncade looked down at his wound. Not deep enough to be mortal Lyncade just came forward in anger. Fayne wanted this hoping Lyncade's rage would make him do something stupid.

Each passing warrior didn't dare interrupt as they seemed alone with the hellacious battle around them still going on. As Fayne continued his nonstop attack he knocked Lyncade's blade away once again and sliced him across the chest once again. With Lyncade now having a bloody X in the middle of his chest he quickly gained control and blocked the second attack as he elbowed Fayne in the face. Stumbling back Fayne turned away as Lyncade swung and sliced him across his back. Fayne turned quickly throwing out his blade recklessly. Lyncade blocked and slammed his blade down on Fayne's as it fell from Fayne's grasp. Lyncade came in for the kill but the champion reached forward and grabbed Lyncade's neck as he squeezed with all his might. Choking to death Lyncade dropped his hands as he elbow shot across and nailed Fayne in the face again. Still holding his grasp on Lyncade's neck Lyncade did it several times until the champion began to fade. With one final shot Fayne let go but not before he kicked out his own foot and kicked Lyncade's hand. Lyncade's blade flew through the air and landed far away from his reach. Catching Lyncade off guard as Lyncade looked to where his blade was going; Fayne punched Lyncade across the face as Lyncade fell to his knees. Fayne quickly pulled a small dagger from his forearm armor and was seconds from stabbing Lyncade in the top of the head. Lyncade fell back to the ground as he took his feet and grasped Fayne's sword. Trapping it between both his feet he quickly jabbed it forward as it penetrated Fayne's armor and imbedded in his abdomen. Kicking the butt of the sword the blade went in further as Lyncade spun away from Fayne and went to his sword.

Fayne grabbed his sword with both hands and began to pull it out of himself. Dropping to his knees as he did Lyncade picked up Soul Stealer and turned around as he saw the champion fading. Quickly trying to end it Lyncade charged as Fayne blocked but seemed drained from his wound. Over and over Lyncade tried everything he could but Fayne seemed to never give in. Even as blood began to pore from his mouth Fayne began to regain his intensity. Lyncade recklessly took a swipe as Fayne blocked and sliced him across the chest again. With this one deeper then the others, Lyncade backed off as both him and Fayne leaned on some rocks for support. Lyncade could barely contain the pain as he slowly stood in front of Fayne as Fayne just looked at him. Fayne smiled slightly as he stood as well. Holding his blade with the left hand Fayne spun it as he came in for a strike. Lyncade blocked quickly spun and cut off Fayne's hand. Lyncade swung low slicing the champion across the kneecap. Dropping to his knees in defeat Fayne looked up fearfully as Lyncade raised his blade and beheaded Fayne. With his head rolling away a bolt of lightning came to the skies. The body of Fayne began to glow as it still kneeled up even with the head of Fayne gone. The head stopped rolling as the tattoos on Fayne began to glow a deep blue as they lifted from his body. Swirling around the corpse they flew at Lyncade and smacked him hard. Flying back from the impact Lyncade was thrown into a hut as the small home collapsed. The sounds of Lyncade screaming could be heard as the effects of the unusual spell faded away. As Lyncade rose he noticed the wounds on his body began to heal on their own and his once white blank skin was covered with the tattoos and ruins of the gods. As he touched his face he could still feel the burn of the markings that implanted themselves there. Lyncade looked over at the head of Fayne as the markings he once had were gone. Each blessing given to Fayne and the ones he had taken were now all over Lyncade.

Artwore entered the throne room as he saw The Dark Lord standing in front of Sygon. The two just stared each other down as Sygon prepared for a confrontation.

"He won't harm you," The Dark Lord assured, "Go to Mayreon and get the information we need."

"You can't touch the ruby and neither can he," Sygon reminded, "Only he who is pure of heart can."

The Dark Lord didn't answer as he just looked at Sygon. Artwore grabbed the drained Mayreon as she looked at him with glazed eyes.

"Search her soul," The Dark Lord told, "Find what I need."

As Mayreon began to fade away from all the energy she used Artwore seemed to get his answer.

"The temple," Artwore replied as he looked at The Dark Lord.

"Kill her," The Dark Lord told.

Artwore removed his blade as Sygon went to throw out his hand. The blast he began to conjure was blocked as a light from The Dark Lord's hand stopped it. Artwore raised his blade just as a dagger flew through the air and scratched his slightly in the neck. Turning quickly he saw Halouse running in as Halouse pulled out his blade.

"Go," The Dark Lord yelled to Artwore.

Artwore quickly ran away from Mayreon as she fell back. Halouse stopped in front of her looking to try and help her.

"I have her," Sygon assured.

Halouse looked at him for a moment then ran off as Sygon began to circle the large form of The Dark Lord. Still staring at each other Sygon began to walk backward toward Mayreon.

"Your powers are no match for mine," The Dark Lord reminded.

Knowing this Sygon readied himself as he continued to keep both his eyes on The Dark Lord. Just as he felt himself only inches from Mayreon he stopped and held out his staff. A large green shield began to form all around him and the comatose Mayreon.

Two more black mists formed next to The Dark Lord as Greco and Korack soon stood side by side with their older brother. Their hands all began to glow as they readied to take on the wizard.

"The shield can't hold for long," The Dark Lord told both the evil gods.

Artwore exited the back of his castle as he began to run down the long stairwell leading to a temple located in the back of the large palace. This temple was called the Temple of The Dark Lord. It is where his mother used to worship the evil god as she practiced her dark arts. The garden of this evil temple was filled with black flowers and had several large pillars holding up the temple. Statues of The Dark Lord stood high in the air as Artwore passed several of them.

The garden he ran through was open to the sky above and stretched out for several hundred feet. Never taking cover to hide from Halouse he knew he would soon need to make his stand. He stopped in the middle of the garden and removed his sword gasping from his run. Halouse ran down the stairs and as soon as he was close to the final stretch of stairs he saw that Artwore awaited him. Halouse slowed down as he tightened his grip around the blade and walked slowly toward the Falmore King. Holding out his arms in the air Artwore could almost smell defeat.

"The Dark Lord is protecting me," Artwore yelled, "Promising me victory over your kind. Swearing land and title once your people are wiped from the earth."

Halouse just stopped as he stood twenty feet away from the Falmore and looked at him intensely. Holding his blade toward the ground he was only seconds from striking.

"Not to worry," Artwore replied, "Fayne will soon kill your king and erase the curse Warad has placed on him. Through his actions I will have my vengeance."

"What vengeance?" Halouse asked, "If one of us here needs vengeance you are looking at him."

"Your two brothers should have stayed away," Artwore replied, "We only needed her for answers."

"She wasn't yours to take," Halouse said.

"And she isn't yours," Artwore reminded, "I see the feelings you have for her even as you look at me now. Her heart is with another and yet you defend her honor instead of her true love."

"He is here," Halouse told, "Would you prefer him?"

"It won't matter," Artwore told, "Here is where I escape. Once your body hits that ground there will be no way to find me."

"How so?" Halouse asked.

"Fool," Artwore replied, "Once I find the ruby The Dark Lord will return and have his power. Then I will watch as all of your people suffer the wrath of his true nature. Here in this temple it lies awaiting me to give it to him."

"Why not give it to him before?" Halouse asked.

"Because before he wouldn't have given me anything for it," Artwore knew, "Now that I know where it is I will hand it to him personally and he will spare me of my death."

"You won't have time to find it," Halouse assured.

Artwore pointed the end of his sword at Halouse and replied, "I hold The Dark Lords sword. Blessed by his hand along with the armor I wear and my helmet. Your brothers didn't stand a chance what makes you think you do? Even if you do win you can't touch the ruby without being of pure heart. Your action for loving another's wife isn't pure."

"I assure I'll be alright once that happens," Halouse replied.

Running quickly at Artwore they clashed with heavy strikes toward the other. Artwore proved quickly he was a match for Halouse blocking every strike Halouse usual killed his enemies with. Standing atop a fountain for a high advantage Artwore swung down at Halouse but Halouse made sure that even the high ground wouldn't give the Falmore King a gain of the upper hand. As Halouse began to use more advanced techniques he began to get the better of the Falmore. As he came in he blocked the blade away and thrust his sword at Artwore. As the blade hit Artwore's chest the blessed armor given to him by The Dark Lord did its work. It seemed unfazed as Artwore used Halouse's surprise to slice him on the shoulder as he spun away. Halouse angered looked at the wound but didn't touch it as he came forward again.

With Artwore staying on his defense as Halouse came in with a counter to knock away his blade once again, Artwore watched as Halouse swiped at his chest. The blade bounced off with no wound coming to Artwore. Artwore quickly slammed Halouse's blade as it hit the ground. Still grasping it Halouse held it up quickly to block Artwore's strike. Just as Artwore noticed the quick block he sifted his strike in the air as it sliced Halouse across the arm. Affecting his left arm Halouse stumbled back in pain as the blade sliced into major arteries. Bleeding heavily he picked up the blade with his right hand as the weight of the sword was weighing him down. Usual grasping it with both he knew he'd soon tire.

Artwore took both his good hands and lifted his blade as he came in with a flurry of attacks. Halouse blocked each quickly but recklessly as his blade almost flew from his grasp with each powerful strike by the Falmore King. Taking advantage of the wounded elf, Artwore reached to his waist and pulled a small blade as he began to strike with two of them. Now having an even bigger advantage

Artwore came in as he struck Halouse's blade away as the second smaller blade passed Halouse's defense and sliced him across his lower neck. Artwore came in again this time attacking the opposite side as he knocked Halouse's blade away with his large blade and sliced him on the other side of his lower neck. The strikes got even closer as Halouse began to get cut all over his body. Never penetrating enough to mortally wound him Halouse's whole body soon began to get sliced all over with the small blade. Artwore continued with the two blades at once as Halouse knocked both away but Artwore took his small blade and swung it up as Halouse was cut on the chin. Backing away Halouse looked at every wound he had sustained. With several slices on his chest and hands he knew he'd lose if the pace continued.

Artwore came in this time though with the small blade as Halouse took his weak left hand and grabbed Artwore's wrist. Seeing and opening Artwore stabbed the larger blade toward Halouse's exposed side. Halouse quickly spun ripping the smaller blade from Artwore's hand. As he spun he stood back to back with the Falmore King and stabbed it high in back of him. The blade entered into the side of Artwore's neck. Artwore threw his leg back and kicked Halouse away as Halouse stumbled forward.

Artwore quickly removed the blade from the side of his neck as he tossed it away weakly. Turning around slowly the wound began to pore with blood. Soaking his robe and his white skin the loss of blood began to take effect on him. Placing his hand to his neck quickly Artwore stopped the bleeding temporarily. Beginning to breathe again Artwore picked up his blade and awaited Halouse as he kept his hand on his neck to stop the blood. Halouse knew now that it was back to his advantage.

Halouse ran at Artwore as Artwore immediately went for the kill swiping at Halouse's head. With a quick duck Halouse pressed forward and sliced Artwore in his exposed ribs. The armor given to him didn't protect that part as Artwore tensed in pain.

"That's for Cloron," Halouse told.

Artwore swung his blade not giving Halouse a chance to attack. With a quick block Halouse ducked the second swipe aimed at his head and sliced Artwore in his other ribs. Backing away Halouse just walked around him as Artwore kept his blade in front of him.

"That's for Hecorus," Halouse told.

"I suppose the next one is for you," Artwore replied as the blood in his throat could be heard gargling.

"No," Halouse quickly answered.

Coming forward Artwore struck at Halouse several times as Halouse blocked each strike, swung his blade in front of him and chopped it into Artwore's shoulder. Artwore tried to stab at Halouse as that happened but Halouse threw out his foot and kicked Artwore's hand. The amount of force made the blade fly from Artwore's grasp.

"This one is for my father," Halouse said as he took his blade and stabbed it through Artwore's collarbone. The armor started just an inch below as Halouse knew every exposed spot of the Falmore King. With the wound from earlier bleeding without a hand pressing against it; Artwore fell to the ground as the pool of blood began to form around his body.

As The Dark Lord, Greco and Korack prepared to attack Sygon they all felt a weird sensation. As they both turned they saw the forms of Warad and Talius. Their hands soon went back to normal as they thought twice about attacking Sygon.

"Fayne has fallen," Warad told, "I have won the wager."

Korack and Greco looked at The Dark Lord in disbelief.

"Tamian?" Greco asked.

"Lyncade," Talius told as she took a step toward them.

"Impossible," Korack said.

"It's true," The Dark Lord said, "I feel it."

Warad raised his hand and replied, "Banishment. I believe that was the agreement"

The Dark Lord yelled in anger as his roar defined Sygon's ears. The Dark Lord, Greco and Korack began to fade as Sygon soon heard the screaming stop.

"If you banished him why can't you just kill him?" Sygon asked.

"Seems so simple doesn't it?" Warad asked, "You don't know the laws of gods so do not judge."

Halouse ran in at that moment as he saw the god Warad and Talius walking closer to Sygon. Sygon began to remove his blue robe and began to wrap Mayreon in it. He was still wearing a white silk robe underneath as he carefully placed it around the half naked body of Mayreon. When he was done Halouse bent down and picked up the unconscious sorceress. Her eyes opened slightly as she looked at Halouse.

"It's over," Halouse whispered, "Rest now."

With a small smile Mayreon reached up and grazed his face with her fingers.

"You saved her life," Warad replied as he looked at Halouse.

Halouse quickly turned to his maker as Mayreon went limp again.

"You are her hero," Talius assured.

"I have saved her life yes," Halouse agreed, "But I will not get my prize."

"Your prize should be knowing you saved her," Warad replied, "She will know as well."

Halouse just nodded as he slowly carried her away.

"Sygon," Warad called, "The ruby is not here."

"Where did it go?" Sygon asked.

"Removed ages before," Warad told.

"Artwore saw it though," Sygon remembered.

"He saw the place it once was," Warad informed.

"Mayreon knows where it is," Talius told, "She will know how to retrieve it in time."

Nodding Sygon turned as the forms of the two gods vanished before him.

Around the Falmore city most of the Royal Elves had stopped fighting. Small amounts of Falmores had lived but quickly surrendered as soon as most of the army was killed. With no hope they had laid down their weapons and submitted to the elves. Lines of Falmores walked with their hands atop their heads as Royal Elf warriors marched beside them.

Tamian looked all around the burning city as he leaned against a wall. With his blade resting against the wall as well he saw Maxus soon appear. Maxus held a goblet in his hands as he handed it to his king.

"Wine," Maxus told.

Tamian took a long gulp as some of the wine came out his mouth and he quickly brushed it away. He looked all around him in anger as he handed the goblet back to Maxus.

"Why so angry?" Maxus asked, "We have won."

Tamian got up from the wall and said, "If you call killing an entire civilization over the actions of a greedy king a victory; then I'd say you are blind to the ways of our people."

"How could you say that?" Maxus asked.

Looking ahead to the hundreds of women and children found by the Royal Elf warriors, they gathered them in the center of the city. Tamian made his way there with Maxus behind him. Tamian saw a woman holding a child in her arms as she looked at the king in fear.

"What do you wish for us to do?" A Royal Elf warrior asked Tamian.

Tamian looked at the woman who still had dried tears in her eyes. Tamian ignored his soldier as he approached the woman. She slowly began to walk backward in fear of the Royal Elf King but soon stopped. Trying to look brave she cradled her child in one arm and stared directly at him.

"You do not need to fear me," Tamian assured in a soft tone.

As the woman nodded she began to break down and cry once again. Regaining her sanity she quickly went back to a stone cold look as she gazed at the king.

"Your people have suffered a great injustice because of the actions of your king," Tamian informed.

"So you destroy all of my people?" The woman asked.

"He captured our queen," Tamian told.

"My husband," The woman quickly yelled, "My husband and three of my eldest sons have died in this city today. With most of the men killed by your army how will we survive?"

"If there is anything…" Tamian began.

The woman came forward and spit in his face as she then replied, "You can die."

Several Royal Elves began to go at the woman but Tamian held out his hand to stop them.

"No," Tamian replied, "She is right."

"Her king was in league with The Dark Lord," A warrior replied.

"My lord," Raven replied as he approached Tamian.

Tamian turned his head and looked at him.

"The city is burning to the ground," Raven told, "What is your command?"

Tamian looked directly at the woman and replied, "Put the fires out at once."

"My lord?" Raven asked.

Tamian snapped his head back at Raven with a look of conviction.

"As you request," Raven replied as he bowed his head slightly and walked away.

Tamian approached the woman again and kneeled before her.

"You may hate me and my kind all you like," Tamian replied, "This I can never take back. The lives of your sons I will never be able to give, but I swear to you now that I will do all I can to repair your city for the future of your kind."

The woman looked down at the Royal Elf King as she just walked away without saying a word.

"My lord," Maxus replied, "Why did you bow to her?"

"Her people have been slaughtered by our forces," Tamian reminded, "Most of these people didn't know the ultimate outcome. They were left in the dark as Artwore tried his quest at glory. They should not be punished for his actions."

"What do you intend to do?" Maxus asked.

"Rebuild their city for them," Tamian replied as he began to walk back to his forces.

"Are you insane?" Maxus asked.

"No I am a man with a conscious," Tamian replied.

"They struck out against our people," Maxus yelled.

"Their king did not them," Tamian replied.

"You are blind," Maxus yelled.

Maxus yelled so loud that most of the forces turned and looked at the confrontation. Tazzill, Drayus, Raven and several Royal Elf Guards looked over at the argument. Lyncade emerged from a crowd and stood next to his king.

"Is there a problem?" Lyncade asked.

Maxus looked at the heavily tattooed face of Lyncade.

"The new blessed warrior shows himself," Maxus replied, "Plan on showing all the new skills you've acquired."

"Not if I don't need to," Lyncade replied.

"He should wipe their children from this earth," Maxus yelled, "They will plot revenge once they are older."

"And what?" Tamian asked, "Attack us on our own ground?"

"You fool," Maxus yelled, "One of them will become king and join with The Dark Lord just as Artwore did."

"When that time comes we shall be prepared," Tamian assured, "I will not destroy a whole race of people for what their king did."

"You are destroying our people with your actions," Maxus said.

"We are making peace with them," Tamian assured.

Lyncade pulled out his blade and stood in front of Tamian.

"What do you intend to do?" Maxus asked, "Kill the highest noble of the Royal Elves."

"Your title has no power here," Tamian reminded.

"But my solders will revolt if I give them my command," Maxus assured, "Do you really wish to have a revolution here?"

"My forces, Lyncade's and the natives outnumber yours," Tamian reminded, "If you wish to have your men slaughtered here then be my guest and do it."

Maxus looked around as several of his forces were mixed in with Tamian's. If he wished his men would die with him. They looked to him never going for their blades. All he needed to do was give them one gesture and the revolution would have begun. Never making a move he stared at Tamian as he removed his blade. Tamian placed his hand on his but Maxus tossed his blade at Tamian's feet.

"Have it your way," Maxus replied as he walked away.

Halouse then began to emerge from the smoky castle. Several explosions and rock throwers taken over by the Royal Elves heavily damaged the palace. Through the fog of the small fires around it the Native Elf brought out the queen in his arms. With a roar of the warriors that had seen him he stood on the high staircase as he looked on. Mayreon awoke that moment and looked up. With her head pressed against his she had looked at the thousands of warriors that had come to her rescue. Still drained and weak Halouse carried her down the staircase to the thousands of warriors below. Still cheering in victory and excited to see their queen alive the warriors deafened the air. The Falmores that remained couldn't help but look on as well. Halouse walked over to Lyncade as both the warriors stared at one another. With his new look to him Halouse barely recognized him. Lyncade held out his arms quickly for his wife but Halouse hesitated. As Halouse briefly looked at his love he handed her to the General.

"What ever you need," Lyncade replied.

"Trust me," Halouse began, "You can't give me what I want."

Tamian came from the crowd and stood face to face with Halouse. With a small stare Halouse finally looked to the ground and kneeled.

"Maybe I can," Tamian replied as he looked down at Halouse, "Tell me this gift you wish to receive."

Halouse rose slowly and replied, "King of Royal Elves, my brothers have been slain and my father has been avenged by my actions. I ask of nothing from you."

"You have saved the queen," Tamian told, "Do not tell me that there is nothing I can do for you. It would be an insult to not consider a reward of some kind."

Halouse thought for a few moments then asked, "Allow me to speak with my father once we go back to Tullian. You will have your request then."

Tamian nodded and replied, "Of course. It was an honor knowing your brothers."

"It was there honor," Halouse assured.

"They see from the afterlife what you have done for them," Tamian assured.

Halouse nodded as he began to walk passed the king. Passing thousands of Royal Elves he came to Drayus who was with the ranks of Natives.

"We have fought turbulently," Drayus told, "All in the name of Calbrawn and both your brothers."

Halouse nodded as Drayus embraced him with a hug. The Native Elves raised their blades and cheered the son of their leader.

Lyncade carried Mayreon through the devastated city as she was still too weak to walk on her own. Mayreon looked at him as he carried her in awe.

"What?" Lyncade asked noticing her stare.

"What happened to your face?" Mayreon asked noticing his tattoos.

"Markings of the gods," Lyncade told.

"You killed Fayne?" Mayreon asked in disbelief.

"It was your safety and love that kept me alive," Lyncade told.

"Stop," Mayreon requested.

Lyncade did as he slowly looked at her. Mayreon softly kissed him as they embraced for several moments.

"I swear on Warad I will never let you out of my sight again," Lyncade promised, "Never again will you be in harms way."

"I know," Mayreon replied, "Nothing will ever happen to me when I'm with you."

With a small smile Lyncade continued to carry his wife away. With the city still burning from the sky above the Royal Elves quickly did as their king asked. The fires would soon be put out. The Falmores would never go into slavery under Tamian and the king would do what ever he could to make sure the Falmores survived. As the thousands who were dead were gathered they were burned before nightfall. The burning flesh of Falmores and Elves could be smelt for miles. Within the hour the Royal Elves began to leave. Several thousands of them would stay behind to help repair the city. They would do the hunting and crops for the local farmers to make sure the woman and children wouldn't starve. On the shores of the beach Tamian and Rakar met as the Forest Elves would sail back to their homes.

"Your men fought very well," Tamian complimented.

"Next to your men we felt like we were in competition," Rakar joked with a small smile.

Tamian joined in as he looked at the young Forest Elf King.

"If ever you are in need," Tamian told as he held out his hand.

"I will hold you to that Royal Elf," Rakar replied with a smile as they shook forearm to forearm.

"What will you do now?" Tamian asked.

"As much as I loved fighting side by side with you I think a little peace is in order with my people," Rakar told, "I will send men here in a few weeks to help yours with the Falmores."

"Thank you," Tamian replied, "I will make sure I came to see you in the near future."

Rakar nodded as he turned around and began to walk with his men to their ships.

Tazzill stood next to several of Tamian's guards as Tamian turned and looked at him.

"What can I do for your kind?" Tamian asked.

"The city is all," Tazzill assured.

"You will have that," Tamian told, "As well as a personal invitation to join me back to my city."

"What if I decline?" Tazzill asked.

"It will be an insult," Tamian told.

Tazzill just nodded and said, "Then I will take your invitation."

Lyncade carried Mayreon onto a ship as she was taking into the deck below. In a private room Lyncade laid her down as he began to walk out.

"Wait," Mayreon called.

Lyncade turned and looked at her.

"Stay with me," Mayreon replied, "Just for a little while."

"As long as you like," Lyncade replied as he walked over and lay down next to her.

Chapter 19

In the Valley of Talius, Halouse and Drayus walked in slowly as the warriors that remained looked at them. With no cheer or reception they watched as Halouse and Drayus walked to Calbrawn's fort. Walking up slowly passed the guards Halouse walked into the room and saw Calbrawn laying in his bed. Looking sick and weak the elder opened his eyes and looked over at his son and Drayus.

"Victory?" Calbrawn asked.

Halouse just nodded as Drayus went to him.

"Not a scratch on you," Calbrawn complimented her, "Leave me and my son alone for a few moments."

"Of course," Drayus replied as she quickly walked into another room leaving Calbrawn alone.

"Artwore?" Calbrawn asked Halouse.

Halouse just looked down and nodded.

"I am proud of you my son," Calbrawn told.

Halouse approached his father and kneeled before him. He picked up his fathers hand and placed it on his head as he looked down.

"What is this?" Calbrawn asked.

"I am not worthy to be called your son," Halouse told.

"You are," Calbrawn replied, "What would make you say such a thing?"

Halouse looked at his father with tears in his eyes.

"You are ready to make a commitment," Calbrawn knew, "There is something given to you that has not yet been asked."

"Tamian," Halouse replied, "He is offering me a title in his lands."

"Will you except?" Calbrawn asked.

Looking away from his father Calbrawn already knew the answer.

"It is not even him that you will accept," Calbrawn said, "But her."

"I feel it my duty to protect her," Halouse told.

"She has protection," Calbrawn told, "From her husband."

Halouse looked around then back at his father still overcome with emotion as he said, "When I picked up that ruby. I knew at that moment what my purpose was. The way I felt about her was pure. It was graceful and not intended for any evil. Warad told me at that moment what I must do."

Calbrawn just nodded as he replied, "If you truly feel that strong about it. Then I must let you go."

"Will I dishonor you?" Halouse asked.

Calbrawn shook his head, "Never."

"Is there anything you need?" Halouse asked.

With a small laugh Calbrawn said, "My time here is almost done my son. Even the life of an elf comes to an end. Ages I have watched everything in this world take place. Fought in battles, laid with many woman all of virtue and purity. Soon though I will be called to the afterlife. All those that live here will look to another for guidance. Halouse you are the last of all my sons. Take our people to the city of Tamian and be their guidance. Unite all the clans as one and become Royal Elves."

"But father…" Halouse began.

"Silence," Calbrawn requested, "Our whole existence we have went against the ways of Tamian. And though I still disagree with those who call themselves king our people will need to be among his men. It is the most powerful army the world of Tullian has ever seen. You will be given a title and you will have say into what happens in the city. Make sure our people are safe. Now that The Dark Lord, Greco and Korack know where we are they will not hesitate to destroy us."

"How long…" Halouse began.

"Not long," Calbrawn told, "I have been weaker then I've ever been these last few days. All I requested from Warad and Talius is that I saw you again. I can die now a happy man knowing that my son has done what I knew he would."

"I wouldn't let you leave this world without vengeance," Halouse told.

Calbrawn looked out the small window as he replied, "All those await your command. I have told those in the council that you now take my place. I am too weak and too old now to try and help our people. It is your turn."

Halouse just nodded slowly as he rose.

"You are now Halouse of the Natives, King of the tribes of Cavell," Calbrawn told.

Halouse nodded as he turned away from his father. It would be the last time he'd ever see him and he knew it. Never looking back Halouse walked out of the fort and began to make his way into the Valley. The thousands of warriors that still remained seemed to look at him. A councilman that Halouse had seen many times took a step forward.

"Halouse," The councilman called, "What is your command."

Halouse with a tear in his eye replied, "We pack our things and we go to Tamian. The Royal Elves will greet us with open arms. All those who are of title here shall be of title there. We must think about the future of our people. The future is with me as I go to the city and call that my home."

"We will follow you to our end if we must," The councilmen assured.

Halouse began to go around to the back of his father's fort as he was left all alone. Trying to clear his thoughts a loud scream was heard from the inside of Calbrawn's fort. Already knowing what had happened Halouse let the tears in his eyes go. Unable to contain himself he dropped to his knees in pain. Nothing was left of the world he knew. Everything he remembered from this place involved both his brothers and his father. Letting out all that he had bottled up he slowly rose and knew what needed to be done.

As Halouse walked out of the Valley and back toward the camp the Royal Elves had made his people looked at him as he passed. With grief in their eyes as well they had felt the news from the Valley. Drayus stood in back of Halouse as she stopped and watched him approach the heavily guarded tent of Tamian. The tent was open with no cloth on the sides. Four large trees chopped from a forest near by holding up a massive tent. The guards slowly moved out of the way as Halouse saw the king sipping wine in a chair. As comfortable as could be Tamian already knew why Halouse had come to him. Adjusting himself from his lazy posture the king sat forward holding the goblet in his hands. Halouse dropped to one knee slowly as Tamian took a small sip.

"King Tamian of the Royal Elves," Halouse began, "I have considered your offer and except with no further hesitation. My people; the tribes of Lycans and the Murkildens of the Cavell territory will march back with your men to the City of Tamian. I will go to war with you when ever necessary and protect the lives of all those who live inside our land and the land of Tullian if commanded by Warad."

Tamian tossed his goblet to the side of him as a servant somehow caught it in midair. He pulled his sword from its case next to him and placed it on Halouse's shoulder.

"Then I pronounce you General Halouse, Nobleman, High Lord and leader of the Lycans and Murkildens of the Royal Elf army," Tamian told, "Now rise and prepare your people for the journey home."

Halouse slowly rose and replied, "Of course, my king."

Lyncade standing near by away from the tent watched the whole thing unfold. Leaning against a rock he looked on with anger. Still having ill feelings toward Halouse he wanted to keep the native as far away from his bride as possible.

"Raven," Lyncade called.

"Yes my lord," Raven replied as he approached his general.

"It will surly be hours before we march," Lyncade told, "We will camp for the night but make sure Halouse sees me in my chambers."

"Of course my lord," Raven quickly assured.

Halouse sat in his tent alone now as he was getting ready to sleep. Seconds later two servant girls of incredible beauty came inside his tent. One held a bowl of water and the other a tray with wine and freshly cooked meat on it.

"Who are you?" Halouse quickly asked.

"Sent by the king himself," One of the girls told, "You are a Lord and General now. We are here to bathe and feed you."

Halouse kind of smiled and replied, "I can do that on my own."

"You do not need to anymore," The other girl replied, "We are yours until you wish us not to be. We will take care of you."

"In all ways that you like," The other girl replied with an enticing smile on her face.

"Do not let this offend you," Halouse replied as he rose, "I do not need servants. I thank you for the offer but at the moment I am quite fine."

Raven then entered the tent and saw the two servant girls.

"Busy are we Halouse?" Raven asked.

"They were just leaving," Halouse told.

"Good," Raven replied as he evilly looked at the girls. In fear they walked away as Raven said, "Lyncade wishes to see you."

Halouse quickly gather some of his things as he began to walk with Raven to Lyncade's tent. There was a cold silence as they walked toward the camp of Lyncade. Something in Halouse's mind told him that Raven didn't like him. With a quick look Halouse saw a look of anger on the face of the captain.

"Is there something on your mind?" Halouse asked.

Raven looked at him incensed and then forward. With a small fake smile Raven asked, "What would make you think that?"

"I feel hatred toward me," Halouse told, "It reeks from you."

"You can find the things that are hidden in people," Raven complimented, "They do not lie."

"Why is this so?" Halouse asked, "I have never..."

"Keep your mouth shut," Raven replied as he snapped at Halouse. They both stopped as Raven looked him dead in the eye, "I do not like you. You can either in turn ignore it or hate me back. One way or the other we must never act upon how we feel because according to Tamian we are one. So let's drop this little discussion and just meet with my lord."

Halouse just nodded avoiding any confrontation as they continued to walk to Lyncade's tent. Lyncade had emerged from a tent next to his that was surly Mayreon's. He saw Halouse escorted by Raven and other Royal Elves as Lyncade looked at Halouse for several moments.

"General," Lyncade said to him.

"General," Halouse said in return.

"Join me in my tent if you will," Lyncade replied.

"Of course," Halouse said.

As Halouse entered Lyncade stopped Raven and the others from following Halouse in.

"I'll be alright," Lyncade assured.

As they entered Halouse just stood near the entrance as Lyncade walked passed him and quickly turned around.

"You and I are men of the sword," Lyncade began, "Words do not make us or tell the world who we are so I will make this quick."

"What is that?" Halouse asked.

"I cannot turn back what Tamian did," Lyncade replied, "He is king and the decisions he makes are his choice and his alone. Supreme rulers make laws without the disregard from their closest advisors," Lyncade got right in Halouse's face and said, "But I know the way you feel for my wife."

"General…" Halouse began.

"Shut up," Lyncade demanded, "I do not feel pity for the fact that you met her after me. I do not care for your longer of her or your infatuation. It will pass in time or it will be your doom. She will be taken to the city and never leave it again. She will be protected by me or my men and them alone. Your services to her are no longer needed."

"Just spit it out," Halouse said in anger.

Lyncade relaxed and backed away from Halouse as he said, "I assure I owe you a great debt which Tamian has already given to you. Title and forces of your own. But if I catch you talking to my wife or even looking at her in a manner I don't like I will kill you myself and post your head on my spear whenever I ride into battle."

As Halouse looked at Lyncade he noticed the recent gift of his tattoos seemed to make him arrogant. Halouse being very skilled with a sword didn't feel like testing it against the brave general. Fayne's skill was told about in stories since he was a child and yet somehow Lyncade had defeated him. Halouse already knew he might never get the chance with Mayreon ever again. She told him that on that fateful night back in the valley. She only let him get a taste of her; a taste he would never forget in a thousand lifetimes. To him it was enough even though he had yearned for her even at that moment. A sinking feeling came into his stomach as he feared what he had the moment he knew he loved Mayreon. Banishment from her presence and a penalty of death. He had already knew it was inevitable and should have expected it. Hearing it even when he knew the words were coming still didn't prepare him for the heartbreak that soon came over him. Hiding his feeling well from Lyncade he softly nodded.

"As her husband you have every right to demand that of me," Halouse assured, "For I would say the same to you if the situation were reversed."

Lyncade nodded with conviction as Halouse bowed his head slightly and replied, "I retire for the night. Have a safe journey home."

Lyncade watched as the honorable Halouse left the tent. Halouse walked away slowly as he heard the laughs of Raven and the others. They seemed to be mocking him even as he left. He didn't let them get to him. Only the sinking feeling in his stomach was all that mattered. He prayed in his mind even then for it to go away. With small amounts of tears in his eyes he went to his tent quickly and sat on the edge of the bed. Thinking of Mayreon he thought of their embrace. One he knew he would never feel again once he went back to Tamian. He wished for her then in his arms but he knew it would never be. She slept silently in the tent next to her husbands as she dreamed and recovered from her long journey. He fought back his emotions as he ran his hands through his face.

"If you can here me now my love," Halouse began, "Know that I will love you always. In this world or the next we will be together. For some reason Warad has chosen us to only be in the same city but not in each others arms like I know we should be. What ever curse has come to me for the things that have happened I pray they have stopped now. Know that even though I will not show it in my face or my words; my actions if you are ever in need will always prove that I love you. Sweet dreams my queen; for mine are filled with demons and haunting that The Dark Lord can't even recreate. If ever I hurt you by my actions I hope you will forgive me."

With that the warrior lay back in his bed and closed his eyes.

Mayreon jumped from her sleep in her bed. Breathing heavily she seemed to be hit with something she couldn't explain. She heard words in her head but they didn't come clear to her. She knew a message was in the air but she couldn't place it. Rubbing her temple the message went away without her hearing. She seemed cursed to hear things but not be able to interpret them.

The only thing she knew was she was sad. A sinking feeling began to engulf her as well but she knew she shared it with someone else. Looking to the top of her tent she wished to call out to the one she yearned for. The burning of his kiss still fresh on her lips. Gaining control of herself she quickly went back to sleep fighting the feelings she kept so hidden from everyone in the world. Including herself.

Many suns had rose and set. The large force of Royal Elves as well as the tribes of natives with their women and children got ever closer to the city of Tamian. There days were long no doubt because of the thousands of villagers and farmers. The native warriors stayed close to them as they marched through unknown woods and trails back to the great city. Days into the march Mayreon had gotten a horse as she rode proudly next to her husband. Grasping hand in hand for a moment not far back Halouse had seen the embrace. Looking down as he rode on horseback Tazzill rode up to him.

"Don't let it bother you," Tazzill told, "Back in your city you will be swarmed with women."

Halouse looked at him with a small smile and asked, "Will they love me for who I am or for what I am?"

"Who cares," Tazzill replied, "They will all claim to love you for who you are. Most will claim to stay by your side even if you had rags and just a small tent for shelter. Love in your world does not exist. They will only be by you for your power until it is gone."

"Is this what they teach human children where you're from?" Halouse asked.

"Humans are taught many things in my village," Tazzill told, "Mostly about the races that are supposedly better then we are."

Halouse looked to the large human warrior then ahead. Soon across the horizon the highest of the castles was seen. Halouse had seen it before as the majestic sight took over Tazzill and several of the natives. Their eyes seemed to almost explode from their heads as they were very much taken by the sight.

"It's beautiful," Tazzill replied.

Looking at the back of Mayreon's head Halouse replied, "I've seen better."

The gates were opened proudly as tons of flower peddles were pored down to the forces as they began to come in. Looking all around his vast kingdom Tamian smiled proudly as the streets were crowded with his people. Tossing thousands of flower peddles from the buildings above they began to cheer his name. The soldiers were greeted as kings themselves. They marched proudly forward and began to go to their families. Those who were commanded were escorting Tamian to his palace. The people roared with cheer the moment Mayreon was seen riding next to their great general Lyncade.

Tamian began to ride to the steps that climbed to his castle as Drizell waited on the top. With a smile that stood larger then the gods they worshipped she was dressed in all white. The dress was long and dragged behind her. Two servants held up the dress to insure she didn't trip and fall. With a blinding happiness she was holding a child. With a stunned look in his eyes Tamian began to walk slowly up the steps as Drizell smiled proudly. Going to her quickly he looked at the child as she held it.

"Why didn't you..." Tamian began.

"And ruin that look on your face?" Drizell asked.

Tamian looked down at the child and asked, "His name?"

"I named him Endore," Drizell replied, "It means worshipped in the language of the gods."

"That he shall," Tamian assured, "He is the heir to my throne."

"We have our prince finally," Drizell replied.

Softly Drizell handed Endore to Tamian as he looked out below the steps to the thousands of his people that stood in front of the castle.

"My son," Tamian yelled as with both hands he faced the baby toward them and raised him high in the air.

The people roared in cheer as Tamian pulled his son toward him and held him tightly. Reaching forward Tamian kissed his wife gently as they began to walk back toward the castle.

"My lord," A noble replied as he approached Tamian, "We need to speak at once."

With a look of confusion Tamian looked at the nobleman and asked, "I've just returned can't it wait."

"No," The nobleman replied, "It is of great importance."

Drizell looked at Tamian angered and said, "Tamian your son."

"I'll see him in a moment," Tamian assured.

Mayreon met with Drizell as she looked at her smiling.

"I told you," Mayreon replied to her about her son.

"I owe you my life," Drizell assured as she reached forward and hugged Mayreon, "It is good to see you alive."

"I will escort you to your room," Mayreon replied, "Tell you of my tales."

"You can keep me up all night if you like," Drizell replied with a smile.

Halouse stood on the bottom of the steps as he watched the woman he loved walk away. A weird sense began to take over him as he looked up the steps at the other noblemen. There was a betrayal that he felt. Quickly climbing up the steps a few of Tamian's guards stopped him.

"The king wishes to be left alone," A guard told.

"I am one of his generals," Halouse reminded, "I must speak with him."

"The nobles will see him first then you will get a chance," The guards replied.

Halouse looked threatening as more guards began to go to where the other two were. Holding up his hands Halouse assured that he had met no harm. Halouse backed away and began to go through the crowds of people. He looked up at the largest castle in the city and tried to think of another way to get in. He began to run around it trying to get away from any heavily guarded area.

Tamian began to walk off with the nobleman as Lyncade was close behind his king.

"Have Raven take Halouse to his courtiers," Tamian commanded Lyncade, "I must speak with the nobles about extending the city as soon as possible. We start building within the week."

"Of course my king," Lyncade told as he walked away.

Being escorted to her room by dozens of guards Mayreon began to get a sinking feeling in her stomach. She stopped suddenly as she looked in back of her.

"What is it?" Drizell asked.

"Guards take the queen away at once," Mayreon commanded.

"What is it?" Drizell asked in a demanding tone.

"I don't know Drizell just trust me," Mayreon begged as she began to walk in the direction they just came.

Six or so guards began to follow Mayreon as she walked.

Halouse began to scale the side of the castle wall careful of every stone he reached for. Moments later he looked down and realized how high he was. Climbing large mountains his whole life he was making an incredible pace as he went further up. Finally coming to a window he went in and pulled his blade from his back. He began to go to where he felt a disturbance as he moved through the shadows hoping no guards saw him.

Tamian went into a room where all the nobles were as he saw one of them facing away from him. With a shocked look it was the man who was dressed in dragon armor in Fadarth. Tamian quickly removed his blade as the door was shut behind him quickly. The guards that escorted him were behind it as they began to pound on the door. The nobles inside placed a large steel lock across the door as several of them pulled out their blades as well.

"What is this?" Tamian asked.

The dragon armored warrior turned around as Tamian saw Maxus.

"Traitor," Tamian yelled.

Tamian felt a blade to his back as he knew the nobles in back of him were a command away from killing him.

"Welcome to the trial of Tamian," Maxus replied, "Here we take you out and replace you permanently."

"What do you think the people will do when they find their king assassinated?" Tamian asked.

"Your latest general Halouse did it," Maxus replied, "Bought your trust in Fadarth and killed you in the night."

"And the guards outside?" Tamian asked.

"I came back to the city last night while you thought I was marching with my men," Maxus told, "Your castle is swarmed with my men. They are killing the guards outside as we speak. By morning your body will be reveled by us with the blade of Halouse in you. Making him a general in our forces helped our plan to take your throne. Thank you for that."

"You will die," Tamian yelled.

"No," Maxus assured, "You are outnumbered here twenty to one Tamian. Not even you with the blessing of Warad could defy those odds. You are cursed remember. To die by the hands of your own people."

Tamian began to get worried as he looked all around him.

"Drop your sword king," Maxus demanded, "There is a paper in front of your chair that needs your signature."

"For what?" Tamian asked.

"To make a law stating that if you are killed I become king," Maxus replied, "Sign it."

"Never," Tamian yelled.

"Sign it or I will rape your wife for weeks and throw your son from the highest tower to the rocky terrain of the streets you built," Maxus replied viciously.

"How do I know you will not do that anyway?" Tamian asked.

"You don't," Maxus replied, "But I swear it will be done if you do not sign that paper now."

Mayreon came to Lyncade and Raven as they came in with a dozen of Lyncade's forces.

"Where are you going?" Lyncade asked.

"Raven," Mayreon called, "Go to Drizell's room and protect her at once."

"For what reason?" Raven asked.

"Do not question me," Mayreon yelled.

"Of course," Raven replied as he quickly took half the men and went to the queen's room.

"What is it?" Lyncade asked.

"You do not feel that?" Mayreon asked.

"No," Lyncade replied, "What is it?"

"Betrayal," Mayreon told.

"Tamian," Lyncade replied.

They began to rush to the meeting room far away from where they were. The men were near Lyncade following him where ever he went. They soon came to many guards as the guards pulled out their blades.

"Maxus' men," Lyncade replied.

In a split moment a ball of green light flew out as the men lifted in the air and were tossed away. Mayreon was this reason as her hands continued to glow as they went further into the castle. Passed many hallways Mayreon could almost feel those who were with Maxus as she immediately struck them with a spell.

Halouse ran through the hallways like a madman as he soon came to the party of Mayreon, Lyncade and six of his men. With her hand out Mayreon quickly stopped it from glowing as they looked at him.

"What are you doing here?" Lyncade asked.

"I feel something," Halouse told.

"The same thing as me?" Mayreon asked.

Without looking at her or excepting her voice into his mind he looked at Lyncade and said, "Tamian is in trouble."

"I'll handle it," Lyncade assured.

"With six men?" Halouse asked.

"I have the blessings," Lyncade reminded.

"I have my sword," Halouse told, "You will need me."

"I have it under control," Lyncade yelled.

"Both of you shut up," Mayreon screamed, "Fighting amongst ourselves is not helping."

Lyncade looked at Halouse for only a few moments before he replied, "Mayreon go to your room now."

"What?" Mayreon asked in disbelief.

"I can't fight off these traitors if I feel you are at risk," Lyncade explained, "I wasn't able to help it in Cavell or Fadarth but I can help it here. You have done enough please do as I ask."

Mayreon looked at her husband in shock for a few moments before she nodded and slowly began to turn around.

"Take her back," Lyncade commanded his men.

Mayreon was being escorted back to her room. For a precaution just in case there were any other men trying to assassinate anyone else besides the king.

"You intend to storm that door with just us two?" Halouse asked as he spun his blade in his hands.

"Let's find out if you're worth your title," Lyncade replied.

"We'll see if you're worth those blessings," Halouse replied as they pressed forward.

As they began to get closer to the meeting room more of Maxus' men came at them. The two proficient warriors killed them with little effort as they seemed to be in competition with one another. Both seeing how short of a time they could kill off the guards better than the other. They seemed to be equals as they got closer to the front door. There standing guard were twenty of Maxus' men. They all pulled their blades at once as they stared down at the two generals.

The guards quickly charged them as at first the two generals stood only a few feet apart. As the guards got about ten feet or so they charged as well. With their swords flying through the air all that was heard was slicing and ripping flesh. The guards began to fall all around them as they wiped through them with little exertion.

Halouse pulled his blade from his final opponent as he looked at Lyncade. Staring at the door Lyncade grabbed it with his free hand but couldn't open it.

"There is a way in other than this door," Lyncade told.

"Where?"

"Around the other side of the castle it will take some time to get there," Lyncade told.

"How?"

Lyncade turned around and just as he did the form of Nagarth stood only ten feet in back of them. With this sword out the tip of the blade was on the ground as he seemed to be leaning on it. It looked as if he had been there the whole time but he some how snuck up on the two of them as they were trying to open the door.

"Nagarth," Lyncade called, "What is this?"

"The dawn of a new day," Nagarth told.

Halouse looked at him with intrigue as Nagarth pointed his finger at Halouse while looking at Lyncade and replied, "I do not want you.

This is between Lyncade and I. Stay where you are and you will not be harmed."

"What is?" Lyncade asked.

"I was sent like a fool to fight off a legion of orcs and goblins that outnumbered mine," Nagarth explained, "While I did that you claimed your prize with the servant girl that we both had our eyes on. You claimed the glory in the end as Tamian fought by your side. I was banished to stay here and watch the city. In the end I didn't get the vengeance for the men that died next to me in the battlefield. Maxus offered me more then Tamian ever did. Once Tamian is killed and you as well, Mayreon will be mine. As well as absolute power of the militia and nobles."

"You fool," Lyncade replied, "You only do this for power. We are elves not human. We are not corrupted by wanting more."

"All men no matter the race want more," Nagarth assured.

"Halouse," Lyncade called, "Go to Tamian's room, and look for the picture of my father. Behind that is a secret passage to the meeting room. Go now and save the king."

As Lyncade said that ranks of Maxus' men came around the hall and stood in back of Nagarth. The amount of them seemed endless as they kept coming around the halls in a vast number. The hallway was surrounded with them when the loud sound of a sword being removed from a case was heard as every one of the men pulled it at once.

"We could have a problem," Halouse replied.

A massive amount of wind soon came from in back of the rank as Nagarth held out his hand to stop it. As he looked he saw Sygon, Raven, Tazzill and Drayus walking toward them. Bolts of blue light began to get fired as Sygon began to cast spells. Drayus aimed her bow as Raven and Tazzill charged with their weapons.

Nagarth picked up his blade and swung at Lyncade's head quickly. Blocking it the two generals began to engage in a mighty battle. Without thinking Halouse jumped toward the hundreds of Maxus' men and began to kill them one by one. Once he got to an open hallway he began to run toward Tamian's room.

Back inside the meeting room the nobles began to hear the battle outside as they began to get anxious.

"Hurry up Maxus," A nobleman yelled.

"Sign the paper," Maxus yelled to Tamian.

"You want my throne you'll have to take it," Tamian replied audaciously.

Maxus pulled his blade and pointed it at Tamian as he began to walk toward him.

"I will rip your son's head from his shoulders if you do not do as I ask," Maxus promised.

"And I will sign if you take my offer," Tamian told.

"What offer is that?" Maxus asked as he stopped in his tracks.

Tamian slowly pulled his blade as the nobles that surrounded him kept a good eye on him.

"If you take this sword from my dead hands the crown is yours," Tamian replied.

With a small smile on his face Maxus asked, "Sign that paper Tamian and I will make this quick."

"Do you not remember what we are?" Tamian yelled, "We are not human Maxus, we're elves. I give every man in this room my word that if you win the crown will be yours. No questions asked. Have everyone here place their blades away; I'll take the paper sign it over there where none of you can stab me in the back and we will clash for the crown."

"Your word?" Maxus asked.

"My word," Tamian assured.

Maxus looked at Tamian then quickly to the noblemen, "Put your blades away."

"What?" A noble asked.

"Do it," Maxus demanded.

Slowly each noble placed their sword away as Maxus picked up the paper with his free hand and walked it over to Tamian. Holding it out for several moments Tamian finally took it and began to walk toward the front of the table. Placing his blade away he picked up the feather and dipped it in the ink. With his signature still wet Tamian removed his blade and took a few steps back.

"The paper is signed," Maxus said to the others, "If I fall kill him."

"You gave your word," Tamian yelled.

"No," Maxus replied, "You gave yours."

With a quick charge the leader of the nobles swung with everything he had. Each violent strike blocked by Tamian but the impact took him off his game. Maxus swung over and over as if he would never tire. Each punishing strike that was blocked tingled in Tamian's hands as he could barely contain the power. As the leader of the nobles kept coming Tamian blocked stepped away from the next strike and sliced Maxus on the side of his ribs. Tamian raised his blade to finish him but a nobleman from behind took out his sword and knocked Tamian's from his grasp. The nobleman looked to be seconds from finishing Tamian.

"No," Maxus yelled as he held his wound, "He is mine."

Tamian was now without his blade as he went for it for a moment. Maxus stepped in front of it as he held his blade out. Almost toying with the king Maxus came in as Tamian was forced to duck and dodge each swipe. Defenseless the king tried to do what ever he could to reach his sword. As Maxus swiped at Tamian's head, the king ducked as the blade hit a column and Tamian rolled toward his blade and picked it up as he rose. Tamian turned just in time to block a strike from Maxus as they both had their swords once again.

Halouse entered Tamian's chambers as Drizell was surrounded by her guards. They looked as if they were ready to attack him but Drizell held out her hand.

"The painting of Lyncade's father?" Halouse asked.

Drizell pointed to it quickly as Halouse went to it. Pushing the side of the painting Halouse went into a dark hallway. With torches every few feet from one another the long hall seemed endless as he rushed down it. He soon came to a wall where another painting must have been placed as he jumped through it.

As Tamian and Maxus continued their battle Tamian once again stopped an onslaught from Maxus, stepped to the side and sliced him in the shoulder. Raising his blade to finish the wounded High Noble a nobleman pulled out his blade and stabbed Tamian in the lower back. Dropping to his knees Maxus rose and hit Tamian's blade. Once again the sword flew from his grasp and landed several feet to the side of him. Maxus pushed the nobleman out of the way as he stood over Tamian. As Maxus raised his sword a painting right in back of him burst open. Halouse rolled forward and quickly got to his feet as he blocked the strike seconds from killing Tamian. Maxus thought quickly as he spun away from Halouse and swiped. Halouse was sliced on his arm as he blocked the next strike from Maxus. With their swords clashed Maxus kicked Halouse in the chest and turned toward Tamian. Tamian ran toward his blade as he jumped for it sliding against the floor. Getting to it Tamian jumped up just as Maxus reached him.

Heavily wounded Halouse got to his feet as the nobleman in the room all removed their blades. They charged Halouse but he seemed too skilled for them as he blocked all of heir attacks. With no way of countering he could only block the dozens of swipes coming at him at once. The skilled hunter kept all of them back as he slowly began to get closer to the door.

Outside Lyncade and Nagarth equaled the other in skill for several moments. Throwing everything they had at one another the generals seemed to know the others move before they did. Lyncade tried every attack he had used in his life but Nagarth always had an answer and a counter for it.

Returning the favor Lyncade could have closed his eyes and still knew where each strike Nagarth was throwing was coming from. The two master swordsmen were like artists among the others that fought around them. Using the columns of the halls the generals tried to ducked behind them and surprise their opponent. To no avail the swordsmen began to pick up the pace. With incredible speeds the swords clashed over and over as the sparks of each powerful strike ignited.

With a simple slip of his feet Nagarth came forward and was sliced on his collarbone. Stepping back the general looked at his wound from Lyncade's blade and quickly picked up a blade from a dead warrior around him. Engaging quickly Lyncade could only back up as Nagarth came with a flurry of both the blades. As each blade was blocked by Lyncade he could only take a step back and prepare for the other. Lyncade barely got away from the battle around him as well as fallen warriors fell in front of him. He pushed them away trying desperately to get away from Nagarth. He couldn't attack with the handicap he had. If he tried to engage Nagarth would surly kill him with the second blade in his hands.

"Lyncade," Tazzill's voice yelled.

Lyncade turned for a moment to see a blade coming toward him. With his freehand he caught it in the air and blocked an attack from Nagarth's second blade only seconds from wounding him. Now an even battle Lyncade began to come forward as Nagarth was forced to back away. Going in the direction they just came from Lyncade could see they were getting closer to the doors of the meeting room.

Trying to end him quickly Lyncade made a mistake as he chopped at Nagarth with his first blade. Easily blocking it Lyncade stabbed the second low as Nagarth dropped his knee into the blade. His shin armor deflected the path of the sword and had so much impact Lyncade lost his second blade. Nagarth took the advantage as he sliced Lyncade across his abdomen. Holding in his pain Lyncade blocked the second blade and began to back away once again.

The battle around them began to decrease as Raven, Drayus, Tazzill and powerful wizard Sygon were killing off all the members of Maxus' forces. The human Tazzill seemed to have no problem as he swung his massive ax at all the guards that came at him. He had suffered his wounds though as several parts of his unarmored body were sliced. Each didn't seem to bother him as the blades that managed to hit him didn't mortally wound him. The guards that were trying to attack Lyncade as he fought Nagarth were caught with perfect accuracy from Drayus. Each warrior that was seconds from jumping at him fell quickly from the arrows that flew with incredible accuracy.

Sygon took on the most making sure that his outnumbered party wasn't killed off. With dozens of bolts of light flying around Maxus' men were hit and killed instantly by the power of the bolts. Raven held two swords in his hands fighting off two of Maxus' men at once. The skilled captain used his experience in the battlefield to his advantage. Most of the warriors he was fighting were only guards and had never seen the battlefield before. Each strike hit his target as none of the swipes got blocked by the warriors that attacked him. As a sword came from his blindside he was so aware of it he either ducked or blocked it just in time.

The two generals continued their battle as Nagarth noticed all the guards around him were dieing at an incredible pace. When victory for Lyncade and his small force seemed moments away Nagarth increased the speed of his attacks with both his blades. As Lyncade blocked one of Nagarth's swords, Nagarth used his second to pin Lyncade's blade to the wall leaving him wide open to an attack. Nagarth stabbed forward but Lyncade moved from the blade. Taking his freehand and taking the blade from Nagarth's grasp Lyncade used that blade to pin Nagarth's on the wall. Lyncade slipped his first blade away, spun and sliced Nagarth down the chest. Dropping to his knees quickly Nagarth's blade was dropped from his grasp. Lyncade held both blades to Nagarth's neck as Nagarth seemed to except his fate.

The final member of the guards fell dead as the halls were covered in blood and the bodies of Maxus' forces. Drayus, Raven, Tazzill and the wizard Sygon stood in back of Lyncade as he stood in front of Nagarth.

"Finish him," Sygon commanded.

Lyncade breathed heavily as he stared down at his once close friend. Nagarth was so helpless as he sat there on his knees. Never in a thousands years would Lyncade have guessed their fates would have brought them this. Having pity on the warrior he had fought side by side in many battles Lyncade kicked him softly in the chest as Nagarth fell on his back.

"Let Tamian decide his fate," Lyncade replied.

Inside the meeting room Halouse finally killed a couple of nobles as he kicked the steel lock as it slipped from the door. He stood in front of it with his sword toward the other nobles. Throwing his foot back the door burst open.

Lyncade looked forward as Halouse was seen battling many of the nobles. Sygon quickly walked forward as he held out both hands. The nobles were tossed from their feet and raised in the air as they flew through the large room and hit the wall on the opposite side.

"Raven," Lyncade called, "Watch Nagarth. If he moves kill him."

"With pleasure," Raven replied as he held his blade toward Nagarth's neck.

Walking forward into the room Lyncade stood next to Halouse as they saw the fight between Maxus and Tamian. Maxus backed away from Tamian as he saw all the nobles knocked out around him. With a look of outrage he came at Tamian with all his anger. The skilled king stepped to the side slicing Maxus in the stomach as he passed. Tamian then spun and chopped his blade into Maxus' back. Maxus threw his blade in back of him as Tamian removed his sword from Maxus and blocked the attack. Tamian spun again and stabbed Maxus in the back for the second time. Pulling it out quickly Tamian walked around the wounded Maxus as he barely stood up in front of the king. Struggling to keep his balance the nobleman raised his blade slowly. As he struck Tamian blocked with his sword and redirected it as it stabbed Maxus in the chest. Maxus' sword fell to the ground as he grabbed the blade that was inside him. Tamian placed his foot on Maxus and pushed him off the blade. As Maxus fell his final breaths could be heard before he gasped and died.

Tamian dropped his sword in anger as he looked all around him. Sitting down on the ground he began to wheeze in exhaustion. Placing his hands to his head he seemed to try to wake up from what ever nightmare he thought he was having.

"Take Maxus' body to the center of the city and post it on the statue on the fountain," Tamian commanded, "I want all of those who think about betrayal to know the penalty. Have all his men tossed into the dungeon at once until they scream for clemency. Let them starve to death for their crimes and never have mercy for their sins."

"My lord," Halouse replied as he took a step forward, "They were only following orders."

"They betrayed me," Tamian screamed.

Halouse seemed to shutter with the comment as he looked at his king.

"He's right," Lyncade replied to Tamian, "Banishment for the remainder of their days is a better castigation."

"Banishment from Tamian?" Tamian asked, "They will leave this place and go to Cavell for safety. Live among the humans."

"No," Sygon replied as he stepped forward, "Imprison all of them as you requested. Banish them not to Cavell, of to Cagore or even allow them near Celladom."

"Then where to?" Tamian asked.

"Porian," Sygon replied.

Lyncade looked at him in horror as the sound of the dark territory even made him give a look of fear.

"Killing them will make the people fear you," Halouse told, "Banishment will show that you do have mercy but betrayal comes with the ultimate price. Let them live and suffer in the lands of the dead."

Tamian starred at them for several moments before he began to node. Holding out his hand Lyncade helped him to his feet.

"Round them up," Tamian commanded.

"My lord," Lyncade called, "Nagarth was one of them."

Nagarth was dragged in by Raven as he was tossed in front of the king. Tamian looked down at him in sadness as Nagarth stared all over the ground trying to keep his eyes off his king.

Tamian removed his blade and kept it on Nagarth's shoulders. Nagarth froze at the notion expecting his fate to come swiftly. Tamian looked at the others and slowly placed his blade away.

"Take him away," Tamian commanded as he just walked passed his betraying general.

Nagarth felt Tamian walk away still not even giving him a gaze. Nagarth was too ashamed and broken himself to offer even a glance. Nagarth fell on his back in pain from his wounds as Tamian was quickly surrounded by several of his servants to take him back to his room. They would surly work on his wounds and make sure he didn't sustain any major injury.

Lyncade slowly began to walk passed Halouse but stopped and looked at him briefly. Halouse returned the stare as the two didn't say anything. It seemed to be some contest as Halouse didn't back away from his glance. Lyncade finally nodded at the brave warrior.

"It seems you do live up to your title," Lyncade replied.

Halouse walked away as well as he and Lyncade went down two different hallways. Mayreon had felt the battle end and was making her way to the throne room. In the hallway Halouse came out of the corner and immediately saw Mayreon. With his heart jumping a little he continued forward. Mayreon looked to him but as he got closer he never returned her glance. Mayreon watched him even as he walked by. In wonder she continued to walk forward trying to figure out why he ignored her so.

Chapter 20

A few weeks later the traitors to the throne were taken care of as ordered. Escorted by thousands Maxus' men as well as any others not loyal to Tamian were being marched toward the territory known as Porian. Porian had been a dreadful place that no one had ever traveled and lived to tell. It was said to be the realm of the dead and all the lost souls traveled there when they died without accepting it. The dark woods of Porian made noises in the night and all those who went there were never to be found again.

The marching Royal Elves would force the traitors down the path leading to Porian and return when the gate separated the two territories was closed. Lyncade was the only one who was allowed to have the key. He rode in the front lines side by side with Raven. Nagarth was not far in back of them chained like the others. His head was still down and he looked like a broken man. Once respected as one of the great generals of the army and not cast away for his corruption.

"What fate lies ahead for these men?" Raven asked.

"What ever it is," Lyncade began, "I'd hate to see what happens to them. I do not think I would give this curse to any of my enemies."

"Not even Halouse," Raven replied.

Lyncade delayed for several seconds as he replied, "Let's not speak ill of a good general."

Raven looked at him in disbelief and replied, "My lord!"

"He is still not allowed to speak with her or look at her," Lyncade assured, "But him and his people are one of us now. He did an incredible thing for our kingdom."

Raven just nodded as they continued their march.

Back in the city in her courtiers Mayreon sat on the bed with the baby Endore in front of her. Sitting up he watched her do small magic tricks that made the babies face light up with joy. Making small insects and birds out of fire she made them fly all around the room for the young prince. In wonder he smiled gentle and even laughed. Mayreon's womb was swelling at this time as she looked at the child and smiled gently.

Drizell walked in at the moment and stopped, looking at what Mayreon was doing.

"He loves you," Drizell told.

Mayreon looked over at her never noticing her stare until that moment.

"I'm good with children," Mayreon told.

Drizell walked over to the bed slowly and laid on it to the side of her son. Mayreon took a ball of blue fire in her hand and made it swirl. The fire then became a bird as it chirped for the prince then faded away.

"I wish I could show him all those things," Drizell replied and playfully said, "You make me envious."

"A child will never love any other woman more then his mother," Mayreon assured.

"Can you watch him for a little while longer?" Drizell asked.

"Of course," Mayreon replied, "What do you need to do?"

"A few of the nobles wish to speak with me," Drizell told, "Tamian is still recovering and resting from his travels and battles with Maxus."

"Horrible thing," Mayreon replied, "The nobles that weren't against him will surly ask for the lands of the others."

"Nothing will come to pass," Drizell assured, "I think he wants a few of the new elves in at power."

"The Lycans and the Murkildens?" Mayreon asked.

"Yes," Drizell told, "Give them the lands and hopefully have full power over all the nobles so this doesn't happen again."

"Sounds reasonable," Mayreon said.

"Giving them power will without question get their undivided loyalty," Drizell knew.

"Why do you need to meet with them then?" Mayreon asked.

"To assure that when Tamian returns from his long rest that they have no worry of being killed," Drizell told, "The ones who didn't betray him need assurance that we know they are still with us."

Mayreon paid attention to Endore the whole time in wonder of the child.

"He's a blessing from Warad," Mayreon told.

"You can't wait for yours can you?" Drizell asked.

"He'll be here soon," Mayreon replied as she patted her womb, "He will be a great general one day."

"High hopes," Drizell told, "I pray you're right so he can protect Endore."

"He shall," Mayreon assured.

Drizell stayed for a few more moments as she kissed Endore on the forehead and began to walk away. Drizell began to go to a room not known to the other elves beside her and her husband. As the guards stayed close behind when she knew she was out of harms way she held out her hand for them to stop. Drizell walked into the secret room and closed the door behind her.

The entire room was filled with candles. The massive space had a large table in it as well as paintings and beautiful marble floors. Small pillars held up the large roof as they were a dazzling royal blue. As Drizell walked further into the room the candles began to dart toward her. A moment or so later a large gust of wind began to take over as she looked around in fear. In a matter of moments The Dark Lord stood in front of her. When she realized who it was she looked at him angrily.

"I thought you said Maxus would kill Tamian," The Dark Lord replied.

"That's when I assumed the natives would have been taken care of," Drizell replied, "I didn't know Tamian was going to make Halouse a general and allow the natives to join our empire. Besides I thought the Falmores would have put up a better fight as well as have Fayne kill Tamian."

"Lyncade complicated things," The Dark Lord told.

"Why wasn't Tamian fought by Fayne?" Drizell asked.

"They tricked Fayne in the battlefield," The Dark Lord told, "Making Raven dress up like Tamian to have the forces attack the city. Fayne was fighting what he thought was Tamian. By the time he realized it he went back in the city and was seconds from killing Tamian until Lyncade got involved."

"Now Lyncade holds all the blessings," Drizell replied.

"A minor problem," The Dark Lord assured, "He can be turned."

"Just like Mayreon?" Drizell asked annoying The Dark Lord.

"She seems to be more important to Warad then any other creature," The Dark Lord told, "She did hold the whereabouts of the ruby but it was lost in Fadarth. It wasn't there not even when Warad told Sygon where it was."

"So she still holds the knowledge?" Drizell asked.

"No," The Dark Lord told, "I didn't have time to find out where it was so I made her pass the knowledge on."

"To who?" Drizell asked.

"Her son," The Dark Lord replied.

"The one she bares?" Drizell asked.

"Yes."

"When do your forces attack again?"

The Dark Lord laughed at the statement and replied, "I was a fool in Fadarth. My forces are banned from Tullian. An agreement I made under false pretenses."

"What?" Drizell asked in anger.

"Not a problem," The Dark Lord assured, "Where one door closes another opens."

"How are they banned?" Drizell asked.

"I made a deal with Warad," The Dark Lord told.

"You are a fool," Drizell replied, "You never make a deal with your maker you will always lose."

"Once again a minor problem," The Dark Lord assured, "Besides how do we really know that Maxus would have handed the kingdom over to me. You have a son do you not?"

"Yes," Drizell told.

"Raise him to hate his father," The Dark Lord commanded, "I will work on Mayreon, Lyncade and their son. Tamian will not hold the throne by the time my forces are allowed on Tullian. This I promise."

"You better be right," Drizell warned.

"By the time my influence is felt your husband will have so many enemies they will be itching to have him removed," The Dark Lord assured, "We must make sure that who ever is given the throne is with us."

"They will be," Drizell assured.

"I will work on influencing Lyncade and Mayreon but be mindful of them," The Dark Lord replied, "For if they want Tamian out they will surly want you gone as well."

Drizell nodded as her and The Dark Lord were unaware of another presence inside the room. The god Warad was well hidden in the shadows and undetected by his son. With The Dark Lords powers only at half in the land of Tullian Warad stayed quiet.

"Leave it to me," Drizell replied, "I will make sure he meets his doom."

The Dark Lord nodded as he faded into a mist. Drizell got up and went toward the door. Before she could open it herself the doors swung open. Dozens of guards stood waiting as Sygon was leaning on his staff giving an evil stare to Drizell. She looked at him in a state of shock. Sygon just continued his long look as Drizell tried to find the words.

"Take her away," Sygon commanded.

Six guards passed Sygon as they grabbed the queen. Placing on shackles she was quickly brought away. Sygon watched the queen get escorted passed him with the same look in her eyes. A state of shock and not knowing what was going to happen.

The King was away in his chambers still recovering from his long days of travel as well as his wounds. Tamian had just been given the news by Sygon about his wife. He was more furious then sad.

"I should have known she was trying something with Maxus," Tamian replied, "I feel like such a fool."

"Your days of infidelity surly had something to do with her betrayal," Sygon knew, "Not that the penalty for what you've done should have been betrayal."

"What will I do?" Tamian asked.

"Do you love her?" Sygon asked.

"Sometimes," Tamian admitted, "I guess now we know why I was the way I was. She had a plan from the beginning."

"You must have a swift penalty," Sygon told, "She can't be banished."

Tamian looked at the wizard and asked, "Death?"

Sygon nodded.

"The people love her," Tamian reminded.

"Not after it is revealed that she was in league with The Dark Lord," Sygon replied.

"But we need a queen," Tamian said.

"We have another," Sygon replied.

"Mayreon is married to Lyncade," Tamian reminded.

"So," Sygon said, "She doesn't have to be your wife to be queen of Tamian. Maybe you make her the queen for the people."

"If she is queen Lyncade will certainly want a kingship," Tamian replied, "That is what he was suppose to get for Arawon until this little incident."

"He cannot be a king in Arawon. You give Arawon a chance to turn Lyncade against you and the entire empire could be at risk," Sygon knew, "It is known that Arawon was very good friends with Maxus."

"You think he wanted me gone too?" Tamian asked.

Sygon shrugged and replied, "Hard to say."

"If Lyncade goes he will surly be loyal to me and me alone," Tamian assured.

"He can stay still be you influence in Arawon," Sygon suggested, "Not a kingship but his presence will be that of yours. Arawon holds a grudge with you, but will not if Lyncade is there. You can have an ally in his city overlooking him to make sure he isn't trying anything."

"Mayreon will not go," Tamian knew, "This is her home."

"He can travel back and forth," Sygon assured, "He doesn't need to live in Arawon for the remainder of his days."

"Keep him in power there," Tamian replied.

"Precisely," Sygon said, "All we need is for him to have control over there so all the nobles in Arawon will be by your side. Lyncade is your most loyal general. He will surly keep the nobles in Arawon in your favor."

Tamian sat silently for a few moments then replied, "Execute her in the square. Same place we laid Maxus' body. Let the people know what happens to even royalty when they betray their people. Mayreon will be announced supreme queen the next morning."

Sygon nodded gently as he said, "Now to our defenses."

"What are these plans?" Tamian asked.

"White towers my lord," Sygon told, "I figure we place them all around our lands. Small armies of thousands even to protect them. Give us an opportunity to take on forces without them coming near the cities. When trouble arrives a lone horseman rides back to us and gives us word on who or what is coming after us. We then leave the city and go and help. This allows our enemies to never get a good jump on our forces to try and take our cities. It will keep the queen and the people protected as well as have them knowing their king is doing all he can. The farmers will return to our lands because of this and surly will know you mean to protect them."

"They should be here," Tamian replied.

"We can't fit the entire population of elves inside our city walls," Sygon replied, "The city would have to be massive. They are some who still live off the land and not wish to be involved with the politics of our empire. Besides the taxes in your city are fairly high."

Tamian just nodded and said, "These towers will cost me a lot won't they."

"They will come in handy," Sygon assured, "This in turn will also prepare for the invasion we will certainly get from Greco, Korack and The Dark Lord's forces in the future. Each white tower will be built a few miles away from the other. Even if they try to sneak between them they can still see it."

"This stops an army but what about a small party of men?" Tamian asked.

"They cannot get into the city and hurt you," Sygon assured, "The Dark Lord, Korack and Greco will not send a few men to try and kill you. They will always battle with an army."

"How long will it take for us to have this built?" Tamian asked.

"A few hundred years but most of The Dark Lord's forced have been crippled," Sygon reminded.

"What else do you propose?" Tamian asked.

"Extending the city of Tamian because of the new arrival of Halouse and the natives," Sygon replied, "We are being overpopulated. I estimate that the city will be over crowded in about two hundred years or so. This building must be done soon and swiftly."

Tamian sighed in frustration as he replied, "The humans want their city and some of our builders are in Fadarth helping the remaining Falmores."

"It can be worked around," Sygon assured, "The architects aren't part of the army there are thousands of them. Besides offer the servants a cut of their time in helping with the construction as well. If they are bound a few thousand years of service before they can become farmers or hunters tell them it will be reduced by half with all their effort."

"Then that takes away from the servants here in the castle," Tamian replied.

"That's where the natives come in," Sygon replied, "Many of their women and children will be looking for work so they can survive or feed their families. As their warriors are away or serving you at the white towers or protecting the human, the women and children will be of service. Higher the tax of all the owners of the taverns and steel mills."

"That will make the people angry," Tamian reminded.

"As long as they know all the money is going back to them then there is nothing to worry about," Sygon assured, "Let the nobles know what you are doing so they can assure their people that it is for them."

Tamian sat up from his pillow and placed his hand through his hair.

"If you also plan to give Lyncade a position in Arawon you will need to consider your next option for a general here in Tamian," Sygon replied.

"Easy Halouse," Tamian replied.

"I do not think that wise," Sygon said.

"Why is that?"

"Halouse is a native. How many of the nobles in Boleadar, Arawon and here will criticize you for such a decision?"

"He has earned it," Tamian assured, "He saved Mayreon on how many occasions as well as myself. If it weren't for him Maxus would have the throne."

Sygon sat silently for a moment and said, "You must remember that you are raising the tax for the people. The nobles control the people. You have to make a decision on a high general that they would approve so you still have them on your side. You do not want another Maxus in the nobles to try and take the throne from you. The nobles fear you for what you did to Maxus as well as the other traitors who haven't shown themselves. You must keep them that way but not too much. Push them but it must be fearful. If they think you're week they will make an attempt on the throne again."

Tamian took in all the wizard said and replied, "If I give Arawon the blessed warrior, I want his in return."

"Xanafear," Sygon knew, "The invincible all powerful general."

"You've heard the name," Tamian assured.

"He's been a noble in Boleadar for some time," Sygon told, "He is said to be very close with Arawon. You don't really believe all the stories about him being invincible do you?"

"Stories come from truth," Tamian reminded.

"He hasn't been in a battle in many years my lord," Sygon reminded.

"When he did see it in years past he was very valiant and fierce," Tamian remembered, "He became a nobleman when he fought with only one hundred men against a force of one thousand orcs and goblins. He and three others remained when the battle was over."

"And there wasn't a scratch on him," Sygon added.

"He will come here and do more for the morale with just his name," Tamian assured.

"Choosing him will also put you on the better side of Arawon and his forces," Sygon assured, "Since you made Lyncade High General he has been angry with you."

"In return I have never asked him or the forces there to fight for me," Tamian reminded.

"They are your men and your people even in the city of Arawon and Boleadar," Sygon reminded, "You must get those forces back in our arsenal. The Dark Lord, Korack and Greco will surly bring in larger forces once their ban from this land is lifted."

Tamian just nodded.

"I will let you sleep for the time being my lord," Sygon replied, "We still have much more to discuss."

"When you leave send in Halouse," Tamian commanded.

"Of course," Sygon replied, "Make it quick with him you need your rest."

Halouse entered at Sygon's command as he walked in front of Tamian's bed and kneeled.

"Rise," Tamian commanded.

"You wish to see me?" Halouse asked as he rose.

"My original plan Halouse was to make you High General of the city of Tamian and of course High Lordship among the nobles," Tamian told, "The plan will be delayed for some time. I will need you to stay within the ranks of the Lycans and Murkildens as their general for a good influence among them. They see you as their new leader and by all means you should be. Lyncade will go to Arawon the High Noble and be my influence in his city. Being my High General when he leave he will vacant the position once I command and I will need a good general here. For the recent problems we are having it is important that I stay on the noble's good side. I have requested them to appoint me my next High General to keep them in my grasp and to assure that I have good faith in them. Arawon and I haven't gotten along in recent years so I must make peace somehow."

"Of course," Halouse replied, "What ever you need me for I will be by your side I assure."

"That I know," Tamian said, "This new general will be the only one to outrank you in the city depending on weather or not Lyncade takes my offer."

"I'm sure he will," Halouse replied.

"That is yet to be seen because Mayreon loves the city," Tamian reminded, "Who knows if she'll accept it or not. Lyncade wants to be by her and if she decides not to leave he won't."

"So if he doesn't leave he'll still be high general right?" Halouse asked.

"No," Tamian replied, "He will accept but Mayreon will be given the title of supreme queen. She will command half the people with me."

"My people hold her in a high regard," Halouse assured, "but she is married to Lyncade."

"I figure a change is in order," Tamian replied, "Half rulers. Mayreon is certainly a queen of the people unlike my wife Drizell. I see the way the people look at her and reach out to her. Because of her beauty there is no doubt why they have that connection. Although most of the nobles will certainly hate me they will not turn down a request by Mayreon. Sygon has assured that she will one day become the most powerful sorceress the world has ever seen. With that power the people will fall to her feet in service. It is quite a shame that she is married to Lyncade but that's just the way the world works I guess. Besides an unmarried king and queen might be better for our kingdom."

"My people already value her and worship her the moment we brought her to my lands," Halouse told, "I assure their loyalty."

"Good," Tamian replied, "You must know that your addition to my forces is a great day to our people. With most of the nobles being banned to Porian there will be many positions open. I am asking you to pick the best members of the Lycans and Murkildens to fill them."

"If I delay it will only be because I want the best," Halouse told.

"Very good general," Tamian replied, "Now leave me in peace."

"Yes my lord," Halouse said as he bowed his head slightly and walked away.

The next morning thousands had gathered in the square of the city. The people who were all present didn't say a word. A sword could have dropped to the ground and it would have been heard for miles. No one said anything as Drizell was carried out to the center stage of the square. Sygon was standing next to her as she was escorted out by many guards.

"Queen Drizell," Sygon replied, "You are here by being executed for betraying your king, your people, your god and most importantly yourself. The crimes of speaking to The Dark Lord about taking the throne from your husband and planning to have him killed are punishable only by death. May Warad have mercy on you once you reach the afterlife."

The beautiful queen began to cry softly but contained her tears. She dropped to her knees slowly as one of the guards forced her to.

Her hair was then placed on her left shoulder clearing the back of her neck for the ax that would soon pierce it.

Slowly walking up in back of her was Tazzill. Holding his massive ax he slowly placed it in his hands and readied himself.

"Any last words?" Sygon asked.

Drizell kind of smiled through the tears building in her eyes as she asked, "The bastard couldn't do it himself?"

Sygon nodded as Tazzill swung. The head of the queen sliced from her head and rolled forward for several moments. The crowd was still silent as they watched the woman they had worshipped for many years get killed before their eyes.

"Let this be known that everyone will suffer a penalty for betraying their king and their god," Sygon yelled.

With no attempt to remove the body all the guards and Sygon walked off leaving the corpse of their queen where it was. Her eyes that were once enchanting were now rolled back in her empty cold face.

A knock was heard on Mayreon's door as she was wiping tears from her eyes. Holding Endore in her harms she looked over to see Tamian walking in.

"Hello," Mayreon softly replied.

Tamian walked to her slowly and looked down at his son.

"I guess you heard?" Tamian asked.

Mayreon just nodded trying to contain the tears in her eyes.

"I can't help it," Mayreon said, "She was very kind to me."

"She betrayed our people," Tamian reminded.

"How can you be so cold?" Mayreon asked as she looked at him.

"She was talking to The Dark Lord about taking over the kingdom," Tamian replied raising his voice, "She would have given you up for her own personal gain."

Mayreon looked down at Endore as she pulled him toward her and held him.

"I know I am putting a lot in your hands," Tamian replied calming his tone, "But put your distain for me away. The future king of our people is in your hands."

Mayreon looked at him and said, "I will raise him as if he were my own."

"You are being rewarded for it," Tamian told, "From this day forward you are queen of the Royal Elves and half ruler of our people."

Mayreon looked at him in shock as she replied, "I can't."

"You must," Tamian told, "You are obviously of great importance to Warad. His purpose for you brought you to Lyncade in marriage and to me as queen. I will not ask for your hand ever again I swear."

"I will never accept," Mayreon told, "Just in case you do."

"I know where your heart lies," Tamian assured.

Mayreon looked up at him and said, "You know nothing about me."

Tamian just looked at her for several moments.

"Raising two children on your own will be hard but I assure I will give you some assistance," Tamian informed.

"I can handle them," Mayreon assured, "You take care of your laws and you empire and I'll do what I can to help you as well."

Tamian just looked at her almost longing for her. Mayreon looked up and noticed his stare.

Her hand began to glow as Tamian took a step back.

"Your charms may have worked on my once but never again," Mayreon informed, "Try that again and I see what will happen."

Tamian just laughed but did so just to hide away his fear of the sorceress.

"You want to hate me Mayreon then hate me," Tamian replied, "I'd prefer that anyway. I want to know your true feelings about anything that involves this empire. Your hatred for me will make you the best queen."

Mayreon just looked at him while she held the prince in her arms. He just smiled a little and began to walk out.

Chapter 21

In the square of city a few days later Mayreon was sitting in a chair next to Tamian. Thousands had gather like they did days before when Drizell was executed in front of them. They were silent again not knowing what to make of the situation.

"People of Tamian," Tamian began, "We have seen more betrayal in these last few days then we would like to see ever again. All those who have been dealt with is a lesson to anyone else daring to do what they did. After long thinking of what to do about the future of our people I am proud to give you your queen.

"She is no stranger to the title and was supposed to rule in Arawon. Now though because of recent events I know I cannot take her away from the empire and city she has grown to love."

A small amount of cheers began to go off as Tamian turned and held out his hand toward Mayreon.

"I give to you the Lightqueen Mayreon," Tamian yelled.

As the words were said the thousands cheered with excitement. Mayreon rose holding Endore in her arms and still swelling in her own womb. Dressed in all white with her long wavy blonde hair brushed back she was as beautiful as the first day the people saw her. A pearled circlet was around her head with many strands falling down her face. At the ends of each strand was a small diamond.

Halouse stood next to her as she rose but never gave her a glance. She walked toward Tamian slowly as he held a crown in his hands. Sygon took Mayreon's hand as she kneeled slowly. With a small smile on his face Tamian bent down and placed it on her forehead.

"Rise my queen," Tamian replied.

Mayreon rose as the crowd cheered louder. The deafening cheer was echoing throughout the land and could be heard for miles. Sygon helped her from her knee as she stood proudly on the stage facing her people.

Not too long ago she had been scrubbing the floors of temples. Cleaning the robes of nobles and sleeping in a ragged, ripped and torn bed. The cloths she wore were dirty and ripped. Now she was an elegant queen that the empire she once served loved undoubtedly.

The months passed quickly in the city of Tamian. Lyncade had come and gone since returning from Porian. He had been traveling back and forth to the city of Arawon to try and make peace between Arawon and Tamian. Mayreon rested softly in her bed as there were now two cribs by it. The child Endore in one, and her own son in the other. Her peaceful sleep though would soon turn into a living nightmare.

On the edge of the territory known as Tamian a Royal Elf farmer and his family were riding on the dark road headed toward Porian. Porian being known as the territory of the undead. Unknowing of this the farmer cautiously looked around as his family stayed warm inside. Looking on into the depths of the dark forest around him he began to get the chills.

Deep in the woods he could hear voices and low screams. Afraid for the sake of his family he stopped his carriage. Jumping from it he began to study his surroundings.

"Warad please don't lead me astray," The Royal Elf softly replied.

He pulled out his blade by his waist as the screams in the forest began to get louder. It was if they were closing in on him. He quickly jumped to the carriage and turned his horses around. Riding quickly in the other direction he began to hear horses in back of him. Looking back quickly he saw three dark riders gaining on him.

Inside the carriage a beautiful Royal Elf woman opened the window and looked out in back of the carriage. The hooded rider's eyes began to glow a deep red as she screamed in fear.

The leader rider rode up quickly and with one swipe of his blade beheaded the woman. The children inside screamed as their mother's beheaded corpse fell next to them. The cries of a baby were soon heard as it pierced into the night.

Far away in the city of Tamian a Mayreon awakes from her bed screaming. Inside her large chambers she looks around at the emptiness inside. It is only her, awoken by a strange nightmare. The two cribs beside her are silent thankfully from her hellacious scream. She jumps from her large bed and with her magic; candles get lit all around her.

"Help me Warad," Mayreon softly replied, "Do not let me see such a thing in my dreams if you can not help me."

Back on the rode the Royal Elf farmer quickly tried to pick up speed. He looked to the side of him as a dark rider raised his hand and tossed his blade toward him. Nailing him in the shoulder he flew from the carriage and landed hard on the ground.

The carriage quickly stopped with no one controlling it. The hooded creatures stopped riding as the screams of the children could still be heard.

Two of the dark riders quickly went over to the wounded Royal Elf man as the third went into the carriage.

"No," The man screamed as he saw the rider enter, "Leave them alone I beg you."

The rider who tossed his blade quickly removed it from the man's shoulder. The screams of the children began to stop as the Royal Elf knew they were being killed. With tears in his eyes he looked up as the two riders raised their blades. With two quick swipes the Royal Elf was killed.

The cry of a baby was the only thing left as the third rider emerged from the carriage with it. Placing the baby on the ground softly the two other riders joined him. They removed their hoods revealing three vampire lords.

"Leave no survivors," The leader of them replied, "Kill the child as well."

A blue mist formed in back of them as Mayreon appeared.

The vampire seemed to feel her presence as he slowly turned around.

"Mayreon," The vampire replied.

Mayreon quickly tossed out both her hands as the vampires flew away from the baby. With one fire of a blue light the leader of the vampires was ripped apart. The other two quickly got to their feet and rushed her with their blades ready. She placed her hands across one another then violently pulled them to the side. The vampires were ripped into peaces just like the other.

She quickly got out of her trance and looked at the carnage around her. With tears in her eyes she soon heard the silent moans of the baby. She walked slowly toward it and saw the small baby girl looking up at her with such wonder. Wiping the tears from her eyes quickly she gently picked the child up. Hushing it to be silent the blue mist formed around her again.

Transporting her and the baby back to the city of Tamian she was back in her room.

"I heard you," Mayreon said to the baby, "Calling me from miles away."

Still filled with tears in her eyes the doors to her chambers burst open. She jumped a little as she saw Lyncade walk in. He was filled with dirt and looked weary from his journey.

The general looked at her eccentrically as she held the child.

"Is their something you need to tell me?" Lyncade asked in an angered tone.

"It's not what you think," Mayreon said to him. She looked back at the baby and said, "She called to me in my dreams."

The Royal Elf Lord walked over to her slowly and looked at the child then back at his wife.

"What are you talking about?" Lyncade asked.

"I just found her," Mayreon told. She looked at him intensely and replied, "You've only been gone a few months I think you would have noticed if I was carrying."

The Lord placed down his sword as he took the child from her arms and held it in his own.

"She called to you?" Lyncade asked.

"In my dreams," Mayreon added, "I don't know how to explain it."

"What are you going to do?" Lyncade asked.

"Keep her," Mayreon replied.

"How?" Lyncade asked, "Where did she come from the sky?"

"I don't know Lyncade," Mayreon yelled, "But I won't just place her in front of a hut in the city."

"I'm not asking you to," Lyncade assured, "But you can't say it's your child what will the people think? They'll know we found her you just had Nabian."

"I found her," Mayreon snapped as she quickly took the baby back, "Besides I'll come up with something."

"What?" Lyncade asked.

Mayreon thought for a moment and replied, "My sister."

"What?" Lyncade asked.

"I'll say it's my sister," Mayreon replied as she rocked the baby and said, "You'll be my sister."

"And how did she get here?" Lyncade asked.

"I sent for her," Mayreon replied still gazing at the baby.

Lyncade just shook his head as he sat on the bed.

"One of these days you'll really need to tell me about your real family," Lyncade replied, "You never did give me the story and if you even did have any brothers or sisters."

"I told you Lyncade I don't remember my parents," Mayreon reminded, "I don't remember them."

"Oh," Lyncade replied than sarcastically replied, "So you were just sent here by Warad then."

Mayreon ignored his rant as she looked at the baby with a large smile on her face.

"Although I'd have to admit I have never seen you so happy," Lyncade replied, "But what is her name?"

Mayreon looked at him then thought to herself. With a large smile on her face she looked at the baby and said, "Maylein."

"Seems good enough but how can we take care of her?" Lyncade asked.

Mayreon looked at him incensed as she replied, "We are Royalty. Do you not remember? If we give her away she'll become a slave or a maiden. I will not have that. For some reason Warad gave her to me and I will not go against his wishes."

Lyncade just got up slowly and went to his wife as she looked down at the baby. He placed his arm around her and kissed her gently.

"I'll tell Tamian in the morning," Lyncade assured, "Do with her what you'd like."

Mayreon looked at him and kissed him softly as she replied, "Thank you."

Lyncade stood next to his wife as he looked at the two cribs on the other side of the room.

"Three children?" Lyncade asked, "How do you expect to do that?"

"I'll manage," Mayreon replied.

Lyncade looked at her and replied, "Why is Endore in our room?"

"Tamian needs his sleep and the servants do need rest," Mayreon replied.

"That's why we have servants Mayreon," Lyncade reminded, "To help us with everything."

"I will not have any of the children raised by a servant," Mayreon replied, "I've heard of kings and queens who do not raise their children. The children grow up envious and have a lot of hatred for their parents."

Lyncade walked over to one of the cribs slowly. Peacefully sleeping in it was Nabian. He studied the boy for some time. Trying to hide the fact that he was happy from his wife he reached his finger down and touch the boy on the face. Not disturbing him Lyncade turned and looked at Mayreon holding Maylein.

"We go from having one child to having three," Lyncade replied.

"We'll be alright," Mayreon assured.

Lyncade just nodded as he went to his wife and softly kissed her on the lips again. Placing his arm around her they looked at the baby girl in Mayreon's arms.

The world was peaceful with the night passing slowly. They seemed to be the only two awake in the entire city as they both continued to look at the baby. As they both laid in their bed Mayreon kept Maylein close in her arms. Lyncade cradled his wife as she cradled the child kissing her softly on the forehead.

The morning was peaceful in the large city of Tamian. Building quickly began to extend the city for the Murkildens and Lycans that now called Tamian its home. The workers would work endlessly until the small portions of the city were complete for the new elves to live in. They were welcomed with open arms by their new king and would die beside him if he so wished.

A small meeting was being held by Tamian in the same meeting room him and Maxus fought their battle. Tamian awaited patiently all alone as he held a small goblet in his hand. Lazily he sat until the others he had summoned came. The doors of the room opened as Halouse entered slowly. He bowed his head slightly to his king and took his place at the table. Seconds later, walking hand in hand, was Mayreon and Lyncade. The crown resting on her forehead could have blinded those who stared at it long enough. Her beauty though at the moment with the outfit she had worn dulled the magnificence of the crown. Her long blonde hair worked on incessantly it seemed by the servants who dressed her. The robes she wore expensive and shaped perfect to her exquisite body.

Her and Lyncade separated as she walked slowly toward Tamian and sat beside him at the head of the table. Lyncade took his seat next to his wife at the top side of the table as Halouse sat across from him.

"My lord," A guard called from the door, "He's here."

Moments later followed by dozens of the men that traveled with him a young general walked in. He stunning feature seemed to place intimidation into the eyes of those who were his enemies. His face had an impact much like his reputation and name. He had never been wounded in the thousands of years he had been alive. His skills weren't heard of being matched in the city he came from or the world at that. A long blue colored cape was in back of him as it stopped at his ankles only inches from hitting the ground. With a war helmet between his arm he looked ahead at his king. The look in his eyes was intense and bitter. He never seemed to smile or laugh even when the occasion seemed right.

The sword that had been soaked in the blood of his enemies was around the belt by his waist. A small blue stone was the center peace of the handle as it sparkled once the light hit it. The armor he wore barely scrapped by past battles and had the emblem of a blue colored snake. This was the Mark of Arawon and the nobles. As he slowly approached he dropped to his knees before Mayreon and took her hand. Kissing it softly he rose and then dropped before Tamian.

"I am honored by the position you give me within your kingdom," The warrior told, "The nobles in Boleadar no longer hold a grudge with you."

"I trust your journey was safe," Tamian replied.

The warrior rose and sat next to Halouse.

"Safe as it always was," The warrior told.

"For those of you who don't know this is our new High General of the Royal Elves," Tamian introduced, "General Xanafear."

Xanafear just bowed his head to all the others at the table.

"What position will my husband take?" Mayreon asked.

"High General of Arawon if he wishes," Tamian told.

"And me?" Mayreon asked.

"You will be queen here," Tamian told.

"I take position in Arawon and my wife stays here?" Lyncade asked.

"This is my home," Mayreon told.

"You will go where I say you go," Lyncade said.

"She has a right to speak Lyncade," Tamian said quickly.

Lyncade looked at Tamian then to Mayreon as she still looked down.

"My lord this is my home," Mayreon began to Tamian, "As half ruler of our people now I demand that I stay among you in your kingdom. I now have three children I am looking after because of Drizell's betrayal. I wish to keep them here where the temple is close. There, Nabian and Endore will learn from Lyncade and Halouse how to fight in battle. For Maylein my sister I will teach her here everything she needs to know about sorcery."

"Your sister?" Tamian asked.

"I saw friends of my mother and father," Mayreon lied, "They died tragically. Maylein was sent to me and I intend to take care of her."

"I was going to bring that up with you," Lyncade told Tamian, "She already has for me."

"Good," Tamian complimented, "Now the problem we had from the beginning is finished."

"What do you mean?" Mayreon asked.

"My intention was to make you queen so you two would have a daughter," Tamian told, "Because you two were blessed with a son it delayed my plans but now that you say you have a infant sister; that brings me back to what I wanted in the first place."

"Agreed," Lyncade said quickly.

Mayreon looked at him in an angered tone. Lyncade returned it as if telling her she had no choice or he would tell Tamian the truth.

"If Lyncade stays," Xanafear began, "What is my position here?"

"High General," Tamian told, "I will not take that away."

"I will not stay," Lyncade informed, "My king feels it best for me to be among the nobles in Arawon and I will go."

"Excepted," Tamian assured, "Mayreon will stay here and be half ruler beside me. Any objections because she isn't married to me speak now."

No one said a thing for several moments.

"My lord," Xanafear said, "No objection here but don't you think the nobles will have a problem with that?"

"That is why you, Xanafear, will now take over the position Maxus once had," Tamian told, "Xanafear is now High Noble of the Tamian, and the Royal Elf people."

"Will they accept my position?" Xanafear asked.

"I'm sure once they know you were close with Arawon they will be at peace," Tamian knew, "That is one of the other reasons I wanted you to take position here."

Xanafear nodded.

Halouse had kept quiet the whole time. Mayreon looked to him every now and again noticing that he stared at the table and no where else. It seemed he was in his own world never even giving a peak to her or anyone at that.

"Halouse," Tamian called.

Halouse's head came up and looked right at the king. Mayreon looked at him to try and see if she could figure out why he had acted so cold toward her.

"Yes my lord?" Halouse asked.

"You are to appoint two leaders of the Lycans and Murkildens," Tamian told, "They will speak for their people and go directly to you. In return you will bring what ever they request to me. You yourself will lead the Lycans and Murkildens into the battlefield as well as be their High Lord."

Halouse just nodded them looked back at the table quickly.

"All of us here will be the true leaders of this kingdom," Tamian told, "I will have all of you as my ears and eyes in the city. You will all be my council for every decision made from now on."

They all nodded as Halouse was the first to get up. The others did as well as Mayreon watched him walk out of the room quickly.

"Shall I take you to your room?" Lyncade asked.

"I must pray in the temple," Mayreon told.

"I will have guards go with you," Lyncade told.

"Of course," Mayreon replied.

Mayreon was escorted by legions of guards as she walked through the city. Hundreds stood in wonder as she walked by trying to get a glimpse of the queen. Many yelled out their undying love for her as she continued to walk with many things on her mind. As Mayreon got close to the temple a priest was there to greet her.

"My queen," He replied as he bowed.

"Rise," Mayreon said softly.

"I had emptied the temple for your own private worship," the priest told.

"I thank you," Mayreon said as she began to go in.

"I must say though that one particular man didn't leave," The priest told.

Mayreon turned and looked at him.

"He is one of those natives," The priest said.

Mayreon thought for a moment then replied, "He is not a native. He is a Royal Elf just like the rest of us."

"I'm sorry my queen," The priest replied.

As Mayreon entered the guards stopped knowing she was safely inside. Mayreon walked a long way into the temple as at the end she saw the back of Halouse kneeling before the large statue of Warad. She slowly approached and stopped a few feet in back of him.

"I have prayed since there was peace for the way I feel for you to go away," Halouse told, "Begging my maker to help me deal with these feelings that I've had to stuff since the time you've embraced me."

Mayreon seemed to fight back tears in her eyes as he spoke. Her emotions were overwhelming her as she looked to the ground.

"The taste of your lips is still burned into my memory," Halouse replied, "It never goes away and I yearn for it again. I know it wasn't sorcery you placed on me but it sure feels like it."

"It is you that has cast a spell on me," Mayreon told as a single tear fell from her eye.

Halouse rose still looking up at the statue and never turning around.

"I was able to grab that ruby because my heart was pure," Halouse told, "I would have died if the way I felt about you was wrong. The gods have told me that they weren't wrong. Yet I still beg for me to hate you instead."

"At least you will feel something for me," Mayreon told, "You haven't even looked in my direction since we left Fadarth."

"I cannot," Halouse told, "I will worship you as my queen but I will never return another glance."

"Why not?" Mayreon asked as she took a step toward him.

"No," Halouse yelled.

Mayreon stopped in her tracks as more tears fell from her eyes.

"Do you not think that the same things haunt me?" Mayreon asked, "The taste of your lips, the feel of your hands on my face. The look of your eyes when you glance at me."

"It cannot be," Halouse told, "Leave it at that."

"There is something between us," Mayreon knew, "Something that has made Warad constantly make us see one another. When we were children in the village, when you saved me on my way back from the temple. The gods know that we should be."

"The gods are only toying with us," Halouse said, "They want us to suffer. They do not love or care for us."

"How do you say such things?" Mayreon asked.

"If I had it my way you wouldn't have been married," Halouse told, "But you are. The gods had us meet but they laugh with the situations that force us to keep away."

Mayreon wanted to go to him but she stopped herself. For the way she felt for Lyncade and because she knew what would happen to her hero if she did.

Halouse quickly turned around and without looking in her direction walked passed her.

"Will you not look at me one more time?" Mayreon asked as she turned and saw his back once again.

Halouse stopped as his head turned slightly. Stopping himself he looked forward once again and began to walk off. Mayreon's heart called to him like his did to her. The love that they kept secret from the rest of the world had died there in Mayreon's eyes. The warrior that had saved her so many times was gone. Only a black face and the back of a general's form remained. Whipping away the tears Halouse didn't see quickly Mayreon just watched her hero walk away. His steps fading away as his from became smaller to her. There was nothing but the silence now as she looked around the massive temple. With the doors closing behind the general, Mayreon screamed in pain as she dropped to her knees. The curse of loving two men still ate at her soul as she wept uncontrollable. The gods themselves seemed to be crying with her as she continued her sadness on the cold floor. The same floor she had once washed with her hands. The world might have been peaceful but her soul was still fighting a war.

A war that could one day kill who she was.

Printed in the United States
109236LV00002B/223/P